ATROPHY: BREAKDANCE

Lucas William Raynal

ISBN: 979-8-218-34726-0

Cover design by: Lucas William Raynal

Everything is intended. The universe flows. The seas flood.

The skies fall. Sleep and then open your eyes.

Enjoy.

THE AUTHOR WOULD LIKE TO THANK YOU

FOR READING HIS MINDMUSH

ATROPHY: BREAKDANCE

Atrophy [n]

1. *Decrease in size or wasting away of a body part or tissue*
2. *A wasting away or progressive decline*

Breakdance [n]

1. *A style of hip-hop dance in which soloists perform acrobatic moves that often involve touching various parts of the body (such as the back or head) to the ground*
2. *The act or an instance of* ***breakdancing***

Merriam-Webster.com

The First Apostle

"The Primal Key will come, turning fourteen. And to you, take her in with maternal instinct. With that, guide her towards me. Use the others if you must. Then, when the time is right, when she is supple enough, bring her to me."

1

Willow

Willows Eve was on fire. The two story farmhouse burst with dark flames, the glass of the remaining windows growing red with the continuous heat of the fire. It almost made a face with the two second floor windows which oozed black death, the open front door making a mouth twisted and horrified. Black wispy smoke danced up towards the glittery sky almost with delight. Breakdancing. Break...dancing- The heat licked at us as we hid behind the station wagon where my family watched. Mom with her partially blackened body had her head buried and shaking deep in Dad's unmoving chest. Her muffled sobs came out in small droves. Dad was trying to console her with empty promises about how everything was going to be alright. I saw his lips quiver as he whispered, never fully paying attention to the inferno raging in front of him. Matt and Jeremey stood by saying nothing. My brothers. I didn't look at them. I didn't want to look at them. I smelled like smoke. I watched.

The house creaked and trembled, something popped within. Willows Eve began to crumble into one big pile of burnt wood and metal and glass and everything that we owned and it was dead. I think I heard my brothers begin to cry but I didn't look at them. Dad said something but fell silent again.

My eyes felt dry as they blinked. My stomach hurt. I smelled like smoke. Everything smelled like smoke. I coughed.

They never found the cause. We moved into a temporary apartment. Dad's not around too much anymore.

2

My eyes were glued to the green wall-mounted phone and it's looping cord hanging and swaying to and fro from the soft wind coming in through the open window, my ears being tuned to whatever was happening behind the door of my parents bedroom, blanking out the occasional car honk and slight buzz of people from the street down below.

They were talking in hushed tones of increasing and decreasing volume. Dad was talking now. Back and forth, from one to the other.

"...house..." I heard Dad say.

"...I don't..." Mom's muffled voice said.

I got up from the couch and tip-toed my way to their door, softly putting my ear up against the wood, closing my eyes, focusing my listening powers to what's going on beyond the thin threshold.

"...that house was in my family for decades. I grew up in that place." Dad said.

"Daniel, please..."

"My Dad grew up there. His Dad built the damn place."

"Come to terms with me here-"

"And I'm the one who let it burn down..."

"Stop blaming yourself!"

"Then who am I to blame?"

"I don't know! Sometimes shit happens!"

"Shit like that? Shit like this? Everything is shit, Mary! Everything has turned to shit! I mean, look at this, this is shit!

Fucking shit! Shit! Shit! Shit!"

"Jesus Christ! Are you seriously acting like this?"

"Yes! How else am I supposed to act?"

"Like a man! Right now you're acting like a fucking baby!"

"Oh really?"

"Yes! God yes! I see how you are now! Don't act like you don't know. Leaving your kids, leaving me to do God-knows-what all day?"

"I'm working! I'm fucking working! What are you saying? What are you saying right now?"

"You barely even come home at night!"

"Don't do this, don't you dare do this right now."

"Do what? Tell you to do your job as a father? A husband?"

"You seriously don't care, huh? Do you?"

"I do! I really do! I know how you feel! But you can't just leave it all behind in your little sad world!"

"Little sad world... is that really how you see me?" He was quieter.

Silence. The TV blared behind me, the sound of car honks grew and fell.

"I...I'm sorry," Mom said. "I mourned with you. I cried with you. I get it, I really do. But please...I...we need you to come back to this world. Our world."

"I am trying...I am...but it's hard."

"Daniel...you're killing yourself over this."

"I named one of my kids after that place."

"I know."

The bed frame creaked slightly like someone just sat down.

"Let's just," Dad said, "look for somewhere else."

"You don't want to even try and-"

"No...I just...I just want to move on. I'm tired, Mary. I want to sleep."

"Okay..."

I laughed. I don't know why. Breakdance.

*

The new house was big. We're scouting the place out. The outside of it was a dark gray that matched the neighboring houses. They were all the same. The word buildinghouses comes to mind. I don't know why. I've never heard someone say that before. Suburban. Suburban breakdance. Beyond the backyard spanned a large stretch of forest, going miles and miles back. It creeped me out. Going back and back and back-

I've never lived in a neighborhood before, Willows Eve's neighbors being miles apart from each other. Mom kept telling me about how many friends I was going to make here. I never really had friends before. Never really thought about it much.

I saw some other kids on the block playing with each other as we explored the house, their smiles and laughs bringing up odd feelings of annoyance. I thought about a moth bumping into a glasslocked flame over and over again. The only other girl on the block was my neighbor.

I ended up getting the smallest bedroom equipped with a slanted roof, a tiny window looking out over the front yard that I called the crows nest window, and a side window with an almost perfect view into the neighbor's backyard which had a large treehouse looking over their tall wooden fence.

I thought of my old room. I thought of the smell of smoke.

Something dark.

Something else.

My head began to hurt.

I shook it away.

Wrapped it up.

I laid down on the bare floor, trying to let my head rest, and stared up at the ceiling. I noticed a tiny little spot. Rubbing my eyes, it was still fogged and odd. It might be a spider or a bug. It looked like it was-

A car honked in our new driveway. I looked outside the crows nest window and saw my family getting situated in the car. I glanced once more at the spot. It was still there, staring at me. The honk came again, more aggressive this time. I blinked and shook my head and ran outside as fast as I could. Dad liked to get angry fast. I didn't want to anger him.

It'll be gone by the time we move in.

*

The spot was still there. It was tiny, barely even noticeable, but I could not take my eyes off of it. It was still foggy and odd, it's aura something I couldn't exactly grasp. Today was moving day, and my bed was finally in place. I struggled onto the covers and tried to get another look at the black spot. On closer inspection, it was just that: A black spot. I tried to touch it but I was too short even standing on the covers, the slant of the roof making it even more out of reach. Something about it...something...

"What are you looking at?" Dad was standing in the doorway. His eyes looked tired but alive.

"Nothing." I said, still standing on the bed.

He walked further into the room and looked up at the ceiling where the spot stuck, both his thumbs rung very Dad-like through the loop of his belt, his hairy arms hanging loosely at his sides, "Huh," there was no recognition in his eyes. "Well," he looked back at me, "We need some help moving the new furniture downstairs, come on."

Mom and Dad bought a lot of new stuff. Couches, picture frames, this and that. All of it made me feel weird. It smelled weird. "Okay," I said, hopping off the bed.

He smiled and turned around.

I took another look at the spot on the ceiling as I was leaving. It was still there, of course.

*

I hated the spot. It was watching me...I think. And something about it made me think and find nothing, which was annoying. It gave me a headache but I continued to look. It was almost fuzzy. Hazy. The smell of the house made my head woozy. The new couches and chairs and this and that. I hated it. My stomach hurt. Give me back the old couch, the one from Willows Eve. It was old, worn in, and smelled good. It smelled like Dad. It smelled like home.

That shiver crept back.

Wrap it up.

Throw it away.

It's been weird at the new house. Jeremy and Matt have seemingly moved on, this new house suiting them pretty well. They go and cry when Willows Eve burns but now they're all happy? Smiling? Running around, frolicking through fields like some jaunty little girls? Maybe not exactly that, but still... why do they get to move on so fast? Back at the apartment they didn't exactly seem to care either. It's been getting harder to sleep, this constant whispering of thoughts that run and bang through my mind whenever I close my eyes. Noise. Earth shattering, constant, and unstoppable. Noise that plays and crashes each and every time I close my eyes. It's industrial, like I'm in the middle of a construction site with jackhammers hammering and screaming as saws and machines go saw saw and beep beep over and over again. Over and over. Over and over. It's maddening. Moth to the flame. Like those kids laughing and screaming in the street. Be quiet. But it's not. It wont. I want to sleep.

I can't sleep-

*

Mom keeps telling me to go out and make friends with the neighborhood kids. Why? My brothers have gone and made friends already, maybe Mom wants me to be like them and forget the past. But I wasn't like them.

I would find myself looking out past the backyard towards the woods. Something about them made me feel gurgly in my stomach. When we first moved in, I tried not to look at them too much, but I can't help myself now. I would picture some type of labyrinth behind that dark veil of trees and brush and green. A green labyrinth. A labyrinth that stretches and moves, making all means of escape impossible. I would get trapped in there. I wouldn't be able to leave. Running and running, moving and moving, pushing and screaming against little and big bushes. Large round trees would systematically block and stop any view of what's beyond them. They're all working together. My hands became clammy. I froze. Looking out into its unending nothingness-

*

I realized how quiet the new house is. I would lay in my bed, straining my ears to hear anything. Even a car driving by. But no. There was nothing. It was odd. My ears rang in the silence. There was always noise at Willows Eve. Animals, the house settling, creaks and cracks. Voices-

My chest hurt.

I felt cold.

I was sweating.

I felt hot.

I was laying in the dark for a while, letting my vision slowly grow better and better. I could barely make out the spot, still there doing nothing, it being even fuzzier and hazier than before. Sometimes, if I stare at it long enough, it starts to form into something in its misty shadow. Something odd and misshapen. With jagged ends and little points that stick out in ways that sicken me. But I would blink and it would all go away. I think I'm tired. I really need sleep. I can't. Industrial noise. Crazy and loud and annoying. Breakdancing?

How long have I been laying here? It must have been ages. I stood on the bed and peered out of the little nest window towards the neighborhood. It was dark. The moon shone down with a pale light as it took its rightful place in the clear sky. Nothing moved out there. Grayness overtaking.

The house was gray.

My stomach grumbled: I was hungry. Walking downstairs towards the kitchen, I readied for a creak of the floorboards with each step, but there was nothing. Quiet. Ears ringing. I wanted to scream. I wanted something else besides this silence. I didn't scream. I didn't want to wake up Mom and

Dad. So I went down the stairs, step by step, making sure that I wouldn't make any noise even if the house already made sure of that. My ears rang to the silence, louder and louder, step by step.

Downstairs rang too, the only sound being my ears as they continued to search for some type of sound. Anything. They started to scream themselves.

Entering the kitchen, I heard the fridge hum silently as it grew colder inside. Finally, some type of noise. I grabbed a something from a cabinet and decided to sit down at the kitchen table, looking past the glass sliding door into the backyard. The backyard was swathed with moonlight, gray and sad. Beyond that was the veil of darkness. The start of the forest. I looked at it. I couldn't help myself. Something about it... The labyrinth constructed in my mind, endless and unescapable.

Something moved in the woods, this small light that flickered and faded fast like a spark. Blinking and rubbing my eyes, I stood and got closer to the glass. Nothing. The veil was left still. Maybe I imagined it. I went back upstairs to try and sleep.

That morning when I was eating my breakfast, I kept looking out into the forest. I saw nothing but trees going all the way back. Leaves and wood and dirt. The green labyrinth unending. I got a shiver and looked away, my appetite gone.

That night a repeat: Hunger. My belly responded, rumbling and moving with a ferocity. Suddenly, there was an empty vastness where my stomach once was. My mouth watered and my eyes opened among the brain noises of industrial machinery. I needed food. I needed to eat. Badly. The spot was still there, up on the ceiling, hazy and misty. I glanced at it, it glanced at me. I left before too long, not wanting to stare at it again.

The ring of my ears started and continued with each step down the stairs, escalating and culminating to a silent scream until I found myself in the kitchen, freed by the hum of the fridge. I opened it, the cold from its belly washing around my legs. The light which beamed out from the door blinded me for a second as I realized that there really was nothing to eat here.

I closed the door and turned around towards the dark veil of night.

Beyond the glass door, beyond the fence, beyond the veil, into the darkness, two somethings were shining and glowing, flickering and lighting, looking at me as I stood.

The labyrinth shot back into my mind, my skin prickled and tingled. But curiosity beat any type of hesitation as I walked forward towards the glass door, eyeing the odd sight all the way.

Their shape morphed slowly with each step closer towards the glass, forming and molding themselves into a pair of eyes. Glowing eyes. They sat and stared, wavering like candles.

They looked at me, I looked at them. Even with the light of the moon, I couldn't see anything else besides those glowing eyes, the dark veil of the forest hiding the rest of whatever it was. Maybe a haze. Something corporeal. Something tangible was there, standing and waiting, watching the entire time, unblinking.

Filth. Disgust. Awful things. My empty stomach felt like it was filling with garbage that gurgled further. Plastic bags and chemical sludge swirled and danced in a brown sea of shit and urine as hills of discarded trash piled high up towards the rotten sky, ew.

The eyes. Two fires. They danced and tangled with the wind as they sat and watched. I wanted to keel over down towards the ground, my breath caught in my throat, garbage in my stomach. But I stood and watched, the sea of filth growing and leaking further down into my guts adding to this overwhelming feeling.

In a haze of shadow and flame, the mass, the eyes, and the fire, rose up into the precipice of the trees and flickered off, extinguished.

I stood, frozen to the ground, my legs unmoving, my hands jittering, the filth still growing and swashing around my stomach, leaking and finding itself in more nooks and crannies.

I had forgotten to blink.

*

I woke to the smells of blood and meat. I lifted my head from a cold, hard surface and found myself in the kitchen, seated at the table. Darkness spread before me as I was the only one in the room, each chair vacant and sad, their table settings all but gone. Some drool was spread on my chin and I wiped it away. Looking down in front of me, I was faced with a large and red steak, its juices dripping out of its uncooked sides which filled in the rest of the white plate that it sat on. I could almost see the smell coming off of it, their lines thick and heavy. My nostrils moved on their own, the little lines finding their way up and up into my brain, prickling my senses and turning something off and something else on. That empty, void-like, hunger came creeping back causing my mind to race and my hands to jitter. My mouth watered as the machinery and noise in my head calmed and my senses dulled. A storm of wants rained down and pooled just like the red juices of the steak on that white, white plate.

I could feel the saliva almost dripping from my mouth as the last drip of hesitation washed away somewhere else, forgotten in this new storm. The wind blew and thrashed, wrecking my mind. My hands jumped. My mouth frothed. I moved.

I tore into it at the rate of the storm, the steaks juices flowing and splashing across the table as I snatched it up like a hawk. It had the consistency of butter and melted oh so good in my mouth. Without a second thought, I took another bite and another and then another, one, two, three, chewing and swallowing and chewing and swallowing again and again one after the other in a cycle of bite and swallow. Red leaked down my arms and down onto my lap as I continued to cycle, chomp, chew, swallow, one, two, three, I continued and moved, my mouth having the ferocity of something godly and I liked it. I continued, swiping the thought away, thinking and moving and going and eating and chomping, still at it. A miraculous pain resounded in my thumb as I accidentally bit down on it.

I stopped.

And looked at it, watching the dark red blood drip slowly from the bite mark. It had a rhythm to it as it dripped, pooled, and dripped once again, making this slapping sound on the floor. It was hypnotic, the pain all but gone.

"Try it-" a voice echoed from somewhere, its smooth tones bouncing off the walls seductively. Deja vu spread in my mind for a second and then disappeared.

I licked it cautiously, lapping some small amount of the stuff. It was sweet and delectable and thick and savory, like everything in one. Jesus. This. Was. Good.

Like a switch, I went back to the steak, adding in the savory and sweet and thick tones of myself. It added to the steak as I was getting down to the bottom of the monster, the hole in my stomach still not satiated.

A knock resounded from behind me as I tore at the steak once more, knocking my transe-like haze out of motion, putting a cog in the wheel of chomp, chew, swallow. I was annoyed. Moth to the flame, again. But still, I turned for but a second towards the glass shield between me and the forest.

It got caught in my throat, the meat becoming a solid, holding my breath and everything else. I couldn't breathe. The fire was there, staring at me, in the form of two eyes hovering above an unsightly black mass where nothing could be firmly constructed. There was something there, but it was shadowed and wispy, like smoke. The eyes danced, their two flames doing a little bit of a jig as if they were having a dance battle...a breakdance battle...huh.

I tried to breathe again, but everything was clogged up and blocked. The storm died right there as I fell to the floor clawing at my neck, desperately trying to force the meat chunk from my throat. They never left me, those two breakdancing flames from beyond the glass. They watched and judged. I looked at them. They looked at me, never breaking contact. I stopped trying to breath, choking and waning, my sight began to falter and a dark haze set in all around my sight. It grew slowly as my body died there on the floor, meat firmly lodged in my throat. One by one, organs shut off, the brain praying for oxygen. The dark rim grew, forcing everything to become wispy and hazy like the monster. Like fire. Like Willows Eve.

The eyes watched and never left, their fires joyously celebrating.

*

The dark spot filled my vision as my eyes opened again, caustic sludge filling my mouth. Frantically, I grasped and pulled at it to get it out. Strand by wet strand, breathing became easier, my hair a clumped and matted mess which had filled my entire mouth, choking me mere moments ago. I blinked and huffed ragged breath after breath, the visage of the dream fading slowly, the kitchen turning into my bedroom, the floor turning into my bed, the flaming eyes turning into the dark spot. My heart slowed and worked itself back into calm order as I worked to calm my breath to a lesser effect.

The steak dimmed and so too did the taste, the tangy pings and savory pongs got lost as I blinked and corrected myself. I checked my thumb to find it perfectly fine, no blood pooling off of it in that rhythmic fashion that it did mere moments ago. Drip, pool, drip. It was all gone.

I laid back, further settling my breath. The spot watched the entire time, almost analytical in its quietness.

I realized that it was my birthday tomorrow.

3

Fuck off. Fourteen? I feel eighty. I never wanted a

birthday party. Almost forgot about it. Breakdancing? Sounds cool.

My parents remembered though, they remembered well. They must have invited everyone from the surrounding blocks over to my house for a party I never wanted. All these nasty kids and their parents who barely even give me a half-glance as they meander around my backyard mingling with each other, gluttonously picking and stealing from these little platters of food scattered about on plastic fold-em tables adorned with floating pink and blue balloons which all screamed, 'Happy Birthday!' in big bouncy letters. I recognized most of the kids there, their shrill little laughs now straight up in my ears. Like that moth to the flame. Bounce bounce bounce; Laugh laugh laugh; Shut up shut up shut up! I thought that Mom and Dad understood me in some sort of parental way. But now here they are, these strangers, invading my everything, let in with open arms and smiles which curled dangerously upwards. Rage and hate and frustration boiled behind my face. I smiled and moved on, trying to laugh.

Above us all like some large hideous flag, waved my face (plastered with a smile) sprawled down in a banner which hung from the back of my house. It wavered and shook in the wind as it held on for dear life, letting everyone get a good look at me up there with that hideous smile of mine. I tried. It was last year's school photo. I really tried...

Mom and Dad would push me to this kid and that, smiling these peeled back, plastic smiles, forcing me to make awkward conversation and shake these gross, greasy, little monkey paws.

"Hello, my name is Willow Pines."

"Oh I know that sweety. Happy birthday! Where's that smile I'm looking for?"

"Hello, my name is Willow."

"Happy birthday."

"Hello, my name is Willow."

Shake hands.

"Hello, my name is Willow."

On and on.

Even the thought of touching those things made me shiver with disgust. I imagined them picking their noses and their asses and going to the bathroom, forgetting to wash afterwards. It made me nauseous, my stomach all in knots of various sizes. Those parents too! How dare you! How dare you bring your things near me. I just wanted to run away from it all and hide in my room. The spot was in there-

This one kid shook my hand and laughed, his face morphing grotesquely as my stomach curdled down and flung this way and that, his spittle splashing outwards onto my face and into my mouth and my eyes. I excused myself and ran to the bathroom to wash and wash and wash my hands, my face, my everything. Scrubbing and scrubbing with soap and sweat to try and get it all off. All of it. Whatever it was, I had to get rid of it. Scrubbing, I thought of the banner of my face with that fake, school smile. I shuttered.

Mom asked me if I was alright, my hands wrought into this pinkish red from all the scrubbing. I nodded and smiled a fake smile. Just like everyone else. Every other fake person here. I was getting tired of all the formality. Why couldn't I just say, 'Fuck you!' to one of the bastards? Oh God, I thought of it though. And more. Much more… more vulgarity.

They thought this was good for me. Talking and meeting all these people against my will. Maybe they thought that I could use some friends from the neighborhood. I wanted none of it. They wouldn't listen! No one would. I was in a zoo. Forced to eat when fed, forced to play ball when fetched, and forced to be happy when surprised with a party. Be content. Be smiling. Be happy.

The party continued on and on, I wanted to run. I wanted to hide. I wanted to lean out one of the windows and set fire to that hanging monolith of me which fluttered as the wind grew.

I felt sick at the thought, the fire moved and smiled

behind the veneer of two dark eyes, my mind growing stagnant, my hands growing taught, my eyes twitched, that pile of garbage grew once again, deep down, in the pit of my stomach-

I glanced out towards the forest and it looked back, the green labyrinth growing behind the veil which darkened slowly as the day progressed.

"Honey, why don't you go play with some of the kids? The adults and I are going to move inside to talk about some grownup stuff." Mom said as I stood frozen, my eyes glued to the darkening forest.

All the other kids were grouped around the fence, talking with each other. I could tell they didn't like me just like I didn't like them. I was an outsider. An outcast. Let's keep it that way. Why couldn't Mom understand? She could see them over there, ignoring me, whispering to each other, peeking over their shoulders at me.

"Okay," I said.

Shit! Why? Why did I cave so easily? I should have told her to screw off.

'Fuck you! And Fuck you! And Fuck you especially!' Right down the line, each and every one getting an increasingly powerful middle finger shoved in their soft, dough-eyed, smiling faces.

But I could never do that. Not in front of Mom. Not around Mom. Her blue eyes watching. My blue eyes.

I was a coward.

Begrudgingly, I walked over to the group of kids, the wind blowing and moving everything. I looked back towards the banner of myself. That was the worst thing. Awful. I wanted to run away from it, but I didn't. I continued on in its unblinking gaze which watched the backyard and beyond.

There were about ten of them huddled by the fence talking with each other. With all of the parents moved inside, it was oddly quiet out here, the wind being the only sound which rustled the leaves with each windy compulsion. I looked back towards the kitchen door. Mom and Dad were laughing and drinking with the other parents. They all smiled. None of them looked out here, towards any of their children. They were in their little world, shielded by the glass and the wood and the warmth of the kitchen.

"Hey," I turned my head to the voice. It was that kid who had laughed at me, "You're the birthday girl, right?"

"Sure." I felt insecure with all of them watching. Why? I hate them even more for making me feel like this. I moved my head slightly, letting some black hair fall further over my eyes.

I glanced out towards the forest, nothing was there. I looked back.

"We're all planning to jump the fence and play hide and seek in the woods, you coming?" He said. "You're the seeker since it's your birthday and all."

I didn't know what to think about that. I remembered the eyes and started to feel sick again, looking out past the fence, through the trees and leaves, deep into the dark woods. The labyrinth constructed once again, green and endless.

"Sure…" I said, confidence not anywhere in my voice.

"You scared?" A girl said. She wasn't our neighbor. Now that I looked upon the group, I realized that the girl next door wasn't here. Did she not come? A well in my stomach started to build. I think I was…a little happy. Or relieved. Maybe both.

"Whatever," the boy said. "Start counting to 30!" They all jumped the fence and ran off into the woods leaving me completely alone. I was shocked, but I couldn't do anything else. I started counting.

10

I shuttered. It was getting cold here. The wind was rising and pushing harder and harder as the night started to overtake day. It was almost October, the month of orange. I liked October. I liked Halloween. The candy was fine. Monsters. Skeletons. Zombies. Ghouls. Maybe I'm too old for it.

20

I looked up at the huge picture of me moving about in

the wind. I hated how I looked in it. The fake smile plastered on my thin lips could tell me exactly how I was feeling that day. Mom would always tell me, in the car, that I would have to smile. It was picture day and everyone had to smile! But I didn't want to smile. All of this...formality...it was killing me. Everything was fake. Nasty.

Matt and Jeremy weren't even here. Damn them.

30

The picture of myself started to sway hard in the wind. One strap fell off and it came apart, the right side moving and covering the left, hiding my face from the world once again. I thanked the wind for that. I'd rather watch the white underbelly of the banner than see my face smiling that disgusting smile.

I finished counting and stood up, looking over the fence off into the darkening forest. The woods danced and moved to the wind's command. I really didn't want to go in there, but some sort of pride forced me to move up and over the fence with slow anxiousness. I thought of the eyes and the fire. I swallowed. Why am I doing this?

"Ready or not, here I come!" I yelled against my will. Damn them.

The first couple of kids were found in minutes. They all stood out like Christmas decorations in the middle of summer. It was sad. Were they really trying to hide? Maybe they shared my thoughts of the woods? The house was still in good view, but each step farther and farther into the woods made me want to bolt back and jump over the fence and yell 'Screw all of you! Find yourselves!' but I didn't. One step after another.

The eyes came to mind. I fought them away.

Don't think of them. That never happened.

Round some trees and under a little burrow, the woods became darker and darker. Found another one. Found another one. Minutes after minutes went by as I slowly conjured each person from their little hiding spot. They never set any type of boundary on where they could go, so some of them could be, hypothetically, miles deep in the woods, far away from the safety of the house, deep in the labyrinth...

I looked back and could still barely see the house, my banner still covered itself thankfully. I bet all of those kids were happy and safe over there, away from the darkening woods. I hated them even more. Weren't they supposed to help me seek?

I still had yet to find that one kid who laughed at me, the thought of his warm spittle which had splattered over my face made me itch. That one girl, too. They were the last of the terrible bunch. I stopped and looked around. It was dark here. I couldn't see farther into the woods due to a combination of close knit trees and the sun lowering behind the Earth. A blistering wind sent a chill right up my back and I turned towards the house. It was mostly covered by trees, I could only spot little slivers of it. I was farther off too, I must've walked much farther out than I had realized. This was my limit. I wasn't doing anything else for these people. I could already imagine them both laughing behind some tree somewhere, waiting for me to search and search. Maybe they snuck back to the house and they all laughed while I continued to search for them.

"I'm going back! You guys won!" I yelled out into the woods. My voice seemed to surround me in a vortex as I spoke. My voice dissipated and I stood in the silent, dark forest waiting for any response. Nothing. The wind blew and pushed some leaves this way and that. I heard a bird jump from tree to tree up above. Some animal moved somewhere. "Hello?" I said. My stomach felt weird and odd, it churned with a force, nauseousness filling the world. Everything was off. I took a step back and started quickly walking back to my house. I could still barely just see it. It was my guiding light back to my safe place. I wanted to run, but I kept my cool and made my way, step after step.

My fingers were freezing, my nose ran cold, my ears burnt with each hollow of the wind as it danced and curled through the branches of the large, overbearing trees. My hands tightened into little balls of fist and worry. They released and tightened again, the process repeated and repeated as I took each step. The house was closer now.

I shuffled through a little bush, almost back to safety, almost out from behind the veil, when I froze, unmoving. My feet felt glued to the ground, my heart quickened. Something was behind me, I could feel it.

"Hello, Willow." It was deep and familiar, from where I couldn't remember.

I couldn't move and didn't, my stomach all turned to knots. There was a newly found pressure below. I needed to pee. Bad. Really bad.

It felt like forever. Wind blew and everything stood with a silence similar to our new gray house. There were no more birds, no more animals jumping from branch to branch. It was all dead. My fingers felt like popsicles. I wanted to blow my nose. I wanted to run away from whatever was behind me. I needed to pee. But I stood, unmoving.

"This is for you."

The voice jumped and danced around me, creating a hurricane of noise.

"Happy birthday-"

I ran, my frozen legs now thawed as hot relief spread out through my body as I put leg after leg, jumping and moving between trees and brush back to my house. I wanted to scream and cry and yell for help, but I focused my everything on running, step after step. All the kids looked over to me as I burst from the trees and jumped the fence, panting and shaking. I crumpled to the grass and breathed heavily, my eyes wanting to cry. I glanced up at my parents laughing and talking in the warm kitchen behind that glass shield. They didn't care anymore. The gray of the house washed over them as they disappeared far back into their own little world of gray and smiles.

"Ew! She peed herself!" One of the kids said. They all

laughed shrilly as I laid on the cold backyard grass, watching my parents laugh and drink. The large banner of myself opened up once more, the wind forcing it back open. It looked down at me with that fake smile and laughed too, deep and thick.

All at that moment, I thought of Willows Eve, the spot, and the eyes of fire. Everything went silent. The laughs, the yells, the people. It all cascaded back down into nothingness.

It all went black, taking me with it.

4

They were gone, those two off in the woods, somewhere, deep in that ever expanding labyrinth of green. Each day went by like a blur of color and sound and talking and yelling. I talked to the police, my mind flashing and forgetting any relevance of the eyes and the fire and the voice from in the forest. Something about those memories...my mouth didn't talk about them.

That day, the parents of the missing would march up to me, their chests all puffed up, their eyes furious as their fake smiles turned down. Their gluttonous maws consumed no more but the air around them, which they sucked in with a fat fierceness. I saw them all behind that glass shield, in the kitchen, all warm and nice inside, each one with a bottle of something in their hands, laughing and smiling as they left their children to the cold of the outside. They didn't care then, but now, right here, in their little minds, I am the one to blame as they screamed in my face. Now they care.

'They are perfect. They are in the right. Their children too, those wonderful things. They are all in the right and I hold all the blame.' Even as I burst into the kitchen that night, they all looked at me with a certain disgust, blame already set in their eyes. My parents looked around, their smiles moving up and down, embarrassment skewed on their faces, their wonderful birthday princess now shaking and panting with piss running all down and around her legs, those long white socks that Mom bought now stained with a yellow that darkened as the night continued on, each hour adding to the stain. 'They are truly in the right. Those wonderful parents who blame everyone but themselves.'

Is that what I'm supposed to say?

No, fuck that!

Suck my fucking dick, bitch! I'm seriously the one to blame? Me? You yell at me, acting all big and tough? You're weak. Have some responsibility you fuck! Yelling at a kid because you're too scared to blame yourself. Fuck you! And fuck your kids too. I see their faces everywhere now, posted up on walls, posts, signs, watching me wherever I go, their beady little eyes still judging from behind those flat paper prisons, blaming me, always. Why am I the one to blame? What did I do? Why me? Why me? Why me- I feel like I'm going insane. They're still alive on those posters. Watching and watching and watching-

My only break from their constant stare is when I go to school deep away from all of this bullshit back where Willows Eve once was. There's a school close by but Mom and Dad are decently adamant about letting me go where I want, and I want to get as far away from this shitshow as I can. It gets me away. It clears my mind. I can finally think, saved from their constant stares beyond the paper prisons.

Mom and Dad are quieter now, our lessening talks becoming rarer and shorter as the days blurred by, their tired eyes looking off somewhere distant all the time. Everything has gotten quieter...

Everything has gotten...gray.

*

"We're moving you and Matt to the school nearby." Mom said bluntly.

We were in the kitchen eating dinner silently until Mom spoke. Matt and Jeremy were gone somewhere, they were gone a lot now. I don't remember their faces.

I didn't know what to say. I took another bite of the pasta that Mom made.

"Willow," Dad said.

I looked up finally.

"You understand why we have to do this right?"

I nodded. I didn't understand.

"It'll be fun..." she looked like she was going to add something, but she stopped.

I nodded again.

The conversation ended in silence. We finished eating.

*

My new school was small, those posters of the missing two were pinned and posted everywhere, in each hallway, each room, each corkboard, each whiteboard. Their names were everywhere, but I always avoided looking at them directly. Their eyes kept talking. They looked at me, same as before. My mind spun. They went here before they dissolved into the darkness of the labyrinth.

No one talked to me. They would look at me but never talk. Everyone was staring and looking and judging. Judging and thinking.

Fire and flame.

Breakdance.

I shook it away and continued on, my steps echoing in the quiet hallway, looking down, avoiding their stare, them and the posters.

*

The house was quiet. The night was especially cold which bit and nipped at me from under the covers. I closed my eyes, trying to sleep against the hum of noise and sound, hiding from the gaze of the spot.

There was a whole school assembly earlier for the missing. Kids got up to a podium and had these little flowery speeches about them, saying these bottom of the barrel compliments that meant nothing. People would glance at me and then look away, glance and look away. It was odd and preachy, the whole event just a giant circle jerk to show off how kind and good and righteous everyone was for caring so much. Screw that. Screw all of it. I bet most of those kids up there were lying to look better. No more formalities. Fuck em'. Fuck em' good. I'm tired of it all. I just want to sleep, but the noise stays consistent. Loud and disturbing and awful. All I can do is think. And think...

Tink.

A tiny little sound.

Tink.

It was coming from my window. I looked up at the small window above my bed and, after another second or two, a small rock clinked against the glass. I stood up on my bed and looked out the window. Everything was dark as pitch, the front yard covered in it especially so. I strained my eyes and continued to look. Then a flashlight beam turned on and off, beaming into my room cutting through the darkness like a knife. My eyes finally made out the outline of a person waving back and forth in big, voluptuous, waves. They said something but it was muffled from behind the glass of the window. The flashlight flickered on and off again, trying to get my attention. Moth to the flame. Annoying.

I opened the window a little bit, "Hello?" I said.

"You're Willow right?" It was a girl's voice.

"Uh..."

"My name's Scarlet. I live next door," she pointed towards her house. "We go to school together."

"Okay?" This was the first time I heard her speak. I saw her walking around school once or twice before, but I never paid any attention to her. I kept my eyes down.

"Good!" She was a little loud, her voice echoed a little in the silent night but she seemed unconcerned with her volume, "Hey, I have something to ask you."

"Um..."

"But first, you gotta come with me, I have something to

show you."

I didn't know what to say. I stood there looking at this person who I've never talked to before. This is the first time I've ever even heard her name and here she is, acting like we're already friends.

"Hurry up Willow, time doesn't wait for you or me, come on!" Again, her voice echoed through the dark street.

Jesus.

"Uh…okay."

I closed the window and put on my shoes and a dark coat. Why was I even doing this? She's out there acting like we're friends which we're not. But some type of deep curiosity pushed me along, step by quiet step.

Opening the bedroom door washed me back into the silence of this house. I walked down the stairs. Not even a creak. I sneaked through the living room and slowly unlocked the bolt shut front door and silently closed it behind me once I stepped outside.

The cold snapped at me as I shut the door. Scarlet was sitting in the same spot as when I talked to her from the window, she waved at me when I stepped out. I didn't really know what to think.

I walked up to her and crossed my arms, "What?" I asked.

She stood up and smiled, she was slightly taller than me. "I have something to show you, follow me." She started walking.

"Where?" I asked, not budging.

She turned around and sighed. "Look," she stepped back towards me, "I know you saw something right? Something out there." She gestured to the woods.

"Uh…"

She leaned in right next to my ear and whispered, "I saw it too."

I moved my head back. She saw it too? Why should I trust this person?

Huh...

Something weird, deep down, tinged when I looked at her. Something primal and hungry. I wanted to follow. *Something*...that's the only word for it...

I followed her. She had this smile of excitement on her face.

"How'd you know that was my room?" I asked her.

"Trust me, I've done my homework."

Weirdo.

She led me to the side of her house where she crouched down and pried open a small rectangular window to the basement. She looked at me, nodded, and then got on her stomach and crawled inside. I stood there for a second after she disappeared into the window, not sure what to do.

"Come on," her voice echoed from the window. "It's cold out there."

I got on my stomach and wiggled in through the window without any resistance. I fell face first onto a soft couch that smelled like musty perfume. There were several candles lit all about it making shadow upon dancing shadow. There was a cozy warmth in the room too. Posters of things that I've never heard of before were plastered all upon the walls. One poster said Divine Burial and had 4 dudes with axes shaped into guitars. Never heard of it. Another poster said Dark Season. Never heard of it. Another poster was of *Star Wars: A New Hope*. I knew that one.

"Welcome to my room." Scarlet said as she sat cross legged on her bed. "Close the window, please." She pointed to the basement window. I got up and shut it. "I know," she motioned towards her entire room, "it's pretty glorious ain't it?"

"Lots of...candles." I said.

"Yea, Mom doesn't like them. She says I could burn the house down but whatever."

Huh...

"You're impressed, right?"

"Sure?" I shrugged.

I sat on the couch across from her bed and tried to warm my hands. Scarlet looked at me for another couple of seconds, a gust of wind howled beyond the basement window above my head.

"You know, a lot of kids at school think you're weird, right?" She cocked her head.

I was taken aback. "Okay..."

"Some kids even think that you're the one who killed Damien and Sarah."

"Why...why would I even kill them?" I asked, crossing my arms.

"Hmm...you hated them for some reason?" She perked up, "Oh! They stole something, like money or, I don't know, something important, you know? You had some type of vendetta on them? You're an assassin and they had hits out on them? They...uh...they-"

I continued to say nothing. She stopped.

"Look, I know you didn't kill them. People just talk and talk, you know? You're way too scrawny anyways."

"Why are you telling me this?"

She made a face like she was thinking of something, "Because I think you should know."

I didn't know how to react. She was the first person to tell me how anyone felt. I already knew how all the kids at school thought of me, but this was the first time someone actually straight up said it. "What do you think?" I finally asked.

"Hmm..." She scratched her chin, "I think you're alright." She smiled. "I'll be your friend."

"Why?" This was weird.

"Because I like you. And because we share a secret."

"What?"

"One second." She said as she excitedly fished around under her bed for something. She pulled out a small lockbox and handed it to me. I looked at the box then at her.

"Open it, silly."

I opened it, clicking the two locks. Inside was an assortment of drawings and photographs of all sorts. I grabbed one of the drawings and saw a pretty decently drawn wolfman with two big red eyes. I grabbed another drawing and there was a pretty good depiction of a mothman with especially ripped muscles. It also had glowing, fire-like, eyes. I picked up another drawing and saw another monster with glowing eyes. There must have been over twenty drawings of different creatures with glowing eyes.

"Those are all artists' interpretations by yours truly." She gestured to herself.

At the bottom of the lockbox was one turned polaroid photograph. I grabbed it and slowly flipped it. The picture was taken from a window, high up. Locked into the middle of the polaroid were two candle-like eyes, their breakdance frozen. They were looking at me again. I screamed and dropped the picture and the lockbox, my stomach turned and gurgled as the garbage grew once again.

A loud, 'SHHHHH' hissed out from Scarlet's teeth as a finger rose up to her mouth. She looked up at the roof and waited. We sat silent for a couple of seconds. There was a little bit of movement from upstairs and then silence.

"Dad's been sleeping in the living room lately and I don't want to wake him up."

I nodded, goosebumps wrapped around my arms. My stomach settled slowly. Scarlet stood up and started to clean the mess of the lockbox.

"You have the same reaction too," she was picking up her art and placing them back into the box. "Do you get that feeling?" She looked at me, "You know, that feeling? Like you're about to throw up but, like...weirder?" She motioned her hands as she explained and cleaned.

I nodded again.

"Yea, pretty weird right?"

We sat in silence until she was done. I was feeling better

by the time she finished up. She sat on her bed and looked at me, lockbox still in hand.

"So I was right. Right?"

"That I saw the eyes?"

"That. But was I also right that you saw what the Monster is? What does it look like? There has to be something there, you know? A body..."

I sat for a second.

"You know," she gestured again, "you were out in the woods when Damien and Sarah went missing. I heard you ran out of them screaming and peeing. You HAD to have seen it right?"

I cringed a little, "No."

"So I was wrong. You never saw it."

"No." I sat for a second.

"Are you saying 'no' like," she started to mimic my voice, "'No, you're not wrong Scarlet. I did, in-fact, see it. And you look like you lost weight too.'"

"No, I'm saying that I didn't see it. I saw the eyes weeks ago." She looked a little disappointed at my answer. "Have you seen...more?" I asked.

"No. Mom got me this camera," she pointed at a polaroid camera on her desk. "I was messing with it one night and I caught the bastard in still-frame."

"Still-frame?" I asked.

"Pic-ture," her words spelled it out.

"Oh."

"Yep..." She nodded.

Awkward. "Have you told anyone else about it?" I finally asked.

"No. Have you?"

"No."

We sat silent for a little bit.

"How do you know it's a monster and not, like, a wolf?" I finally asked.

She looked up at the ceiling in thought, "Well, whatever

it is, they were way taller than a wolf, so there's that-"

"I'm not saying it's a wolf, I'm just saying it doesn't have to be a monster."

"Yes, but think- What kind of animal known to man is that tall?"

I thought for a second, "Bigfoot?"

She laughed, "Bigfoot isn't real."

"How do you know?"

"Look, even if bigfoot is real, and that's a big if, bigfoot is just an animal. Why would its eyes give off this weird feeling where even a photo of them can make you scream bloody murder and almost wake my Dad up? Also, there's thousands of bigfoot sightings and none of them are like this."

She had a point.

"Also, I don't think bigfoot would be able to make two kids completely disappear off the face of the Earth without anything left behind. Do you know that even two weeks after the disappearances, there has still been no evidence found at all? No tracks, no blood, no nothing."

"And how do you know that?"

"I keep up." She smiled.

"Well...why would that monster specifically be able to make them disappear completely?"

"Look, it's a monster and it probably took and killed Damien and Sarah. I don't know why or how, but the proof is right here in this pudding."

I felt a pit in my stomach, "I don't know..."

"It's a saying. The proof is in the pudding-"

"I get that, but I don't know about this whole...monster thing. Isn't that kinda jumping the gun?"

"Fuck it, man. Let's jump a hundred, no, a thousand guns." She smiled. "And besides, life's a little more magical with a monster lurking about."

Huh.

Scarlet sat quiet, looking over me. She liked to talk, that was made clear instantly, but she also seemed to know when to shut up.

"Well," I finally broke the silence. "What do you want to do about it?"

She nodded, "Follow me."

5

Scarlet opened the window and we both squirmed out back into the cold night. I could barely pull myself up and she had to grab my arm and rip me from the window, almost spilling us both on the ground.

"Where are we going?" I asked, standing up.

"I have another cool thing to show you."

She led through the side gate of her house to the backyard. "Don't worry," she said. "We're safe back here."

"How do you know?"

"Eh." She shrugged as I followed her.

"Eh?"

"Eh." She shrugged again. "Check it." She pointed to a singular large tree growing from the center of her backyard. Atop the tree was a large treehouse which shimmered with a glow from the inside. I had forgotten about it.

"Jeez," I said.

"I know, right?"

I looked past the tree to find that her fence was way higher than mine. Almost as tall as the treehouse. I had forgotten about that too. It felt much safer compared to ours.

She led us up the tree ladder into the increasingly impressive treehouse. She opened the hatch and I followed her inside. It had a modest interior with these nice little lights which lit up the ceiling. There were openable windows with wooden covers, a small couch, a stereo, a desk, and a lantern in the center.

"Watch this." She said and turned on a heater stuffed in the corner. "Dad set this up last week."

"Isn't that dangerous?"

She pulled out a small fire extinguisher from under the couch and smiled, her eyebrows dancing up and down.

"But still..."

"You worry too much, Willow Pines."

I moved a little towards the heater, fighting off the cold. "So, what are we doing up here?"

She nodded and opened one of the wooden window covers, "Look."

The window gave a perfect view over the fence into the dark forest. I stopped looking. "Okay..."

"You don't understand?" she frowned.

I shrugged.

"Are you saying, 'No I understand' or-"

"I'm saying that I don't understand what the purpose of this view is." I cut her off.

She smiled, "Okay, you may want to sit down for what I'm about to say."

"I think I'm gonna stand."

"Sit," she commanded.

I sat.

"Okay. We're going to get evidence of the monster." She let it sizzle.

I didn't know what to say so I proceeded with saying nothing.

"I got a camera and everything! Pretty rad right?" She definitely thought she was some sort of hero.

I didn't say anything.

"What do you think?" she asked.

"I think that's...kinda dumb."

"Ouch. Why?"

"I don't think it comes out during the day so it's going to be dark. We're never going to get good enough pictures of it. And it's also...kinda dumb." I shook my head, "You really want to chase this thing?"

"Yes. I do. Oh yea, I forgot to show you this!"

She stuck her arm under the couch and deftly pulled out a huge flashlight and hefted it onto the desk with a huff. She patted it like a dog. "When we see the eyes, bam! One of us shines this beast at it and the other person takes a picture," she motioned to the polaroid camera that hung from her neck by a thick black strap. "Cool right? It's a two man job."

I sat and stared at the mega-flashlight.

"Here," she lifted the flashlight onto the window, pointing it out towards the woods, "I'll give you a demonstration." She turned it on and a beam of light lit up the entirety of the forest beyond the fence, destroying the seemingly indestructible curtain of darkness. "And this is at its lowest setting." She was very proud of her hyper-flashlight. She turned it off, "So?"

"I mean..." I just wanted to move on.

"Come on, it'll be like we're monster hunters."

"It's dumb..."

"So?"

"Why do you even want to do this with me? We barely even know each other."

She deflated with a deep long breath as her face fell. She sat next to me on the couch, placing the flashlight down on the desk with a bump, "Well...I know you more now." Her brows lowered slightly as she looked off somewhere towards the window. "And...you're the only person I can talk to about this. It gets, I don't know...lonely? Just having someone who...you know...understands. I guess..." She looked at me, "It feels good having someone else around." Her eyes left me, wandering back down to the floorboards.

We sat there on the couch for a little bit without saying anything. The heater sputtered a couple of times, the chilly wind continued to blow in through the open window, fighting with the warmth of the heater for dominance. I don't really know how I feel about Scarlet. Can someone even be your friend right after meeting them? And this whole monster hunting thing? Sounds like some kids' story that I want absolutely no part in.

I want to move on and forget about it, but can I even do that? It keeps swimming around in the back of my mind, sometimes getting close and sometimes going far away, its strokes becoming a loud continuous splash or a silent skate like a water strider. I know I can't talk about it with anyone else. They wouldn't understand. But Scarlet's too ambitious. She wants to capture it. That's all her, not me. That's not something that I do. I just don't. I deal. Deal with it just enough. But it was catching up. Slowly. Very slowly...

Maybe I...I don't exactly know. But, the more I think about it all, the more I want to help her in this stupid quest. It's not mine. It's not something I want to do. But something about her... Her ambition? Her confidence? Whatever it was, I think I was starting to like her, even with her annoying antics. I've never had a friend before.

"Something talked to me-"

"What?"

"That day," I swallowed and kept going. "Out in the woods, when they went missing, on my, uh, birthday it, uh, spoke to me."

Her face stayed still, her eyes watching, no fire behind them, "What did it say?" she finally asked.

"I...it..."

"It's okay..." She looked at me, sincere and purposeful, silently and still.

We sat for a little longer. The wind blew beyond the treehouse, shaking it slightly.

"You know," I said, "why not?"

She nodded, "Good." She said nothing more. She got up and closed the 'woods window' as we came to know it. She sat back down.

A thought just came to mind as she sat back next to me, "That picture you took of the eyes. Did you take it from that window?" I pointed.

"Yea. It's fuckin' tall, right?"

Tall was an understatement. This treehouse was almost as tall as the house before it. I remember it rising up into the trees when I saw it. Was it crouching? Flying?

"What happened after that?" I asked.

She looked at the closed wooden window covers, "Mmm..." she hummed out like she was thinking. She glanced at me then looked away. She never answered. We sat some more on the couch and took in the warmth from the heater.

"So you coming over every night?" She asked after a little bit.

"What?" I asked.

"To stakeout. We need to get on the grind, you know? If we're to find evidence of whatever this thing is."

I thought. Maybe this was it. This was the unbeaten path to having a friend. She smiled at me as I contemplated. "Sure." I answered. Scarlet didn't seem like she needed much sleep either. My stomach grumbled.

*

It was cold once again as we left the treehouse. I still don't know much about Scarlet. I wondered how she was going to treat me at school now? Maybe she will ignore me like some, or stare like the others. Either or, either or. Maybe she would come up and talk to me.

We came around to the front of my house and she gave me a nod, "See you tomorrow," she said. It was Monday tomorrow.

"Good night." I walked back to the front door and found it still unlocked. How long was I out?

I creeped back upstairs and nestled back into my bed. Things felt like they were moving fast. I didn't know how to think about it.

I closed my eyes, expecting the noise of the machinery to boom back, but it didn't.

Silence...and then some more. Continuous-

I opened my eyes again. The spot was still there, watching.

I closed them, the silence still there.

6

I got ready for school that morning. I was worried. 'Friend'. It's an iffy thing. Would she forget about me? Ignore me at school? So many little things can go in so many little ways today. If she forgot all about last night, would I even care? Would I be relieved? Maybe. I've never had a friend before. That fact was finally dawning on me. I've really never had a friend... huh.

I looked up at the hazy spot. It looked back, saying nothing.

The doorbell rang and I heard Mom go and open it. I listened deeply, trying to figure out what's going on down there. Mom yelled upstairs.

"Willow, someone's at the door for you!"

"One second!"

I finished getting dressed as quickly as I could and went downstairs to find Scarlet standing in the doorway talking to Mom. Her eyes lit up and she waved at me. She was wearing ripped jeans with a metal shirt of a band I've never heard of.

"I asked your Mom if we could walk to school together."

I stood there staring at her.

"I didn't know you made a friend," Mom said with a smile. "And such a sweet one at that! Of course Willow will go with you!"

Mom practically pushed me out the door without a word. She never liked the idea of walking to school even though it's only a ten minute walk but now, with Scarlet, she seemed quite sure of it.

Scarlet and I walked silently for a while. There were other kids walking in front and behind us and on the other side of the street. The warm morning sun shone down along with the cool wind which blew past us, filling my nose with the fresh scent of the morning dew.

A couple minutes from school, I finally asked her something I've been thinking about, "How much was that giant flashlight?"

"Dunno."

"Then where'd you get it?"

"Dad got it for a camping trip but we never went. Now the flashlight is mine."

"I've never been camping." I said.

She looked at me and smiled, the sunlight beaming through her hair making a darkish glow, "Maybe we'll go one day."

*

I forgot about all the looks and stares from the other kids that day. It was just Scarlet and me, us, as we walked throughout the halls. She never brought me to any friends or acquaintances. It was just us, alone, in this world of eyes lining hall after hall, classroom after classroom. I felt better. Safer.

We were in some of the same classes, some different. All the same, we would reconvene no matter what. It was almost robotic in its naturality as if it were meant to be. Whatever the case, we went on, walking and talking, standing and sitting, ignoring and laughing, it was great.

It all continued until it didn't.

And then school was over.

*

That cold Monday night was our first coveted stakeout in the treehouse. We talked about its logistics as we walked home together after school. She wanted me to bring some food for the night. I was supposed to sneak out at 12. I was thinking about grabbing the half full box of Cheez-Its from the cupboard before I left. There was still the distinct feeling of anxious nerve running my body cold as I thought about it more, laying in my bed, waiting for the right time to go. Mom asked me all about my new friend when I got home. We talked a bit, then it went quiet and then we stopped and then I went upstairs.

The mechanical and industrious sounds were gone, at least for the moment. It feels weird, closing my eyes to a pure silence. Deafening silence. Ringing silence.

I looked at the spot. It was there, hidden, somewhere in the darkness, just a shadow, looking and watching, thinking.

It was time. I hopped out of bed, already decked out in my cold clothes. I grabbed a beanie too, just in case. I was ready. I made my way downstairs, grabbed the box of Cheez-Its and made my way outside.

She was waiting by the backyard gate with a puffy sweater and sweatpants. I followed her to the treehouse as we shared our hellos. She saw the food I had and nodded approvingly.

The heater was already running and the tree fort was warm and toasty. Both the flashlight and the polaroid camera were sitting, ready, on the table. The stereo was playing some gruff tunes, some guitars strumming and drums bam bamming in the background to a quickening beat. I noticed her backpack was sitting on the couch too. She saw me looking at it and said, "I still got homework, so might as well do it while we're here, you know?"

"Sure," I nodded.

She opened the woods window and set another chair by it, "We could take shifts." It was getting a little colder in the treehouse.

"Okay, I guess I'll go first."

"Sweet." She sat down and took out a folder and a pencil, "This math homework is kicking my ass."

I grabbed the flashlight with a heft, sat at the window and pulled my beanie a little more tightly over my head. She turned up the music a little louder. It was definitely some metal song.

"Can I see your homework?" I asked.

She handed me the paper and I looked over it. Math was never my forte. "Yea, I don't understand what's going on here." I handed it back to her.

"Me neither," she said.

After about 30 minutes, she was done with her math homework. Nothing had changed outside the window, past the dark curtain of definite black and more black. We talked here and there. She started working on some other homework assignment.

"What band is that?" I asked.

"Oh, that's Divine Blood. They're pretty rad right?"

"I guess," I said, "but I don't think it's really my style."

She stood up from the desk, "Here, you might like this." She walked over to the stereo and moved around a stack of CDs until she pulled one out, "This might be more up your alley." She replaced the Divine Blood CD with this one and hit play. The first song started with a couple lofty guitar riffs into a smooth melody.

"What is this?" I asked.

She sat back down at the desk, "Radiohead."

"Never heard of them."

"You'll like it," she smiled.

I looked back into the darkness and saw something move. I felt a weight drop in my stomach. Movement, just beyond the black. I wanted to throw up, the garbage pile building up once more, weighing my stomach down with its lofty weight.

I swiftly clicked the on switch for the mega flashlight and the entire area in front of us lit up into bright light. There was a deer who lifted its head and stared at me, frozen. Relief washed through my bones. Scarlet stood and excitedly looked over my shoulder, camera poised in her hands, ready to snap.

"It's just a deer." I said.

This flashlight really meant business though, I could see everything with this thing.

Another hour or so went by. Scarlet just finished her homework and stretched out on the back of her chair.

"Jesus, that shit sucked." She stood, "Hey, I think I should take watch for now."

I enjoyed my post. I liked the calmness of it all. I liked the coldness of the air. I liked listening to Scarlet curse under her breath as she struggled with the homework. I enjoyed the new music that Scarlet put on, we let it repeat through the hours. I wanted to keep looking into the woods. I felt brave doing it. I had a big flashlight with me. I had someone else with me too. I was always lonely, I never realized it until recently. It hurt to think about it. I should cry, right? People cry and then other people listen. But the tears never came. I'm human too.

"It's okay, I can watch some more." I answered.

"Here," she pulled her desk chair next to mine. "Scooch," she commanded. I grabbed the bottom of my chair and moved over a little.

She put the chair down and zipped her sweater up a little bit. "Damn, it's cold here," she said with a chill. "That beanie is a good idea."

I took it off and gave it to her, "Here."

She took it with a smile, "What a sweetie-pie."

We sat like that next to each other, the album still playing on repeat, looking out into the cold. Scarlet reached over and grabbed a snack.

"Why did you move here?" She asked, chewing.

I sat for a second, pulling together the past, "My...my old house burnt down."

"Oh," she looked at me. "Well at least you're here now, right?" She smiled.

I had expected her to say something like 'I'm sorry' or 'that sucks'. I was happy about that. I've heard enough 'sorrys' in my life from people who really didn't give a shit if I died the next day or not.

"Yea," I said.

She leaned over and turned on and off the flashlight, "I'm just checkin.'"

"Why didn't you come to my birthday party?" A cold gust of wind hit my face. "I'm pretty sure my parents invited every family on the block and then some."

Scarlet sat there for a second. She took another bite of her snack, "Why would I go to a random kid's birthday party?"

I smiled real hard, thankful that at least one other person understood, "Right?"

"Cake?" she questioned. "Maybe they wanted free cake and ice cream?"

"Maybe."

"Man, now I can't stop thinking about ice cream." She stretched over the back of the chair, "What's the best ice cream flavor?"

"Uhh...I don't know...chocolate or pistachio."

"Eww, pistachio," She made a stink face. "And here I thought you had better taste Miss. Pines."

"You barely know me. What's your favorite then Professor Good Taste."

"Well it just so happens that my favorite flavor is also the objective best flavor." She let it simmer.

"And?"

"Strawberry." She was confident in her wrong opinion.

"And I have bad taste?"

She laughed, "Whatever nut job."

"What?"

"You're a nut job. Get it? Pistachios are nuts."

"I think they're seeds."

"No they are not. As I said. Nut. Job. That's you and you're only proving it."

"I'm pretty sure they're seeds." I shot back.

"Look, seeds, nuts, it doesn't matter what they are because you're still a nut job."

"Shut up, dick."

We laughed out into the cold night.

"Hey," Scarlet said. "Wanna arm wrestle?"

"Why?"

"Because I think I'm stronger than you."

"You're bigger and taller, you're gonna win."

"So? Let's see."

We turned our chairs over to the desk behind us. She scooched hers over to the other side of it so we were looking at each other face to face. She put her arm up and I did the same. Her hand was sweaty. It was kinda gross. But it was comforting too.

"Okay," She started. "One...two...three."

I instantly knew I was going to lose. I pushed as hard as I could but her arm didn't budge. I felt her strength pushing against mine and I was losing hard. After a couple seconds of struggle she finally slammed my arm onto the table, victorious.

"Well," I rubbed my hurting wrist. "You happy?"

"Yea," she looked satisfied with her victory. "I think I am."

She stood and turned around towards the stereo, "What's your favorite band?" She was changing the CDs. Metal music started blaring out.

"I don't really listen to music," I propped my head up with my arm as I leaned against the desk.

"You're really easy to read, you know that right?"

"Why's that?"

"Dude," she sat back down. "You just are. With just a glance, BOOM! I got you on lock."

"So you're a god?" I asked.

"Something like that."

"Well...then tell me something about myself that I haven't told you yet?"

"Hmm," her brain was chugging along as she tried to think of something, "Ah!"

"What?" I asked.

"That you're a loser," she laughed.

"You're the one hanging out with a loser."

"Losers are cool."

"I'm pretty sure that, by definition, a loser is not cool-"

"Okay!" She stood up. "Stand up!"

I stood, not knowing what was going to happen.

She held out her hand, "From this day on, we will be some badass losers. Let's shake on it."

I hesitated for a second, but screw it: I grabbed her hand and we shook a hefty shake.

"Fuck em'," I said.

"Fuck em' indeed," Scarlet said with a nod of her head, her dark black hair waved back and forth.

A little bit later we were back to sitting and looking out into the veil of the woods.

"What time is it?" I asked.

She had a watch and checked it, "3:30. You tired?"

I shrugged, "Not really."

She kept looking into the darkness, "Me neither."

We sat there a little longer.

"Hey," Scarlet said. "Me and my dad are going to a corn maze for Halloween next week. Do you wanna come?"

"Corn maze?" I asked.

"Yea, it's a maze...in corn...a corn maze? It's fun."

"So we just fortuitously wander around some corn?"

She scrunched her face, "For-tu-i-tously?" She sounded out. "You even know what that means?"

I thought for a second, and then another. "No-"

"Smartass," she smiled.

"What about trick-or-treating?" I asked, steering the topic.

"We can do that early in the day. So? We doing this?"

"Why not?"

The rest of that night we chatted about this and that, but we finally decided it was a good time for me to go home at 5:00. That way we could try and get a couple of hours of sleep and so my Mom wouldn't freak out if she saw me missing in the morning.

We saw nothing during the night. Nothing but darkness and that one deer. The eyes of fire glowed in the back of my mind, but I shooed them away every time, fighting off that feeling. I don't want to be judged anymore, not by them.

Breakdancing? What? Sounds cool.

When Scarlet and I parted ways at my house that night, I felt accomplished. I wanted to go upstairs, lay in my bed, and think about everything that just happened. I wanted to drink it all in and retain it in my brain, almost like these experiences were going to be deleted, never to be had again. Like I'll forget them somehow. I wanted to hold onto them and never let go in fear of losing them like how I lost Willows Eve. Fire is the destructor.

I stopped myself, my mind starting to turn.

Wrap it up.

Forget.

I wanted to cherish it all and keep it close, so I did. Scarlet, Scarlet, Scarlet, my mind all a mess. I had never had a friend before...really? Are you shitting me? My heart bumped.

In all that cherishing, deep tiredness started to black everything out.

I closed my eyes and waited, the silence consuming me once more, the machinery gone.

I felt myself drifting off into sleep, my mind finally at rest.

"So? You like her, right?" A voice shot out from the darkness.

My eyes opened violently, my heart started up again, like a pulley engine going off. It whirred and continued on, faster and faster, second by second. I tried to move, but I couldn't.

"It's easier now, right? To sleep? And all after meeting her..." It was deep and soft, it was smooth and rough, like fine sand and rough gravel, it went into one ear and stayed. It reminded me of my dream. With the steak. With the meat. With the eyes of fire.

"I feel like there's...I don't know...something special between you two." It sauntered.

I tried to move again. Nothing. Again. Nothing. My heart whirred more, beating faster and faster, this voice almost bringing up memory after forgotten memory. Stuff and more stuff piling. Stuff I didn't want to remember-

"Be calm, Willow. I'm only trying to help you here..."

My head felt lighter, my body untensed itself, my lungs rattled less, the whirring of my heart lessened, the cord being released.

Thump-thump-thump.

Thump-thump.

Thump.

Thump.

Thu-mp.

Thu-mp...

"There you go, Willow. Breath a little. It's going to be alright. I'm only here to help...."

I tried to speak, but nothing, my mouth locked together by mesh and pins and needles and string all working together. They stopped me from speaking. They stopped me from moving- All encased by this voice which calmed continuously, one second after another.

Where is it?

"Where am I?" It asked. "I'm up here, Willow."

The spot? It hid in the darkness of the room, barely visible. There was something around it. Something... ethereal...dark...

"Yes, up here."

A memory almost breached the surface, only to be pulled back, down to the depths, forgotten once again.

"We should help eachother out...a sort of deal? Yes. A deal."

Deal?

"I help you and you help me."

What?

"I can help you...with Scarlet. I can help you...be you. You see all this fake around you, right? The smiles, the faces, the world... It's all fake, correct? You hate it all. I can help... with that-"

What do you mean?

"What I say. That's what I mean. I want to help you. Why would you slap away an upturned hand? That would only be rude. Just say yes."

I don't know who you are...

"Who I am doesn't matter. All of this is only for your benefit, Willow. Just-"

Yea, I don't think so.

"Willow, please..."

Fuck off man, I'm trying to sleep.

No more formalities.

7

"What are you going to be for Halloween?" she asked me one night while reading a comic book on the treehouse couch.

"I don't know. You?"

"I'm in between a couple of ideas. I kinda want to be, like, Frankenstein or a mummy. Something like that. Maybe we can both be monsters?" She flipped a page.

"I could be Frankenstein and you can be Frankenstein's Monster?"

"What do you mean?" she asked, looking up from her comic.

"Frankenstein is the guy who made the Monster. The Monster doesn't have a name."

She looked at me for a second, blankly. "You're a nerd." she finally said.

"I'm pretty sure most people know that."

"Whatever. Yes, we can do that. You can be a crazy scientist and I'll get some monster gear together."

*

I finally had my costume for Halloween. Mom and I went out to the costume store to find what I needed. She was ecstatic that I was finally spending Halloween with a friend.

We tried to talk about it but, slowly, it sizzled out into silence.

We found a nice set of crazy scientist gear fit with a white and frizzy wig that smelled like death. I was digging it.

We walked to school that Halloween. She showed up to my house wearing really tall shoes which added a couple of inches to her height. Her hair was slicked back and had gray streaks all throughout it. She was also wearing a purple coat with holes placed here and there and her face was painted gray with specks of red blood on each side of her mouth. She looked like some weird amalgamation of each monster from Dracula to Frankenstein's Monster to some type of zombie. I was even shorter than before, her stilt-like shoes adding a newfound height which was a little intimidating. I was dressed in my lab coat with a fake white mustache. I ditched the wig because it smelled like shit. I bet it had asbestos all over it like one of those horrible plastic halloween masks.

At school, people seemed to ignore me more than anything now, their scathing eyes turned away instead of at, those posters of the missing slowly being taken down and, with them, people's memories. It wasn't even that long ago, their flowery speeches of love and remembrance, friendship and companionship, fun and laughter, now all but gone in the mist of time, proven only to be fake feelings just to show everyone how much they cared when they really didn't. Like I said: Giant. Fucking. Circlejerk. People seemed to move on too quickly. They hate when everyone else hates, they stare when everyone else stares, and they forget when everyone else forgets. It's all a cycle of the masses blanketed by an overwhelming plastic wrap which covered and suffocated the life out of all beneath it, slowly turning everything into this shiny and smooth and safe little playground where no one can get out of line.

And as I said, no more formalities. I'm done with all this dogshit and I'm not going to hide it anymore. Fuck everything.

And as school finished, as the bell rang the toll for everyone to leave, I found the last poster of that kid who went missing and, in my scientist outfit, ripped his fucking face down, the corners of the paper leaving the only remaining marks of him left in the entire world.

*

The spot was watching me as I did homework. Right behind me.

That voice kept coming back, echoing deep in my mind as it tried to make me remember something. I wanted to shiver but I didn't and then I got annoyed.

I spun in the chair and flipped the fucker off. Damn right.

*

I found Scarlet waiting for me out in my front yard.

"Yea, the stilt shoes are a no go. Those puppies hurt like hell." She said, rolling her ankles around.

"I noticed."

"Walk and talk with me, baby."

She started walking, I followed her.

"So, I got this entire thing planned out. Trust me, we're gonna get some serious baggage." She said with a skip in her step.

"Sure-"

"And remember to act cute," she told me as we walked. "These oldies suck it up."

"Cute?" I asked. "What do you mean?"

She stopped walking and looked at me, "Like this," she made a puppy dog face. In her amalgamated monster costume, her cute face looked almost twisted, "Twick or tweet," She said in a baby voice.

"Fuck off!" I laughed.

"Just watch! It wins hearts and candy."

To my surprise, Scarlet was right. She would tweak her words just enough, make a face just subtle enough to where I don't even think most people understood that they were being punked. And, to my surprise, as we walked from one house to the other, I noticed the heft in her bag compared to the lightness of mine.

"Don't worry," she said. "We'll split all of our candy later."

I forgot to respond. I realized that my fake, white, mustache was gone. It must've fallen off earlier, lost and gone in the October wind. Whatever.

We made the rounds. With each round, our sacks of gold grew in size. As our gold grew, we grew happier. As we grew happier, we got more gold. It was a devious little cycle that only spurred on our tricking and treating.

We eventually made it back to her house and got ready to go to the corn maze with some time still left in the day as the sun still danced somewhere in the sky, a couple more hours left in its waltz.

Scarlet's Dad was still doing stuff in the house so we decided to wait for him and count our loot in the treehouse. It was a little bit of a struggle to get up the ladder with the increasingly heavy bags of candy but we eventually did it. We both poured our bags of candy on the desk and started to systematically separate them by chocolate and non chocolate, brand, and size. We got a decent amount of full bars which I planned to give to Scarlet once we finished.

"You know," she said as we counted. "You could really pull it off."

"Pull what off?"

"The whole cute thing, you know? You got good eyes."

"Oh...yea I don't know about that." I shook my head.

"I'm serious!" She punched me in the arm.

"Ow!" I yelled.

"That didn't even hurt, come on."

"You're stronger than you think, Scarlet."

"I wont punch you again if you do the cute face."

My face said no.

"Come on. Pweese!" She made the cute face.

"Stop! That's annoying!"

"You're prettier than you think, Willow. Come on!"

"Dude..." I sat, looking at her for a second.

"Dude...I'm totally going to punch you again-"

I took a breath, "Okay, but just this once."

She smiled and nodded.

"And fuck you by the way," I said.

"Fuck you too, little miss badass. Now hurry up and do it."

I steeled myself. I was already embarrassed just thinking about doing it. It's uncomfortable and out of my zone. But Scarlet does have a mean right hook.

I made my best impression of that terrible terrible face, "Twick or tweet." I said in that awful baby voice. A scream of embarrassment shot out of my mouth as I shoved my face into the safety of my hands.

Scarlet started laughing, "Holy shit!"

I was still hiding in my hands, "That was awful!"

"Aw, come on! You loved it!"

"Jesus..."

A banging on the tree trunk shook the treehouse slightly, I jumped out of my seat in surprise.

"Scarlet!" A man's voice rang out from below, "It's time to go!" It was Scarlet's dad. He was banging on the tree trunk. Scarlet started laughing more.

"Alright Dad, one second!" She held her hand out and helped me get up. I was still a little shook and a little embarrassed. "Don't worry Willow, we're safe up here."

"Screw off."

I started to leave the treehouse when Scarlet grabbed my arm, "You know I was serious, right?"

"What?" I turned back around to face her.

"You should be more confident, Willow."

A second passed. I didn't know what to say exactly. She watched me.

"Alright, Dad's waiting. Let's go see what this maze is all about."

*

Scarlet's Dad was much more talkative than I thought he would be. He was a bigger guy with strong looking arms. He introduced himself as Mike. He was wearing a cheap Thor costume which had some plastic hammer that hung from his belt.

"So, Willow," he turned to look at me in the back seat of his old Carolla. "How'd you and Scarlet meet?"

"Uh…"

"School-" Scarlet butt in. She hasn't told her parents about our late nights in the treehouse. I haven't told mine either.

"Ah, well I'm glad my pumpkin got a friend, finally."

"I've had friends before, Dad."

"Well, you've never brought those friends home before. Your old man wants to see who you hang out with."

"Dad."

"No, no. I get it." He was feigning a sad voice, "You hate your Dad now, I get it."

"Dad!" Scarlet started laughing.

"I kid, I kid!" He glanced back at me, "Well, I'm glad Scarlet has taken a liking to someone who looks like they have a little class, right Willow?"

"I guess."

"Oh come on, don't sell yourself short. I can tell a smart kid apart from a dumb one."

"And how do you know that?" Scarlet butted in jokingly.

"Because I have you!" They both started laughing, the car swerved a little bit. I didn't really get it.

I listened to Scarlet and her Dad talk for the rest of the ride. They went back and forth with each other, joking and laughing. We started to go through fields and fields until the car turned into a gravely pathway that could only fit two cars going either way.

Slowly, from each side, we were enveloped in trees of long jagged arms which ended in little hands of spikes that stuck out in all directions. They were jutting out, trying to touch the car with their little fingers. I watched them speed by as Mike said something that I didn't hear. It made Scarlet giggle her little laugh, but my attention was still on the trees, their hands of spikes getting closer and closer and closer. Then there was nothing but air.

We drove into a large grove of dead yellow grass with about 50 cars parked neatly upon it. In front of the makeshift parking lot was a large field of corn with several food venders and little theme park games spread out before it, the type of games where you have to pay a dollar to knock over a rigged bottle to get a five cent plushy. Mike rolled the window down and the smell of popcorn and cotton candy flooded into the car. He quickly found a parking spot, rolling over some little yellow bushes in the process, killing them further.

He gave us five dollars and left, disappearing off towards the litany of food carts, leaving us to our lonesome. We waded into the mess of bodies, alone, just us. There were a lot of kids there, all walking and talking, all loudly laughing and spitting everywhere. It was almost too grand, and loud. I wanted to cover and stuff my ears to stop all of it from flooding straight in. Just the constant buzzing of talk from one person to the other, voice after voice, was all, nothing else, all right into the depths of my ears, right into the brain.

It was getting colder. It was getting darker. The wind grew. It reminded me of-

"We haven't gone into the maze yet." Scarlet said, rubbing her shoulder after throwing and missing our last minigame.

"Should we tell Mike that we're going in there?" I asked.

We both looked over at the food stands. Mike was standing at a cart, turned towards the person behind the counter.

"Nah," Scarlet said.

She grabbed my hand and hurried us to the entrance of the maze. The sound increased and decreased, swelling in my ears and then deflating as we pushed and squeezed through several packs of kids and adults. Scarlet's hand stayed firmly in mine as she led us on the expedition, tensing and tightening as we firmly squeezed through the last group.

The silence was astonishing as we popped out into this new area in front of the corn, away from the packs of people who buzzed and talked with every word ever. There was a pimply teenager standing at a podium which sat next to the front gate. Behind him stood an army of overwhelming corn stalks which swayed slightly in the wind, their dismal shadows starting to dissolve into the night as the sun dropped lower and lower, deep in the horizon. The podium had a sign that read, 'Must be 16 or older to enter without parental guidance.'

Scarlet pulled us up to the podium, "Yo, we'd like to enter the maze please."

He squinted, "You have to be 16 or older without a parent."

"We are 16."

"I don-"

"Dude, we're 16. Just let us in." Scarlet said.

He looked tired, "Okay, whatever." He opened the gate.

"Thanks!" Scarlet smiled as she pulled us quickly past him.

It was even darker on the inside, walled in by corn which, even a couple of steps in, began to cover much of the lingering light. We walked further, silently. All the insufferable sound earlier was now completely gone as if it all vanished into a void of nothingness.

Each step brought up the idea of another turn, another path, another false ending. And then another. And then another, going on and on until the labyrinth started to construct deep in myself. We were going down its dark green hallways of trees that rose so high up, they blocked out everything from the sun to the moon. And deep in those cold hallways, deep behind the trees and the brush and all the plants and animals, they were there, glowing and dancing behind glimmering eyes. They smiled at me. I stood still, my legs, my arms, my fingers.

"Hey," Scarlet shook my shoulder.

I was back in the corn, standing in the middle of a junction which swayed this way and that, the sun still slightly in the sky, still falling.

"You alright?" Scarlet asked.

"Uh," I shook my head a little bit, "Yea. Yea, I'm good."

"Okay...You better not be going coo-coo on me."

"Nah man." I looked around a little more, "So..."

"You wanna split up?" She looked at me with a smile.

"Fuck that."

"I'm just messing with ya," she nudged me. "So where should we start?"

We stood at the precipice of a four lane junction, looking from path to path as the wind blew colder.

"What about that one?" Scarlet pointed at an extra path that I didn't notice before.

Cut diagonally between two of the more traditional paths, grew a thin and misshapen rampage which destroyed corn all along the way, leaving sad and fallen stalks dead all throughout in its wake. Something deep in it pulled at me slightly, this small little sparkle shone at the end. My mind started tumbling slightly.

"Nah," I shook my head. Stop thinking.

"Why?"

"I don't know..." It started to pull again. I looked away towards another dark corner.

"Pussy. Whatever, let's go right."

We went right, turning away from the crude little path into the wind which pushed us back as if it were prodding us to rethink our decision. But we trudged through it, forcing the wave aside, telling destiny to go and fuck itself. The corn danced with each step and we took them good and heavy.

We took a swift left at the next junction, leaving the wind to push at our sides. Quickly, the wind increased tenfold, turning everything into a gail of noise and sound which only grew with each fledgling step.

"The fuck is with this wind?" She almost screamed, her voice carried off somewhere deep into the corn.

The next junction careened into sight and the wind increased, pushing and pulling against the corn whose dance became more sickly as they began to bend and snap with each scream, it now becoming a sturdy fist, punching and ripping as it got stronger. My entire face began to freeze in the cold. My fingers stiffened. Scarlet yelled something that got blown away somewhere.

If we jumped, it would surely take us along with it, deep into the dark sky, up past the atmosphere, to only disappear forever into the void of space, forgotten and frozen and stiff and quiet.

And deep within that space grew something big.

Something dark.

It's always 'something'. Something unrecognizable. Something...up there...on the ceiling-

"Shut the fuck up!" I screamed into it, filling my mouth with air and dust.

It stopped, dying instantly.

We stopped.

Everything fell and nestled into silence. The dirt rested, the corn stood, my ears swirled and hummed, and my eyes stung with each consecutive blink.

"Holy shit," Scarlet looked at me. "You're a fucking wizard." Her hair stood aimless on her head, jutting out this way and that. She slicked it back with her hand. "What the fuck..." She looked around.

"Let's just..."

"Go." She finished.

I took a breath of silent air and started walking again. Scarlet followed behind until we hit the upcoming junction and-

There it was, again, cut diagonally through the more

conventional paths: Crude and sad, the stalks laid dead across this path which cut deep somewhere off into the corn. The light was slightly brighter now at the end of that path, its pull even stronger. I looked away again, not wanting to follow it.

"You wanna try it now?" Scarlet asked, motioning towards the peculiar path.

"No," I answered quickly.

"Dude, come on. What's to be afraid of?"

I looked up at her smiling ghoul ridden face with all of that gray and red makeup. Her dimples perked up slightly as her pearly whites shone too, pulling.

I followed as she started to trek down the path, stepping over stalks of corn which half covered the dark earth. There was a lot to be afraid of.

A Lot. Like fire.

We went in formation down the path, her in front and I closely behind.

"You see that down there?" Scarlet asked.

I didn't answer, my attention on the close walls of still corn that stood all around us, their height seemingly growing as we took step after step over the fallen corn. The stalks continued to rise, making the world darker, veering on complete blackness, sending us to the void past the veil, deep into the forest. My heart began to flutter, my breath quickened, my eyes stung, a well of thoughts flooded in as I continued behind Scarlet's quickening pace.

Back in the labyrinth. Back in the darkness.

I could see them, deep off in the corn, glowing and dancing, the wind no longer able to blow them out. I blinked and they were gone and it was dark again.

"What is that?" She asked to no answer. I wasn't looking.

We emerged from the crude path to a crude little opening, completely encircled by the tall corn, the only exit behind us where we had just come out of. I looked back at the path as Scarlet walked over to the other end of the circle, intrigued by something that I didn't care for. My legs tingled as they got fueled with little pokes and prods to run.

"Willow," Scarlet said behind me. She was crouched over looking at the ground. She motioned for me to come over.

"What?"

"Check this out."

I walked over to her, eyeing past the dark openings in the corn, trying to think of nothing.

In front of her sat a little Jack-O-Lantern which glowed from the inside, illuminating its pumpkin smile with yellow, dancing light. There was no wind.

"This is weird, Scarlet," I tapped her shoulder. "I think we should go back-"

Back into the path. Back into the corn. We had to get out and escape, back. Back there-

The silence talked as the corn around us settled in the lack of wind. All spoke in little creaks and cracks that told me to leave. They told me to run. Something in the dark, in the corn.

I tapped Scarlet's shoulder again.

"Give me a second," She said as her hand grasped the stem of the Jack-O-Lantern and pulled it off.

Her scream echoed into the silence as she fell on her ass, flinging the top out deep into the corn, pushing herself back with her hands.

"Holy shit!" she yelled as she pulled herself across the ground away from the Jack-O-Lantern.

I was frantic but curious, and looked inside the pumpkins headless top.

I stopped thinking, my brain becoming murky.

And slowly...

The thoughts of...

dark things came to-

...like the veil

...like the forest

...like the eyes...and the fire

...and...up there, high on the ceiling, watching, and

dark...

And they continued, the thoughts, slowly dripping and dropping here and there, all about my brain. One dropped hard, splashing wide, spreading everywhere, dark and endless, eating silently back in the reaches of the psyche. It tickled.

Inside the orange pumpkin, it moved.

It danced.

There was a finger deeply infused into the white bottom. It swayed slightly in a dead and still wind. It was loose and pointless as it fluttered, blowing against its own bone structure in a gelatinous mess of pale flesh which pulsed slowly every other second with silent life. Like a heart, it beat steadily.

It looked warm. And soft. And dark-

Scarlet got her bearings and stood next to me. We stared into the finger fueled Jack-O-Lantern. It was transe-like and unusual. This was not right. This was wrong. Very wrong. But deep inside...inside my hands, inside my brain, inside my heart, inside my everything, was a driving inclination. It pushed and gnawed at me, forcing my mind full of random thoughts that machine gunned drivel at a quickening pace-

'What is this?' One thought shot out.

'Run!', another thought screamed.

'Touch!'

'Touch!'

'Touch!'

'Be QUIET!'

'Touch!'

'Touch!'

'QUIET!'

'Stop!'

'Stop!'

'Touch?'

'Stop!'

'Stop!'

'STOP IT! STOP I i i i i i i i ii i i i i ii i ii i i ii i i-

Ah! Ah! Ah! Ah! Ah! Ah! Ah! Ah! Ah! Ah! Ah! Ah! Ah! Ah! Ah! Ah! Ah! Ah! Ah! Ah! Ah! Ah!Ah! Ah! Ah! Ah! Ah! Ah! Ah! Ah! Ah! Ah! Ah! Ah! Ah! Ah! Ah! Ah! Ah! Ah! Ah! Ah! Ah! Ah!Ah! Ah! Ah! Ah! Ah! Ah! Ah! Ah! Ah! Ah! Ah! Ah! Ah! Ah! Ah! Ah! Ah! Ah! Ah! Ah!

All became one; Ah! Ah! Ah! Ah! Ah! Ah! Ah! Ah! Ah! Ah! Ah!; screaming and yelling, continuously fighting each other for dominance; AAAAAAAAAAAAAAA-

My head began to throb with each little yell; AAAAAAAA!; and each little scream. They continued on and on and on and on and on and on and-

None found victory, all eventually dying out in a crass whisper that ended in a slow, smooth, seductive voice rolling out one little phrase that stuck, "Don't..."

The voice soothed, calming and sedating...everything.

How long were Scarlet and I standing there?

Watching the finger pulse and move around in its little pumpkin prison.

I tried to swallow. My voice returned from the sea of others, which silenced themselves slowly, their screams becoming whispers, like a series of lights turning off one by one. Some still remained, but they got quieter and quieter...

aaaaaa-a

I spoke-

aaaa- "Scarlet, we should go." aaa...

-and my stomach flipped, my foreign voice running my body rampant as cold nauseousness flooded my stomach, rolling all within, reviving the garbage pit which began to erupt. That feces colored water... Saliva slipped down my throat as I sucked the thought back down with another halfhearted swallow of everything in the entire world, right down my dry throat, right into the brackish brown water-

"Give me a second," Scarlet retorted.

She crouched back down closer to the Jack-O-Lantern, closer to the finger.

"Scarlet, we're not meant to see this-" I said.

"What do you mean?"

"I don't know..."

"I...I don't know either...like-" She suddenly looked around at the corn stalks. "Willow...where are we?"

"What?"

"Is it...Halloween?"

My eyes started to burn.

"Willow...are we..." She looked back towards the finger.

My head hurt.

"Everything looks so..."

The world seemed to swirl around.

"Why..."

My legs hurt.

"-does everything-"

My heart hurt.

"-look so-"

My body seized-

"-weird?"

She reached out and touched the finger and everything stopped.

The whispers of the corn oozed to a silent mumble which became deep and then became nothing and then sound stopped altogether. Scarlet sat unmoving, bent over the pumpkin, her hand still reaching inside. All parts sat still. My eyes, unblinking. My arms, unmoving. My body, frozen. I tried to breathe. Nothing. The air was unresponsive. But after a minute, my lungs stayed calm and I continued to not breathe.

"He found you..." The smooth voice echoed out. It was the only thing moving fluently within the continually freezing world.

I tried to speak, but my mouth didn't open.

"I did try..."

What?

"But...just be patient."

Fireworks began to blast out in my head, tickling with each pop and crackle. Each thought made another pop and each pop made another thought, continuing in a cycle of bright explosions going off as it all began to slow and freeze along with the world around it. Synapses fired off: Boom! Crack! Like a big party, it started out loud and brash but slowly, it became dead and dull, the fireworks growing slower to go off. One. By. One…until they stopped in a dead silence.

My heart gooshed out one slow pump and then went silent. Blood expanded out from it in a network of systems going every which way. Each vein had a feeling and each feeling slowed, becoming…eventually…silent.

"Willow," The voice slowly pushed out of the muck, freezing too. "You have to-"

Silence.

Nothing moved.

My mind stopped.

My body frozen.

Everything still…

"...trust me."

My head exploded in a cacophony of noise as all the fireworks exploded at once, sending my body turning and my stomach writhing as I felt everything start to come up with a forceful wave of nauseous bewilderment. The corn's silence broke as their whispers began to scream back into my ears so loud my legs deemed to buckle. Into the corn, everything came flooding out like a firehose, painting all in front of me in a thick sludge of garbage and filth and stomach acid which dripped down the long placid stalks.

The world spun as the fireworks popped mercilessly ringing everything as the whispers of the corn became a steady scream.

"Willow," I heard Scarlet say.

I turned around, dazed, as the world spun in every way imaginable.

Scarlet sat there, her hand still in the pumpkin, looking away from me.

"Who am I?"

A spike shot out from the corn stalks in front of Scarlet,

impaling her through the chest and exploding out between her shoulder blades, lifting her high up off the ground. Blood rained down from her perch, pelting the entire area in thick heavy droplets. A red film washed the world in a pinkish glow as the taste of copper bloomed in my mouth like a brass flower. My hands shook and my head rumbled and my stomach ached and my legs stood still as I watched her sway silently, a nest of gore hanging around the exit wound, puffed up with a juicy red rose of ribbons which followed and wrapped around the shaft of the spike. A shotty gurgle rumbled out from her throat as she twitched and then hung loose, sinking slowly, leaving a sticky red sheen painted down the mass of the shaft.

My stomach tumbled some more, washing and drying and moving whatever was left in it, frothing and bubbling it all up and down, percolating, in my throat.

Per-co-lating-

A shaky step followed mindless instinct, causing a wet slosh as I waded into a thick pool of Scarlet which stained and flowed, filling the brown dirt with years of nutrients. Another slosh, wading further into the swamp that started to radiate the smell of blood and…and…

Something else.

Something…

-I licked my lips-

Sweet?

"Run! You shit!"

My mind awoke, sending the thoughts flying away into nothingness, the taste and smell all but gone as I started to splash and wade wildly through the pool, sending red splashes to the wayside, coating the growing ramparts of corn that circled all around. There it was: The opening. The escape. I just had to run and force my way through the thickening goo. Don't think about anything else. Just move. Leg after leg. I could feel her in my eyes, in my hair, in my mouth, in my throat, deep down in that ever tumbling stomach which turned on itself consistently.

And then it came up.

Again.

It flooded out of my mouth, burning my lips, adding a brownish red seasoning to the red pool that I waded through, one slosh after thickening slosh-

One snag, and then I fell facefirst, deep into the pool. Darkness covered the world, all sound quieted and muffled as I opened my eyes under the rising goo which seemed to grow more to the consistency of pudding.

It was all red, deep down here, where no sound prevailed, where the world hid. The goo crawled deep into my ears and past my eyes, boring deep into the soft membrane behind them. From all directions, it pushed into my brain, eating and thrashing all in its grasp. They tore.

Then there was nothing.

The bottom stretched away, deepening and disappearing all the same. I was in an ocean of the stuff, drowning, far beneath the red surface. I tried to swim towards it, my lungs pumped and pushed at my chest as air slowly became less and less. But it was getting harder to move. Scarlet started to thicken and mass around me, forcing my arms and legs to push harder through the stuff, using up more oxygen. Tiredness racked my brain as it ran out of the means to continue, my arms growing less ambitious to move, my legs feeling almost the same. I started to sink down as the red turned to black, and it all turned to nothingness.

And then, there was something.

There was a shift below me, a certain centrifuge of water that moved from a giant force that pushed me slowly one way. It was big. I could feel its closing presence below me as my heart whirred again and I started to kick wildly, flailing my arms like useless little fans which only made it harder to move. And then I stopped. And sunk slightly. Unable to move.

Looking down. There, emerging from the twilight zone, where even the dwindling sun could barely reach, it was there. Floating and undulating. A black mass that pulsated with delight, the size of the world and everything within it, right below me. A mass. It both rose and fell beneath the dark line of the ocean as it got closer, its tentacle-like fins consuming half my vision.

It got closer.

I clawed out of the scarlet pool, grasping and pulling at the moist dirt that pattered the entrance. Everything hurt. Every. Little. Thing. From the little nerve running and twisting throughout my middle finger to my oxygen starved brain which hungered for more fuel as I spit and gasped on the shore of the scarlet lake, blowing chunks out of my clogged nose, ripping small ligaments which spun deep down my ear canals, and wiping my caked face of her. She was all over me. All in me. Writhing. Gnawing.

The wind started up again. Soft and slight. It tickled my wet face, filling my nose, and cooling my entire body. I didn't tell it to shut up this time. I didn't tell it anything, my mind blank of what to do.

And, through my empty mind, I forced myself to stand, and I walked steadily down the makeshift path between the corn, stepping over the dead and stalking under the alive, cast in a deep night as the sun finally dipped below the horizon.

I stepped out from the path. And sat. On the dirt.

Behind me. The path disappeared. Zipping itself back up; Hiding from the world.

8

My throat scratched with a rasp, the entirety of it padded with a rough sandpaper, clawing with each attempted swallow. Spit like honey. It dripped down the sandpaper tube. Echoes of a metallic flower. Echoes of a thick dredge. Echoes of sweetness...smokiness...Scarlet...ness. It hurt each time, but it kept coming and dripping. Swallowing. Flowing past puffed up taste buds which tingled as it fell down the sandpaper tube deep into the acidic and empty wasteland of the garbage pit.

It was sour and then it was sweet. Brass and copper. Changing with each consecutive Swallow. It fluttered and flaunted its wings. The taste bird looked out west, towards the taste horizon. The Swallows chirped and flew by, diving and playing with one another.

Waves collided below, pushing and pulling against each other, slamming on the rock face and then receding back out towards the deep ocean. Within all the blue, there was something past the horizon. It began but a speck and then grew slightly with each blink of the eye. Willow watched, I watched, the corn seemingly gone. Without a concrete form. It consumed the blue ocean below just as it consumed the blue sky above. Same with the sun and same with the pale blue moon. Deep within the void, I saw it. Dancing and moving. Bright and red. Breakdancing-

'Congratulations!' A big buoyant sign screamed at me as I turned a corner. 'Free candy on the left!' It was the exit.

Through the exit, I found candy on the left, spread about on a big plastic table.

I walked over to it. There was a girl standing behind it in some sort of costume.

"Are you supposed to be a zombie?" She asked.

I grabbed a random piece.

"It looks really good," she said.

I put it in my pocket. It mushed around, raw and meaty.

She sniffed the air for a second and revolted back, her face turning green.

I walked away, down the path, towards Mike. The smell of popcorn and cotton candy fluttered back.

I could feel it under my nails. In my teeth. Between my toes. She was everywhere, chafing as I walked, step by step, squishing between crevice and crevice.

I turned a corner and there they were: The food stalls. And standing at one was Mike in his Thor costume, eating something.

I walked over to him.
He smiled a big smile.
"Willow! How was the maze?"
....
"How was the maze?"
....
"How was the maze?"
....
"How was the maze?"
....
"Hey, how was the maze?"
....
"Willow, how was the maze?"
....
'Willow...how was the maze?'
,,
'"Hey, how was the maze?"'
....
How was the maze?
Was it everything you hoped for?
Did it-
Did it taste good?

"That scary huh?" he chuckled.

You liked it. The honeysuckle sweet tang. The orangy booms and the tart suckers.

"...why don't we get you home?"

You loved it, didn't you?

He ushered me to the car. The engine turned and roared, jittering the chassis.

And then we left, turning right, out silently into the rows of spiked trees which jutted out at us. Looking at them, the taste came back, hitting notes upon notes. My tongue rolled and dragged mindlessly across the clogged teeth, clawing at the little chunks stuck between them.

Mike was quiet. He smiled, his dimples like Scarlets. They perked slightly, proud. His spotty beard was gray here and there. His hair waved black this way and that. His hands stuck at a perfect ten and two position on the wheel.

And the entire drive, his smile never wavered.

*

The car stopped with a jolt. My house was dark from the outside, empty.

We sat in the car, his smile stark and my head weary. The world gently swayed as we sat completely still.

"How was the maze, Willow Pines?"

"I don't know."

The car door popped as I pulled the handle and stepped out into the cold night.

It lolled gently down the road until it pulled into his driveway. The car went dark and then nothing.

The inside of the house was silent. There was a paper on the kitchen table that read, 'Gone for the night.'

As I put the paper back down, I saw a red splotch which stained the white.

Everywhere felt sticky and mushy.

I went to take a shower, up the stairs, thinking about nothing, on each step, step by step, thinking. About. Nothing. Nothing nothing.

The mirror of the bathroom beckoned me as I turned the shower handle which began to relentlessly spray water into the white linoleum tub.

I found a little monster in the reflection, its eyes peering out in a deep blue the color of the ocean. Its long hair, black, now matted its way down to the small of its back, curling and looping in certain ways that made it look like little fireworks went off within each little strand. Little chunks adorned it like red diamonds that shined and reflected the bleak bathroom lights. Its pale skin was now stained with an adornment of colors which zig zagged across the rainbow, never fully getting each and every statement. Its face sat still as it looked at itself, judging every little thing like how its nails were filled to the brim with sinew and dirt or how its clean white lab coat was now a pinkish red which still dripped or how the bags under her eyes were growing or how she looked much skinnier or how how I left her there.

Or how I'm struggling to remember her name.

Or how or what or who...wait? What talked?

Or how I thought she tasted.

She tasted...for a second...right then and there...

Each part of my clothing slapped against the floor with a weight to them. First, the lab coat. Slap. It was meaty and heavy, leaving a red spreading mark that covered the instant area. The shirt which clinged to my body, still wet and grabbing. Slap. It coiled over and rolled to the side, leaving a wet streak in its wake. Shoes. A moist sludge dribbled out from them and my socks which I peeled off quickly. Slappity-slap. They were much heavier than before, filled with something that left a thick syrupy slime that slathered whatever was inside them with a firm coat that buffered the floor with each sockless step. And each sockless step left a footprint, small and distinct, that filled itself in as if it were alive. But it wasn't. Dead things are dead.

I stepped over and into the tub and right into the boiling water.

It burned and cleansed my skin, boring down deep into the crust that laid on top. It spread and watered down with each little droplet that got hotter with each passing second. Each second slowed, becoming a minute and then two, three afterwards, continuing on until there was no more sight, no more sound, just the water and I and the stuff which found itself all over my body. Scarlet. It went past the skin.

I cleaned under my nails, scrubbed my hair, and buffed my arms and legs. I drank and spat the running water until my teeth were clean again and continued to scrub and buff, more and more. But still, it was there, deep down, in my skin, digging deeper, past the skin, somewhere else.

It needed to be hotter. And it got hotter. And hotter. Burning every little follicle. Shrinking the skin it chased after the slowing filth. That scarlet filth. That deranged filth which once covered me under its mass, showing me things I never want to see again. A red ocean with something dark down under and a burning horizon. Two opposites pulled into the same realm. The realm I liked to call: Fuck you territory.

Fuck you. That's what I thought of it all. Absolute and complete bullshit. All of it. I shook the daze from my head spraying water everywhere. A big fat 'fuck you!' to the psyche, a fat suckerpunch to the gut which brought up everything. And I mean everything. From dinner to breakfast to those little chocolate candies that melt in your mouth, they all come up the same and they taste like shit. Holy and godly shit. Acidic and disgusting and filled with little pieces which tickled my throat as they came rocketing right up and out of my lips. Fuckin' Amen. Even the goddamned thought made my stomach tumble slightly, but I knew there was nothing left in there to spew otherwise this white tub would be stained with more than this caked on dogshit.

But...

But there was something there. It took until now to fully recognize it-

In that catastrophic shit, came a sort of...flavor. A little tinge of...a little tang of...it tasted liked... It was fucking delicious. Delicioso. And it was there, in that scarlet ocean, where I tasted it. Was it her? The woman strung high up on that rod?

It was her. It had to be her. But who was she?

I realized something right then and there.

The water was fucking HOT!

"Holy shit!" I lunged at the handle and turned the shower off.

*

I turned off the light and nuzzled into bed, tired.

The world was heavy along with every little thing within it. The sheets below me sunk deep as if a weight hung off of it somewhere down below. The covers that laid over me molded around my body and weighed me down deeper into the sunk sheets. Above me was that spot, still there, on the ceiling, like always. And then he spoke to me. Something about…

"...and I was wondering, Willow...do you remember her?"

Do I? Who?

"You know…her."

Oh…yea? Maybe?

"And do you remember me?"

I saw you…down there…I think.

"And-and how did it all taste? The feeling…"

It tasted like…fireworks. Right on the fucking dot.

"So you would…"

Wait…why can't I remember her?

"No matter about that…"

Yes, matter. I'll matter all about that. I can see her, right there, on the tip on my tongue. She had...these green eyes and…deep black hair. Raven black. Her smile had these goofy dimples which looked good on her. She was very…I don't know but god damn it, what was her name?

"I can show you…then, afterwards, I want you to think about all the things we've talked about recently. Can you do that for me, Willow?"

I don't know, man. I'm not fit to make deals with strangers.

"Strangers? Oh we go back a ways, Willow."

We do?

"Oh yes…"

Whatever you say, man. What's your name anyways?

"My name? You couldn't say my name. I'll spare you that at the least."

Well, if your name is so special...I don't know…you sound like a…Garry?"

"Garry?"

Yea. Garry. I'll call you Garry.

"And the clock strikes twelve. Here she comes, knocking

on your door."

It's not even twelve-

Knock

"Do you hear that?"

I do. My door shook rhythmically.

"And do you hear that? The walls shifting?"

I do.

"And do you hear that? The whimpers beyond your door?"

I do.

"And do you feel pity? For her and yourself?"

I do.

"And do you want to get up and open the door?"

I do.

"And do you want to accept my deal?"

I don't.

Everything went quiet. The bolt of the door clicked aside and it shifted slightly, opening but a crack, revealing only darkness beyond the thin little veil. And then it opened a little more, widening the crack until it was open, wide. A person stood right beyond the doorframe.

Oh yeah...that's her name-

"Scarlet? Scarlet Miller?" I asked out into the darkness.

"Yo," she walked into the room. "You disappeared earlier."

"So you broke into my house?"

"I mean," she sat on the edge of my bed, pulling everything down. "The door was unlocked."

She wasn't wearing her costume anymore, her usual whiteness spread all over her face.

"You alright?" She asked.

"Well...other than you scaring the shit outta me, yea... I'm alright."

"Jeez..." she studied my face. "You look a little...wack right now."

"Wack?"

"Yea…your eyes look much more…I don't know. But you're sure that you're alright?"

"Yes. I, myself, know that I am alright."

"Hey, don't get all bitchy with me. You know there's something called denial."

"Denial? About what?"

"About your true feelings and all that shit. Read a dictionary, I don't fuckin' know."

"Gee, thanks doctor."

"No problem. Hey, weren't you the doctor earlier?"

"Yeah, but I lost my medical license."

"Makes sense."

We sat for a second as a car drove past, screaming beyond the closed window.

"Well," she patted my bedsheets, "I'll give you a break tonight. But tomorrow, we gotta get back in the treehouse."

"Hmm."

"Hmm?" She asked. "Never seen you so…fucked up tired. You should sleep." She stood up and started to walk out of the room. "Also, You should get an exterminator. Heard something in the walls." The door slammed shut and the silence came back. I didn't hear her go down the stairs.

And, lingering in the room, was a very certain smell. The scarlet ocean. The Scarlet Ocean. It wrapped around my nose like a tangled fishing line. That was her, swinging up there, in the maze. That was her who died…that was her who tasted so good.

Something…intoxicating.

Like a big chunk of meat.

A big ol' tasty one.

A juicy one.

A scarlet one.

"Denial…" I whispered.

"Garry?" I asked.

"Yes?" He answered.

Who killed Scarlet?

“The one out in the woods. The one you seek. I can help you-”

Thanks.

I closed my eyes.

Sleep started to take hold. She was right: I was fucked up tired. The sound of the industrial machinery is still completely absent. And, as I fell faster and faster, there was another smell on the brink. It smelled like...popcorn?

Somewhere in the distance, soft carnival music played. It bopped up and down in a quickening tempo and then went silent with a bump...

“Willow? Where are you going?” Garry’s voice was distant and fading.

“Willow!” His scream was but a whisper. And then it was gone.

And then the song started up again, quicker. Louder.

9

And louder. Continuing with its veracity and distaste as the tempo gained, vibrating my ears and shaking my senses awake.

My fingers curled deep into a moist sand that coated the entirety of the ground. My eyes opened to a bright white which blinded all sense of sight. I couldn’t see shit. But I could hear that shit being spewed out from an increasing noise that shook the ground. The screams of a crowd. Thousands of shit filled mouths yelled all around me. And louder they got, filling my ears with more than my blinded eyes could ever see.

“And here are the amazing Marrion trapeze twins!” Some voice screamed out, distorted and stretched from the microphone that it spoke into.

I heard them before I saw them as they grunted and pulled above me, flying from one point to another, getting close and then falling away, the crowd screaming the entire time, blaring in my ears. The white blind fell away: I was in the center of an arena, fenced in with a high wall that nauseatingly had a repeating white and red stripe pattern along the entirety of the rink. And above that rink sat all of them, laughing and screaming and clapping, sending noise this way and that. I wanted to bury my head in the cold sand that I sat on, my cardinal senses coming back one by one. Touch: The sand that fell through my fingers. Sound: The crowd screaming, and bleeding at my ears. Smell: Manure and popcorn and sweet smells of cotton candy. Taste: Uneven rocks broke between my teeth, I ground away at them, unknowing. Dust and rocks. Sight: Everything opening to the tune of pure and utter white. The dark crowd shrouded themselves behind the floodlights above me. The Marrion twins wore purple spandex suits which covered their entire bodies from the neck down. I could see their rockin' bulges from down here. I bet some chicks in that shadow crowd would fuckin' love this spot I got.

As quick as it started, the show was over, the two trapeze twins and their bulges jumped away, leaving an abusive wave of clapping which boomed out from the audience, dazing me even more, sending my poor ears into even more of a fright.

"Wow! Wow! WOW!" The same microphone infused voice blazed out again and, with it, a tall man in a tall top hat and a black suit waltzed out into the center of the sandy arena, waving his white padded gloves around, a microphone held tight in one. "And now, folks! We have a special guest with us here today!"

He stopped next to me, still crumpled on the ground. I could see my reflection in his shining black shoes. My entire face was covered in red and white and blue paint which scrawled a big frown that stretched down past my lips. I found a large red clown nose suckered over my small pale human nose which I didn't notice before. *Honk*. "Come on, stand up," he whispered away from the mic. I didn't budge. He sighed and pulled me up with a hearty yank. "And," he continued towards the feasting crowd, "We have a new act prepared for you all! Please put your hands together for-" he shoved the microphone right in front of my face, still glistening with his spit.

I didn't know what to say. My ears hurt, my eyes stung. My mouth slapped dryly as I thought. "Uh..."

"Your name is 'Uh?'" He laughed and the crowd laughed with him, the pure sound boiled the sand below our feet. "That's no name! Now come on! Give us your actual name!" He put the mic back in front of me.

"I..."

"It looks like our guest is a little shy! Come on folks, give her some encouragement!" he screamed into the microphone, causing a cacophony of yells to boom out from the crowd once more. Deciphering them was hard. They said everything at once from this to that and that to this, continuously, but they all sludged together into one giant soup of sound that poured in through one ear and spilled out the other right onto this slurry of sand and other stuff.

"Come on!"

The soup emptied and the crowd made no noise. All stopped at once, even the wind dared not defy this sudden silence.

"Don't you things love carnivals?"

I looked up towards the ringmaster, up towards his top hat hidden face. "Hey," he dropped his microphone hand down to his side. "You like carnivals, right?" He fingered the brim of the hat, pushing it up revealing his eyes.

They were dark and deep. Two black little marbles which continued on forever, a nebula both deep and deeper. Infinite. But, deep in that infinity, was something. There was fire.

"Or, do they like roller coasters?"

The world snapped into darkness for a second and then wind splashed against my face as the world zipped by in a cacophony of color and sound. I was on a rollercoaster going down an infinite fall, speeding faster and faster.

"Oh! I love this part!" A voice next to me screamed into the wind.

Colors meshed into one, creating a shotgun blast of visual sensory en masse that exploded as the velocity increased.

My stomach tossed and tumbled with each turn, with each movement, I could feel the garbage heap spilling and popping up and down in my throat.

"You don't look so good! Maybe we can try something else!"

Black. Again. And then-

Water. And lots of it. I was deep in the stuff. It filled my nose and flooded my lungs, bypassing all. I started to drown, dying, lost in a black mass of black water. My eyes popped, propelling from my skull out deep into the murky depths. My ears imploded and burst, all sound stopping at once. My tongue expanded and swelled in my mouth, making it impossible to close, and then a voice wiggled somewhere in my dead brain-

"Oops! Too deep!"

And then it was all cold. My skin bubbled as I felt the blood boil underneath. A hollow noise sounded out from somewhere and then all went quiet.

"Too high!"

The black went even blacker and then it all stopped.

The smell of smoke was the first thing I noticed as I shuttered awake in a soft wooden chair which sunk downwards into the deep padding. I was in front of a desk. A wooden desk. On it sat a couple of loosely scattered papers and a smoldering cigarette that sat nuzzled into the indent on an ashtray, its filter pointed out towards me. The room looked like a 1950s detective office, brown and wooden, with windows that had lowered blinds which filtered in these thick rays of light.

I squeezed my hands and felt the warmth of my skin. I touched my eyes and felt their gelatin exterior. My eyelids closed and opened and beyond them I could see. In the corner of the room sat a little phonograph that spun a little black disk. Out of it played a soft little piano tinged tune that alternated between slow and fast notes. Sultry and whimsical, I listened to it as I realized that I was alive.

"*Clair de Lune*," a voice said. Behind the desk, sitting across from me, a black mist began to grow from the dark. It sizzled and moved like a smoke with an endless and cycling wind. I could see through the haze to the dark oaken wall that stood beyond it. It was thick and human-like, except much, much bigger. And above that mist, sat two dark eyes. And, in those eyes, they danced. Bright and glowing the fire walked. "Isn't it just beautiful?"

"Holy shit!" I stood from the chair. That garbage pit filled and moved like on the rollercoaster, I could feel it bouncing in my throat. Here it was. Here this fucker was. I started to think it was all...

I don't...

What do I...

"Jesus! Are you done? Are you done overreacting?"

"I..."

"Look, just please sit down. We can hash this whole ordeal out." It reached down and put on a pair of phantom glasses and shuffled some papers on the desktop. "And sorry about all of that earlier. As you can probably tell...I'm not too good with kids or humans for that matter."

I took a breath, my mind grew calmer and I sat, staring at it all the way.

"Good. Are you hungry? I got coffee and tea...maybe a danish?"

"Fuck you man! I don't like any of that shit! The fucks going on?"

"Then what do you like, huh? Dolls? Skirts? Little pink things? I don't know...I thought you were different. Right? That's why you're getting that special 'deal' and all of that? Right?"

"Fuck you man! You killed Scarlet!"

"And...how did you feel about all of that?"

"I..."

"Right? You don't know. Why? Why do you think all of this left your mind?

"I..."

"And, why do you think I would kill her?"

"You killed those kids."

"Did I? Did I really? Why do you think I would do that?"

"I don't know, I barely know you."

"Ah! See, that's what I'm trying to do. I know you don't easily fold, but, and here's my proposition: Let's be friends."

"Friends? No thanks, dick."

"Harsh. Rude. I get it, I really do. I'm the whole catalyst for your new friendship. You guys wanna catch me and all of that. Well, WOAH! You caught me! Here I am! Woo hoo! You guys did it. And guess what? This 'monster'," It pointed to its misty chest, "has feelings too."

"What?"

"I'm just saying that you guys hurt my feelings."

"Dude, I couldn't give a single shit about how you feel."

"I can see that. I know I'm not as...manipulative as that thing on your ceiling-"

"Garry?"

"Garry? Is that what you're calling him?"

"Yea."

It chortled, deep and weird, "Well, good enough. Oh yea, if you're calling him Garry, just call me Mark."

"Sure..."

"Alright, I know that we're not best buds yet, but I would like to get down to business," it fixed its floating glasses. "Alrighty...I guess we'll just get right down to the brass tacks: That 'deal'? Yea don't listen to that, excuse my language, bullshit."

"And why should I listen to you? Can both of you weirdos just leave me alone? And, really, fuck you, man."

"Woah! Calm down there."

"No! You killed her!"

"Did you really not listen to me before? You got the wrong guy here!"

"And why should I trust you?"

"You're really going to put your trust in Garry? Never trust a Garry."

"Hell no! I don't trust either of you. And, dude, the fuck were you doing looking through our windows at night?"

"WOAH! Okay, you can call me a lot of things, but accusing me of doing any of that maliciously is a no-go in my books."

"I'm not accusing, I'm stating the facts."

"Hey, don't get mad at me for looking in at the new family that just moved in."

"Then why do you gotta be so...creepy."

"Rude...that hurt. I don't try to be creepy. I just am...me? Look, I'll apologize, okay? I'm sorry. Does that make you feel any better?"

"Fuck no! How about you tell your little friend to get the hell out of my life."

"WOAH! Okay, let's get one thing straight here: I'm not friends with that guy, okay? That dude's a serious basket case."

"And you're not?"

"NO! Am I trying to get you to accept some no-clause deal? Hell no! I'm trying to dissuade you from accepting."

"And why's that?"

"Hey, it's just my job alright. I know I said we should be friends, but I can tell that's not gonna happen. Just don't accept that deal. Please. Pretty please?"

"Dude, I was never going to accept that deal, that shit sounds scammy as fuck."

"Well...there's something else I should tell you..."

"What?"

"You see, Scarlet's going to get...irresistible. Might take a week. Two. Maybe three, but you're gonna notice something different about her...something..."

"Tasty?"

"My god, he's already on it."

"Wait...Garry wants me to eat her?"

"...it's a little more than that, but that deal will get harder to...not accept."

"I think I'll be fine. What's the deal even for?"

"Ask him. I don't rightly know, I just know that it's fucked up, excuse my french."

"Wait...wait...who the fuck are you guys?"

"Hmm...he's the bad guy and I'm the good guy. That good enough?"

"No. Everyone's the good guy in their own eyes."

"Well...just look through my eyes for once-" The fire moved heavily, growing hotter in the two large eyes.

"And, what's with the eyes-" I asked.

"Okay, that's enough. Don't take the deal, don't listen to him. That'll be all."

And everything went black once more.

*

The first sense to regain consciousness was smell. It smelled of freshness. Leaves and green and cool wind which fluttered by my face. I rolled over, feeling the tickle of grass and forest floor beneath me. It was cold to the touch. The slight rustle of trees and leaves above me. And then it all came together as I opened my eyes: I was beyond that dark veil, behind my house, where the monster- Where Mark presides. The slight well of fear boiled underneath me and then went silent. It was gone. Dissipated to the wind, sunk into the ground, gone with the very darkness of the night. It was over. That overwhelming fear that I came to know so well before. Now it's...gone. Dead. Buried. And now, what replaced that fear was much more palpable: Embarrassment. Why was I so fucking scared of that loser? The labyrinth fell apart right at the seams scattering everywhere, sinking into the depths of the folds.

I trudged back to my house, over some fell saplings,

over some bushes, under the trees, under the night, smiling the entire time, laughter almost bursting. And like I said many times before: Fuck You.

10

"Hey," Scarlet said as we walked the sidewalk. "Really, where did you go last night?"

"What do you mean?" I asked, hopping over a slight crack.

"What do I mean? Whatever...you know I'm the best thing in your life, right?"

"Really?"

"Yes, sir-e."

"And why is that?"

"I don't know why, I just am."

"Wow, very cryptic. You're oh so cool, Ms. Miller." Sarcasm thick on my tongue.

"I know, I know," She bowed and followed up with an impression of The King, "Thank you, thank you very much."

"Can I please have your autograph?"

"Sorry baby, I gotta go and slug back a bottle of pills and hit the ho-ha!" She snickered.

"Don't do that routine around other people, they'll beat your ass."

"Yea, yea, whatever. Besides, I know I can kick your ass any day."

"Whatever you say, King."

"And you best not forget it," her foot kicked high as she mimicked a dance move which followed in a resounding POP! and a resounding fall as she fell down to the earth, holding her leg. "Ow, shit!" She gasped.

"The King smite thee," I laughed.

"Jesus, I need to stretch." She reached her hand out, "Wanna help me up?"

"I guess so," I grasped her hand and pulled her up.

And in that little interaction, it was there. She stumbled into me, as I pulled her soft hand, and it was there too. That one little smell. That one little tinge, deep in the background and then it was gone.

Don't think about it.

We walked to school.

*

"Wow, so this is your room?" She asked, dropping her backpack on the floor.

"Dude, you saw it last night."

"Did I?"

"Yea..."

She looked off, scratching her chin, "Hmm...I don't remember..."

"Seriously?"

"Nah, I'm just shitting with you," She smiled and sat on my desk chair, sitting and spinning continuously. "But, this is the first time you've actually invited me to your room."

"Uh, huh. Figured that you've earned the right."

"Oh wow, so prestigious! I could die happy right now!"

"Suck my dick," I sat on my bed.

"You don't have any balls, dude."

"Literally or metaphorically?"

"Both."

"Says you-"

"Oh I got giant fat fucking herculean monster balls ridin' right here, between these beast thighs, swingin' and danglin' all around not like your pussy ass."

"Impressive," I nodded. "I'll be sure to tell your parents about that."

"Go right ahead, I got nothing to hide. And hiding these fat fuckers would be impossible anyways." She stopped spinning, "So, we doing homework?"

"Yea, yea..." I rustled through my backpack, grabbing and taking all the things I needed out of it. "Hey, just a question..."

"What's up?"

"What do you remember about last night?"

"Huh?"

"Just answer the question, Monster Balls."

"Uh: We tricked and we treated...went to the maze which kinda sucked...and then we drove back and then YOU disappeared on me."

"Uh huh-"

"Hey, don't get all accusatory on me. Remember: Denial-" She practically sang the last word.

Then the spot spoke:

"And denial you are in..."

Be quiet

"You've stopped thinking about it..."

Shut up

"But I know you can smell it..."

Snap

And I opened my eyes to Scarlet's hand, snapping again in my face, "Hey...Earth to Willow..."

"Uh...yea..."

"Zoned out on me for a second there."

"Sorry...guess I'm still pretty tired."

"Whatever. Hey, can I stay for dinner tonight? Mom and Dad are out later."

"Sure."

*

Dinner came around to crickets and wind and whispers as we all sat down at the kitchen table.

"So...Scarlet, how has school been?" Mom asked, passing the grub around.

"It's been fine."

"Good, good." She smiled.

"How has...work been?" Scarlet asked.

"Oh, good. Yea, it's been alright."

"Good..."

And then the conversation went back to the wind and

then the crickets, both sounds growing and feinting with each other, one growing and then one shrinking, back and forth along with the sounds of chewing that growled out from our jaws, feasting in silence.

"So..." Scarlet started, "How is Mr. Pines?"

Her eyes opened wide as she swallowed a hearty mouthful, "Oh...Mr. Pines has been...good."

"I just don't see him around a lot...just hoping that he's...good."

"Oh no," Mom started, "He's just working overtime most nights. No need to worry about him." Her lips flapped a word silently.

"Ah, okay...and where are your other children? Don't see them around much either."

"They're...fine. So...Scarlet, Willow's told me so much about you."

"Really? What has Willow said about me?" She glanced in my direction.

"Ah," Mom started, her mouth opened and then closed as she looked off somewhere. "Oh, just lots, it would take practically forever to tell you all of them."

"Oh, no problem, Ms. Pines, I think we have all night," she smiled.

"Oh...I've been told that you're so...nice?" It was basically a question.

"Really?" Scarlet looked at me again. "I am known for being quite the philanthropist around the ol' Miller household. Please, give me another thing that your loving daughter has told you about me?"

"Oh...oh," She looked around. "Won't you excuse me for a second, I have to use the ladies room."

"Sure thing Ms. Pines. We'll be here, waiting. For you. To finish."

"Ah, surely."

She left. The bathroom door opened. The bathroom door closed. I turned to Scarlet, "The fuck was that?" I whispered.

"What?" She fiddled with her fork.

"What?" I retorted.

"Look...you don't have to tell me your whole...situation, but I can read it like a fuckin' book."

"Seriously? You're being kind of an asshole right now."

"Yeah, I know. Goody two shoes philanthropist, right?" She rolled her head to the side, "You and your Mom never talk, huh?"

"Fuck you."

"And you have brothers, right?"

"Yea?"

"Where are they right now? I never see them around."

"They're...you know..."

"And your Dad? Where is he?"

"I..."

"And don't give me that BS about overtime."

"He's...he's uh..."

"He's? Come on junior! Spit it out!"

"I don't know."

She took a breath and put her hand on my shoulder, "Look, kid: I know it's not my business and all of that, but when you're rollin' with me, we can't take this dogshit. And I, specifically, am not going to let you take this absolute dogshit."

"What?"

"Look. At your hand. Look at it."

I lifted it and I looked at it.

"Okay, now open it-"

I did.

"Now, in my long, wisdom-filled years, I've come to understand that life should be taken in with an iron fist."

"What are you on about?"

"I'm serious. Like Otto von Bismarck said: 'Iron and Blood' or something like that."

"Are you on crack or something?"

"No, no. I'm just saying that you can't let anyone, not

even your family, walk all over you like this."

"They aren't walking over me."

"Jesus, open your eyes, girl! Your brothers ditched you, your Dad is completely absent, probably drinking or cheating or both. And to top the whole shit pie off: your Mom is a total bitch."

I swiped her hand off my shoulder, "Shut up!"

"I can tell you've thought about this before, Willow. I get it. We all want to act like little princesses, but that's not who we are. That's not who you are. Let me ask a question: How did your Mom and Dad react when those kids went missing?"

"They..."

"They distanced themselves, right?"

I didn't answer.

"And your brothers?"

"They...left."

She smiled, "Now close your fist-"

I hesitated.

"Do it, Willow."

I did, hard, whitening my knuckles.

"That's life, right there, in your hand. Squeeze that shit until it pops."

I kept squeezing. Harder.

"There you go, now fill it with everything you hate. Everything and everyone that's done you wrong. Every little person who's even looked at you the wrong way. Every person who's thought wrong about you. Every little whisper. Every little pompous betterment. Every little push and each pitiful smile. Put all of it in your little fist and fucking kill them all."

I did, squeezing harder, filling it with Mom and Dad and Matt and jeremy and Garry and Mark and the entire fucking school and all the people who I fucking hate in the entire fucking world fuck fuck fuck you fuck you fuck you fuck all of them right now I wish they all died in a world wide blaze of wind and fire and drought and hunger and all of the sins and all of the famines and all of the terrible things that could happen to everyone. Scarlet didn't die. They lie. They're all in my head and all they're doing is FUCKING WITH ME. I can smell her from here. Put that in here, that scent. Her skin looks better now, with a sheen of goodness spread all upon it but SHUT THE FUCK UP WILLOW! SHUT UP! PUT ME IN THERE AND KILL TO SHUT MY DUMB FUCKING MIND UP BE QUIET BE QUIET STOP THINKING ABOUT THOSE THINGS SHUT UP SHUT UP SHUT UP SHUT UP SHUT UP-

"Woah, you okay?"

My transe broke and my brain cooled quickly. I felt like I was about to take a shit.

"You looked like you were gonna explode there."

"No..." I took a breath. "I'm alright."

Her hand patted my shoulder, "They're all dead."

"Now what?" I asked, releasing my fist.

"Willow, what we do now is the most important part: We fuck shit up. Iron and Blood baby." Her hands mimicked putting on some badass black shades.

"Iron and blood? What does that even mean?" I asked.

"Dunno. Sounds fuckin' rad though, right?" She leaned back in her chair. "Rule number two: When something sounds cool, say it. More rules pending."

And then the bathroom door swung open and Mom scuttled back into the room.

"Sorry about the wait, girls."

"No problem, Ms. Pines! Oh man! This food is to die for! Willow told me so much about your cooking!"

"Really?" Mom sat, poising her hands across the table top.

"Oh yes, absolutely!"

Scarlet glanced at me, smiling her dimple filled smile.

I couldn't help but to laugh.

*

"Do you feel it?"

Shut up, I'm trying to sleep.

"No need to be so rude, Willow."

Shut up, I know what you're trying to do.

"You know he's lying right? Poisoning your mind with those false little lies..."

Lies? Like how you're trying to get me to eat Scarlet?

"What? You really think I would be that...depraved? No, I'm just positioning your greatest and most dear desires. Think about the deal-"

My most inner desire is to eat her? Yeah buddy, I don't rightly think so.

"You should listen to Scarlet, Willow. Denial gets you nowhere..."

Fuck you and your denial. I'll deny it all if I have to.

"You know, he's the one who killed Scarlet, right? You shouldn't listen to him."

She never died. It was all in my head.

"Is that what he told you? You're putting your trust in him and not me?"

I don't trust either of you dickheads, can you please shut the fuck up?

"Okay...goodnight Willow."

Have a bad night Garry. Suck my dick.

Monster balls.

*

"Ah! So that's what he thinks of me!" Mark bellowed.

I opened my eyes in the chair, slightly spinning, waking from a shallow sleep. Smoke spun from the still lit cigarette in that same ashtray. The same sun beamed in from the shaded windows in thick and deep shafts of light which overshadowed everything. The same monster-thing was sitting across from me and the same me sat across from him in my PJ's, rubbing sleep from my eyes. "Dude...can I not get any sleep around here?"

"Sleep? Oh yea, sorry about that. I forget about your whole...bodily needs part. Ah phooey! Sleep is for suckers, am I right?"

"Whatever... So, more of the same today? You gonna

just tell me more about how Garry is not to be trusted and all of that jazz? Cause, like I said, I don't trust him and I don't trust you."

"Almost. You see, for us to be a righteous team against the dark forces of evil, I think we need a little bonding session. With just the two of us...pals. You'll learn to trust me."

"Pals?"

"Yes! Pals! Buddies! Friends! Buckos! Look, I need you to trust me and, yes, I may have jumped the gun last time when I said that we were not going to be friends. For that little falter, I sincerely apologize."

"Apology-"

"Up!" He put up his ghastly, see-through, hand. "No need to accept. Apologizing is just what friends do."

"I was going to say-"

"First things first: Where would you like to go?"

"What?"

"How about a little getaway? Just us pals?"

"I think I died the last time you took me anywhere..."

"And how does that make you feel?"

I thought for a second, "Eh," and shrugged.

"Interesting," He moved a couple of papers, "Well, don't worry about this time, I got it fully under control."

"Uh...no."

"No? What could you possibly mean?"

"No."

"No?" He asked again.

"No."

"No?"

"No."

"No-"

"No! I don't want to go anywhere you dick, just let me go back to sleep!"

"But sleep is so...paltry? Boring? Bland? Tell me when I hit the right word here-"

"Necessary! To get away from you two fuck faces! Get

out of my head!"

"I-"

"You know, she smells really good now. Like a god damned fuckin' glazed ham on Thanksgiving. Every time she gets near me all I think about is not thinking about that fucking smell. FUCK!"

"Yea..."

"Is there something you could do? To help? If that's your job and all? Maybe take this whole...sensation away? Cause eating people is, like, totally fuckin' nasty...but I can see it... eating...feasting" I wiped my mouth-

"Hmm..." He picked up some papers and shuffled them around, looking through some of them. "Yea," he sucked in a breath, "here." He reached out a ghostly hand and started to physically vibrate, his shadowy mist bouncing and wafting up and down, "ZzzzzzzzhhhhhhhhaaaAAAAAAAAAAAAAAAA!" he screamed loudly.

I stood and watched, confused.

His ghost arm dropped back down and he fixed his glasses. "Did that do anything?"

"No." I said.

"No?"

"No."

"Yep..."

"Wow, big help you are, huh? Are you really here just to remind me to not fucking eat her or something?"

"I'm here to advise, not remind, and that's why I want to bond with you. To advise better. To understand your predicament better."

"Bond? You're acting like an estranged father."

"Well, your whole fatherly situation right now isn't too good sooo...maybe I can be your new Dad! Eh? Pretty cool right? I can be a cool ass Dad."

"No."

"No?"

"No."

"Well...okay...Tell me about her."

"About who?"

"Scarlet."

"Why?"

"Just tell me something about her. Then I'll get you back to sleep."

"Fine...Scarlet is kind of...an asshole. She talks too much. She doesn't really care about personal space. She has Monster Balls, I don't know. But all of that makes her her, you know? I guess I really respect that? Now can I go to bed or do you want an entire ten page essay about the ethics of the universe or something on that astronomical level?"

"Good enough."

And then it all went black.

Addendum

Addasaeh awoke to the deaf callings of his mute flock, "It is here!" they screamed in alignment between their sewn lips. "The second coming!" they continued, muted and silent.

And, in their calls, Addahsaeh calmed all with his voice, saying with commandment, "For the time is nigh, my weary flock, stick with me and flourish until the very end, for so it may be when it spins and circles until it is found before us, in a mere five years.

Calm and wait. Be patient. Look towards the future. Stay with me and only then will you find peace and godhood for then, when the worlds align, is when she will be ready. Wait my flock. Be patient. And salvation will come."

He then closed his godly eyes once again, waiting until the next brokered peace.

11

Mark

As the months spiraled down into the depths of winter, Willow Pines found herself in a mental torrent of mockery. Mockery from her parents. Mockery from her brothers who never come around anymore. Mockery from her senses as they fall and revive with an unusual purpose. A purpose that makes her breath tickle a little harder. It makes her hairs stand on end and her fingers to curl into little fists which curdle white with a squeezing force as all she thinks about is not thinking. Not thinking about that one…little thing- But she makes it well enough, after a couple grueling days. She holds onto it with stout purpose now, never letting the cracks grow.

And in this cold spiral, it talked little nothings into her ear, the thing on the ceiling, about this and that, each and every night, constant and annoying. Maddening and writhing in both ears.

And I quieted down, watching her condition grow. Waiting. What one little change can do to someone. It eats at them and slows them down. But she…

One must stay patient. Wait and see. Open conversation soon enough.

She has been cursing much more frequently. Is that due to an outside factor, or are we to blame for this sudden shift?

I wonder what she thinks of me now? That I've given her a little bit of space-

Willow

"FUCK YOU, CUNT!" I screamed.

"There you go! Again!" She screamed.

"FUCK YOU!"

"Fuck yes! Again, even louder!"

I took a breath, "I think I'm good- FUCK YOU!"

She laughed, "FUCK YOU!"

"FUCK YOU!"

"FUCK YOU!"

"FUCK EVERYTHING!"

"FUCK EVERYONE!"

"And, sincerely," I put my hand on her shoulder and whispered, "Fuck you. Again."

"Fuck you too," she whispered back.

Then we laughed to the tune of the movie playing on her television before us. Her living room was empty, her house was empty, her parents were gone for the night as the snow slapped silently against the living room window.

"Yo," Scarlet started, "I've been wondering: Has your Dad even come home, like, once in the past couple months?"

"Um..." I thought, "I don't know."

"Interesting...What do you think of following him one day, you know? Skip school and track him after his work?"

"I don't know about that...we don't even have a car."

"Yea we do," She stood up and walked over to the window. "This bad-daddy," She flaunted her hand elegantly at the car sitting in her driveway. "Mom and Dad are gone on a business trip for the week, so we got this beast of a car."

"And do you even know how to drive?" I asked.

"Of course I know how to drive. I'm just missing that core component: A license."

"Well thats a pretty fuckin' important component."

"Nah. We'll be fine. Come on! You know where he works, right? Let's just follow him. Do a car stakeout like some detectives or something!"

"I don't think I even want to-"

"Pweese, Wiwwow."

"Stop with that fucking voice."

"I'll shtop if ywou say ywes-"

"Fine, sure, yea. Just stop with that."

"Great-" She smiled.

"Hope you don't get us killed."

"Oh, I'm an expert level driver over here. I've done it tons of times."

*

The car swerved and jittered as it almost hit a mailbox.

"Jesus!" I screamed.

"It's fine! I got it!" She pulled the car into the lane and continued slowly.

"You sure you can drive?" I asked.

"Yea, yea. Dad let me handle the wheel once."

"And the other times?"

"Video games..."

"Holy shit, we're so boned."

"Have a little faith, Willow."

"Faith? You almost crashed backing out of the driveway!"

"That's faith! Iron and Blood baby!"

"I'm missing a math quiz for this-"

"Dude," the car slowed down to a start and stop at the stop sign, "You're such a nerd."

"Fuck you."

"Okay, you gotta be my co-pilot. Directions, now. Please."

And through the snow laden roads, Scarlet barely managed to keep it steady as I guided her to where Dad worked. It was some brown bricked office building that reached up towards the gray sky in two stories of bleak office space and, as we pulled into the parking lot out back, we found the station wagon sandwiched neatly between a couple of small cars. I've never asked him what his job was before. It was always: Dad went and he WORKED and then he came back. But now, he barely comes back. Shit. In his suit and tie and all these black suitcases. Sounds boring as shit. And Scarlet is right: What is he doing? Not coming home most nights? Barely talking. Can't let people walk all over you...can't let family walk all over you.

I wanted to hate, really. And in some aspects, I do. But, and I hate to admit it, I love him. And Mom. And my brothers. I was...worried. But I also didn't want to see what he was doing after work or where he was going. I would rather not. And then I look over towards Scarlet and see her leaning into the back of the fabric car seat that has a couple deep stains set in here and there. And then I feel confident again. To see him and learn. Learnnnnnn...

"Yo, when does he get off?" Scarlet asked, popping the chair, causing it to fall back.

"Dunno."

The pitter patter of snow fell softly on top of the car. We sat and waited.

Mark

Willow Pines waited in that corolla with her friend, watching the snow fall about them, clogging the windows, forcing the wipers to spout out and furiously spread the white powder around and around, until it was mostly off. It clogged the door handles and blocked view from the four side windows that followed the car down, making the inside colder with each minute. Willow donned her gloves and pulled them on even tighter as Scarlet shoved her hands far into the reaches of her coat, nuzzling her face into the collar of her multiple undershirts.

And here I am, tasked with watching these two on their little adventures. The Key. He wants her on close watch to progress her. Five years is what was stated all that time ago. An unknown time ago. An odd time ago of black and swirling moons and darkness and accretion disks. But for these things, time is weird. Peoplethings? -Yes- One hundred years and then they're over. But all is necessary for the conjunction.

He chose well. Or was it prophecy? Both? But to watch

her struggle, or lack thereof, is truly an achievement. Trapped in that car with *her*. At first, she was windpipped, or, more like, flabbergasted, this whole new sensation rocking her world for a mere couple days. But she pulled it together, fighting against *that* and It, on the ceiling. She can ignore it well, not think about it too much, of course. But how long until she does think about it? Until it washes past her mental barrier and into the limelight? Months? Years? Possibly. But this is not the end. Nowhere near. To truly find out if she is the one, to make fact concrete, we must continue with the process. Continue with progress. Test her more until it is time.

And they keep talking with each other. About random little things that make no sense to really talk about. Why? Some paltry entertainment of the smallbrain? Does this make them...un-bored? Happy? Interested? How, no... Why? That is what it is to be a human, to be a peoplething, I must really guess, to continue on with unobvious nothings until they die. When time is so fleeting, what else is there to do in your little meatbag body, full of sinew and pulp, running with fleshy veins, all commanded by a bulge of mass and folds at the top of it all. And in the end, all that complex structure of evolution ends with decay and dirt and forgettence.

Seriously, what are they talking about, this nonsense:

"Okay," Scarlet Miller started, "Aliens?"

"What," Willow asked, a confused look on her face.

"Are aliens...here?" Her muffled voice raised out of her undershirts. "On this pale blue dot."

"Uh...no."

"No!?"

"No..."

"Dude, what about Roswell?"

"Weather balloon."

"Phoenix lights?"

"Government training."

"Nuremberg sightings?"

"Mass hysteria."

"What about the Gatling International Treaty?"

"The what?"

"Look it up."

"No."

The 'Gatling International Treaty' was completely made up. Why? Why make falsehoods just to prove oneself right? There's no need to lie when one thinks that they're in the right. Right?

And these languages too: How coy. All of them a network of confusion; All of them tickle the metaphorical tongue. To physically speak instead of do. Interesting, very interesting these meatbag peoplethings.

Is to speak to feel? Is it the same as I with another one of my brethren? Are what they doing...is it feeling too? Does her mind not move as her mouth? They are two separate entities with two separate minds which both bow to one internal mass of mind and wanting/un-wanting.

I've stayed distant from her the last couple of months. I could tell that she was getting annoyed at me. Well...she did tell it or scream it right in my face. So I let her sit and fester without my help. But soon, she'll come to me. And then will I get the full scope of her mind. Soon. Soon...soon.

It'll be subtle, like the others, but it will grow in its grandeur, all under the will of Him, deep in the veins, down under. Subtle, not enough to be instantly mindbending, but just enough to get the engines rumbling just slightly. That rumble will grow steadily throughout the years.

And, as I think, they continue to talk with one another. About what? Random nothings. I cannot understand mindless chatter. Sweet talking. Why must you know what the best 'Ice Cream' is? Or what they think about this or that? It is incessant. It is unneeded. But, as I watch, I cannot help but to feel...something churning deep down below. Something in this corporeal form that I've been conjured.

Must figure out what it is.

Must watch.

Willow

"...and that's why-" Scarlet's eyes opened wide as she swiftly ducked, "Shit! Get down!"

I ducked low below the dashboard before thinking, knocking my head on it hard. "Ow!"

She laughed, "Dumbass bitch."

"Eat one," I raised a middle finger and slightly peeked over through the snow drizzled windshield.

Dad waded carefully over towards his car, holding a bag in his left hand and a set of dangling keys in his right. His suit was covered up in a long gray coat which dragged across most of him as it trailed slightly on the snow that plastered the ground. He didn't seem to notice us as we both hid and watched him from our little stakeout spot.

"Turn the car on," I said.

"I know, I know," her hand fumbled towards the key as the engine turned over with a rumble.

Dad opened the door, got in, and closed it.

We all sat there, waiting for something. Has he caught on? Has he seen the neighbor's car dubiously parked a lane down from his? It was a decently common car with a decently common color on it. We blended in perfectly nice, or I thought so at the least. Maybe he did see us-

Nope! His car turned on and immediately started to back out of its snow padded spot.

"Go! Go!" I screamed.

"Hold on!"

Scarlet rammed the stick into reverse and pumped the accelerator, sending the car from a standstill to a speedy and slidey reverse which narrowly missed a parked car behind it as Scarlet tugged the wheel harshly downwards.

"Fuckin' hell!" I screamed.

"Fuck yes!"

And in all of this commotion, Dad's car slowly crept down the parked cars towards the outlet.

"Dude, he's barely moving!"

"Maybe, but whatever," and the stick pumped into drive as she slammed the petal again, sending us speeding down where we started to follow Dads car which went slowly and steadily towards its destination.

Scarlet kept on his tail, sometimes riding it and sometimes swerving a car or two behind, always near.

Mark

The lively danger of the situation seemed to stay nowhere near their minds as an ill-licensed Scarlet Miller pulled in and out of this lane and that, no blinker in sight.

"Yo, be on cop watch," is what she told Willow Pines, as she moved another lane, keeping, as they would probably say, 'On his (metaphorical) ass.'

There was some danger lurking in Willow's mind as she looked from window to window, watching for any inclination of an enforcer of the personlaw of this little world.

These types of actions could kill someone. And as we know, these things live short lives as it is, so where is the reason for putting more people in danger just to shorten their already short lives? Does Scarlet Miller even see the future where she has a chance of ramming her death vehicle into another death vehicle filled with an entire family of four single minded, thinking, peoplepeople? Killing them all as her front bumper slams through the side doors, smushing and burning the occupants inside, moving their hard bones where they shouldn't?

But I digress, as that didn't happen. They followed and followed until they found themselves nestled in an alcove of concrete street and large wooden buildinghouses, parked on the opposite sidewalk as her Dad opened the door and walked down the pathway of a large suburban house that was surrounded by several more large suburban houses all caked in a thick snow. Willow thought, *This spot looks way better* until it turned into a sort of parlay rage. Lots of things followed in to her mind as she and Scarlet watched Daniel Pines open one of the two front doors, scuffed his boots on the outside mat, and stepped inside, closing the door behind him.

It would be hard to categorize her exact thoughts which shotgunned as she watched and speculated. Some were hopeful (more like a small amount), a couple were sad, but most were a stark rage, continuing the previous bout of rage, making it all hotter. But, like a human, her face remained calm as her mouth moved, "We should get a better look."

But contrary to herself before, Scarlet Miller found her mind empty of the extreme bravado of before. She liked to put on a big game of, as she says, 'Iron and Blood, baby!', which is probably followed by a whole slew of crass 'language' afterwards, just to show how 'cool' she is. But inside she could be nowhere near that. Her stomach dropped when they stopped at this exact spot. Her mouth went dry as she pulled the parking brake into ready. Her eyes blinked several times in disbelief as she grabbed the ignition and turned it off. She tried to play it off though, "I don't know…" she said.

"What do you mean," Willow was more abrasive. "We're here."

"Yea, but…I didn't think…" Scarlet's mind shook for a second. She never thought that in a thousand peopleyears, that this whole affair of fatherly affairs would have actually happened but now here they were, watching the impossible. What was she to do now? "I'm not sure."

"What?" Willow's features contorted into annoyance, her white face growing a slight tint of red as her dark eyebrows furrowed down and her mouth moved inwards in disgust. "You were the one who said we had to do this!"

"Yea, but…I didn't think that…" she tried to look anywhere but Willow, but she couldn't. Scarlet had always liked her deep blue eyes.

"What? What are you saying?"

"I…didn't know that we would ACTUALLY find him… you know."

"No. I don't know." Her body shivered slightly. Was it from the cold which bit or was it the boiling feelings which raged deep down? But what could she do with that rage? What would she do when she eventually looked through that big window of the living room of that big house that her father had just walked into. Where could all that rage go if not out? In?

"Whatever," Scarlet finished, her bravery all funneled out.

Willow shook her long black hair which she quickly tucked into the furrows of her clothing. She opened the door swiftly and then slammed it shut as she trudged through the bright evening snow towards the house. She didn't look back as she trudged through powder.

Scarlet opened her door and stepped out, following her hot headed friend who blasted in a quick pace towards the window. She didn't run to catch up though. She stood and watched with maybe a paltry step or two forwards.

Willow knew past all those little thoughts that ran rampant in her head with each trudging step, but accepting the fact was another battle. If her father was going against the marital oaths of conformism, then what would that say about her further about life at home? It would confirm it all. Every little lingering fact that Scarlet told her during dinner all those nights ago. And her mind went blank as she hid behind her fathers still warm car.

Scarlet watched her peer over the hood, looking into the house that was way too big. Scarlet watched her head recoil back and her eyes widen as she almost fell back onto the ground. Scarlet didn't know what to do in a moment like this. She was scared of what to do next. She likes to act confident around others. *Why*? She would think. *Why can't I just, I don't know-* but then she would keep acting like this. She knew her abrasiveness was never the most attractive to potential friends. And here, in front of her, in the trailed snow, she watched her only friend in the world confirm to herself what words could never.

And she was scared.

I'll get her...dinner? She thought as Willow began to crawl back towards her. Then she stood, then she slammed the car door without saying anything, her face a mist. Scarlet stood outside the car a little bit, leaving Willow Pines alone, watching the light beam out from the window of that large house.

Willow didn't know what to do either as she sat in the shotgun seat, breathing hard. Her hands shook, her eyes hurt, her stomach tumbled slightly as she thought of random soliloquies deep in the recesses of her mind that raced here and there, trying to solidify themselves. Scarlet's outline darkly shrouded the driver side window, but she didn't enter.

And, in that emotional little outburge, her wall broke just slightly, with a little crack and all. She thought, for one picosecond, *It smells good in here.* As she leaned over slightly, sniffing the air around Scarlet's recent seat.

And then she pulled back and punched herself in the face. I smiled.

*

They both sat silently across from one another at some booth, looking over an expansive menu of this and that. Other people inside the diner chatted away and moved around, bustling around the silent duo. Willow Pines sat with a slight bruise on her cheek and Scarlet fingerpoked some menu item, I think it was pancakes.

"Yea, that's the one," she said. "That's fuckin' it right there. Some butter n' shit."

Was she speaking to Willow or herself? Or no one. Or me? No, she forgot. She doesn't remember. Soon. Someday.

Willow didn't respond, a tired look upon her face, a light purple dusting below her right eye. Scarlet didn't mention it when she sat in the car, and has still yet to mention it. She noticed, for sure. It was the first thing she noticed. But her mind kept somewhere else. On pancakes and...no, really just pancakes.

"What are you gonna get?" Scarlet asked.

"I...uh...the...steak?"

"Diner steak? That shit is probably nasty." Scarlet responded to the slow speech, quick and loud. Some denizens nearby heard. Some of them were, in fact, eating the steak. But she didn't care if others heard her.

And Willow didn't respond to Scarlet's comment. She put the menu down and fiddled with the large sugar dispenser that young people used to pour loads into coffee and old people ignored.

Willow, like Scarlet, didn't think about much. While her mind wasn't on solely pancakes, it was on some comubulous assortment of nothings that fleeted constantly. What was one supposed to think about after finding her worst fears visualized? The anger that she had in the car boiled away quickly. Especially so after she gave herself a sucker to the cheek. But now what was left? I couldn't rightly tell and I don't think she knew much either. Her soliloquies lessened into nothing as she sat and fiddled with the sugar dispenser. She poured a little out onto the table and drew little lines in it as she sat.

They ordered soon from some preppy waitress and then continued to sit there quietly.

Scarlet built it back up, her slight confidence that she used to finally broach the topic which Willow was waiting for. "So...wanna talk?" she asked.

"About what?" Willow asked, drawing a face in the sugar.

"Don't BS me. You know what."

"Ah...yea. Saw them in there."

"Them?"

"Dad was sitting with...a lady. And there were...some kids running around. And then I left. Good for him, right? He got away from his first mistake of a family, right? That's what everyone else is doing. How long till Mom leaves? Right?" She slouched even more and drew another face, "I deserve it."

"I..." Now it was Scarlet's turn to rage. It forced its way past the recesses of scaredness and tepidness that found itself consuming herself before. "Really?" her mouth flashed, her eyes angry.

"I guess," Willow continued to draw in the sugar, not caring to look up.

Scarlet looked around the restaurant, eyeing and sizing up this person and that. Two old dudes sat at one table, talking with one another silently. A family sat a couple of booths down, eating. The cook in the back rang a bell as the waitress ran over, grabbing whatever food item was placed below the bright red warmer. At that moment Scarlet knew what to do. All this comforting and all of this oo-y goo-y stuff about making your friend feel better in moments like that, they really weren't her style. She didn't know what to do on the quiet drive over, she didn't know what to do when they sat down, heck, she didn't know what to do a mere second ago, but she knew exactly what to do, right at the very moment. And she smiled, *Screw it.*

"Fuck you!" she screamed loudly, making everyone in the diner look at her.

"What?" Willow finally looked up.

"Yea, you heard me. Fuck you!" She stood and placed her hands heavily on her waist. "Come on, tell me off. Give it to me!" Her waist buckled to the side as her head cocked, waving her black hair to and fro.

"Scarlet, what are you doing?" Willow whispered louder, bracing her hands on the table as she leaned over towards Scarlet.

"Oh, what? You wanna play with your little sugar? Fuck you!" She quickly swiped all the drawn sugar off the table in a mist of white powder, much like the snow outside. "Come on! What are you gonna do?"

"I..." Willow stood quickly.

"You bitch!" Scarlet forcibly pushed her back down,

"What are you going to FUCKING do? You pansy little girl!"

Willow stood again, her eyes annoyed and cold, "Stop!"

"No! Do something about it!" she pushed her again, but Willow only wobbled back as she caught herself with the heel of her boot. "You weak little shit! Do someth-"

Willow's small fist connected with the upper cheekbone of Scarlet's dimpled face, sending her almost flying backwards, her body slamming harshly on the ground. The diner sat silent as the family of four watched, the coffee dripped as the two old men looked back, the cook stuck his head through the slit in the wall, and the waitress itched her head. On that gross cold ground, Scarlet started laughing as she pulled herself back up, rubbing the side of her face. "Maybe you could kick my ass," she laughed. Willow started to smile.

As if nothing had happened, everyone else in the diner turned back to what they were doing previously, the life of small chatter seeping back.

Scarlet scootched back into her seat, still rubbing her cheek, "You hit hard."

"Sorry," Willow said, still smiling.

"No need to thank me," Scarlet raised her hand and the waitress came sauntering over. "Yo, can I have some ice, please?"

She nodded and left.

And the two sat in a light silence once more, looking at one another, smiling and eyeing around.

Willow's mind rested for now, finally gone was the forlorn lonesome of sadness which left her through one balled up fist. She rubbed her aching knuckles below the counter as she sat, thinking about not her father. Thinking about... something...I don't exactly know. That's weird. She leaned back and felt energy surge through her bones, her smile growing larger.

Scarlet got her ice and pressed it to the spot on her face which hurt like someone had just punched it really hard. And she smiled some more, breaking the silence, "So, how do you feel?"

"Eh," Willow shrugged, "Hand hurts."

"Face hurts."

They both bursted into another fit of laughter. Soon, their faces would have matching bruises to boot, a perfect little couplet.

And soon their food came around in white plates of stuff. Scarlet had a stack of processed flour and churned milk and sticky sugarsyrup which laid in front of her.

Willow, in front of her, sat something strikingly similar. A fat and juicy steak, slightly browned on the top and leaking red juice. A bottle of A1 sat next to the plate as she grabbed her fork and knife.

They both started eating, Scarlet feasting and Willow poking and prodding.

"I feel...like I wanna, I don't know, do something." Willow said, sticking the knife into the meat.

"Like what?" Scarlet asked, a sticky mouthful congealing the words.

"I don't know...like...wanna party or something?"

"Par-tay?" Scarlet's eyebrows rose high. "Well, I do declare," her impression of a posh southern boy from Manilla started to come through, filled with molasses just like her mouth was filled with syrup. "I would never have thought to see the Willow Pines exhibit in the Par-tay."

"Well, just us." She took another wispy bite from the steak, clearly not enjoying it.

This was the start, but keep it low and slow. One at a time. Not too fast.

"Oh, you're so sweet," Scarlet said, rubbing her cheek again. "You love me."

"Shut up," Willow smiled and pushed the steak away. "Also, this food fuckin' sucks."

"Told you the steak is dogshit."

Willow slapped her mouth, testing this new taste that entered. It was an odd taste. Unpleasant.

Slowly. Over time. Let it drip in.

12

Snow gusted in through the open front door as Willow and Scarlet floundered in, tripping over each other as the wind slammed the door wide against the wall. Scarlet turned around and grabbed the door and pushed hard, concentrating everything on her upper body and, step by step, the door finally closed with a clink and a thump as Scarlet slid down the wooden frame, sitting on the floor in exhaustion. "Jesus fuckin' A."

"How'd we even get here without fucking crashing?" Willow asked, her breath still catching as snow started to bead into little crystalline droplets on her thick winter coat, the warmth of the inside coming to fruition, warming their hands and faces.

"Are you really shitting on my perfect driving?" Scarlet started to stand.

"Yes. Yes I am."

Willow

Scarlet smiled, the bruise on her cheek a remnant from my still aching fist, "You know, thinking about it," she took off her powdery coat and threw it to the side, "I could totally beat your ass."

"Even after I grounded your fat ass?"

"Abso-fruit-ly, my friend."

"I know. So..." I looked at the television, the window behind it a blanket of cold white, "We watching a movie?"

"Eh...Oh, I got an idea." She pushed past me and walked towards the kitchen to which I followed suit. "Okay," she said as she pulled open a cabinet and reached inside, "now, I know you're a pussy, but I want you to think about this good and hard," and out came her hand holding a long pale bottle that sloshed around as she set it on the center table.

"Alcohol? Really?"

"I mean-"

"Only degens drink-"

"You said that you wanted to party, so..."

"Yea but, that was in a moment of sincere adrenaline."

"Sincere adrenaline? You fuckin' punched me right here!" She motioned to the purple mark on her face.

"Yea. Sincere. Muthafuckin'. Adrenaline. Sincerely."

"Sincerely my ass. Whatever...hey, lets call it sincere reimbursement."

"What?"

"This fuckin'," she shook the bottle, "booze right here. In my. Hand."

"Why reimbursement?"

"To reimburse you for this whole...you know?"

"For my Dad banging some bitch?"

"Basically..." She pointed to her bruise, "He basically gave me this bad boy up here."

"Jesus, you really gonna keep pointing it out?"

"Having a mark of the beast right on your face is never something to be ashamed of." She cocked her head, "What about this thing, right here?" and she poked my face, causing a ring of pain to wallop out from where I had punched myself. It was a fucking stupid thing to do, but...

Stop thinking-

"Ow!" I screamed, repelling my head from the pain.

"Dude, since all the awkwardness has gone away, why the fuck did you punch yourself? I get it, you were all mad and shit but...actually, that's a pretty wicked thing to do, in all my honest honesty."

"Thanks."

"Sure thing," her dimples showed. "So..." and the bottle slid a little farther on the oaken table.

"I don't know, that shits nasty."

"You ever try it?"

"No."

"Well...how do you know you hate it without even trying it...just a little."

"I know what you're doing."

"What am I doing Ms. Willow Pines who is currently being a total bitch ass pussy hoe ass bitch ass-"

"Peer pressure is what you're doing, cunt."

"-dumbass nerd ass stupid ass silly ass-"

"Silly ass?"

"Shut up, I'm not done- really really stupid dumb dumb ass ass stupid pussy bitch hoe ass bitch dummy dumb hoe."

"You done?"

"Ehhhhh- bitch ass stupid ass reallllllllllllllllyyyyyy dumb. Ass."

I looked at her.

"I'm done."

"Uh huh..."

"So, you drinking or what?"

"...no."

"Dumb ass bitch ass-"

"You're really back on it?"

"Dude, I have a whole assortment of 'asses' to go through. You may as well bite the bullet-"

"No."

"-ass ass hoe ass ass ass hoe ass. Bitch. Stupid."

My arms found themselves crossed, "Really?"

She nodded, "Dummy dumb dumb stupid dumb dumb, bee bee boo boo haa haa hee hee-"

"What are you doing now?"

"-pee pee-annoying you-poo poo ass ass."

"Dude."

"-pee pee -you'll see- poop he he hapoopoo lalalalala-"

"Stop."

"La-no, fuck you-lilulelo-"

"You're seriously doing this?"

"-ass ass-yes-ass ass-"

"And this isn't going on long enough?"

"-dick-suck-dick-my-dick-balls-dick-"

"Your Monster Balls?"

"-hoe-yes. You bitch."

I let her go on for another minute.

"-ass ass ass ass... Man, I'm thirsty."

"You done?"

"Whatever, you win."

"Yep," I finally sat down after all the annoying torment.

She coughed deep into her arm, "Bitch."

*

We found ourselves sitting in her bedroom, listening to the wind blow harshly on the one rectangle window which braced against a powdery white wall that pressed harder and harder as the night continued. In both of our hands were some dull steaming cups of hot chocolate which emptied consistently. Dull. They didn't really taste like much, but I drank nonetheless. I guess Scarlet's Mom skimps out on the good hot chocolate or something.

I just took the final sip when another howl of the wind rung from beyond the window. "You think that's gonna hold?" I asked, looking at the window.

"Probably," she took a final, ninety degree sip.

"Probably?"

"Yeah. Probably. Nothing's one hundred percent good sir."

"Okay...that's...not promising."

"Eh. Oh, here, I got an idea- truth or dare?"

"Truth or dare? What are we, like ten years old?"

"Holy shit! You're like fourteen!"

"And you're also like fourteen."

"Yea! Willow, you can't try and skip this whole 'Having fun as a kid thing', let's just have a little fun. You skip drinking, which is the adult fun, now truth or dare, that's our only option left-"

"We can still watch-"

"Movies? Nah, man. We can't just be sedentary settlers

here, we havta do something. Something. Something..." She echoed her voice in a lax effect.

"But we are sedentary. Right here. In this room."

"Yea but you get what I mean, right?"

"I guess..."

"Alright, all we got left is truth or dare. Pick one. Now."

I made an unknown face as I finally gave in. "Truth?"

"Okay...why did you go into my room that one night when we first met?"

"Uhh..."

"Cause, I could have been totally some type of ax murderer or something, you know?"

"I just kinda...did?"

"Wow," she slow clapped, "Really juicy here."

"Your question was dogshit."

"Oh really? Then ask me one."

"Okay...why did-"

"Woah woah woah! You're missing the rules, Ms. Pines."

"What?"

"You gotta ask me the pinnacle question: Truth or dare? Go on..."

"Fuck me. Alright: Truth or dare?"

"Dare."

"Okay...breakdance."

"Breakdance?"

"Breakdance."

She stood up and got down. "Give me a beat."

"What?"

"Beatbox. I need something."

"Sure...uhh-"

"Jesus, Willow! You want me to bust a move or what?"

"Okay, okay!" I cleared my throat and started what I thought sounded like some type of guttural tunes, *"Boots n' cats, boots n' cats, boots n' cats-"*

And she started to bust a move, right there on the carpeted floor. Her legs went twisting as her body wriggled and slammed several ungraceful times on the floor. Her hair twisted this way and that, tangling with itself and her clothing as she started to breathe harder with each consecutive *'boots n' cats'* that came out of my radio of a mouth. Soon, she started to get some type of rhythm with the shotty dance moves. They refined slightly and the ungraceful became a little more graceful. She continued, scraping her arms and head and neck on the floor as she pulled one final half headstand and tried to spin herself on only her head. She fell quickly after as half her body sprawled onto her unkempt bed. My beats died down as her breathing slowed. We both sat for a moment.

"Holy. Mo'fuckin'. Shit goirl." She said, her voice bouncing, her body still sprawled everywhere. "That. Was. Radical!" She spun around and stood up. "How'd I do? Did it look sick?" The lengths of her forearms were a rashy red and her hair spun out of control in a black nest of sweat and breakdance.

I stood, the wind howled. Only one word came to mind-"Disco." I said.

"Disco." She nodded.

"Disco world of the eighth dimension."

"Disco king of the world of the eighth dimension."

"Disco God of the world of the eighth dimension."

"Disco God emperor of the universe of the eighth dimension."

"Disco king God emperor of every universe in every dimension."

"Infinite universes of disco."

"Fuckin' disco King," I nodded.

"Disco fuckin' King," she nodded.

"Breakdance retribution."

"Breakdance revolution."

In that moment we stopped and looked at each other. Her eyes, green, watered over. I hugged her.

"I'm sorry Willow."

"It's okay."

Addendum

And Addasaeh spoke, calming all around it, a god amongst men,
"Close thine eyes, for the future goes and ends with a blink and a whisper, but be calm and reassure all around you: The phoenix comes. And with a fire and a destruction, it destroys all."

Through it all, they found it, under the coxsum and through the spindel. One button press from some hidden plight, whatever it may be. And how long ago was this that he spoke to them. Hundreds? Thousands? Millions? Billions?

His disciples stayed all along, his closest compatriots, hitting the ground and burying with him, deep into the whateverground of the old earth.

With the seeds of prophecy, came the key to unlock rebirth. The conjunction to save all and send all into salvation.

All that was needed of the key was to resist and to keep resisting. Continuously. On and on. Until their potential is ready.

13

"Alright, this is starting to get mad gay," Scarlet said.

"Yea. I need some water."

Scarlet went and sat back down on her bed, looking sad at her empty cup of hot chocolate. "Yo, get me more hot C, pweese."

"Hot C? Hot chocolate?"

"Yea, duh."

"How hip."

"Hip is my middle name, diggity-dawg."

"Oh, you're sooooo hip girl."

"Now, get my hot C, peasant."

"Yes, me lord," I said with an impression of some farmer of the dark ages.

I went upstairs and I went through the process of creation: Breaking out the hot chocolate package and the gallon jug of milk and, finally, the microwave. I combined the three and after a minute or two it came out steaming and hot and mixable. I put a little bit of whipped cream on the top of it and a sprinkle or two of cinnamon which dotted the white melting cream. I poured a glass of water and made my way back down the mess of dark stairs, back to Scarlet's room.

"Yo," I said, entering the room.

Scarlet didn't respond as she stood facing away from me, looking at her bed.

"Yo?" I asked.

"Dude. You gotta..." She took a deep, deep breath, "I don't really know...but, okay-" she finally turned around. Her face looked paler than usual, "Can you...look under my bed? Please?"

"What are you talking about? Also," I handed out the hot C. She looked at it confused for a second but then nodded and took it.

"Okay, okay...so while I was waiting for you to come back," she took a sip, making a white foamy mustache, "I guess I got some really really fuckin' weird feeling. Like some inclination or something-" she stopped.

"Huh? What's going on?"

"Okay, so I got this weird ass feeling, like I almost threw up, but I really wanted to look under my bed which is where I kept that lockbox with all of the...you know-"

"Yea," I nodded.

"So I...so I did and I...look, dude, just look for yourself," she stepped out of the way, her hand beckoning me to crouch down and look under the dark reaches of the bed.

"What is it?"

"Just look."

I put the water down and grasped the edge of the mattress as I got down on one knee and looked under.

It was almost too dark to see anything then I found it amongst the strikingly empty space. Sewed deep under the bed, into the carpet, was a little red button. It glowed silently and misty, slightly sticking out of the beige carpet like a little red tongue from a mouth. "Uh...what's this?"

"What's it look like," she said behind me.

"It's a...button?" I stood back up and looked at her.

"Willow...am I going crazy or something because, and I swear to the almighty, that was never there before. And the fuckin' lockbox is gone!" She put the hot C down and hurriedly looked under the bed again, "The complete FUCK is this? Where is all of my stuff!" She stood back up frantically, "Willow, I had a ton of shit down there, I swear! But now it's all gone! Did I...did I get robbed or something? While we were out earlier, maybe someone busted in and stole all of it, or...or..."

"Hey," I smoothed her arm, "take some breaths. We'll figure it out. But first-" I got down again, "What is that button?"

"I don't know man..."

"What was under here before?"

"All of my school stuff. My backpack and shit. Some other stuff, but they're all fuckin' GONE! Like, where the fuck!? I promise that I didn't do anything-"

"I know! I know! I trust you, man. Just...let's see what this is first."

"I...I don't know, Willow."

I looked back at her, "Now you're the pussy?" I smiled. I felt...good. Confidant. Fuck fear.

"No...I'm not a fuckin' pussy..." I could see it in her eyes, she was about to say it. And, in unison:

"Iron and blood."

"Iron and blood."

It was too tight under the mass of the bed for someone to crawl under with their own willpower, so we decided that I, being the smallest, would get under and she would steer with my legs, all in tune to press that dumb fucking button.

"Just a little farther!" I yelled and with a force my head rammed hard into the wall.

"Like that?" she yelled back, her voice muffled.

"Uh..." I shook my head, rubbing it all the same, "Uh, just a little to the left!"

"Okay!"

And my body forcibly went left as Scarlet jammed my legs in that direction, locking my knees in some uncomfortable 'they're going to break!' type of way. But I said nothing, focusing on that misty tongue poking from the carpet.

At first, we didn't realize how deep it was in the reaches of the bed which we heaved back and forth until, right this second, the tongue was in my grasp, right under my fist that had socked Scarlet's face mere hours ago. It still ached slightly but I didn't think about that either.

"I got it!" I slammed it with a balled fist that barely fit underneath and...nothing happened. It popped back up, still glowing red as if nothing happened.

"Did you press it?" she asked. Her voice felt distant as it traveled through the length of the bed.

"Yeah!"

"Did anything happen?"

"Uh..." I looked around. "No!"

"What?"

"Yea!"

"What? Did something happen? Yes or no!?"

"Uh...yesno?"

"Jesus Willow, press it again!"

"Okay!" I slammed it a couple more times, the tongue bobbing up and down each time.

"You hit it again?"

"Yea! Nothings happening-"

And the floor swiftly opened up underneath me as I slammed my face on the curve of a very hard stone step. Blood filled my mouth in that instant as I tongued a definitely chipped tooth. "Fuck!" I yelled into the step.

I could feel the constant up and down of the rough and jagged steps that made its way down into complete darkness, I forced myself to stand, more like crouch, on the top step, my head hitting the underside of the bed harshly, but I paid it no mind as I eyed out through the shining crack of the bed. Scarlet's upturned face filled the light as she bent over to her side, her long black hair coiling up on the ground like a mess of snakes.

"Holy shit! What happened?" She hollered.

"Why'd you let go of me?"

"I was adjusting my shirt. Is that an opening?" Her eyes shifted.

Crouching on the cold stairway, still sucking back the newly found copper taste in my mouth, the world still slightly swirling, I padded the bottom of the bed with my hand. "Uh... yea. I'm kinda in it..."

"So...what is it?"

"Uh..." I looked down and saw black. I caressed a rough

stair step. “I think this is a staircase or something.”

“Seriously?”

“Yea, but it's too dark to see anything.”

“Jesus fuckin’ A, Willow! The robbers dug a tunnel to snatch my fuckin backpack n’ shit!”

“You were almost pissing yourself moments ago.”

“Yea, well I can’t be a pussy in front of the Pussy Master.”

“Am I the Pussy Master?”

“Oh, absolutely.”

“Thanks, Monster Balls. But…now what?”

We sat quietly, looking around the darkness. I touched the step a little more, staring into the darkness beyond. A hollow sound leaked out from that black in slow and droning echoes. Sounded like wind or something. My curiosity only grew. Fear should have been there, for sure, but I don’t care anymore. I thought of that motherfucker on the ceiling and that asshole in the office.

“Here,” Scarlet said as she stood and lifted the entirety of the bed, hauling it on its side, making it rest on the wall, releasing me from this darkness.

I stood up, “Why didn’t we just do that earlier?”

“Eh,” she shrugged. “Just thought of it.”

She walked over and stood next to me.

In this new light we could see a tiny bit more: Dark and rocky and chipped steps moved downwards until they hit an immediate bend, turning off somewhere else. Stale air.

“So…” Scarlet started.

“What do we do?” I finished.

“I guess we go. I got flashlights somewhere.”

“The giant one?”

“Smaller ones.”

“Lame.”

*

The beams of the flashlights cut through the darkness like a hot knife to butter as we made it to the first bend around the corner. Drips and creaks echoed. The smell of mold and stale air wafted down the length of the cracked stone which glistened in the light with some type of constant moisture. Just like a disco ball.

"Jesus," I said. "Was this always down here?"

"You asking me?"

"More like I'm asking the world."

"Ah, well, the world speaks in riddles, my friend."

"Thanks Tolkien-"

And we turned the first bend, shining the flashlights down another long and dark cauldron of disco walls. The rays of disco seemed to tell us to stop, telling us that we're not supposed to be down here but we didn't care anymore. Fuckin' Disco dancin'. I wanted to bust a move if anything.

"Hey," Scarlet's voice echoed out. "What if there's like some monster down here?"

"Then, I guess we'll beat it up." I shrugged and shook my 'punching Scarlet' hand.

"Sure thing, boss. Hey, now that I think about it-"

We turned the next dark bend and faced another declining set of stone stairs.

"-Oh, watch your step, they're wet-" she shined her flashlight hard on the steps which all breakdanced back their own reflective disco shrouded light.

"Yeah, yeah. What were you gonna say?" I asked, stepping lightly on the top step, feeling its exterior with my shoe, making sure I wouldn't slip.

"Oh yea: you think that monster thingbitch is down here?"

"The what?"

"The whole treehouse thing, you know, before it started to get mad cold."

I did remember. I thought of him, in that little detective room. His annoying glasses and his...what a joke. I buried my embarrassment and told Scarlet, "It probably wasn't even real. We were kids, right?"

"Well, that was like four months ago and, Willow, we

still are kids."

"Yea but, you know..."

"You're probably right-" is the last thing she said when we hit the bottom of the stairs and came to a large steel door which seemed to jump up at us from nowhere. Our lights shined over it hungrily, eating the inlay designs. Little figures danced along the bottom touching one another, following the length of the floor and the sides until they hit the top which was filled with swirls and outpoking little dots which pulled and dragged at little metal fingers that followed the length of the door. My light hit the center of the door and held there. Stretched across the main length of the metal was the etching of a long coiled finger that looped within itself once in one large swirl. The notches of the finger joints lined many as it extended down and into the large circular opening that made the handle. I slapped my lips, there was a sweetness on my tongue. I spit. Fuck off. Scarlet didn't say anything.

I grasped that cold handle and pushed it open with a grunt. Scarlet pushed her shoulder against the hard wood as we both forced the heavy door open. And then it hung loose, all of its resistance gone as it creaked and then stopped. Slowly, the smell of mold and stagnation wafted in through it, revealing nothing beyond its dark exterior.

I looked at Scarlet and she looked at me, her green eyes sparkling in the flashlight's artificial light. She looked like she was keeping it together but the color of her face was a different story. "Uh...are we goin' in?" she asked, peering into the darkness.

"Yeah..." I said.

Walking under that heavy door, we softly spilled out through an umbral opening, the beams of light no longer hitting anything right in front of us as they reached across a long cavern filled with hulking pillars and long stretched walls that rose higher than our flashlights could reach. We had only gone down a couple of staircases but those walls looked like they went up and above where the house was supposed to be.

Almost infinite. Further off, a dull thud echoed out, "What is that?" Scarlet whispered to no answer as I looked around more intently.

It all reminded me of something spectral in the back of my mind, but nothing answered. Fuck if I remember. At the back of the room sat some type of scrawl that spanned the entirety of the wall. It was dark and weird and it stretched up beyond where our lights reached, up into eternity. As I looked at it more, meanings started to emerge. Little knowledgeable facts that entered and stayed. The world spun slightly.

It was a tasty warm in here, I realized. It was hot and humid and smelled of something nostalgic. Like I was back there. Fuck...everything started to get all...why do I know that? I tried to stop looking at that sprawl but I couldn't.

Mark

And Willow's mind went blank as she stopped thinking the normal peoplethoughts, the fiendish thing. But, finally, they were here, all for the sake of knowing her future role in the hulking cosmos. This, being only one node of a network of tunnelveins, it is of sheer pleasure that I invite not only one down there, but two, allowing them the splendor of viewing the mantra of Him. And yet, He still sleeps, waiting for the very moment that she is to be of favor for us.

Willow took the first step in the space, her lurch echoing and bouncing off the fleshy walls that oozed in delight at the first entrance in thousands of years. It was of his flesh that spread out from his holy corpse. But, sadly, time is only finite as like a peoplething in their own life. Once this is over, the node will expire and sink back into the mirth, along with the very prophecies that contain them. A sad thing indeed, but a necessary thing nonetheless. Slowly, the other nodes will crumble on eachother, hundreds of them, giving back to the Father.

And then Scarlet followed her through the pillars and dark mud and stone which etched along the floorplan. They found the end of the cavern. Willow never looked away from the written wall and Scarlet looked everywhere but, *Are the walls moving?* she thought. But then Scarlet started to think of other things. A monster of the night. A bump under the bed. She started to wonder about the intricacies of this whole situation. And her mind finally landed on one very specific mark: *The fuck is going on?* And then she asked, "You think I should tell my parents about this?" trying to take her mind off the situation.

"Uh..." Willow started, but never finished as she shined her light up towards the large sprawling walltext prophecy.

The wall spoke in large commanding sleuths of cosmodic script, unrecognizable to the human eye. But Willow eyed it a little farther, her silverblue peepers bestowed the knowhow of cosmodic coxsum. The script waved this way and that, almost a smear on the wall to the uninitiated, representing thousands and millions of peoplething books and movies and culture and more all encapsulated in one small area saying everything at once, something only a god could decipher with their kin eyes...or a Key.

"The fuck is that?" Scarlet asked as Willow stood motionless and studied the wall, her flashlight dashing from one end to the other in erratic readings.

"It's a..." she shook her head, "It's everything."

"What?"

"From the start of the cosmos to the end, the set time of each and every planet which all escalates into the formation of nothing and everything. Scarlet...I..." Out of Willows small nose came these thick heavy red droplets of blood as her peoplemind began to crumble under itself, the amount of pure knowledge spread in that one splotch enough to kill a normal thing, but things normally couldn't read such script. But she was the Key.

"Woah," Scarlet grasped Willow's shoulder, "You alright, man?"

"I...I'm better than alright. Scarlet!" She wiped her nose,

spreading a heavy smear of blood over the course of her pale face. "Can you not read it?"

"Uh...no. Looks like a shitstain..."

Willow pushed her back hard, "Stop!"

"The fuck?" Scarlet rebounded back to a steady stance.

"You must not make fun of the everythingtables."

"The what-the-fuck-tables?"

"Everything," Willow touched the wall, "Oh, Scarlet... you know so little...you know not your false purpose."

"Huh?"

"You know not that you died before, only you are but some false little clone of meat, your mind conferred to the Third. Only you are meant to be a tool to construct the will of I, the Key," she giggled. "Infinite amounts of universes stretched across the universal plane, if I had the power of one of They I could send us to any single one!"

"Willow, you're being, like, super fucking weird right now."

"Weird? What a small little word." She walked over to the other side of the sprawl which expanded out on the further wall horizontally and vertically and she started reading it, her nose gushing even more, slapping and corroding the gray floor with her red. "The Third, The Second, and The First are all part of the same pie."

Scarlet stood there staring at her bloodied friend, her eyes hungering as her nose leaked even more. Scarlet didn't know what to do. She watched, saying nothing, only watching her friend turn back towards the wall that, to her, looked only like a large black scrape of nothing.

"Abundance. Conjunction. Primal. Key." Willow whispered loudly to herself, her shoulders jittering as her hands caressed the walls of the cave. "Breakdance."

As she whispered, Scarlet heard the beating walls grow louder, steadily.

Then Willow dropped harshly to the floor with a wet slap as she went motionless, blood still pouring from her nose.

Scarlet stood, unmoving, unsure of what to do. And then she took a step. And then another.

14

"So, Willow..." I fixed my glasses and sat back into the soft fabric chair, "Tell me exactly what happened. From what you remember, of course."

"It was..." she laid further back into an ergonomic therapist chair, tucking her legs under herself, "Really dark. Like a void."

"Really dark...can you expand upon that?" I asked, tapping the clipboard I held with a pen. It said absolutely nothing on it, but everything was about aesthetic to these peoplethings, even the Key.

"Like...absolute nothingness. Dead. Stark. Empty."

"I see. And is this after the whole...episode."

"Yes."

"And can you tell me about that?"

"No."

"Okay, we'll go at your own pace. But please, in that 'void', was there anything else?"

"It was...there were things there."

"What things? What did you see in there?"

"I saw...planets."

"Planets? And what else?"

"And...they were close. So close...like I was falling into them."

"And what else did you see? What else was there?"

"I could see the horizon somewhere down on their curve, but they disappeared into something else...something swirling and dark. But it was...so...absolute. But it was bright too."

"Interesting...can you tell me about that?"

"It was...all around that black mass was some infinitely

wide whirling light. I...I could barely see because it was so bright."

"And how did that make you feel?"

"It made me feel...I don't know..."

"Would you say that it made you feel empty?"

"I guess?"

"And what else happened? Elaborate."

"I, uh...fell into it, flying past that bright light and deep into the dark...ness."

"And what did you see in that darkness?"

"A...there was something there-"

"And what did you see in there, Willow?" I leaned in, pretending to write something on the clipboard, my dark hands almost see through.

"I saw-" She stopped, looking off, squeezing her legs deeper into her little ball.

"What did you see, Willow? What did you see in there?"

"I saw a-"

"Tell me, what did you see Willow?" I leaned in further. She was much smaller than I. Well...all of them were.

"There was a face."

"And what did that face look like?"

"It was...gigantic."

"How so, Willow? How big was it? This face?"

"Its nose was like the pillars of creation."

"And?"

"It had a beard, like a galaxy."

"And? And what else?"

"And its eyes were like..." She finally looked up at me with that pale face, her blue little eyes set behind those dark thick eyebrows. Those dark indents of sleeplessness were stapled almost purple below her eyes in stained bags. She was a paltry little thing wearing this black-set onesie pajama set that was dotted with constant little stars that followed from her feet up to her long pale neck. Frail and insignificant. Small. Meager. "I don't think I want to talk anymore, Mark."

"And why's that?" I asked.

She looked around, that annoying confused look spread upon her face, "I don't remember coming here."

"And why's that?"

"Mark," she sat up and looked around the room. "Why are we in a therapists lounge?" Her mind seemed to empty from the sludge which slopped metaphorically from her ears. I could hear it from over here.

"Ah, I felt like you needed a little more of a safe place compared to that grungy detective's office."

"Uh huh."

"You wanna go back?"

"Whatever," she coiled her long and dark hair up and heaved it over her slight shoulder, caressing and smoothing it as she uncurled from that little ball, crossing her skinny legs.

"Well, let's bring it around: How is Scarlet doing?"

"Why don't you tell me?" She looked up, squinting down on her slightly larger nose that almost didn't fit her face. Her mouth was terribly flat too, making a straight line across her paper face that still ebbed zero to no color. I was getting a little more annoyed than I should.

I fixed my glasses, "And what do you mean with that?" I asked, clasping my hands together over my misty black lap.

"Who even are you?"

"I'm sorry for the length of time from when we last talked, I never wanted to annoy you, so I waited until you seemed like you wanted to talk."

"Uh, huh."

"But I'm serious: Scarlet?"

"Why do you care?"

"Because I do. Please. I want this whole thing to work."

"What thing?"

"Us. You and I."

Her head peeled back slightly as her thick brows lowered once again and, finally, a sly smile formed on her thin, flat, mouth. "You trying to get in my pants?" A small amount of black hair fell over her eyes.

"Huh?" I was honestly confused. What does that mean? I shook it off and pulled it back together within the microsecond. "No. Please, I'm being serious here. Let's talk. Actually talk."

"Actually talk about what?" She leaned back in the chair once again, her confidence obviously gaining. She saw that she got to me, I could read it and feel it radiating off of her as she thought about how dumb I was. She was the one wearing onesie pajamas.

"You want to know what I am?" I finally said. Should I make something up or tell her...she seemed to forget her experience in the vein.

"No. Not really. Not anymore. You know what? I've come to realize that this whole thing," she pointed her finger erratically. "This is all below my paygrade, man. I'm over it all. I know what you tried to do when I first saw you-"

"You're-"

"Shut up. You know exactly what you're doing here. Trying to fuckin' wrangle me in this way or that? Well I can feel it. And you know that because I can feel you too, watching the entire fucking time. You know how I feel about Scarlet and you damn right know how fucked things are getting. But guess what fuckface," she sat up and leaned in, that smile still plastering her face, farther and more verbose this time. "You're not gettin' me." And behind that smile, I could feel that most of her was confident in those big-boy words, but, and she knew that I knew, there was a part that tripped over itself. She leaned back again, *So what, man?* She thought and smiled some more, knowing I could hear it.

"Uh huh..." I had to admit that I was slightly flabbergasted. But if she was going to act this malcorrectionificient, then I had to respond with the same query. "How's food been tasting?" I wish I could smile back.

Her flat smile dropped, "Whatever, man." She looked away, indignant.

"Have a good night, Willow Pines. Don't let the bed bugs bite...or the monsters." I leaned in farther, almost whispering, "Especially that one on the ceiling."

I sent her back, laying under that one to continue the sleepless night.

Willow

My eyes opened and then instantly closed when I saw Garry looming above me.

"How's food been, Willow?" He added.

*

I poked and prodded at breakfast, unwilling. A set of two eggs with a smiling bacon mouth stared at me wordlessly.

"You don't like my cooking?" Scarlet asked, pulling out a chair and sitting down at her own plate.

"Just not hungry I guess."

I was eating over at her house during the first warm Saturday afternoon in the last three months. The snow started to melt and flow throughout the running sidewalks and deep into the storm drains, making this gurgling sound. But this warmth was not to last, the rest of winter was still to come. Over the past couple of days we talked little to none about that night. Mostly it was a huge blur of nothing. But something happened. I remember a dark hallway and flashlights. How did we even get there? Was it a dream? No. Breakdancing. I woke up in her bed that night with my shirt covered in blood and my face caked in the stuff. She was standing over me with a white face, but we didn't speak as I got up and went to the bathroom. And I still never asked her about it. We act the same, but still, I can see it deep within her green eyes when we're laughing and bantering. Something that she would never show. What was it?

I thought that I'd be able to sleep more since the mind construction ceased deep in the recesses of my brain, but it's been replaced. A whispering constant from the ceiling. Garry. Whispering nothings into my ears. Loudness replaced with softness. Annoying. I can't sleep anymore.

I refuse to entertain the voice from the ceiling, but it's there and it's gnawing continuously. Maybe it'll go away after a while, right? Maybe not. Maybe I am to grow these bickering bags under my eyes until they swallow my entire face in a purple black scab.

I popped one of the sunny side up eggs and watched the yellow yolk ooze out from that thin membrane shell.

And then there's Mark who only talks every so often in some vain effort of gaining my trust. He thinks he's slick, but he's not. And I confirmed that thought last night in that fuckin therapist office. It was a random accusation, but the way he acted...it makes sense now, those weird inclinations. And DUH! Fuck, Willow, how have you been this stupid? The comments about Scarlet and all that, how would he even know it? Because he's been watching me! Duh duh duh, Jesus H Christerini! He can probably get into my brain and control it in little ways. Those inclinations-those inclinations-those inclinations... He knows without a shadow of a doubt how food has been tasting. Like shit. Bland tasteless shit. It started with the steak but now everything has lost its flavor. Even these yellow eggs are gray, and I continued to prod them with tired anguish, dipping the tip of the fork in and out of the yellow froth as it rivered down towards the smiling bacon.

And Scarlet is getting harder to reconcile in my mind. I see it clearly now, I can see where it's going. First its smell, gone to the wind and replaced by this other smell which solely emanates from her, sitting across from me, eating some food that she had just made. Now taste is becoming gone all the same. What's next? Sight? Sound? Touch?

I leaned in and smelled the bacon. The scent was kinda there, but not much. I took another sniff of the bacon and that *smell* was there. The smell emanating off of Scarlet. My mouth started to water and I flushed it down my throat with the nonchalance of a toilet.

And, next question: Why? Is it really Mark doing all of

this or is he some watcher or observer? Garry? He seems like the main one, the one that Mark says is doing this, but I'm not trusting either of them. Whatever. In the end, all I have to do is put my head down and say 'Fuck all of you!' in loud words. I've been keeping it all trapped up over the last months but it does feel good to categorize them all in some mental list. I can withstand whatever onslaught they put against me. All of it is fake. Surly. First Scarlet dying in front of me in October and then her smelling like some irresistible piece of meat and now food losing its taste and then some slurry afterthought of a deep dank crypt somewhere below the depths. Maybe that was a dream, maybe it wasn't... All that blood... Scarlet and I have not brought it up to any further extent. It was probably a dream. Most definitely a dream. Maybe not, actually. Shit! Make up your mind, girl! She would have brought it up by now, for sure. For absolute sure. One hundred percent. But her eyes say something else, even now, with a piece of bacon sticking out of her chewing mouth, her hair pulled back in a ponytail that slunk behind her back. Wait...she was wearing glasses...these large oval shaped thickset sumbitches-

"What's with those glasses?" I said.

Her head popped up like some gofer sticking his head out of a hole, and then it became slightly red, "Oh...I forgot I always wore contacts around you."

"Huh?"

"Yeah, you never seen me pull them out?"

Did I really not? I feel like I would have noticed her at least once taking them out or putting them on or wearing fucking glasses in front of me.

She pulled them down to the bottom of her nose. "What? You likey?"

I did like the more casual look. It magnified her eyes so they looked giant and pretty and green which emphasized better with her broad shoulders. "Yeah," I nodded. "I do." And then I smiled back at her and at the dying breakfast smile sitting in front of me.

You know what...I don't care anymore. Fuck it. Fuck all of this. Maybe I was just being inattentive. Yep that's all. It doesn't have anything to do with all of this bullshit around me.

Ludicrous bullshit.

And Mark, if you're listening to this somehow, if I'm right, which I know I am, *Suck my nuts, bitch.*

Mark

Rude.

15

And the winter turned to spring, melting the cold fronts and sending it deep back down into the hungering grasses, plants, and roots of the Earth. The sun stayed for longer and the days grew slightly hotter. Within that newfound heat, Willow Pines found herself in a drought of food and sleep, still holding somewhat strong, always with Scarlet Miller now. Willow's house only became colder as the days became hotter with the absence of everyone except her quiet mother. Willow wanted to leave like her brothers, absconding her sad mind over to Scarlet's house more often, sleeping there sometimes in a vain hope that the one named 'Garry' wouldn't find her with the whispers during those long nights as she fruitlessly shut her eyes against them. It would tell her to get up and go over to the sleeping Scarlet who laid right next to her. Unspeakable acts it would describe. And, after one or two nights over there, the thick headed Willow didn't sleep over at the Miller household anymore.

She was starting to look more frail now, the gaunt skeleton face even more pulled in while her ribcage must have looked like a set of piano keys. But those blue eyes and thick brows never faltered in their hate for everything around her, that sheen of resistance never faltering...much. There was never a big slip up with Willow, but sometimes she would skid, just slightly. Sometimes she would get lost in Scarlet Miller's smell or, once, she would wander her thin face dangerously close to Scarlet's long black hair, giving her a good smell or two to which Scarlet would respond jokingly, "What are you doing?" She asked as they sat around in the newly opened treehouse, the cold being less and less of a problem.

"Oh uh," Willow pulled back, embarrassed, wanting to slap her little face with her little hands that looked like five tiny sticks glued to a thin little branch of an arm that stayed set in a large and baggy sweatshirt. She was beginning to like big baggy sweatshirts.

"Do I smell bad?" Scarlet gave a quick whiff of herself. "Because I totally forgot to shower this morning."

"Uh, no. It's nothing." Willow looked away, tucking her little arms under each other, thinking about me for whatever dubious reason.

"Jesus," Scarlet smiled and pushed Willow's shoulder with a friendly gist, "You're a wacko."

But behind Scarlet's smile, she thought of that one wintry night, deep in the caverns that dissolved. Scarlet was frightened, still remembering those words that Willow chanted at her, entombed by the magnificence of something that she couldn't understand anymore. She thought about how she dragged her shaking corpse from the vein and how the walls pumped as if they were alive. But she thought about it no more, shooing it away, still dazed at the fact that the red little 'button' as they called it, disappeared as did the return of all that she thought was stolen, all back under her bed where they belonged. Except I kept that picture of myself. Looked quite dashing if I do say so myself.

Scarlet Miller's been interesting too, watching her grapple behind that mask of bravado and saysoship of random little 'cool' things that she heard. She's been scared, watching Willow continuously refuse to eat. And the whole smelling thing put her in another mood. As she called Willow a 'wacko' and pushed her with friendly abandon, she thought of Willow eating her insides, like some monster from down under. But, like the other thoughts, she pushed them away all the same as she thought about other little things. And then she looked into the avoidant eyes of Willow that Scarlet continued to like very much and that almost made her forget for a second.

And that was where I found it was time to continue.

One cool day, as the wind danced around them, sucking in through their long hair and their nostrils, after a long day of learning, as the school year was coming to a supposed end in the next few peoplemonths, they found a white sheet of paper with big words scripted all upon it, stapled to a long wooden pole, buzzing with lines of electricity that dipped up and down, trailing the streets, weaving in and out of buildinghouses that went down the sidewalks methodically in samey rows.

Willow

"Look at this shit-" She pushed a black and white poster right in front of my face that sprung out with a large ***'YO!'*** in golden letters. ***'Let's get this spring on with a BANG! Let's show the world how to PARTY like back in the OLDEN DAYS. Drinks are on us over at the Marsupial graveyard on 8th and 5th Ave! Be there on March 30th!'*** and in very small text on the bottom, ***'This is a church sanctioned event, please be respectful to the graves or we're screwed.'***

"That looks so lame." I said.

"I know, right? We have to go." She nodded, her glasses stuck to the thickest part of her nose, unmoving. She's been wearing them more often now. She looked better with them.

"The only people who go to things like that are these pseudo-bohemian losers with more dick than brain. Total hormonal toilets." I looked at it closer, "Also, why are 'olden days' capitalized?"

"I don't know," Scarlet looked at the poster and squinted her eyes. "Maybe they're racist or something. Whatever, we have to go!"

"Seriously?"

"Yes! Can you imagine the types of losers that we'll see

there? It'll be like a museum of assholes just for us!" She waved her hand slowly through the air as if to represent these 'assholes', her eyes full of excitement.

"I don't know..."

"It's a church sanctioned event, what can go wrong?"

"Molestation?"

"Maybe," Scarlet said. "But who cares? We going or what?"

"To get molested?"

"No, to the fuckin' church sanctioned event." She shook the poster, "In a graveyard for whatever reason."

"To get molested? In a graveyard?"

"Okay, here: Would you rather go to heaven or hell?" Her hands rose up, one representing heaven and one hell.

I thought for a second, eyeing the poster. "What if all the prunes go to heaven, right? And all the rad fuckin' dudes are in hell, rockin' out with Satan?"

"Yea but isn't Hitler in hell?" Her head cocked to the side.

"Eh, you can probably avoid him or something."

"So you want to be with the prunes or Hitler?" Scarlet asked.

"Neither. I'm just joshin' with ya, home doggy dawg." I made a peace sign. "Eh, maybe heaven actually. If hell is a huge ass party, I'd rather chill with the prunes."

"Boom! Now to get into heaven, we havta go! To. The. Party. Tonight."

"So to get into heaven, to hang with a ton of molesting prunes, we have to go party at some graveyard?"

"Hell yea!" Her hand raised in an unmet high five.

"Why?" I asked. I wanted to mention that we had homework but I didn't feel like getting called a nerd by her swaggering mouth.

Her hand drooped limply to her shoulder and her face sunk slightly, "Look, Willow. I'm trying to have us some fun. Okay? Fuck me, man. Who cares about heaven or hell or all that fucking bronze age bullshit," she pulled her glasses down to the edge of her nose with her other hand. "Let's have some fun."

I looked around the empty street and then back at her green eyes masked by those large and black oval glasses. My face must've said something because her large smile dimpled back as that limp high five became erect once more, raising almost too high to where I couldn't even reach without standing high on my tippy toes. "Alright, we're going." I submitted and high fived her hand.

*

The rumble of the ground shook the graves as the horrendous beat of the dance music boomed these sonic pulses out, shaking the dirt and concrete slabs that surrounded us. Tens of people danced and talked amongst the gray stones which stood vertical and horizontal, the dead all resting unpeacfully below them. In the center of this supposed church event was a large and locked crypt that held the dead of some rich family...probably. We stood side to side at the edge of the little circle of graves and people, her in some dark clothing, her contacts in, and I in some baggy sweatshirt and jeans that hung loosely even belted at the last rung. Instantly I wanted to leave, the music was too loud, the mess of people I instantly disliked as I looked them over. Again: Church event? All these people looked like they've never even seen a church. Tattoos and spiked hair and bottles of alcohol and the overwhelming smell of weed hung over the topless air. My stomach felt queasy and unfiltered looking at them all. And how old were they?

"I don't know about this, Scarlet!" I screamed in a whisper, my voice barely rising above the music.

She looked at me all the same, her eyes unmistakable, she kinda liked it. Poor Scarlet, stuck to me most of the time. I could tell she wanted to join them. But she never said anything from her mouth, her eyes doing all the speaking. They also said, *I don't like you*, in some weird way. They silently whispered it deep in the depths of them. I shook my head from the thoughts. I figured that I best watch over her as some type of guardian. The wind picked up slightly and the disgusting weed smell wafted away, only to be replaced by something sweet. And then it was gone as we both looked back at the people.

I wanted to tell her to leave with me, but I couldn't. I couldn't leave her either. "Hey," I yelled, "you go ahead, Ima check something out first!"

She smiled that smile. Shit. I had to do this in some way.

And then she was gone somewhere, like a blink and whoosh of the wind. Then there she was, walking over to some spot. I'll just keep an eye on her. I pulled my hood up and covered my poor ears from each pulsing beat of the music.

Boom! Boom! Eert! Eert! Skkirrrttt! Boom! Boom! Eert! Eert! Skkirrrttt! Boom! Boom! Eert! Eert! Skkirrrttt! Over and over. Was it a new song or what? Fuck, man...I walked over to the big monolith with that big gate and tried to look through the confines of the iron that guarded the entrance. But it was dark in there and nothing but silence beyond the cold gates said, 'Go away,' in its shadowy language. I wish I was in there, in the cold and silent darkness that only eats noise and light, maybe the music would shut up just a little bit. Maybe Garry was in there but so what? Or Mark or whoever fuckin' weird ass thing, I don't care. All liars. All fake probably, all of my fucked up head. But I kept it locked like this fucking gate. And I shook the iron, hearing the lock jingle and jangle with a guttural metal rasp.

The air started to smell like heavy and hearty shit, all the weed now wrought in a thick wave of nose hair sizzling horror that culminated in a thick shadow behind me that stretched and warped in its absence of light.

There was a big, meaty hand on my shoulder as I turned around quickly, looking up into the fat sweating face of some flat nosed stranger cast in darkness. He breathed heavily as thick nasty locks of unwashed hair plastered his forehead. He looked into me with these dark, unsightly eyes. "And what's a young girl doing here?" He asked, his breath smelling of old fish and rot, his face devastatingly close, his large fat back arched over, his height unobtainable.

"Uh..." was all I could spit out before he spoke again.

"Hmm..." He whispered as his eyes undressed me past this sweatshirt. My mouth watered in disgust as I felt like hurling my guts right up into his rotten smelling mouth. "Hmm..." he hummed out again. "Won't know till...hmm..."

And then I found my courage back and pushed him hard with all my strength, somehow forcing him back a few steps, "Fuck off dude!" I screamed into the louder air.

He stopped backpedaling, the light finally consuming his shadow, his breathing growing heavy. More clearly, I saw his mouth first, full of rotten and split teeth that rowed back in missing gaps here and there, his tongue bulging between them, swollen and massed as a purple thing, the veins curling through it like little thick worms. His upper brow slouched down in a patch of dark and black skin, dead from decomposition and those eyes were black shells of nothing as the right side of his nose hung by a lengthy strip of sinew that waggled back and forth with each of his hoarse breaths. The plastered hair on his forehead was his only hair, as it stuck in a lengthy widow's peak resolving in nothing. "Jeez," he said, his rotten eyes stretching in offense. He wiped his belly, smoothing the protruding fat folds that mixed into the linen of the shirt, eyeing me all the same with a deep and dark belly button which ate at the cloth. He fixed his collar and walked away into the further recesses of the party, off somewhere, in the direction that Scarlet disappeared into.

And I stood there. "Huh?" And then shook my head. Zombie? And then I shook my head again. No, that's stupid. But then I looked around more and found more of them. A couple in front of me, almost balls deep in each other making out in a disgusting French style, their sounds slopping over to where I stood. The man's lips were cracked and erased, revealing white sets of bone and teeth through them as the woman underneath him slobbered her forked tongue through them. One of her eyes drooped outwards of its socket as the other leaked viscous white fluid all over their faces, messing their rot into one sludgy black tangle, their faces almost melting together as thick black blood slapped with each mouthful. Looked like two plates of black mashed potatoes being squashed together. Near them a man stood, his shirt all ripped and shredded as his stomach underneath loomed hollow and black, his disconnected spinal cord hanging precariously and casually at the same time. He took a sip of his drink and it spewed out of his bottom, slapping against the brown dirt below him. A couple paces to the left stood a woman who looked more skeleton than woman, somehow gripping an ice cold drink between her bone hands and her cheeks gave way to nothing as her mouth fell off in a mass of flesh with each word she spoke to some other fleshy creature without a set of shoulders.

And more and more, all around I noticed them more, people rotting and falling apart, their decaying bits protruding and messing off in large amounts of skin and sinew, some lingering and sticking together by just a hair. Some laughed and cackled over the music which seemed to slow and beat just a little quieter.

"Huh?" I said again.

I looked over to where Scarlet disappeared, a mess of bodies and skeletons and rotting flesh, but no Scarlet Miller.

And I...didn't feel anything. Sure, the stink smelled worse and worse as more people began to skelify and rot, and the music was still annoying, but what was I supposed to do? Scream and run around? I don't know...I was really tired and thought about nothing else as I wandered away from the party, to the fringe, and found some quiet plot and a stone grave to rest my quiet head and stone ears. 'Here lies Chett Morfield, a brave husband and loving father. May he rest in peace. 1948-1989'

"Hey Chett," I whispered as I laid on it, trying to close

my eyes. Maybe Garry couldn't get to me here...

"Hey, who are you?" My eyes opened. It wasn't Garry's voice. It was close and far, muffled and right in my ear.

"Hello?" I said, looking around to no one except the darkness around Chett and I.

"You know, it's rude to be sleeping on a grave, right? Moreso, specifically, my grave."

The voice was coming from below me, "Chett?"

"Yep. And you are? You are sleeping on my grave, but what's your name? Maybe I can convince you to find someone else's resting spot."

"Uh...Willow."

"Nice tuh meetcha, Willow."

"Hello Chett."

"Well, why are ya sleeping on me grave, Willow?"

"I'm tired..."

"Well, I can see that, Willow."

"Can you?" I tapped the hard concrete that I laid upon.

"Yea...well kinda. My eyes, you see, are gone. But I can see you still. You got that?"

"Uh...maybe."

"Well...how's life been Willow? It hasn't been treating me too well lately!" He laughed.

"Bad."

"Well I can see that lass! You're talking to a corpse!" He laughed again.

"Eh...I kinda want to eat my best friend. Saw her die too, but she's back now and now food tastes really fuckin' bad and she smells so so good and I try to ignore it but its hard even though its easy too, right? And I can't sleep anymore because some demon or god or something else keeps talking to me all night and then there's another one who is annoying too, trying to be my friend and now I'm hungry all the time and tired all the time and she smells so good and now everyone looks like zombies or something and I don't know if anything is real or fake anymore. Dad's cheating on my Mom too, but that's a little more mundane. Yeah...but I bet my lifes not even that bad compared to some other people, right? I hate this self pity-baiting bullshit, but it does feel nice to say it outloud. Even if it's to a dead man."

"Yeah, that sucks."

"Well...how's death?" I asked.

"The man or the Man?" He laughed.

"What?"

"Oh nothing...but, to be honest, it could be worse. But me family don't come 'round much anymore. It gets lonely down here in the dark. Worms ate the eyes right outta my sockets!" He laughed.

"Oh, sorry."

"Oh, no need to be sorry lassie!" His voice echoed, "That's the way O' life. You'll see one day. All men must die."

"Yea but I'm a girl."

"Boy, girl, don't matter per se. No one's wriggling outta Lady death's cold hands. Whether it be a car crash or a heart attack or...or a...finger?"

"What?"

He stayed silent for a second and then continued, "Huh...sorry bout that, something came over me fer a second there."

Mark or Garry, either one. Maybe they're working together or something. *Fuck you or YOU or YOU especially!*

"Willow?" He asked, his hoarse voice a raspy question, muffled by the stone.

"Yea?"

"How old are ye?"

"Fourteen."

"My God- Fourteen? You speak like a lass full grown. Look, Willow...I know life can be hard and all, you're talking to a corpse for Christ's sake," he laughed, "but still, just use yer head once in a while. Many a young-un goes dough eyed in the brain. Don't be like those ones a couple plots down with their raving music disturbin' me and my friends down here, all smoking their devils lettuce and drinkin' their ale. Maybe if I were younger or...aliver," he laughed, "I would tell you *'do what yuh want'* but in me older and more rotten years, I'm pleadin' with yuh to not get roped into stuff like that. Life's hard, but there's no need to ruin it all for yerself."

"Uh..." what was I supposed to say to a corpse's DARE speech? "Okay," is what I said.

"Now can ye get off a' me grave, young lass? Tryin' to get me eternal rest o're here!" He laughed again.

"Yea sure, just one question, Chett."

"Yes lass?"

"Why are you talking like a pirate?" I asked.

"Hey! It gets boring down here, let me have my fun!" Chett laughed again and I could feel the slight rumble of the slab beneath me.

"Bye Chett."

"Be seein' yuh around!" Chett laughed again as I sat back up and stood off of his pirate accented grave.

And then I saw her standing far back in the darkness, a plot or so down. Scarlet Miller, her green eyes like spotlights in the darkness that surrounded her, the moon dead behind the mess of trees all above us. Besides her shadow, nothing was there. Was she rotten too, like the rest? Sight was now. Probably sound next. *Don't lie to me.* And then the shadow took a couple of steps forward, sloshing and biting through the darkness around her, those green eyes growing bigger with each step.

"Scarlet?" I asked, dusting my ass of grave-dust.

"Sup."

"What are you doing?"

"Your Mom," she stepped out of the dark shadow.

Her boots rode high up to her knees which were strapped in long black stockings that ended in a short pair of jorts. Her black shirts hung on her lengthy body as her arms crossed themselves. Her face sat still and white, whole without rot anywhere in sight as her eyes sat looking, still shining,

"Where'd you go?" She said, brushing a swath of black hair out of the green.

"It was too loud and I was too tired."

"Yea," she sat down on Chett's grave, "those dudes were all mad creeps."

"Are you satisfied?" I sat back down on Chett's grave. Sorry Chett.

"No. But thank you," she looked at me.

"For what?"

"Coming along, even though I know that you know that I knew that you'd hate it."

"Yea, sure, okay."

"Sure sure sure," she mimicked as she laid back, her head hanging off the end of the grave, "Man, my back is killin' me."

"Let's go," I said.

"Hole up a sec, home-dawg." She stretched a little farther, barring her back into the cold stone beneath herself, "Hey, Ghosts or nah?"

"Uh…naw."

"Nah?" She sat up, her face a mock surprise. "Actually, that makes sense to you at least." She stood, "Aliens and now ghosts? They should call you Willow Boringass or something. You think the ghosts all around here aren't watching us?"

"Not ghosts," I looked at Chett's cold grave, "Zombies."

"Huh…"

And there, as she sat, she seemed to glow just for a second as if the moon pushed through the dark bramble above.

16

"So what? Zombies now?" I said.

"No, not 'Zombies'…" he paused for some sort of effect, his fire eyes glowering in it, making little pops and crackles. "Xombiez!" His black frothy hands exploded in a mess of excitement as his non-face made whatever amount of a smile that he could. "Huh? Funny right?"

"What? I don't get it."

Mark

Dumb girl. How could you not get it? Stop it, stop it. You're trying to appeal to *her*. Her face leaned on homely and comely as the white of it teemed a light hue of purple as this vein and that stained in little putrid lines which trailed this way to that across her taut skin. Her nose seemed even bigger now as the depth of her thick brows only grew as her stomach stretched back due to malnourishment. I'm not one to judge, especially for these things, but compared to some of the others of her race, she was not the most...sightly, especially now.

Her eyes crusted and blackened further underneath but interestingly enough they sat sharp. I could see it in her fold-brain, she didn't get it, the joke that I've been working on since last night when the plan continued. Her reaction to the hollow people of her mind was lackluster to say the least. It takes some effort to do this, so a little more acknowledgement would be nice.

Whatever, she already seems used to it, all those people around her looking like some sort of amalgamated monster(s) of nightmareland. She did have some wide eyes when she saw her mother earlier, almost made me laugh, but then I realized that I couldn't laugh, or, at least, didn't know how to...

"With a X. Zombie...but it's spelled like-" she didn't care. "Okay, look," I grabbed a clipboard at scribbled down 'Zombie' in the peoplelanguage, and then below it I wrote 'Xombie'. Her face didn't change as her mind still stirred to nothing as I showed her the miraculous text.

"Huh?" Her mouth opened and stood still as she stared at the very funny joke. She thought of nothing and then she looked at me, "I don't get it."

"Want me to explain it?" I asked.

"No, not really," and then she sat back into the swirly

chair and began to spin in it. "You know...well -you absolutely do know- but," she twirled some more in the spinny chair-

Willow

"I think I'm gonna get used to it all just fine. I don't think I need to eat much. Or sleep much. Or even smell much. And you know the funny thing-" I stopped spinning, padding my bare foot against the cold wooden floor of the detective's office, looking at him. "I think I'm starting to like you."

"Really?" Again, if he could smile.

"Yea. Why not, man? Fuck it all, right? Let's be friends, huh?"

Mark

She was lying. I could see it in her mindspace, but, even then, she began to think something else, *you can hear this. I know you can,* she thought out, her annoying eyes looking at me further. I dropped the clipboard on the desk and sat back.

"Yes, I can," I responded to her thoughts.

Willow

Fuckin' knew it. You can hear this too, huh?

"Yes." The fire sizzled slightly in their dark spaces.

"Hey, I've been wondering, and I bet you know too, right? But anyways, you're lying about Garry, huh? And that deal too, right?"

"...-"

Mark

Shit my breeches. Do I tell her? No. But what? Is the key to know?

Willow

He sat silent, saying nothing, his fiery eyes silently popped as the smoke of the still lingering cigarette swirled and moved up and around, disappearing barely halfway towards the ceiling. Then he sat up in the chair, the bulk of his mass almost herculean in size, the ceiling growing to accompany it. I would have been scared before, some time ago, but now I didn't care. Kill me for all I care too, and I don't care at all. Everyones a zombie now, their smell almost unbearable, my only solace being the ham-like scent which emanated off of Scarlet who still had all her perfect meaty skin right where it ought to be. She looked juicy and plump all the same. Fuck me, I wanted some. But I didn't.

And all the while, the thing that was Mark continued to creak and stand up, almost growing leagues in size and, still, I felt like I should shoot out some witty remark about this thing or that thing, but he knew everything I was gonna say before I even said it, *right*?

The dark and red fire in his eyes singed and began to turn blue. All sat completely still. The phonograph in the corner stopped playing its endless rendition of *Clair de Lune*. The cigarette smoke froze. Heart stopped. Time froze. Freeze.

I was right.

Time continued. His eyes red once again.

I smiled and spun in the chair.

Then he sat down again.

The First Apostle

"Yes, Willow Pines. You are correct in your stupid assumption."

"Stupid? Really? HA! I figured your ass out." Her voice weaved in and out as she spun.

Her spinning was beginning to annoy me. "And what did you *figure out*?"

"That you'd been lying the entire time, bro. And since we're friends now, I'm gonna shit on you even more, man. My first decree as The Pussy-Master-" she stopped spinning with a halt, "Suck my nuts." She laughed shrill and annoying. She stopped, then started up again, "Oh, you're soooo mad!" she continued and pointed, laughing that shrill child's laugh. I could read her nonetheless. She was purposeful in these feeble attempts at annoyance, but I was not to be fooled by this thing. A lamb. But still an important lamb.

"Really? Is that it?" I answered.

"I don't know. I feel like I should ask some hard hitting questions about, like, 'Why are you doing this?' or like, 'Is any of this real?' or 'Why is everyone a zombie now?' or, as your lame-ass joke put it, 'Xombie!'" She laughed again, "That's not a joke, man! Fuck me, you suck!" And then she started to spin again, her feet kicking up in the air, spinning faster and faster. "But, hey, here's an actual question, *Mark,*" her last word spit out as much venom as some slithering cobra, and she stopped spinning again, somehow not dizzy, "What is your actual name?"

"I cannot tell you."

"Uh huh. Well, I know it's not Mark, that's for sure. Well, what do you even do? Your real purpose? Hey, why not just tell me, okay? Already goin' cray cray over in da he-zizzle, if you get my drift," she laughed again.

"I cannot say."

"Jeez, hey, give me like one word. Or two. Or three. Or four...something that I can identify the real you with, now that you seem to be out of that fake persona you so horribly held onto earlier. We're friends now, right?"

"The First-" I spit out, but stopped, the image of the Holy One on my metaphorical tongue. Is this right?

"The First?" her mind twisted around as she tongued her cheek, thinking as her eyes swept this way and that. "Eh, better than nothing. So, Firsty, now that everyone looks like a zombie, what's next, huh? My bed feels like nails? Garry's little whispers everywhere? Huh? Come on, give me the deets, broski. Broskilla. My home doggy-dawg. Hey-yo! Wazzup my home dilla-"

"Enough!" Was all I could say to clear her annoying little voice. She knew what she was doing-

Ha! The bitch is getting annoyed. *Fuck you, man!* I laughed. It felt good. Refreshing like some cold drink of water. Oh, and I gulped it down hard and fast.

I stopped, staring at the thing known as 'The First'.

"Aural is next." He spoke with some authority.

There we go.

*

"Alright, dude. I'll bite." I spoke to the ceiling dot. "That 'deal' shit is bullshit."

"Hmm..."

"Hmm?" I asked.

"Hm..." He answered.

"H-"

"You know Willow Pines?"

"I am Willow Pines."

"No-"

"First off, what's your name? Real name. Now."

"You don't have authority over me."

"I do."

He cackled, the first time I've heard him do that over the long months of whispers, "No. You do not."

"I sooo do."

"You do not."

"You know that you're, like, super creepy, right?" I asked.

"I care not."

"You wanna watch me masturbate or something? Is that what you're out for?"

He didn't respond for a second, "Uh..."

"Hey, I get it. It's lonely up there, right? But lusting after some kid, even for you man, that's low."

"That's not-"

"Now that I think about it, you've totally seen me naked before. I bet you watch me shower too. Does that get you off or something? Do I perk your stiffy?"

"No, I-"

I'm getting to him, the bastard. "Oh, you don't need to explain yourself," my arm feigned over my eyes, "I know what's up with you man: You got a crush on me, huh? Well, sorry dawg, but I don't like your dog-ass."

"That's not-"

"I bet you got a tiny dong too, even as some ethereal thing. Maybe you don't even have one. Does that make you sad that you cant fuck me?"

"QUIET!"

My ears rang and shook as my pillow became wet under my head and then a dull ringing followed suit and then silence.

"Hello?" I asked, barely even hearing myself.

Nothing responded. I touched my ears and found dark blood which seeped out from them, staining the white pillow below.

And then I laughed and then I slept for the first time in six months.

The First Apostle

That bitch. "GO BACK THERE NOW!" I screamed into his posh little face.

"No."

"By a little girl? What would He think? You're all spasmed by the mere peoplewords of such a little thing? Can't you control her? Put her in a trance?"

"First One...she does not respond to my control... anymore."

"WHAT? AND THIS IS THE FIRST TIME YOU TELL ME?"

"I..." his purple eye beamed this way and that, "I thought I could fix it."

"But you did not. And now she is SLEEPING? And to think we are one in the same. You disappoint me."

"I'm sorry First One, but I-"

"And you won't go back?"

"Not tonight, First One. I have to...fix myself."

"What did she say to get under yourself so much? You don't have any of those primitive organs that she was mentioning! That's all human silica and disgusting strata!"

"I..." he looked around again, his phantom leg kicking as it crossed the other. "I've never had one of them...talk so brash to me before."

"And that's what got you?"

"Y-yes..." his eyes darted from mine to the floor.

"Might as well send her some nice little dreams of flowers and rivers and castles and princes. Would you like that?"

"No..."

I wanted to take a deep breath, but I had no mouth so I sat back in the chair further. What to do, what to do? She was strong enough, her fear dropping away like an anchor, but still, in that mind, there was nothing. And as she dreamed, it was of black. "Hey, look at me, Second."

He did, those purple fringing sparks casted in a large oval shadow that fed into a large gray body which slumped tiredly in the chair it sat in. The one that Willow sat in all those other times. "Yes, First One?"

"I need you to be headstrong for this, okay? This is the final case and you," I pointed at him, "are a crucial part in all of this."

"Yes, First."

"And I trust you, okay? We can do this, for Him."

"Yes, First. But why do we even need to speak this nasty peopletongue while we talk amongst ourselves?"

"We must take every chance to learn their ways."

"Why?" His form shook, "I get this gross feeling when I speak it."

"It is better to understand than not. Only a couple more short peopleyears and then the world will be awakened."

"Yes, First."

"And Second?"

"Yes?"

"Go back. Now."

The Key

"Fuck!" My hands slammed against my crusty, blood dried ears as the loudest fucking sound ever screamed out and shook my skull and everything within it. And then it stopped. Night was still around, the slight silvery sheen of the moon casting a wide shadow through my open window that sparkled as I sat up, my six month late sleep disrupted.

"Ah ha ha HA!" Garry's voice shot out, thick and bound with spite which bit hard with each revolting convulsive laugh. "Oh, you should see the look on your face right now!" And then he laughed some more. "Well, since formalities are all gone, and since you know the other, why not rue the name 'Garry' and just call me Second?"

"Second? Sure, why not, man."

"You remember me, don't you?"

"Nah man," I shoved a pinky in my ear, picking at the clotted blood, releasing some tension that was there. "But, dude, you really had to fuck my ears up?"

"Whatever, it doesn't matter. But think back to those dark memories. You remember me. I know you do, First told me so."

"Man! Garry -oh- *Second,* you sound so much more relaxed my man. Did that spoon finally fall outta your ass or what?"

"Hmm...well, if I had an ass, then I would guess yes. But I do not have any of those human extremities if you really cared so much, so of course I would not want to couple with you or any of your kind. Almost makes me want to throw up. Ew, you humans really get into my head. Why would I have a mouth? Or a head?"

"Well, you're speaking right now. Humans, me, speak with our mouths," I opened my mouth and pointed at it, "Shee? Got good teef too-"

"Close that disgusting hole."

I did. "Man, you didn't need to get so offended, Second."

"But, really, you must think back. You. Remember. Me."

"Mmmm..." I thought back. "Nah," my head shook, "I do not."

"Remember how your old house burst into flames?"

"Yea."

"Remember me? Huh? Come on, you must've just shut that thought away. But I know it's there."

"Dude, I'm not playing your games."

"This isn't...you are annoying, aren't you?"

"That may be the game-plan."

"This 'game-plan' you speak of...what do you hope to find at the end of it?"

"Dunno. Don't really have a plan, but that is the plan, you smell me?"

"No I do not...smell you...ew. Let me ask you a question: What do you think we want?"

"To get me to eat Scarlet or something. Fuck my shit up, my man, cause I'm not doing it. You guys have been slick though, making her smell delicioso, and then making food taste like shit, and then now everyone looks like some zombie except her. And what's up with that 'Xombie' joke?"

He laughed instantly, hearty and true, stopped, and then started up again, continuing with the hiccuping laughs. "Oh, Willow!" He continued to laugh, "I didn't take you for a comedian!"

He laughed some more. "Thanks, Second."

His laughs slowed, "But seriously," he cleared an invisible throat, "You are dead wrong."

"What do you mean?"

"I thought you were so cool that you didn't care anymore?" He asked, indignance all throughout his real voice.

"Eh," I shrugged, "you're right, Second."

"And again, what's at the end of this careless road?"

"Peace and quiet."

"Willow...for once, you are correct."

"OOOOOOHHHhhhh...spooky," my hands waved around. "And what now?" I asked.

Everything sat silent again. Wind blew against the window and beyond, yet the house sat still and silent like it's always been. "Much, much worse." He finally answered.

And then he started screaming again.

*

The First Apostle

"Brilliant! Art! This is it!" I screamed as I started to elaborate upon an elegant dance, a shining dance hall set about me, its pillars sparkling white marble which reached up towards a high roof that hung with several silver and gold chandeliers which reflected the ruby and yellow light that cascaded off the stained glass windows that followed the entirety of the wall, all the way down, depicting everything in the universe all at once. The glass danced with me, leg by leg, move by move. "Join me!" I opened my human hands and gave her the opportunity to grab on which she did. I pulled her in with me, in this circle of dance that followed about in this large and stretching hall and she followed suit, moving and jiving and hitting the right motions at the right moments, like a clock tuned perfectly down to the millisecond.

One and two, a twirl, one and two, a twist, one and two, another, one and two, another, one and two, and then she tripped over my foot and slammed her face into the hard marble floor, her black hair mopped all over unmoving head, her white flowing and bespeckled dress drooping and dying like a carpet on the hard floor.

"Ow..." she moaned, still unmoving.

"Are you okay, Willow?"

"No." She pushed herself up and onto her bottom, crossing her legs and rubbing her nose. "I'm not good at this stuff."

"But this is the best thing that a bipedal thing can do!

The Dance! In all forms, it's elegance, its perfection, oh! This is really the only redeeming aspect about you things. And I say this with both chalance and nonchalance."

"Uh huh..." She brushed her hair out of her face. *Why?* She thought.

"Good question, even if you are too proud to spit it," I smiled. "Why do I like this art-form? A core, two arms, two legs, a head, physicality. Hands to grab, feet to walk, skin to feel. While these gross things may make you lesser creatures, it does make the art of actual movement a joy."

"Don't care."

"Yes you do," I raised my upturned hand again confined in this golden-pale humanskin. I was shrunk to regular humansize. Just for dance. Only for dance. Breakdance?

"Screw it," she wiped her mouth and took my hand again and we continued.

Camille Saint-Saëns' masterpiece, *Danse Macabre*, started from nowhere, only growing louder and louder with each string of the violin and brash excitement of an orchestra. On and on, with each little spin and each little falter, each start and stop of the Danse. An orchestral swirl and she grew better, her annoying-ness gone even slightly and in her mind, as I could see it, she was starting to have a lick of fun. Her heart grew fast as her legs moved more and I grew more ferocious with my movements and follow-ups, baiting her to fall again, to have her face slam into the hard floor. A boom from the music and another bait for her to fall- but she never did, almost once or twice, but my feints and purposeful trips made her only stumble and find her footing once more.

Her breathing grew and fell, a step here and a step there, the light of the stained-glass making a circle around us as the light all lowered down to a whisper and in this little circle of light we continued our dance, as inelegant as she was. Her mind spoke and sputtered as she dodged myself, *Oh you asshole,* she thought, stepping over my black shoe. *I know you can hear thi-* and then I got her and she buckled slightly, but her hand slipped and grabbed my junk, hard. It squeezed and gripped my balls, almost popping the poor things. Of course, I felt nothing, this human puppet form I used back in the carnival was only a shell to make her more comfortable. Using them as leverage, she tugged the two little things in that sack to bring herself back up in a standing stance, moving back with me within the moment. This Danse slowed into the end of its third act.

"I applaud your move," I said, grabbing her hand and pulling her this way.

"You didn't feel shit," she exhaled, pulling back on my hand.

"How did you know?" Her foot just missed mine.

"Any real man would've fuckin' died because of that," I grabbed her slim waist and she kicked my shin as she leaned back.

"That is because I am no man, Willow. Like you are no woman."

"So you-" we pulled this way, "Do wanna get in my pants," her breath quickened.

"And what if I did?" I pulled her close, her steaming breath upon my face. If she wanted to play ball, why not? Even though I could never.

Her face went a stark red, she didn't expect it. I smiled.

"Do you know your worth, Willow?" I got closer, "Do you want to know?" I whispered. And then I dropped her to the floor with a meaty slap against the waxed and reflective marble. The Danse ended with a couple last whimsical strings from a violin. I brushed down the silken shirt I wore, the top button unclasped, took a breath with my proxy human mouth, and watched her stumble back to her feet and smiled as she finally stood, locking my hands behind my back.

"Thanks," she said, rolling her shoulders.

"Uh, huh. I got you, didn't I?"

She only stared with those stark blue eyes. I could tell what she's thinking.

"You see? I can also play the game too." And then I paced to one of the high pillars, "You see, this whole little world," My hands raised precariously, "I can create. And you see how good it can be when you want to be friends?" My hands twirled me around the white pillar, gravity pulling me all the way, "And you're so hot and bothered now, huh? I can see all your thoughts, as you found, so don't try to hide it."

"I won't, Firsty. I admit, this skin you wear is really handsome. That make you happy? But you," she pointed, "are all moldy on the inside."

"You would, wouldn't you?" My finger waved back and forth, "Tsk, tsk, tsk. You nasty nasty."

"First off, I wouldn't. Second off, why are we doing this? Whats the purpose when you want to make me fuckin' insane."

"Mmm..." I scratched my chin and took a long stride towards her. "Maybe love drives insanity too?" I grasped her sweaty hand.

She pulled it away quickly, "Ew...dude, you're like a thousand years old. Also, you literally just proved that you're trying to drive me crazy."

"Willow, I care not about these petty little secrets anymore. You're already too far in the process for anything or anyone to help you." *Except me,* "Any question you ask, I will not hesitate to answer with full sincerity."

"Sure dude."

"Oh, I'm honest too. And I can see that you do want to know. Here," I grabbed her hand again, harder, "I'll stretch an olive branch to you, just to show you that I am serious."

Her hand tried to pull back, but I didn't release it. "Stop looking in my head!"

"No. But I will tell you," I pulled her head past mine and whispered deep into her ear, "It's all real."

She pushed back and I released her, watching her stumble a couple hearty steps backwards, catching herself eventually. "Fuck you." Her eyes teemed with blue hate while her brain scrambled with unsure thoughts, zip zapping this way and that. And then she stood up straight, looking around and then back at me. "What am I?"

"Ah, finally you care." I smiled again. She liked when I smiled with this luscious face, I could see. "You are the Primal Key made specifically to bring back my god. For your metaphorical blade to be sharpened enough, your mind must walk through enough mental torment. Then is when you will abide by me and then He will come back. That is your purpose. That is the reason you live so. That is why all of your perceptions are becoming one with our touches."

"What?"

"You already saw it in the vein. You remember? Underneath Scarlet's house. Your human-sided brain blocks out the memory because it nearly killed you. But you were convinced then and that is why I am convinced now that I can remind you, in your waking brain, without you dying untimely. I have confirmed it: You are perfect."

"Then you must really love me then."

"In a cosmic sort of way, yes." Even though she is becoming more skeleton than person, this is the first time I've seen her in a dress instead of thick jeans and t-shirts and sweatshirts. It was...interesting. "You aren't really reacting in any sort of way. What do you really think of that?"

She smirked and crossed her thin arms, "You already know, bro."

My head shook, "No, no, no. The mind is a mess of thoughts and images. I can get some sort of picture of how you feel, but I can never be one hundred percent sure until you specifically tell me. So please," I gestured, "tell me." It was a blatant lie, but she would never know. I want to hear it from her own mouth.

"I think..." she looked back up towards the stained-glass, trailing up and down, watching and eating the light that changed through their panels. "I think I hate dresses," She nodded.

She didn't want to admit that she liked it. She liked

being important in some sort of way, even if she still hates my guts. This wont make it any easier. It may even make it more troublesome, perhaps, but, in the end, having a willing key makes the process easier for all parties. Still, with this newfound idea in her head, we can only press her harder over the next couple of peopleyears. She must be ready by then, and I am sure of its further success. But now, do I tell her what will happen to her at the end? That she will die in the process? "Mmm..." I hummed, cocking my human head.

"What?" she looked back at me.

"Nothing."

You're totally all over me.

"No."

"Then what's all the staring for?"

"I'm just looking at your potential. And how much you like it." I smiled.

"Whatever man," her tired blues looked away as she tried to hide her face. "Is that really Scarlet?" She finally asked.

"Yes and no."

"What?"

"She both is and isn't-" A Third until the conjunction... but I didn't tell her that. "In one way: She is Scarlet Miller, girl next door, your new bestie. And in another way: She is Scarlet Miller, a girl who died, rotting beneath the dirt of some old raggled corn. But, in every living way, she is she. If that's what you're asking."

"So you did kill her?" she asked, her voice echoing as she still stared at the stained-glass.

"Not exactly."

She stayed quiet, looking away. I decided to pull out of her peoplemind and let her think, if just a little. The creaks of the massive hall echoed out as the wind blew past, making some sort of droll hollowing sound. It almost made me sad. Looking further at her ears, I found the dry streakings of red which had never been fully washed off. She looked much smaller than she was, her slight shoulders stood bare as the dress made little straps across them leading into a dress that almost fit her exactly. But it looked odd as it washed her in a bright white which she was so unaccustomed to. This silence seemed odd too, when I was so used to her flying insults and talking about 'dickbags' and 'assholes' and the whole lot of holes and bags and others. I did call her a bitch barely a couple of days ago. Not to her face exactly but, thinking back on it, I wanted to apologize to her.

She turned around and looked up at me, "Wanna dance again?" she asked, putting out her hand.

And I took it, "Yes, Willow. I do." And smiled again.

*

Her ears rang slightly as the bodiless words began to swell up within her empty and bloody canals, riding deep towards her brain. The aural bit started, harshly. 'Hey, Willow!' they would say from the corner of her room and she'd look to find nothing. Just little tiny things to erk the mind, little words placed here and there to dwell into nothing, and she began to play the game. She ignored and stopped looking at most anyone as they slowly decomposed directly in her eyes. Someone would ask her a question and half their face would slough off and slap against the ground, meaty and true. And the smell...the hallways that she walked down during the average school day looked like a path of meat and massacre as the smell wafted down deep past her nose, her feet trying not to slip.

But she never said anything about it to anyone and, in return, no one would ask her why she has stopped eating anything or why her eyes look like black marshes or why she never looked at anything happening. People just stayed silent. Scarlet wanted to say something, but never found the courage to.

They sat in her room, doing homework one day. "KILL HER!" A voice barked from behind her, but she didn't look, didn't even flinch at it. Scarlet's room smelled like a cookhouse, a shining light amongst the dark stench of the world. And

Willow couldn't help her mouth from watering at the constant smell. But she just swallowed more and thought about it less.

"Hey," Scarlet said.

Willow ignored her.

"Hey," Scarlet pushed her shoulder slightly, causing Willow's tired eyes to look up at her finally. Scarlet's mind, for one little second, saw something hungering within those blue things, something that wanted to eat.

"Yea?" Willow said.

"Wanna go camping this summer?" Scarlet thought that this might be good for her friend who she should have really just asked, 'Are you okay?' but never did. "My Dad already has a plot."

No, Willow instantly thought, betraying her feelings as she didn't feel completely sure if she could control herself out in the middle of the wilderness with the succulent Scarlet. But, instead of saying no, Willow answered, "Yea, sure." She had never been camping before.

And this whole thing swirled, like always, down into a pit of desire and want. Willow was strong minded though, as annoying as she claims to be, and continued with a metaphorical strong back, as her real back is weak and paltry. She would come home to find her mother gorging herself halfway deep into some pint of ice cream, her skin molding and festering off all over the floor and into her sugary sustenance. She would walk down the street and look at the other kids on the opposite side and see them falling apart at the seams like little threadbare dolls. Scarlet would invite her over to dinner as much as she could but Willow would only find one full person amongst two corpses who sat at a table, devouring worms.

Scarlet's parents would lean over to their daughter after Willow has left, barely touching her food, and they would say "Is Willow okay?" with their sweltering mouths that slopped off onto the white linen table. Scarlet would say, "I don't know," her mouth still intact.

And then, that night, Willow would go back to her house, trudge up her cold and silent stairs, lay in her hardening bed, and close her eyes as the screams started once again and she'd sit through it all the night, uncaring, unable to sleep, thinking about the world falling apart, bit by bit. *You happy?* She thought beyond those tired eyes.

I should be. Everything was going perfectly in accordance with the conjunction. But I wasn't. No, Willow, I wasn't, if that's what you're getting at. You asked for it, right? It was going to happen this way nonetheless, but still, this is the first time...I've wanted to say sorry. Makes me feel knotty even thinking about it and I took a deep breath with my mouth to settle my stomach. I shouldn't say sorry. This is her purpose, she will be grateful during the conjunction, for raising Him back from his cold godly depths. She should take her duty with a smile and a nod, blessed to be the most important person in the world. But she wanted to dance instead...stop. Stop thinking about all of this. A glass of champagne should be my reward, not sorrowful thoughts. Have I grown soft? Perhaps being in that humanskin those couple of times softened my inside and made me a little more Man than I cared to admit. But, no worry, once this is all through these unwanted thoughts will leave my head.

But...in the humanskin...I felt...good? Having skin. Having a mouth. Those little peoplething extremities. Feeling... It was nice to feel, for the first time in my life. In that echoey hall I felt something towards Willow...it was interesting...something I've never -wait- feeling? All I've ever felt is towards Him and Him alone, in his magnificent light. Prayer and praise. But this feeling with Willow was something besides praise and prayer...makes me want to throw up, I think. I should tell her how all of this ends. I have to. But I can't. The Key can't know. Her death stays until the end.

Bah! Get it all out! Think not on it. I shook my head and ran my hands through my thick locks of hair, trying to calm my mind. Her supposed friendship is getting to you.

Watch and wait. There is no more reason to reconvene with her anymore, her path is steady, without requirement from me anymore. But still...I wanted to dance with her again. And touch her skin and feel something...STOP! No more 'buts' and 'waits'!

I grabbed a pen and paper and scribbled something down to keep my mind but it was illegible as something odd happened to me. My sight became all blurry and wishy-washy. I touched my eyes and found water. I was crying. How could I be crying? I don't have tear ducts. My hand was pale and skinny and wrapped in epidermis. I was in the humanskin. I could feel this heart pump faster where there wasn't a heart before. I could feel my brain and its many folds thump and echo with a budding headache. I could feel the clothes touching my skin, caressing and warm. I could feel my tongue running along the back of my teeth, almost odd, like some monster stuck to the back of my throat.

I tried to tear it off instantly, but I stopped and found my reflection. Long curled locks of golden hair fell around my strong shoulders. My face stood firm with blue eyes, set brows, a set of luscious fairytale lips, and a stern commanding jaw. I wore a thin Victorian dress-shirt that made a V showing off a defined chest. I looked like some knight from a story. My fingers curled through my locks, letting them wind and fall back gracefully to my shoulders. I opened my mouth and prodded the perfect set of teeth, all white and healthy. My finger caressed the underside of my eyes, feeling the warmth and watching the milk pale skin turn white and then fill with red as the blood coagulated to the correct spot.

I was beautiful.

I was human.

I almost retched. The feeling of bile in my human throat became all the more real as I looked at myself, too scared to pull it off, scared of what was beyond it all, this pale epidermis of silky smooth skin. This layer of vulnerability. This...my skin. A skin that was able to hold all these feelings that I've never had before. Things that I've never wanted, but want...

A thick white substance spewed from my new lips, seeping into the wood of my desk. I fingered it and rubbed it between my fingers, smelling it, tasting it with a new tongue, weird and foreign in my new mouth. Maybe I should try to eat something. What was this viscous plasma substance? It was thick between my new strong fingers. I flexed my biceps and stretched my long muscular legs.

For the first time since the beginning of the universe, I was scared.

"Huh?" was all I said.

17

The Key

It was heavy. Pulling with all my strength, the large travel bag lifted steadily off the concrete. The trunk bounced up and down as Mike opened the door and stepped out. Bits of his meat stuck and stretched onto the car door as he slammed it leaving behind a small circle of blackened rot. He walked back into his house, leaving a slug trail of goo up to the front porch. I put all my concentration into pulling the bag steadily into the trunk. Sweat accumulated on my forehead as I heaved. Finally, the bag slid into the trunk, clinking and clanking with all the other bags in there. The summer was hot and humid at the same time, causing my sweat to stick and sap all over my body as it made the smell of rot even heavier, like a weight pressing against my chest.

I wiped my forehead and slammed the trunk closed, eyeing warily over towards my gray house where my Mom sat somewhere inside, pounding food into her maw as she falls apart, stinking the place up. Dad's still gone. The cold winter turned to hot summer. Still gone. Matt and Jeremey...haven't seen them either, and I'd rather not, their bone structure not something I really wanted to examine indepthly.

I was hungry. Really hungry. These pains became almost

regular and natural to my everyday life, my mouth barely wanting to feast and stop those pangs that rummaged out in my midsection. But eating was getting harder with food tasting worse and everything smelling so damned bad, this viscous stench layering the world in a jelly-like thick substance of smell that both made my mouth water and curl as I wanted to vomit, consistently. But I kept my head up and moved on, not trying to think about how Scarlet is the only one left. Her face, her body, her legs, her smell, they were all intact, like some shining light in the dark. But then I would look too intently at her from time to time, at her juicy steak of a leg and those long muscles that beat under her pale skin. But then I would look at her smile and look into her green eyes that whispered something, pushing my feelings back into the dark depths of the mind.

"Hello!" Someone shouted out, their voice unknown. I didn't look though. Enough of these unknown calls from nowhere. That and Second and First, all of them almost ignored in some sort of way. Second, who was Garry, now only screams throughout the night, deep into my ears. First, who was Mark, has been quiet since the winds of spring, our little dance turning to just a figment of memory. These new voices, screaming. I try to ignore them, and I do, and it feels weird... really weird.

I'm really hungry. I'm really skinny. My fingers hurt too. They crack weird like I'm eighty-four instead of fourteen. I don't feel fourteen but I am, and all I do is recess back into my mind and try to think of nothing or I try to talk to Scarlet if she's in the vicinity. Poor Scarlet, always something in her eyes saying they're worried for me. If my non-eating hasn't become obvious already, then my constant fluttering into sleep-land as I talked, the black bags under my eyes still growing being the ultimate kicker. It's almost become a game with some of these people, I'd give another point the more they'd look at me, almost say something, and then say nothing. Scarlet did it too, not of her own fault though. She had a good heart, but she hid it behind her mask of trying to act 'cool' or something of the sort. I don't blame her.

What about me though. Am I at fault for all of this?

No. They're using me. Torturing me. Primal Key? What is this bullshit? I'm not letting them win. I may be a loser, but I'm not going to lose this. Fuck em'. But the day is hot and the smell is even worse, and I should smile and laugh with Scarlet, my light, as she takes me camping with her dad who is falling apart. I could see his flesh still sizzling on that car door, his slug juice of decomposition still matting the stone walkways to the front door. And she was inside, still packing. The car ride is a couple of hours. Who cares? I can handle a corpse, even if the car will smell like some stinking rotten armpit filled with milk and onions. Man, I was hungry.

I licked those crusted lips of mine and got in the car, waiting, not thinking of anything. Not even the part where Scarlet and I would share a tent together. It made me think of some pizza oven, with her on the bow, that smell radiating off of her, filling the canvas and all within it with everything but layered and rotting stink.

A shock came to my mouth as I bit down hard on my tongue, my teeth forcing those subtle thoughts that pricked and prodded. And my blood tasted like shit.

*

The air that steamed by the windows was good and I stuck my wagging tongue out into that air, tasting the freshness that flowed by the lakeside road that winded up and down, left and right, swirling in view and out of view of this gigantic blue and emerald ripple of a lake. That rotting smell of the neighborhood and the city and everything back there was gone, freed and freshened like a trustled up pillow, nice and fresh.

"We're close," Mike's jawless mouth petered out, the sound beating the logic of the situation, but I paid it no mind and tried to open my mouth even wider, wanting this air to be my new source of food, but it was fruitless in the end, as my mouth was only so big and my appetite so small. I stuck my head back into the confines of the stinking interior and padded my mouth with it, replacing the dried gums with wet pillows, my salivary glands doing their gruesome job.

Then we made it to the camp. A small little plot like some undug grave. It was enough space for two tents, a firehole, and a couple of chairs to sit around that smokey hole. And they were up and then the sun was down and then it was night and then we were sitting around that fire. They were eating and I picked little spoons here and there, fighting the overwhelming taste of awfulness. I could see Mike's milky eyes glancing my way, his mind probably thinking about broaching the topic of 'Hey, why aren't you eating?' I wish he asked, oh I did. I wanted to say, 'Oh, I dunno, it tastes like SHIT! EVERYTHING DOES! BUT I HAVE TO EAT A LITTLE BIT SO I DON'T FUCKING DIE!' But he stayed silent, turning his eyes back down to his bone riddled skin which flaked off in small little pieces here and there, muddling in his bowel, adding to the thick brown stew. That's one point.

I try to eat. I tried to take a couple good spoonfuls of this meaty bowl of brown that warmed my cold hands but, after the first spoonful, I almost vomited. I sucked it back down and closed my eyes, trying not to think about it, my stomach rumbling from disgust and hunger, both wanting to spew and suck. And nothing worked, it all tasted the same, no matter how hot or how cold or how well seasoned or how well made. It just did taste...like shit. Hot shit, cold shit. Shitty shit. Shit shit shit. Even with a burnt tongue, it all tasted like absolute dogshit. And all this talk of shit made me all the more hungry as I forced a long and slow sip of this brown bowl of shit, feeling the little chunks and the little slimy ropes of whatever was in it slide past my tongue and down the back of my throat. With a hearty swallow, it dropped into the vast pits of my stomach with the weight of an anvil. SLAM! Garbage pit revival. Sounds like a band.

"Ohhh..." I said, rubbing my tummy-wummy.

"Are you okay?" Scarlet asked.

"Yea. Maybe a stomach ache or something." I set the bowl on the ground and sat back, stretching my legs, these shoes sliding on the dirt layered ground.

"Don't get diarrhea on me, man."

"Why?" I looked over to her, "It'd be kinda funny."

Her dimples grinned, "Yea, maybe."

"Hey," Mike swallowed, the ligaments and muscles of his open throat stretching and bounding as the brown shit leaked and fell beyond it. "How about a scary story, eh?" His lipless lips tried to smile.

At least this fire and its smoke helped drag the smell that Mike brought on, even as pieces of his legs drooped and sloughed off in meaty chunks that laid around the entirety of the campsite. He was a big guy, he wouldn't miss those little bits. I didn't want to hear a story. I almost told him off too, 'No, not really,' is what I almost said, but I didn't.

"Yea, sure." Scarlet told her stinking father, her eyes not seeing the corpse in front of her.

Oh god-gods? God-s? God? Whatever, this story was gonna suck.

And..

....

...................................It did.

"That sucked!" His daughter laughed.

"Well, with that magnificent story, I am calling it a good night, my darlings." He stood, leaving a plain sleet of slimy film on his chair which hungrily soaked it up. "And I bid you two adieu," he did a mock bow, shakily hanging some tendrily flesh and then promptly left with the opening of a zipper and the closing of a zipper, disappearing into his tent. A slight snore whittled out from it soon after.

Scarlet and I talked for a bit, then bit the bullet and went to bed which opened with another long zipper that seemed to get caught on each and every little nook and cranny that it wanted to, only making the inevitable even more inevitable as I tried not to think about stepping into that dark baking tent with her. Her and that smell. And that weird feeling that itched in the back of my mind. But I was going to sleep and I was going to sleep good. The screaming tended to be less loud over the months and my eyes became more heavy and they got heavier as we both kneeled in the tent and the zipper began to close, catching and releasing like it did before. I let Scarlet deal with that bad boy and laid down over the top of my rough spun sleeping bag, not even bothering to get in. Second could scream all he wanted, Scarlet would never know. She never heard his whispers either when I slept over at her house those couple of times, trying to maybe follow my father and my brothers lead in ditching that cold and gray house for somewhere else, leaving poor fattening Mom all by herself.

As my eyes closed, I thought of her for the first good time in the last couple of months. Maybe I did feel bad for her, my Mom. I saw her eyes grow glazed over the months as she silently realized that all of her life, her flesh and blood, all of it, was gone physically and emotionally. Maybe...just maybe...I should say sorry...the world started to turn black, the screaming distant and unknown, my body forcing sleep amidst the noise, and the last thing I thought of was my Mom...maybe I should talk to her. Maybe I should feel bad for her...

In the dark, a voice shot out, thick with lust and uncaring, forcing my eyes open with a shock to a whole new light, all of that weighted tiredness gone, replaced with annoyance and...excitement? A smell wafted up towards my nose. A smell that wasn't shit. My mouth already started watering.

"Hellllllllllllllllllllllllloooooooooooooooooooooo, my lady! Please take a seat! Oh-" The voice giggled like some little schoolboy, "You're already seated!" and giggled some more.

The light finally processed in my brain as I recognized it all. There was a wide table before me, long and flat, made of some dark wood, maybe walnut, but it smelled good. It smelled like a forest. I shoved my nose deep into its knotted exterior. On top of the table sat food. All the food. Shining food. It exhausted the tablespace of the stretching table. Silver platters of duck and goose stood fully roasted and coasted, right on their platters, each surrounded by fields of green leafy things. Near them sat piles of fruit which spilled out of larger and larger cornucopias. Pies of all sorts pittered and pattered the dark table, their steam wafting and caressing my nose so heavily that I almost fainted as the smell activated some sort of hungering beast in the breeches of my entire body. There was more and more and more over there and more over here, all sorts of meats, all sorts of desserts, all sorts of everything. Giant mounds of little donut-hole things sat piled on one another, a film of light caramel spider webbed down the surface. "That's a croquembouche, my lady." The voice said. A tiramisu here and several piling cakes over here. Meats and meats. Rice with things in it. Spread entrees and trays of little hand pastries all delicately inlaid with thick creamy butter and smothered in chocolate and buttercream. This and that and this and THAT!

And then I looked up at the man sitting across from me. He looked like someone I knew, clad in a large and black tophat and a skin tight three-piece suit that weaved around his bulky shoulders and toned chest. Oh yea. I looked past his trilling locks of blonde hair and his fake blue eyes, past that perfect mouth and perfect teeth, and he smiled that perfect smile. I felt a shiver and noticed I was in a deep black dress inlaid with rupees that followed the seams all the way down. The collar puffed out in a large white bloom. And my hands were both held in long see-through black gloves with white storms that pattered here and there. I lost my appetite.

"What's going on?" I asked, his smile never wavering.

"I...would like to propose a toast." He raised a wine glass.

And then I found a glass of my own in front of me, filled almost to the brim with some wavering purple substance. I grabbed it and smelled it fruitfully.

"Grape juice," he smiled some more. "I know you don't partake in that humanly custom, even while so many do."

It smelled...good? Like a grape field. It was grape juice. And I took a careful sip, never heeding his toast. It was so sweet that I got dizzy, the world swinging around me as if I just drank an absolute shit ton of alcohol with that one meandering sip. But it was just grape juice, sweet and tangy and biting. My tongue reveled and each taste bud expanded and stung at this new sensation that wasn't shit. It wasn't shit. IT WASN'T SHIT.

"I toast to us," he finally said, watching my face probably explode in expressions of whatever. Wait- to us?

"To us?" I eked out, my tongue still uncooperative for the most part.

"To us," he took a deep sip from his glass.

My mind stayed for but a second of time, one tiny microcosm that didn't last as I remembered the food in front of me. And then, there was barely none left as my mind was left awash with no memories of engorging myself on most of everything on the table. My fingers, in rubbing them together, closing and tensing my hands, felt rubbery and coated with grease as my mouth felt thick and gelatin. Empty plates and trays sat beneath me as the entirety of my stomach felt about ready to explode, or implode even, the condensed force of it all in there tight enough to make a mini black hole of food. The goose was gone, the duck half there, its neck shredded into two and its haunches savagely bit into with the force of an ape. But it was my mouth and my teeth that sunk into it. I could still feel it between my teeth as I tongued the little flecks of shitless meat lodged all up in there. It all tasted so GOOD. My mouth slapped as I reached for another ball from the stupidly named 'Croquembouche', but even the movement made my stomach stitch and hurt like I was actually about to explode.

And with a flash, First sat closer, as if the table suddenly became a whole lot shorter in an inch of time and he was still smiling in that dumb black suit and he was still wearing that stupid human face. I thought he hated humans or something.

"Satisfied, my lady?" he asked, cocking his head, causing the tophat to slide so elegantly to one side, revealing a perfect ear studded with a small jewel that crested its upper half.

"Why are you-" a MASSIVE burp flew from my lips, still coated in a thick grease. It smelled good, like food and not rot or shit or all of that bad bad stuff that wasn't good good food.

His smile only grew, "Excuse you, my diamond."

"What are you talking about?" I finally got out between labored breaths and meat sweats. My finely crafted black dress was starting to smell almost like a pig. A succulent pig roasted on a spit with some garlic and onions. Mmmmm...

"My lady, do you not find me attractive?" He asked, pulling that top hat off and setting it on the table top. "And no need to lie, I already know what you want to say."

"I think that skin is attractive, but whatever's underneath is full of black and fire."

"Ah, very poetic, my lady."

"Stop calling me 'your lady'!"

"Why?"

"Dude," another nasty burp-

"Excuse my lady."

"Dude," I swallowed and sopped the meat sweats from my forehead, "What are you talking about?"

He took a deep breath. "I have come to find that this...let me rephrase...I have come to find that I am, let's say, interested in your little human world."

"What?"

"Mmmm...maybe...let me put it this way...before I lose the chance when the conjunction occurs...I would like to understand this...human thing aspect better."

"Why?"

"I would like to know better. That is all."

"Okay?"

"And," he sung it, "I would like you, Willow Pines, to teach me. If not, just a little bit. Please."

"Huh?" Damn, I keep asking fucking questions, tell him off!

"Would you refuse one who has fed you so handsomely?" He smiled.

"Yes. Screw you, man."

"Harsh. Like always. Willow Pines, The Key, proceeds to, as the kids say, 'tell me off'. Again and again. Why? Why do you hate me so?"

"You know," I could feel my face scowling.

"Huh...I do. But what do you want me to do? Not approve of your true purpose?"

"Torture is my true purpose? Fuck off."

His hands rose up defensively, "Ah ha! So I see that your silly little 'no more formalities', farce is still in effect. No need to kill the messenger here, Willow. We're friends too, am I not right?"

"Messenger? You're the fuckin' leader here. The corroborator. You have no message to tell."

"And that," he pointed his thick, strong finger my way, "is where you are wrong yet again. I only serve to pass on His message. I am THE messenger. But, still, only a messenger."

"Well, 'His' message can go right up your ass, brah."

"And it well does, my lady."

"Why do you keep calling me that?"

"Hmmm...if you don't find this so curt, I have found that romance is the first thing noticeable for your species. And we, my lady, are on a date."

"A-" My head shook with disgust. "-Date?"

"Yes, my flower," he reached out for my hand, but it shot under the table, hiding. "Why do you reject me so, Willow? I know we have never had the most respectful friendship, but I mean to right that wrong, to fix what has been broken between us, and to serve you to Him when the time is right. This human species, is so inclined to loosen their belts and start, as you would say, 'Fuckin' like dogs'. Why do you hide from my touch so much when I am everything you want?"

"Dude...I think you're a little too old for me, man. I'm, like, fourteen."

"What does that mean, Willow?"

"What does...I'm too young, dude. How old are you?"

"Old? I don't exactly understand. I was born with the universe. Time both is and isn't and I both see and don't see it all at once, as time is relative to mass, to which I have none. These years you speak of are only relative to this planet as it revolves around that sun, to which there are an infinite amount of plants and suns in the universe, all with their own different revolutions and years. So these years mean nothing to me, as I do not understand nor do I feel them as you do. You may be 'fourteen' on this planet but five-hundred on another. But, please, explain to me, so I can understand better, or at least try to."

"I...uh...okay. So there's something called age of consent in human society."

"Go on." His head cocked again, sending golden locks this way.

"And you gotta be a certain age for that. Eighteen or something."

"Uh huh...and you are only fourteen?"

"Yes. I am only fourteen."

He nodded, "Then I am sorry to have made you uncomfortable. Please, excuse my ignorance, Willow Pines. I am sorry again and again."

"Uh...apology accepted?" Did he even understand what I was talking about when I was making fun of him for 'trying to get in my pants'? Did the other one? The one who screams?

"This will no longer be a date in romantic terminology, but it will be a knowledge filled lecture! Please, go on with more human stuff."

"More human stuff? Like what?" I gave a quick whiff at my pits. They did, indeed, smell like sausage links.

"Hmm...what makes a human tick? Why do they want to live so much when they die in the end?"

"Because people want to live."

"But, and herein lies the question: Why?" He moved his chair further in. "Why? Why does a human want to live?"

"Because we do. It's hardwired into our brains."

"Why?"

"Just because. Because we want to live. Sleep. Smell. See. Love."

"Interesting. Are you becoming less human?"

"...I don't know."

"You see, Willow, the longer I stay in this humanskin, the more it connects to me. The more I feel it's wants and needs. I ate for the first time just a while ago because I felt the want of hunger. Do you understand how weird that felt? Having a stomach and a full stomach nonetheless. I took a nap earlier and experienced my first dream. You were in it, Willow. You see, that was my inspiration for this folly-es date. I can prick my skin now and understand pain, when I had never before. Would you say, Willow, that I am becoming human?"

"No."

"Stark and quick. Why is that? I look the part, yes? And I am beginning to feel the part, yes? So what makes me any less human than you?"

"You just aren't."

"Really? Can anything in this infinite universe be slotted to 'justs' and 'onlys' without any real explanation."

"Yes."

"Interesting. Would you say that, if I got the feeling of lust, love as you put it, then would I be more human? Would I finally understand your previous japs about wanting to get into your pants?"

"I..." My face betrayed me, even though he could read my fucking mind.

"I guess time can only tell," he smiled again, that big fat disgustingly beautiful smile. "And I wonder, Willow...when the time is nigh and you are ripe like a cherry to be plucked," his hand made a soft plucking motion, "Will you fall unto me?

Will I be able to finish this whole mess and bring Him back? Or will this human side of me stop my cosmodic side?" He cocked his head to the other side, "I guess only these earth years may tell."

And the stink flowed into my nose once more, and my stomach was horrifically empty, gnawing at itself when it was once full to the brim and then I smelled her, fast asleep right next to me, her fat and juicy haunches of meat right next to me, enough to make my mouth drip and filter with saliva and want. I reached for her arm and caressed its milky and silky exterior, the darkness of the tent almost making it glow, the gnawing of my stomach only increasing in its veracity. I grabbed at it and lifted it to my nose, smelling it like a big long juicy sandwich filled to the brim with meat and vegetables and everything, thick with sauce and dripping all over my hands. DRIPPING.

I felt my mouth open and then close, deep into flesh, filling it with a wash of thick and juicy blood...that tastes like shit. I opened my eyes and found my teeth deep into the thin band of my arm. And I sucked at it, dragging myself across the tent to hide in the corner, sucking more and more blood from my own arm. I felt like crying, but I didn't. I sucked at myself. Sucked, sucked, sucked, letting the blood trickle down my pale forearm and drip from my elbow, patting softly on the black tent floor.

And I sucked some more, mouthful after mouthful, thinking not about First or Second or Scarlet laying so meatily across from me or my teeth which still bit harder and harder into my arm, bleeding it dry, sucking it down with a shit filled hunger, trying not to think about the feast or how full I was or the Key or the world or the universe or anything about whatever in whatever whatever whatever...whatever... Monster Balls, big and juicy.

Addendum

Addah fluttered and flew upon the heavens, speaking with reverence
Making the other Gods wholesome and peaceful, with smiles
That made the world spin in another way
Until he didn't
Dropping down to the brown mirth of Earth
Under the thoughts and death of others, he was not seen again
Only to be forgotten by the world, sunk under the sea of influence.

4 YEARS LATER. 4 YEARS LATER. 4 YEARS LATER. 4 YEARS LATER. 4 YEARS LAT,,,ER. 4 YEARS LATER. 4 YEARS LATER. 4..YEARS LATER. 4 YEARS LATER. 4 YEARS L,,ATER. 4 YEAR S LATER. 4 YEARS ,LATER. 4 YEARS LATER. 4 YEARS LATER. 4 YEARS LATER. 4 YEARS LATER. ... YEAR S LATE..R. 4 YEARS LATER. 4 YEARS LATER. 4 YEAR4 YEARS LATER.4 YEARS LATER.4 YEARS LATER.4 YEARS LATER. 4 YEARS LATER. 4 YEARS LATER. 4 YEARS LATER. 4 YEARS LATER. 4 YEARS LATER.4 YEARS LATER.4 YEARS LATER.S LATER. 4 YEARS LATER. 4 YEARS LATER. 4 YEARS LAT ER. 4 YEARS LATER. 4 YEARS LATER. 4.YEARS LATER. 4 YEARS LATER. 4 YEARS LATER. 4 YEARS LATER. 4 YEARS LATER. 4 YEARS LATER. 4 YEARS LATER. 4 YEARS LAT,,,ER. 4 YEARS LATER. YEARS LATER.,,4 YEARS LATER. 4 YEARS LATER. 4 YEARS LATER. . ..YEARS LATER. 4 Y,,,EARS LATE,,R. 4 YEARS LATER. 4R. 4 YEARS LATER. 4 YEARS LATER. 4 LATER. 4 YEARS LATER. 4 YEARS L.ATER. 4 YEAR S LATER. 4 LATER. 4 YEARS LATER. 4 YEARS LATE4 YEARS LATER. 4 YEARS LATER. 4 YEARS LATER. 4 YEARS LATER. 4 YEARS LAT,,,ER. 4 YEARS LATER.R. 4 EARS LATER. 4 YEARS LATER. 4 YEARS 4 YEAR LATER. 4 YEARS LATER. 4 YEARS LATER. 4 YS LATER. 4 YEARS LATER. 4 4 YEARS LA . 4 YEARS LAT,E 4 Y....EARS LATE,R,.RS LATER. 4 YEARS .4 YEARS LA.R. 4 YEARS LA,. YEARS LATER..4 YEARS LATER. 4 YEA. L,,,ER. 4 YE,RS LATER. 4 YEARS LATER. 4 YEARS .LATER. 4 YEAR.S LA.TER. 4 Y..ARS LATER. 4 LATER. 4 LEARS YATER. 4 YEARS YEARS YEARS YEARS YEARS YREAR YESYESYESYESES EYSEY EEYE EYE YESRS YEARS LATER.

18

"FUCK! FUCK! FUCK! YOU!" I slammed that fucking fist down repeatedly on the porcelin sink as the music blared thick and heavy in the background from beyond that awful fucking door.

BOOOOOOOOOOOOOOOOOOOOOOOOMMMMMMMMM BOPPPPPPPPPP BEEP BEEP BOOOOOOOOOOOOOOOOOOOOOOOOOOOOOOMMMMMM MMMMMM BOPPPPP BEEP BLAH BLAH BLAH!

"SHIT UP! SHUT UP, I MEAN!" But I only spoke to myself, screaming into a nothing that no one could ever really hear. But I was looking at myself in that mirror, looking at that disgusting face in that mirror. Looking at the face in that mirror, in the mirror, nasty nasty.

"Stop it, man. Get your head straight," I said to myself, rubbing my nose and tugging my hair back over my shoulders. "But that music is so FUCKING LOUD! But hey, Scarlet's here, right? In all that dogshit, right? Hey, hey, you're alright, dude. Dude dude, chillax. Take a breath." I did and almost vomited at myself reflected in the mirror. The air smelled like shit, all those things out there falling apart handedly, messing about the floor with their parts. "Yea, not a good idea. Okay, small breath." I did. "Ah! There, that's better. Small little baby bitch breaths." My face moved closer to the mirror and I felt the dark patches under my eyes, "Jesus, Willow. 'I know I know'," I said back. "But sleep is for losers, right?" I tried to smile at myself, but found a pair of thin lips folded together which pressed up two dark eyes and some unkempt eyebrows that Scarlet always tells me to let her fix them up. Fuck me up, I say! And I laughed then and now as I thought about it.

The First Apostle

"Hey First," said Second, sitting across from me.

"Yes Second?" I had my feet all kicked up on the desk, a juicy plum in one hand and a book in the other, *Frankenstein*. But Second was mussing it up and I let it fall out of my view ever so slightly to look into that purple, annoying eye.

"I know I asked you about this before, but why are you still in the humanskin?"

"Research, Second." I brought the book back up and took a fat bite out of that plum, its insides filling and exploding in my mouth.

"But...wouldn't you say that it's useless now? Everything is ending soon so our knowledge of the peoplethings doesn't matter anymore, right?"

"Humans, Second. Not peoplethings."

"What?"

"Respect. Now, please, I am trying to read. Have you ever tried to read one of these 'books'? Fascinating stuff, haven't put them down in the last couple of years."

"No...First, are you okay?"

"Yes I am, Second. Better than okay, actually."

A wash of sound and noise filled my head, making me stop and gawk, unable to move. As soon as it began, it ended and I looked up at Second and his purple eye. "What was that?" I asked.

Second began to laugh, "A joke. A bad one at that!" And he laughed some more. "Something I came up with earlier."

Then it hit me. "Second, can you give me some privacy, please?"

"Sure thing, First." He was gone in an instant.

The world became blurry. I couldn't understand him. He spoke in cosmodic and I couldn't understand him. My own native speak...what I was born with with the universe all around me...then I shit myself, filling my trousers with everything that was human.

The Key

"Hey, yo!" I said to one drunk, his forehead precariously meandering away down towards his mouth, leaving a thick red slime which drooped as he waddled past towards the bathroom door. "Just took a mad dump!" I yelled to his back, his hair almost all fallen off, the wave of stink that filtered off of him was worse than any dump in this entire stinking universe. Then I was off in search of Scarlet who liked to disappear at these little parties that she would always drag me to. Always leaving me to the rot of everything else. If she knew that everyone looked the part of a zombie in a Romero film then I'm sure that she would think first before bringing me to these human hotboxes of rot and filth. And then there always came a time like this where I had to pool through a sea of corpses, all standing and swaggering to the tune of alcohol and dogshit music.

She drank too much at these things to my annoyance as I always had the job of dragging her corpse-like drunken body out of the mess. And I would just shove my face into her hair, like a human gas mask, fighting away this smell of awfulness that follows anyone anywhere, except for Scarlet, who still looks as human as ever, thank the God, am I right? Nah, just kidding, fuck that guy. If I'm his key, like First says, then I'll let the fucker know, whenever I'm supposed to be of service. If ever. First keeps saying, 'Soon,' while he lounges back in whatever chair he has in that fake body that he's become strikingly accompanied to, never taking it off for the last couple of years.

He tells me each and every new feeling that his skin gives him from the shits to the jiggly bits. I would tell him to go deal with it himself and he would be all like, 'Bro, what the frick?' and I'd be all like, 'Suck it, nerd!' Something like that.

"Willow!" It was a deep and rough voice, right in my right ear. That was a common one, one that I knew not to look at. The voices were still there, always screaming something or a whisper once in a while, but amongst the smell of rot and decay and all the unsultry little bits of everything and everyone, I don't think I really give a damn.

"Chett! Looking fresh, dawg!" I said to some bare skeleton held up by a large stick. Oh, that's an old out of season Halloween decoration. I patted him on the shoulder and walked towards the stairs in my further search for Scarlet. Get this: This guy in front of me, white dude, big eyebrows, kinda regular looking, red solo cup in hand, this dude had his wang out, balls flopping everywhere, trying to grab onto this one corpse that slammed her jeaned ass into his bare dick. "Nice cock, bro!" I yelled out to him, he glanced at me and then away. I was lying though, his cock was a stump of festering mold that leaked all over the floor as his skin took on this green hue. Pretty nast. But, respectable nonetheless. If I were a dude, my wang would be sealed up in this fortress of solitude down here.

But I reached the steps and walked up them, the music pounding in my ears. BOOOOMM BAMMMMMMMM AHHHHHHHHHH! That's all it is, over and over and over and over again again again. "Kill them."

Did I say that? No, no I won't. You see, they're already dead, all zombified or, as First put it, 'Xombified', whatever that means. "No, I won't," I responded, out into the bank of thick heavy stink and music that hit both my ears and my nose. Headache. I gave my temples a rub, two fingers on each, and each step the music became lesser and lesser, and then I took a turn and the music slowed, only becoming a dull repeating thud on the second floor. I went door to door, opening each like some operative, "Breach and clear!" Someone said as I pushed in a white door. Or did I say it?

"Hey, Willow, I gotta ask you a question real quick." Something said, but I didn't pay it any mind, opening another door to this unknown house. Still, Scarlet was gone somewhere. "Willow! Hey, are you even listening!" Then I recognized that voice.

"What, First? I'm doing something," I practically kicked open this door to nothing except two corpses going at it. They didn't even look at me, but I stood and watched a little, waiting for First to finish his annoying annoyances. He probably wants to tell me another thing he found out about history or his own fake body. Something that I always had to listen to. 'Hey, Willow! Did you know cork comes from a tree? They just drill it right out of the base! Isn't that interesting?' Or his book recommendations...my god. And I never read any of them. My mind has enough going on to think about some godly book club with some obsessed dude who wasn't even a dude.

"Am I a good person?" He asked.

"No," I said and moved on to another door. How many doors, what the hell? "You aren't even a person."

"Oh, yea...hmmm..."

"Willow!" another voice slurred out from somewhere behind me, but I moved on. "Willow!" and a hand grasped my shoulder and practically spun me around right into the slobbering face of Scarlet Miller, alcohol thick on her breath, her knees bobbing and wobbling with a festering blood alcohol. "Follow me!" She grasped my hand with an iron vice, and led me to a room. My legs moved forcefully so as not to be dragged. Then we were in a room alone, the door shut, the beating of the floor the only sound other than her rasping breath and my headachy mind. Her hands cupped my face, her right on my left and vice versa and she smiled that dimpled smile with those perfect teeth that spewed out alcohol induced stank, her green eyes magnified by those big oval glasses, "Hey Willow," she whispered between those teeth.

"Am I a bad person?" First asked, almost at the same time.

"Hey Scarlet. You look kinda drunk."

"Hey Scarlet? Talk to me first, First." I ignored him.

"I ammmm..." her face got all sad. "I'm sorry Willow...I

know you don't like it when I do this."

"It's okay." I moved a lock of her black hair out of her glasses, smoothing it behind her head.

"No...it's not. You're, like, my best friend in the entire world, and I keep disappointing you..." She usually gets like this afterwards.

I grasped her hands and brought them from my face, trying to smile that nasty smile I had, "No, baby Scarlet, no."

"I am a baby..." I could see her eyes welling, magnified by her glasses, like big old emeralds dripping after a storm.

"Maybe. But you're my baby."

"You know Willow, I've been thinking about all of this recently...I've been a shitty friend to you..."

"No you haven't, Scarlet. Don't give me that bullshit."

First started up again, right in my ear, "Willow! I have to talk to you, really! Before its all-"

Scarlet thankfully cut him off, "Willow, I've been scared this whole time." Her head rolled a little, drunk on its neck. "All that shit I spew is all fake. I just wanted to look cool."

"There's nothing to be scared of," I said, and for the first time in the last couple of years I thought of that meager corn maze and her dead body skewered. She smelled really good. I put that thought away.

"There is, Willow...I never told you about that place... with that door...with the finger engraved on it..."

I only remembered bits and pieces, but we never talked about it.

"I've been scared to tell you about it, Willow."

"It's okay, we can talk about it later," I didn't want to though, and didn't plan to bring it up when she was sober.

"Nope! Not enough time!" A voice screamed out.

Scarlet's face scrunched up, confused, "Did a voice just come out of you?"

"What?"

"Alright! If you're not talking to me, I'm coming out!" First screamed, even louder.

The First Apostle

First a finger popped out of Willow Pines ear, then a hand, my hand, wavering about, feeling the stagnant air of the room. It was all muffled up in here, but I could hear the panic coming from both of them, Scarlet drunkenly screaming and Willow yelling something that got caught up in her ear canal as I pulled myself further out of her stinking head of nasty thoughts. I'd never thought to do this before, no reason either, but the conjunction was at dawn, and I needed to confide in the only human I knew. I shoved my arm with a force, widening her head with it, using my legs as leverage to push with all my human force, making her head stretched and weird and warped as my own head crowned. I saw Scarlet for the first time with these human eyes. She wobbled and catered this way and that, those glasses on the ground and her face turned into a position of horror. I would be screaming too if I hadn't been focusing on pulling out the other shoulder as well. Willow became deathly quiet as her head had no choice but to fall to the floor as it birthed me from her waxy canal. And that wax was sticking to me like molasses, gross and putrid smelling. "Could you not have-" I grunted again, popping my entire shoulder out of there as well, "used a cue tip or something?" Her head looked like a mop of sullen skin, all pancaked to the ground, her eyes all stretched wide and her mouth no longer fused to her face, and it made a funny whiskery breathing sound as she tried to speak. It was hard to birth an entire human sized human out of one little ear, but if the cervix could do it, I had no doubt that the ear canal could do the same. And I was right. I finally stepped out of it with a meaty slurp as her head loony-tooned back together like some silly putty, slapping this way and that, finally coming back to her own face as if nothing had happened.

Scarlet fainted on the ground, or she just passed out drunk, it was hard to read them from physical-view. "Ew," I said, wiping one of my black catered dress shoes on the floor, spreading yellow viscous wax from the bottom. Willow behind me was grabbing handedly at her reformed face, trying to contemplate with her folded brain what had just happened. I let her grab around for a second or two, then I finally spoke, "Mothers usually have maternal instinct to hold their child, well here I am mommy!" I held out my arms. But she didn't hear, her mind still reeling back, her entire world still puzzling itself back together. "Huh..."

I crouched over Scarlet, looking at her for the first time, the locks of my golden hair falling in droves around my face. Interesting...she was shapely enough, strong arms with quite the comely face to boot. I grabbed her fallen glasses and fitted them to her unconscious face, wrapping the frame delicately over her ears which seemed just a tad too big for her face, but it gave her a more...how do I put it...less contemporary face? Maybe. But the facial structure was much more robust. A strong chin and a symmetrical face overall. A shame, really, her humanskin looked so nice for the Third piece-

"-THE HELL!" Willow screamed behind me, still touching her face, making sure every little proportion was intact.

"Oh stop being such a ninny!" I shooed my hand like some aristocrat. "You wouldn't answer me, so I came."

"Out of my fucking ear!"

"Yes, how else?"

"I...you..." her back stood straight as she found her footing, "Is it time?" she asked, her face still, her blues watching behind those black barriers and sullen face. She looked better, more full than those years past, only as she got more used to the taste of feces.

I nodded. "By dawn. It will be no sooner. And this night will become hell. I..." I had to look away, "I'm a bad man, Willow. I'm sorry."

"You're not human."

"I know."

"So...what happens? When dawn comes." Her face sat

still, but I could hear her heart beating behind that chest.

"Your use will be needed."

"I'm ready?"

"Yes. You have gone through almost it all. All of everything will convene soon, and you will meet Him."

"Huh..." she looked away and then back, "Am I going to die?" she asked.

Yes. "I cannot say." My new human stomach hurt, but I had to do it. I went this far, torturing a poor girl for years. This is it. Soon. "But there will be one more push needed."

"What sort of push?" She scowled.

"Soon."

A sudden breath shot out from behind me and Scarlet sat up, her hair all amess. And then she looked at me, the knowledge behind her eyes still unkempt. "Did you just climb out of her ear?" She asked, a look of nothing upon her face.

"Yes. Yes I did," I held out a princely hand, "I am First. The voice in Willow's head."

She grabbed it quickly and stood with my help. "Huh..." her face puzzled. "Do I know you?"

"Maybe. Maybe not. But all will be revealed later, when it climaxes."

She looked over to Willow, still standing there, and said to her, "This dude talking about sex?"

They both chortled and I didn't. I wish I wanted to. I understood. I understood glands. I understand the complexities after much experimenting. But I wasn't talking about sex. This would be bleak and bloody and the end. "Maybe," I said, trying to smile. The humanskin was hard to take off, especially after four years of wearing it. It made me feel sad. But I still couldn't understand what sad meant. It was empty and void, but it was also sad. Weird, weird.

"Any other questions?" Willow asked Scarlet.

And she shook her head in response, "No. Not really. I... something about all of this reminds me of something... I think I know you," her hand pointed at me.

"And what do you know of me, Scarlet Miller?"

"I...I don't know...but looking at you gives me this weird feeling..."

"I know, I am quite the looker-"

"Oh, shut up, man." Willow walked steady over towards Scarlet, took her hand, and walked her to a corner of the room and they whispered, thinking that I couldn't hear every little thing they were saying or thinking.

The Key

"Scarlet. I gotta tell you something."

"Like who that dude is? I already know. He's the voice in your head."

"That's not it. But, seriously, you're just going to take it all at face value like this?"

She nodded, "Yep. I'd probably go insane or someshit if I didn't. Look, you already knocked me sober with your head getting all flapjacked like that." She smiled, "I'll be by your side until the end, man."

"Well, that's what I've been meaning to tell you. I...I think the world's going to end in a couple of hours. And I'm going to kill it."

"Hmm...You're the Key, right?"

"The...what did you just say?"

"I..." she looked around, then past my shoulder at him then back at me, "It just kind of came up in my head. I don't know why but I think I'm taking this all really fucking well. I don't know how to explain it, it's like I've already known this the whole time."

"Scarlet. You died four years ago. Do you remember?"

"Hmm..." she nodded. "Yes. I do."

"Huh..." was all I said.

"Man, I feel fuckin' good. Like I just downed five cups of coffee or something."

"It's starting," First said behind us. "You guys best get something to defend yourselves."

"What?" I tried to turn to him, but Scarlet caught me in her strong hands and shoved her face into mine. I couldn't stop myself from falling into it, her mouth opening mine. She pulled back softly and smiled behind those fogged glasses.

"Why did I do that?" She asked.

19

The first head exploded with the velocity of a bullet, propelling the brain and stem fluid all over the ceiling, painting it in crimson. The body fell to its knees, no longer a human but a husk of nothing and then it fell to the ground, spreading more matter from the coldening mushy husk-hole. The next popped like an overfilled balloon, blasting out everywhere, making shadows of blood and viscera on the walls outlined by the others it hit. And then the next one popped, and with each step we three took down the stairs, another one popped. None of them seemed to notice, still dancing and partying with music that was no longer there. One flopped like a fish on the ground, trying to find some sort of tune to the wind, and then he or she exploded from the side, still leaving the left half which still grooved as it massed out onto the carpet.

I was the head of the group, my foot only on the second stair down. "Can you see this?" I asked no one in particular.

"Yes."

"Yes."

I turned and they both huddled behind me, like I was some sort of shield. "First, why are you scared?"

"I...I'm not. But you are the one with the baseball bat."

I was. We found it in the closet stuffed away with some other baseball equipment. "Then why don't you leave that form and turn back into that weird fire-eye thing?" Another pop from down below.

"It's harder than you think. And I also...look, never

mind my reasoning. Can we move on?"

I looked at Scarlet who sat quiet, staring out at the mess, "You okay?" I asked.

"Is this what you've been seeing and," she covered her nose, "smelling this entire time?"

"Yep. Except for the whole popping part." Another pop, this was a juicier one, probably some fat kid or something. "Why do I need this bat?" I looked over to First.

"You just do."

"What?"

"Just move down the stairs!"

And I took another step to another pop, and then another. Pop! Step. Pop! Step. Pop! Step. One after another, pop, step, pop, step. At the bottom of the stairs, some dude who was busting a fat move, his ass cheeks all out and crusted from layers of rotting shit, popped! right in my face, filling my eyes, my hair, my mouth, every little orifice with his thick and cold blood. I spit and almost retched, wiping my eyes of the stuff. "Ew! Fuck you!" I swung hard at the bottom half of him which still busted a move on the ground and broke his knee the completely wrong way, but he still persisted which earned some respect. But all that respect was stuck in my hair and in my teeth and made the world red in my blinking eyes.

We chugged through the rest of the party, pushing and galloping our way into the bloodbath. One dude looked at me, his eyes popping out of his noseless face, "Hit him!" First screamed. And my muscles reacted almost instinctively, like his words forced them to fire and I swung hard, blasting his brains and his eyes from that fruitless skull all over the ground and on the other rotting and stinking partygoers.

"Hell yea!" I screamed and swung again, muscles firing, and blasted another dude this time, knocking his jaw off and felling him to the floor. Another pop! and another spray of internals from somewhere far off in the bodies. Again, I swung for the fences, smacking this one girl's head clean off. It soared through the air and crashed through a window, shattering it.

"Home fucking run!" I yelled and then swung again and then again, beheading and splattering all of these fuckers who've been in my eyes for what felt like my entire fucking life.

"Another!" First screamed and my muscles answered back, clocking this one dude in the face. Another swing and then another pop! That dude with his wang out lumbered right towards me and bam! With one mighty swing of my bat, his wang was soaring through the air, festering and disgusting as it was. And then I swung again, higher, smashing and caving the right side of his face in an avalanche of puss and brain membrane which sent the bastard and his wangless doo-dad almost into an elegant soiree through the air.

"Another!" I swung. "Another!" I swang. "Another!" My arms began to throb. "ANOTHER!" No matter how much blood got into my eyes and my mouth, I swung at them, cratering their heads and breaking their limbs, sending their insides to their outsides, killing and killing and killing like that pull of a trigger, each command I answered. I swung again.

"DIE!" *Crack!* "DIE!" *Whap!* "FUCKING DIE!" *CRRRRRRRRRRRRAAAAAAAAACCCCCCCCCKKKKK!*

The bat broke in half on some lady's shins which splintered and fractured, leaving her crawling and boogying on the ground. I took a deep shaky breath and looked behind me at the red carpet of bodies laden like felt, blood everywhere. What was once white was now red, and crimson, and scarlet, soaked deep to the core. All along myself I felt the syrupy stickiness which inked down my arms and my legs and down the concaves and convexes of my face, getting in my eyes and my mouth, making all of this red tang with the taste of shit. The splintered bat jingled on the ground as I dropped it, opened the front door, and led the party out into the cold midnight air.

And then I collapsed down the long rod of a tree which sprouted out from the ground. "Jesus fuckin Christ," Scarlet started, her entire self splattered with bits and pieces of the partygoers inside.

"Yea," I took a breath. "Where to now?" I asked First.

"Well," he brushed his shirt, which gleamed perfectly clean, "follow me," he smiled.

*

The First Apostle

The steps echoed slightly and I could even smell their remembrance as we went down the cold icy stairway which circled upon itself, enveloping step after step, circle after infinite circle. Willow and Scarlet smelled like death too, the blood drying and attaching to their skin as they walked further from that messy room of stank and stink and popping little corpses, their lifesblood sinking deep into the soil, trailing into Him for use later once the time has started. But until then we walked and with each step we sank farther and deeper into the central vein.

"Hey," Scarlet asked with an echo. "Willow, why do you want to destroy the world?"

"I don't want to. I was born to do it."

"But why? Beyond duty, beyond birth, why do you want to do it?"

"Hey, hey, hey," I chimed in. "This is a rebirth for the world, not an end."

"But, Willow, why?"

"I don't know..." her voice trailed off. "Maybe...because I don't care anymore." I could hear her shrug through the muck on her body. "I used to be adamant about 'winning' as I called it. But now...eh? Why are you so nonchalant about it?"

"I...I don't know." Scarlet answered and then stayed quiet.

That quiet continued as we circled the last few times, sinking deep within the confines of the earth and of that vein. At the bottom stood a long and sprawling door engraved from top to bottom in little budding fingers, eventually growing into a large fat finger that swirled down the center towards the buckling handle which I clasped and pushed. It creaked and bellowed under its own weight, but spurred on, eventually opening to a large room. We stepped in and adjusted our eyes to the darkness, revealing large monolith statues that symmetrically catered the room all the way to the end, making a path of limbs that led to another door at the far end.

I expected one of them to speak about what they were seeing. I could see it in their minds, even slightly, that they wanted to talk about something as their eyes watched the sprawling monuments that ended in pointed fingers, but they never did. All three of us trudged towards the far end in more silence. There was a wooden door fitted with several bands of hard copper to keep it sturdy. I pushed it open and it slid without a sound. Beyond it sat an immense light that almost blinded me and my compatriots, but I stepped in without a word and they followed.

The door slammed shut behind us and clicked, locking itself. This was really the end, but the light lessened and we all began to see the spotty openings of a small room. It was sparse, with a few pictures on the wall here and there and a couch that sat in the center, well worn. A couple rooms sprouted off and a staircase led upwards to a possible second floor.

"Holy shit," Willow started. "This was my house." She went and sat on that well worn couch with a puff of dust. She coughed, "Yep, this is it," and waved her hand in front of her dust filled nose.

"Thought this place burnt down," Scarlet said, walking over to one of the walls, studying some of the pictures. "Yep, there's you. And there's you." She pointed.

"Alright, First. Why are we here?" She looked over at me.

"Eh hem," I cleared my throat, "follow me ladies. Let's have a good talk over some good food." I looked at Willow's face which did nothing, not even move once, her mind nowhere near the thought of taste or of tasting. Shit. She tastes only shit. I led them to another room and the three of us sat at a long table and then there was silence. A couple candles whiskered in the corners, and two more candles sat in the center of the table, thick and collective.

"I don't remember this room," Willow broached, shifting her seat. It was nothing other than a comment. She had no more questions, nor does she care to ask them anymore.

"That's because," I looked at her candle light smothered face, "this was never a room in that old house. That 'Willows Eve'. A confusing name considering that you are the one named Willow."

She shrugged, "Eh."

And here it was, "Do you remember what happened here all those years ago?" I looked at Scarlet who hid behind her glasses, her mind running thoughtfully with nothing and everything at the same time, she remembered me.

"It burnt down," Willow answered quickly, not even thinking about it for a moment.

"Do you know how?" I asked.

"Yes. I burnt it down."

"Uh huh...how does that make you feel?"

"Eh," she shook her head, "Don't really care to be honest."

"Do you, if anything, remember why or how you burnt it down?" I laid my firm chin on my robust hands which laid crisscrossed on the cold tabletop. I had to mask everything.

"I remember a voice. It told me to play with matches. So I did. Then it told me to drop one on the carpet, one of those long carpets with fur. So I did. And before the fire could get too big, I grabbed it back up and ran upstairs." She made a face, "It wasn't you that night...it was another one. Second maybe?"

I looked towards Scarlet. Her mind cranked and chugged along, trying to understand who I was. I let her think and turned back to Willow. "How were the last five years?"

"Eh," again with the 'ehs'.

"That's it?"

"Eh."

"Eh?"

"Eh. Fine I guess."

"Are you fine with giving your being to Him?"

"Sure. I lost. I don't care anymore." No hesitation, her mind calm, not even thinking about anything in particular.

"Huh..." What was I supposed to say? "Why don't we eat?"

"Pickles," said Pickles who stood tall in the doorway. He was wearing a black and white clad butler's outfit: An open satin coat and a frilly white center that went down to a dashing pair of pants. Not the most handsome of men, but serviceable.

"Ladies, that is Pickles. He will be our waiter tonight. He only says Pickles."

"Pickles?" Pickles asked.

"Yes, Pickles." I nodded. "No worries, he can understand what we say well enough. Go ahead and order whatever you want. Tonight, you can view it as the...last supper of sorts."

"Why does he only say 'pickles'?" Scarlet asked.

"He just does. Now Pickles," I clapped twice.

Like a hammer to a nail, Pickles spurred on and went around the table, first asking Willow The Key, what she wanted to eat.

"Nothing," is what she told Pickles. Pickles face went red, his brows furrowing down. Was he confused?

"Nothing?" I asked.

"Pickles?" Asked Pickles.

"Nothing," she nodded.

"Why?" I knew why.

"Not hungry."

"I assure you, this feast will taste like...food. Not what you've-"

"You know what? I don't really care. Pickles? I want absolutely nothing."

"P-pickles?" He turned to me.

"Pickles has no idea what it means to have 'nothing' as you put it."

"Well that's what I want: Nothing. Absolutely nothing, man. This is your crusade."

My head shook, "I know you're hungry, Willow. I can see it in your mind and hear it in your stomach."

"Pickles!" Pickles nodded.

"Yeah," Scarlet started, "just listen to Pickles, dude. Just say something to make him happy."

"Pickles!" He nodded in approval, flashing Scarlet with a set of browned teeth. "Pickles, pickles."

"Alright. Pickles." Willow said.

"Pickles?"

"Yes. I want pickles."

"Pickles?" he asked me, pointing at himself.

"No, Pickles. She doesn't want you, she wants pickles, the pickled food that has been... pickled, you know. In a jar."

"Pickles?" he asked, shaking his head.

"Willow, he doesn't know what a Pickle is."

"He doesn't know?" she asked.

"No, say something else."

"Fine...kimchi." She smiled.

"Pickles!" He exploded in excitement and wrote it down in his little notebook. All he wrote was pickles.

He now turned to Scarlet, "Pickles?"

"I'll take a quad burger with extra thousand island and...hold the pickles." They both laughed as Pickles looked back at me, pointing at himself.

"No, Pickles. Just...don't worry about it. Go," I shooed him. "Make their food."

"Pickles?"

"Oh yea. Coq au Vin. Extra sauce please. Oh and a glass of the red. Whatever cask, I care not."

"Pickles," Pickles said, "pickles, pickles...pickles." He nodded and left the room.

Scarlet looked at me for a second. I thought she was finally going to say it, but instead, "Cock und Van?" she sounded out, "Cock in a van?" They snickered over there.

"Yes. I put my cock in a van."

"How is that thing anyways?" Willow asked. "Dude," she looked over to Scarlet, "You know he tells me all about his dong."

"Really?"

"Yea, pretty weird right?"

"Maybe. Kinda rad though."

"Why?"

"Dudes never talk about their wangs to me, bro."

"Well," I chimed in, "If you would like to know, it has gone quite well. I see no shame in talking about these bodily extremities that we all have."

"Yea but we don't have dongs, dude," Scarlet said.

"I know, but we're all humans, right? Does it matter the sex?"

"No," Willow shook her head. "You're not human."

"Mmm...that's another question I've been meaning to ask you. Why am I not human? I look like one, I act like one, I piss and shit like one, I taste like one. Why am I not a human if I feel human enough? Tell me that? I may not have been human then, but I feel human now."

"Because, that's only a cheap covering. It doesn't hide what you really are and what you really are is some backyard monster obsessed with some god."

"Aren't you the one willing to give yourself to this god?"

"Yes, not because I care about it. I'm not obsessed. I lost."

"But, like Scarlet asked earlier, why does birth matter? And I don't want to hear about you not caring anymore. There must be more to it than that."

"Why do you care, man? You were the one torturing me all these years to give in and believe. Guess what? It worked. I'm like this because of you. All the torture, all the years of sleeplessness, all the voices, all the constant preaching with you. It's all come to this, to a point where I just don't care. You made me want to eat Scarlet. You made her smell so fucking good to where I almost ate her because she seemed like the only fucking thing left that was edible in the universe. But instead I got this," she pulled her sleeve down and revealed a faint mark like a row of teeth that followed down the small length of her arm. "I had to fucking bit the shit out of myself to not eat her. And now I don't care. I couldn't care. Fuck everything. Kill them all if you want, I don't care about all of this 'rebirth' dogshit. You could have told me that this god was going to kill everything in the universe and, at this point, I would still do it. All because of you," she pointed a gaunt finger at me.

I swallowed a ball of spit and took a breath. It was me, huh? I am a bad person. But still, fate must proceed. Dawn is coming. I looked at Scarlet, "Any questions?" I asked her.

"No...I...I think I already knew all of that. It's all... weird. Something's right there...its...a spike...I fucking died... I remember forgetting...I remember the pain and the numbness...I..." her eyes went wide. "Oh my god. I know who you are."

I tried to smile, "Welcome back, Third."

"First?" She asked.

"What?" Willow asked.

"Willow...I have something to tell you, "She lowered her glasses. "I think I...it's still wavy...but I'm not Scarlet, I don't think."

"I... You killed her?"

Scarlet nodded, "Yes. I think so. I relinquished mine mind with hers and lost myself in the humanskin. Even to the point where I couldn't even read the everythingtables." She looked at me, "The humanskin does much to block our minds, right First?"

"Indeed. They are dangerous things. Addictive even." Willow sat quietly as I eyed her, "Are you okay, Willow?"

"Y...es. Yes." She took a breath and said-

Willow

"I don't think I care." It all etched away at me, maybe a

part of myself knew the entire time. I was surrounded in a lost war. First's face looked sad for a moment then reformed into a smile.

"Willow-"

"Pickles!" Pickles, that dumb boy, strode in with a cart blanched in a white drape that covered everything on there. He stopped at me first, layed a silver food cover on top of a silver plate. And with a show, he pulled it off, "Pickles!" and there was a jar of kimchi sitting underneath, smoke emanating around it like some fucking cray-cray item from a game. He went to Scarlet-Third, next, and did the same routine. Silver platter, shing! And then a giant burger was beneath, the pickles all but gone. In front of First was some fancy ass looking food and a wine glass filled absolutely to the brim.

"Thank you Pickles," said First, "now you may go."

Pickles bowed, turned, said "Pickles," one more time, and then left promptly.

"What a fine lad," I said, rimming my finger around the edge of the kimchi jar.

"I'm sorry, Willow," First said.

"About what?"

"About what has happened. About everything. I just want to say that I'm sorry."

"Why? I thought this was my purpose."

"It is, but I just want to..."

"What? You're losing yourself in this whole facade. Just stop and leave that fucking skin for the good of all of us. I can't take you seriously anymore." I looked at Third with her skin of Scarlet, "And you too, just get out of it. Stop acting."

She looked like she was about to say something and then stopped dead still, her burger completely untouched. She disappeared without a sound, absolutely gone, like she was just deleted from the world.

"Uhh...where'd she go?" I asked.

"Third is now dead." He answered, coldly. "A third of myself."

"What?"

"She was the first to go. Second is next, then I am next, then you. Time is almost up. Above us, the sky will soon turn a mix of orange and yellow and red, and then the world will be reborn."

"Where is Second? If this was the last supper, I'd have liked to say fuck you to him just one more time for all those nights..."

"He is preparing. He knows he is next, only to be consumed into the will of Him. Then I, then you. We will all be one."

"Gay."

"It is beautiful," he took a sip of his wine. His face twitched behind that smile.

"Is it?"

"Yes."

"First?"

"Yes?"

"Do you want me to call you Mark?"

He blinked, his smile dropped, the glass of red in his hands unmoving. "Yes, Willow. That would make me happy."

"Mark?"

"Yes, Willow?"

"Are you okay?"

He sniffed, "Yes, of course. Why do you ask? This is all I've ever wanted. This is what I was made for, just like you." He took another sip.

"Mark?"

"Yes?"

"Why are you crying?"

His eyes welled, like two big droplets, he wiped at them, "I'm not crying. Only," sniff, "relieved that this is all over, that the god is coming back." He rubbed at his eyes a little longer, sniffing all the same.

"Mark?"

"Yes?"

"You're lying."

"No I am not. I loathe being in this humanskin. I hate having these feelings that only plague me." He sniffed a little more, still rubbing his eyes, "I hate having skin, I hate having feelings, I hate having a mouth, I hate having eyes, I hate having hair, I hate having a heart and organs and those little pains after sitting for too long or the headache I get from reading so much or tired after watching a movie. I hate the taste of food and I hate the cravings for food. I hate those little pieces of meat that get stuck between my teeth. I hate the feeling of love, I hate this world..."

"Do you love me?"

"I do. Like I said, Willow. But now it's different. I hate looking at you now and how it calms these fake veins and I hate how my heart jumps and rests when you speak, I hate having tears for some fucking reason. I hate everything to do with being human. I am not human. I'm fake. I hate it."

"Mark..."

"Yes?"

Something came over me. A calm to the storm that was my life. There is really no use in struggling anymore. My stomach lightened and my head felt light. "Maybe you're human enough." I smiled.

"I...am?"

"Maybe."

He stopped rubbing his eyes, "I hate it...I hate it...I hate it...even this feeling of hate, it makes me so...happy. I want to leave but I can't. I don't want to leave. I want these feelings. I hate how much I love them. I hate how much I feel. I hate how I love dancing. I hate how much I love bantering with you. I hate how much I love you."

"But it all comes to an end, right?"

Sniff, "I suppose so, Willow Pines. I...I don't want to leave. I want to stay."

"Then we can stay here until the dawn. Until we need to go."

I held my hand out across the table and he took it. It was warm and soft but big and strong. I squeezed and he squeezed back.

20

"You know...I really like a good pancake." He said, his blonde head laid out on my lap as we sat on that old couch that I burned down all those years ago.

"Pancakes are good," I smoothed my fingers through his blonde beautiful curls.

"With some of that really thin syrup. I think it comes from Canadia-"

"Canada. It's called Canada."

"Yes, Canada." He breathed out. "I want to go."

"Then go."

"But I am stuck to you, Willow."

"Then I'm sorry."

"Don't be sorry."

"I hate you," I said. "I still do. But there's no use in struggling anymore."

"Mmm..." He smiled.

"What are you?" I asked.

"Human."

"Hu-man. Has a nice ring to it."

"Ah!" He ringed out in pain.

"What?"

"Second is...dead."

"You're up next."

"Yes."

"Why did all those people start popping? Back at the party?"

"It is the first step. All will be reborn through soil."

"So everyone in the world dies."

"To feed Him. Yes. But they don't actually die. Their

minds become one inside of Him. Rebirth. You are the only one left, Willow. The last human on Earth. Your Mom and Dad are dead. Your brothers. Everyone you knew at school. Every single person you saw in a movie, everyone. All except you."

"Do you really think you're human?" I asked.

"I...don't know."

"Do you believe that stuff about rebirth?"

He took a long time answering. "I...don't know anymore."

"Then I'll ask you: Why are you doing this? And I don't want to hear that you were born for this."

"I...don't have anything else."

"You got me."

He looked up at me just a little bit, piercing me with those eyes. Then he looked back somewhere else.

"Then there's no reason to think about going back, right?"

"No..."

There was no sound in the constructed living room. The windows that usually went to the outside were covered in a thick blackness. No wind, no animals, no nothing came through into this sad and cold and silent room. Everyone else was dead, what was there to do? What was going on up there? Was everything being destroyed, or was it all quiet and spartan, everyone just popped like little balloons. It was probably peaceful out there. The birds maybe sang...if they didn't all pop.

"Hey...why the spike?" I asked.

"It is a conductor. It moves the mind to the disciple that takes in their memories and their personality. The entire self. And they put it in an exact humanskin. Once worn, it gives you the memories and thoughts and personality of the recent occupant. And then you lose yourself, just like Third did."

"Did Scarlet feel any of that?"

"Oh, immensely. But, even then, her blood was taken by him. She is in the mindpool with the others. The place you are destined."

"And I am the one needed for Him to come back, right?"

"Yes. When a key is birthed then we must react."

"I hate you."

"I know."

*

The world began to crumble around us. A rumbling beneath and a push and we were rising up through the ground. The pressure mounted less and less as we rose through the Earth, silently, us both without a word. And like a shadow in the night, we popped out. It was familiar out here. Rows of gray houses cascaded down a long street, all samey and boring. I looked behind me and found a long stretch of forest. A forest that I remembered. Oh, this was where my house is or...was. All the walls were knocked down, spread out upon the ground around us and all was silent. No chirps from the forest or rustles from some blowing wind. Nothing. It was all still and stagnant. The sounds of people and planes and cars were all absent. Peaceful.

"This is it, Willow." First said, standing from the couch. I stood with him and nothing happened.

"What do we do now?" I asked.

"We wait."

A man grew from behind a long blink of the eye as if he were standing up from a curtain unfolding. He wasn't and then he was, out of nowhere.

"She is ready." He told the man. His voice sounded shaky and hoarse as if he were acting on stage for the first time. First turned towards me and whispered something that I didn't listen to. Behind him I watched as the shadowy mass blinked in and out of sight once or twice. First whispered something again, something that I definitely heard. "Kill me."

"What?"

"KILLMEKILLMEKILLMEKILLMEKILLMEKILLMEKILLM EKILLMEKILLMEKILLMEKILLMEKILLMEKILLMEKILL

MEKILLME. Kill me."

Darkness.

21

What a wonderful day out here! The sun is shinin' and the streets are burnin' with that hot sun and cool summer wind. I love my work!

*

Wow! I sure do love the warm sun and the cool wind. It makes me smile!

*

I saw Mr. Eggers over there. Working.

*

Ms. Herschel was walking past me earlier without a smile on her face. I was confused but now I'm happy to do more work. More work. I love my work!

*

Sometimes I find myself frowning.

*

I saw Ms. Herschel looking at me with that face again. Why does she do that so? She should smile, like the rest of us.

*

I haven't seen Ms. Herschel in a while.

*

I think I like my boss. He's blonde, blue eyes, a Golden Man.

*

We funnel into a large factory every day. I don't remember my job.

22

"Hyuk! Hyuk! Hyuk!" Ms. Herschel laughed as we passed each other on the street, a smile finally on that downer face.

"Why do you laugh, Ms. Herschel?"

She stopped and looked at me, "Hyuk! Hyuk! Pssst, Willow..."

"What did you just say?" I am Sarah Johnson.

"Ha ha, you're sooooo funny!" She grabbed my hand and pulled me closer, "Hey," she whispered. "I'm here to get you out of here. Willow, yo, you there?"

"I...what are you talking about?" Breakdance.

"Holy shit, you're really fucked up."

"Language."

"Jesus, follow me." She pulled my hand hard. I tried to pull away, but it was useless. I wanted to scream for help, I saw Mr. Eggers on the other side of the street on this hot and cool day, but I didn't say anything for some reason.

She led me through a yard, out to the forest behind it all. It muddied up my clothes, "Why do you have to do this, Ms. Herschel? Why don't we go back home?"

She tugged again, real hard, "We're not going back, Willow. Just shut up and follow me." She took a sharp turn and forced me through a mess of brush.

"The Boss told us never to go into the forest! Ms. Herschel, please! I don't want to go!"

"Just." *Push*. "Fuckin'." *Pull*. "GO!"

I went flying over a log which introduced my face to the ground. "SHIT!" I was shocked at both the pain and my newfound choice of language. I could almost see this woman smile as I cussed.

"WHERE IS SHE!" A brass voice trembled the ground

and shook the earth. The Boss.

Like a lightswitch, the day turned to night and everything went to pitch. I almost said something but Ms. Herschel covered my mouth with two hulking hands that stopped me from saying anything to anyone. I feel as if I should fight but something deep down stopped me. *Willow*...I know that name. Ms. Herschel had pretty eyes. Should she be wearing glasses? Those would have made her look better. "You gonna come with me?" she asked.

I nodded and her hands raised from my mouth. Something compelled my psyche to speak, "BOSS!" Yelled a voice that sounded like mine, controlled by something that was not me.

Her hands came back in a rush as she looked left and right, "Screw it." She said and raised her hand and lowered it swiftly in a grueling punch that hurt like hell and reeled my brain to the front and back of my skull. "Dammit. You're supposed to be knocked out." And she punched again and again and again until it all went black like this new night that surrounded us.

*

Scarlet

Jesus fuckin' A, dawg. Jesus fuckin' A.

"Jesus fuckin' A." I said out loud as I looked down at the swelling face of Willow, my best friend, I think. I shook my hand and took a step out of her cell and made my way down the cold stone hallway towards the bathroom. My knuckles hurt like fuck but it always felt better to run some good cold water over them. That's what I was doing earlier, trying to wrap my mind around whatever the hell was happening while waiting for Willow to wake the hell up.

The water was cold. I watched the blood trickle off and down the sink hole. It was a dance in a way. A weird dance. Breakdance. And I sat, watching it, thinking about what I was going to tell Willow to try and convince her ass that we need to get the hell out of here. And I think I know how. But I have to convince her first. I remembered her better when she was younger, but we've both grown up I guess. Her a little taller, not that much, and her face got more defined too. But nothing else really changed about her. It was her, even with these muddled memories. It was her! I fucking know it is. Not this wack Sarah Johnson BS.

There was a sudden pounding down the hallway. There she was slamming her hand on the metal door to the rung ladder that led up and out of here. Good thing I had the key for it, she wasn't getting out.

"Yo, you're not leaving, man!"

"Let me out of here! I am Sarah Johnson, not some Willow or whatever you're talking about! I want to go back to work!"

I walked up to her and threw her down, she was still light and I knew, for sure, that I could kick her whiney ass to kingdom come if I wanted.

"Ow! Stop, please!"

"Willow!" I grabbed her shoulders. "Look at me. Look at my eyes!"

Her squirming lessened. I could see it in her eyes, those blue annoying things, she wanted to recognize me. I broke through that first dogshit barrier. "Better?" I smiled. "Hey, I'm sorry for beating you senseless earlier, but I wasn't getting caught." I was sorry, her face was swollen and purple, especially her left eye, but fuck her anyways. "You do know who I am, right? I am Scarlet Miller. We were neighbors. I'm your mo' fuckin' best friend."

"I...I know no neighbor like you...I...I..."

I pulled her up like some little kid and brought her back to that cell with her bed, "Sit down. Now!" I practically threw her onto that hard bed and pulled a chair out, sat, and kicked my boots up. "Alright. Now you know I will beat your ass senseless again. Now listen to me, please. Willow."

She pouted with her swollen face, but didn't say

anything more.

"Alright, good. Ima try to categorize this shiz in the best way possible. Okay, I remember seeing you move in. We hanged. You were kinda weird but just what I was looking for if that makes any sense. You were good to talk to, good to feed off of and regurgitate. Weird way to say that I had fun bantering with you. You were a small little thing, scruffy black hair, dark blue eyes, and pale ass skin, but either way, I liked that look. It was cute. I only knew you for like a week but I felt it was good enough to invite you trick-or-treating. I mean, I didn't really know anyone else to invite so good enough, right? We went at it and you were exactly how I thought you would be, shy and scared to do the routine. *Whatever*, I thought, I was all like, *whatevs dawg, lets go to that corn maze I talked about too.* It was pretty lame, but I remember dying there. I remember forgetting who I was. Scarlet Miller but with a big ass spike running through my chest. But, even still, does dying mean forgetting? It was weird, like my mind was getting sucked out like some vacuum. I felt that fucking finger picking through my head, finding what it needed and taking what it wanted. Of course, I remember now. But, suddenly, I found myself in this weird neighborhood. Looked 1950's-ish. And I thought I was called Grace Hershal. And I went by that for...I don't know how long. I abided by The Boss and worked happily with these fucking uncomfortable dresses and I remember loving it.

And then I saw you walking down the street on one of those work days, and all thoughts of happiness left my small fucking brain and I almost fucking fainted from how much my head hurt as I started gaining all of these weird memories with you that I thought I never had, but they were there, and I knew that they were there and I knew that they were fucking fucking FUCKING real. And then I remembered that I was Scarlet Miller. And that you are not Sarah Johnson, but Willow Pines. My best fucking friend. I remember everything. I remember disappearing and I remember kissing you. I remember all of it even if I'm still not sure what this whole fucking place is. I ran and jumped into the forest like The Boss said not to and I found this place, under some leaves. A hatch into a layered fuckin' nuclear armageddon hideout. And I got some other stuff to show you. But first, I need you to remember who you are."

"You...what...I...you..." she looked away, "I don't know..."

Fuck it. Last resort. I grabbed her annoying swollen face and just slammed my lips against hers, tongue and all. It was awkward and gross and uncomfortable, but I kept at it and she didn't stop me. Afterwards, I wiped my mouth and wanted to spit. Her gums were bleeding. But I swallowed instead. "So?" I asked, brushing some hair out of my face.

She nodded slightly, "Yea... Holy shit, what's with this fucking dress?" She picked up the bottom with disgust.

"That's my girl," and I smiled.

*

"You said you knew a way out of here?" Willow asked as we walked and talked down a stairway to the magnum opus of this little complex.

"I did. But it'll require a little bit of...training."

"What?" she asked as we reached the bottom door.

"One second please," I fished through a small ring of keys that I found when I snuck in here. It opened everything around here, but the annoying part of it all was finding the motherfucking correct key. None of them are labeled! But I found the right one, I memorized it like some smart mo' fucka, and slotted that bastard in. One satisfying click later and I pushed open the door and stepped inside with a fat smile crossed on my fat lips, "This, Willow, is the fucking ARSENAL!" I spread my arms out and screamed the last word which echoed along the pure length of the room. On the back wall sat racked thousands of guns all lined up and ready to go, an almost infinite amount of ammo sitting below them. Handguns, SMGs, rifles, automatic and bolt and semi. Heavy machine guns that even I couldn't even lift. Further down sat rocket launchers, racks and racks of all kinds of grenades from white phosphorus and smoke and flash and HE. Further down sat rows of especially sharp knives and tactical vests of all sorts. All clean, all ready, all amazing to look at. On the other wall sat ranges going meters to leagues back, some as long as football fields, practice for close quarters combat, practice for long range, practice for each and every type of gun and CQC possible. Dummies sat further down, ready to punch as well as bags and bags of punching bags and wraps for hands. The door on the other end led to a matted out training room ready for practice in wrestling, boxing, each and every type of martial arts under the sun also fitted with a giant weight room filled with all kinds of racks and benches and plates of all weights and sizes. Deadlift racks and squat racks galore meant for tens of people and not just two. A kitchen stocked with every food imaginable and cabinets and cabinets of food for days. Blenders and mixers and fruit and vegetables for smoothies. And it was all wrapped up in a surrounding white that reflected everything off of everything, each wall was pearl and bone colored. Perfect. It. Was. Perfect. "This is the plan, Willow." My voice echoed even more, off of all the guns and ammo and amazingness. It smelled like life.

"Your plan is…to kill everything?"

"Yes sir. But we have to train. There's a kitchen stocked, there're guns for days, and theres just us to fucking fight our way out of this hell hole and get back to whatever the fuck is going on on Earth."

"Scarlet…everyone is dead back there on Earth. I don't know what else to say. I killed them all."

I shook her, "Willow! Even if that bullshit is true, which it's not, would you rather stay here in ditz-land? Working in some hot dress all day long, slaving under some fucker who calls himself The Boss? Like, we don't even know what the fuck is going on or why there's this giant fucking range of guns or all of this food or really anything, but its here for a reason. Also, have you seen The Boss? He looks like that First Disciple. Don't you see? That is him! He fucking has you in some vice-lock!"

"But I...what's the reason anymore...what's the purpose of all of this? What's the purpose of even trying when everything might be dead? He told me about a land after death called the mindpool. Maybe we're here. Maybe that's what this is. Maybe we can be with each other for the rest of time."

Oh I wanted to beat her ass again. "Aren't you tired of bending over backwards for these people? For these things? For The Boss who is really just First, or the First Desiple or whateverthefuck? All to be just thrown in some fairy land after being tortured constantly for five fucking years? Let's kill them all! Kill the Boss! Have some fucking payback! Listen: All of that stuff back on Earth, or outside of this fucking weird loop-land, it was all bullshit with a giant capital B. Bull-fucking-shit. Didn't you see what they did to you? They fucking ruined your head."

"How do you know he was lying?"

"BULLSHIT! TORTURE! That's what it all was! Lie after lie after lie, messing your head. This 'Key' thing? Bullllllllllllllllllllllllllllshittttttttttttttttttt! And you know it. None of us are specially born from some hole! None of us are born special. Not some special birth or some special prophecy or some god changes any of that because you are you and I am me and I am getting fucking tired of all of this. I look at this world, this one little neighborhood, and I want to vomit. And even if it is true, who cares? Let's kill him! I can see you back there on earth or whatever, I can see your mind, I can see how the world treated you, I can see how it all fucked you up all because of him. Are you going to let them get away with all of that? ARE YOU? NO! I'M NOT LETTING IT HAPPEN AND NEITHER ARE YOU! GET FUCKING MAD! GET MAD AT THEM USING YOU. GET MAD AT THEM LYING TO YOU. GET MAD AT PEOPLE WALKING ALL OVER YOU. DON'T JUST COMPLY, FIGHT. FIGHT FOR YOU, FOR ME, FOR THAT FUCKED UP FAMILY THAT YOU THINK THAT YOU HATE. FIGHT! LET'S TAKE BACK WHAT'S OURS. OURSELVES. OUR LIVES. OUR LIBERTY. OUR LOVE AND OUR HATE. OUR SMILES AND OUR FROWNS. MY LIFE AND

YOURS. WE WILL TAKE IT BACK AND RE-ENTER INTO A WORLD DESTROYED OR NOT BECAUSE WE WILL NOT TAKE THIS SHIT ANYMORE." I swallowed all of this spit that almost frothed at this raging mouth, "Willow. Don't you see that this is our last chance. Maybe we won't find out what this world is or what happened to earth or why there's a giant bunker down here with all of these guns and all of this random ass dogshit. I think I'm tired of asking questions. I remember being killed. I remember the pain. I remember working here for some odd amount of time, all happy and shit. But when I saw that face of yours, I remembered all of these thoughts that I never had. I think that 'me' back on earth, wasn't really me. It was another one of those things, Third, they called it. Another disciple. They killed me, took my body, and pranced around with it for all of those years hypnotizing you to follow their commands. Even if you think that you were fighting it, you weren't. And thinking about that makes me angry. It makes me so fucking mad that they got me so easily and I fucking LET them. And then I see you: five years of torture and it makes me almost want to cry. I want to go and cry like some small little girl because I'm really fucking scared. I want to cry because I love you. I want to cry because I think of all those times where you felt so cold and sad, awake all night, hungry and drained, where I never went to help you. And we let them win. He won. He won then and he may still win in the end, but Willow, I don't want him to win anymore. We were losers for all of this time. Losers at school, losers in life, losers to these monsters who take what they want and don't fucking care. Willow, I'm tired of losing. And even if we die out there, even if this is all for nothing, I want to try." I held out my hand, "I'm scared Willow. I don't want to be scared anymore. Let's be winners for once."

Willow sat there for a long while. I wish there was a clock up on the wall so we could hear that droning tick and tock as we stood in this vast expanse of guns and training equipment, but it was all quiet and still. My mouth was dry and my eyes hurt. Her eyes lulled into mine and I could see her thinking, but those thoughts were hidden. Her lips quivered and her eyebrows moved up and down just slightly like a little tiny shutter as her mind rolled. It was annoying.

"Scarlet," Willow finally said. "I don't know about all of this and I still don't really understand what's happening," she smiled, "but if I could see that bastard squirm, then I'm all for it." We shook good and hard. Her hand was soft and brittle, but that was all about to change. "What now?"

"We train. Let's get fucking jacked." Oh I wish I had some cool ass shades or something.

"What about The Boss?"

I laughed, "The Boss won't find us till we're good and ready. Let's kill that fucking bastard piece of shit."

23

Mark

The hatch popped with a *chi-cink* and opened to a moon veiled night froth with a boiling mist that muddled and pondered through the trees around them. Off in the distance was the target: one singular neighborhood ending in one large factory that spewed out a large red carpet from its metal maw, like a beckoning felt tongue. It fed on all of these people, if that's what they were, stuck in this weird little world created by this man coined as The First Disciple or The First Apostle or The Boss. They were going to kill him though, they both were thinking about it as one slinked out of that heavy hatch and the other followed suit, letting it shut with the help of her strength, closing it without a single decibel of sound.

They were suited in black from head to toe, two ninjas clad in the very night that they stepped through, dodging from tree to tree, trying to see their objective in front of them. Underneath their tactical vests they both wore a thin stab-proof vest appropriated for movement more than safety. At the smaller ones waist was strapped a Walther PDP handgun, loaded with 18 rounds and a Glock 34 handgun, 17 rounds and a classic 1911 pistol, .45 acp, 8 rounds. Slung over her shoulder was a M24 bolt-action sniper rifle. At her right shin was strapped a long sharpened buck knife and on her left, under the pant leg, was a Glock 43 micro-handgun. On her chest, the thin tactical vest she wore held several handgun and M24 magazines and bullets. And on her face she wore a grimace as the first moments of their plan started to tick into action.

The taller one had two Glock 34 Pistols strapped to her waist as well as a Smith and Wesson Model 19 classic revolver ringed with 357 magnum rounds fitted with a walnut grip, tucked neatly into the belt at the back of her pants, polished to perfection. Both her legs were strapped with several types of knives. Slung across her wide shoulders was the slick Benelli M4 semi automatic gas-operated shotgun, a HK416 assault rifle, and a large duffle bag filled with even more ammo and mags and grenades ranging from High Explosive (HE) to smoke. On her chest was a thick tactical vest that held all the mags and ammo that it could, wrapped up with a bandolier of shells that would slide into the Benelli M4 with the speed of a puma, as she practiced for days on the end of days to get it right and efficient.

After a day or two (or three?) into training, she cut her hair short and kept it that way. The long strands annoyed her to no end as she trained. She wore a black bandana tied around her forehead and her face painted almost completely black, her emerald eyes the only color there.

As they stealthily hopped a fence, Willow knew they were here: This was her old house. "You okay?" Scarlet whispered, adjusting her shoulders. Willow only nodded and moved on to the glass back door that she remembered looking out of all those years ago when she first saw The First Disciple or, as they finally dubbed him, 'The Enemy'. And The Enemy only deserves one thing: death.

It was quiet tonight as it has been since Willow's escape. It sat silent and still as if it were stuck in time, waiting for her to come back. They tried to explore deeper into the forest some nights before, scouting the world but, a mile or so in, it ended in a thick black wall that reached up higher than the tallest tree. Willow laughed quietly to herself as she remembered being so scared of that forest all those years ago. A labyrinth she called it, only for it to just end abruptly in a black wall. That black wall ringed around the entirety of this place, trapping them all. *Screw that wall,* she thought and then she shrugged and thought again, *Eh, fuck that wall.*

Scarlet tugged slightly at the glass door, but found it locked. She grunted in annoyance and zipped open the duffle bag and brought out a cordless, absolutely silent, drill and started to get to work breaking a deathly quiet and careful hole into the glass door. "Why don't we try a window?" Willow asked.

"I didn't bring this for nothing," Scarlet said, smiling.

As she got to work, Willow thought about the time that has gone by in that bunker. Each and every day they trained with each other for 18 hours, or what felt like it. Every day was the same down there, fulfilling and tiring. They woke at 6 am with a four mile run which they could barely even do when they first started. Then it was on to a large breakfast of protein and oats and fruits and vegetables, eggs and rashers of bacon, sometimes protein bulked pancakes and waffles if they were feeling a little saucy. Then they went to the range and practiced trigger safety, what not to do with a gun, how to use it, trigger discipline, and, finally, shooting. They both found what they liked: Willow liked the more elegant art of ranged shooting, finding joy in calculating bullet drop and velocity. She liked the feel of the stock bucking back at her like some type of controlled bronco. She liked watching the practice targets of sandbags and straw melt with only the slight tug of her finger. She imagined shooting The Enemy many times.

While Willow took the ranged assignments, Scarlet took on, as she called it, the 'bruiser' archetype. She loved the close quarters affairs: shotguns, knives, shoulder throws, all of it.

The power of both herself and her weapons put a lovely smile onto her face when she thought about it. Willow remarked at her all this time later. Not only did she seem taller, but she was bulkier, with arms like corded steel, a stomach of abs, and thick meaty legs. She always beat Willow in their spars, but Willow too gained some muscle. Where she could barely bench press a weightless bar to now, where she could rack and max 185 pounds with little stress. She was proud of herself. Her mile times soared quickly going from 15 minutes to 10 to a constant 6 as her flab turned to ab. Food tasted like food and sleep was found quickly at the end of the night. Her eyes no longer bulged with black masses of tired accord, but now they stood sharp and awake with awareness. She almost reeled at the taste of food, forgetting completely how good it was to actually eat. Smell has come back, with Scarlet no longer smelling like Thanksgiving while these people of the neighborhood didn't look like zombies. The world smelled clean, the only shit coming from the thought of The Enemy.

Scarlet found a delight in the art of weightlifting, quickly finding that she was a natural at it. Her squats got heavier, her deadlifts soared, and her bench presses felt healthy as she went from chest one day, to legs the next, switching Romanian and traditional deadlifts up as much as she wanted. Arms the next, finding a good rhythm with her barbell curls and EZ bar tricep presses, her partial deadlifts and low pulley rows built her back as her wrists got even stronger with her love of wrist curls fitted with a weighty barbell, and her core only built in strength as she easily popped hundred pound cable crunches and hundreds of incline sit ups, russian twists, you name it. Her shoulders bulged with strength, the weight of all of the stuff she was carrying barely even noticeable. *Glad she's on my side,* Willow thought as she watched her finish her drilling. Scarlet brought out a small metal bit and slid it easily into the hole until the bulge of the bit hit the glass, stopping it halfway through. "And here we go," Scarlet whispered to herself as she brought out a micro hammer from the core of her duffle bag and, with barely any of her massive strength, she tapped the hammer to the bit. *Poof.* The glass fell to the floor without a sound, leaving a clean and glassless opening for them to slip into.

The inside of the house was dead and silent, something that Willow remembered without eagerness. Thoughts of her Mom and Dad and those two brothers who she can't even picture in her head anymore. Were they dead on some dead Earth? Or was The Enemy lying? She didn't know. The stairs made no noise like they thought, and each step brought them closer. "We're killing all of them," Willow remembered Scarlet saying as they planned last night.

"But…is that right?" Willow asked, taking a bite of her sandwich.

Scarlet checked the slide of one of the Glocks. Her arm rippled with muscle. "Yes. They're probably all fake or something."

"But you're here and you're not fake. I'm here and I'm not fake. What if those people are…people?"

"Maybe they are, Willow. But look at it this way, we're freeing them. Or, maybe, they have to die to leave this place, eh?" She looked up with her short hair. Willow had just gotten used to it. "Or don't think about it at all, that's what I'm doing."

"But what if…The Enemy doesn't actually die here in this fake world?"

"He probably won't. We don't know what he is. He probably has like fifteen contingency plans. But who cares. I need some payback. Can't just live life with a 0-1 score in his favor."

They just reached the top of the steps and looked out towards all the doors that Willow remembered. Her room, Matt and Jeremy's which always sat empty back on Earth, and her parents room which turned into her Mom's room once her father disappeared.

"You take those two, I'll take these two," Scarlet whispered as she softly set down the duffle bag, her rifle, and her shotgun on the quiet quiet floor.

Willow nodded. She was clearing her room or...what was her room and Matt's room which sat close. Unslinging the M24 sniper, she leaned it on the wall and carefully unsheathed her buck knife, relieving a small weight tied to one of her legs. It felt good in her hands. Weighty and shaped exactly for killing. She remarked at all the knife training they did in the bunker. She tried to suck her nervousness down as she started with Matt's room, her hand reaching towards the door handle. She never wanted to kill anyone before and she had decided to not think about it much, trying to uninvite her mind to that discourse of morality but, in that moment, she started to think about it: *Maybe they're all fake people. Maybe they're not. Maybe you're going to be a murderer. Maybe-* "Shut the fuck up," she whispered at herself. Her stomach swarmed with annoyance. *He fucking hypnotized me* she thought. She wasn't nervous anymore.

The door handle clicked and swung open slowly, the knife in her right and her left up, ready for anything. She only sparred with Scarlet before and always lost, but she was sure she could take on someone who's never done any type of training in their life. She was ready for this, she had to be. There was nothing but dust in that small enclosed room. She left, closing the door behind her slowly. Scarlet was still gone in one of the rooms. Willow turned towards her own room, the last one she had to check. The one she slept in screaming dis-delight for years and years. A room that made her heart thump with a whirr and it flooded her veins with heat and fire. She was mad.

The door opened and she crept in, slowly, making sure not to trip over anything. It looked as she remembered, but with some weird 1950s posters all around. That was the thing that weirded her out the most about this new place, it looked like a contemporary neighborhood but everything was in this weird veil of the 1950s. She shook her head and, step after step, went to the bed. There was a bump under the covers, thick and wide and moving up and down with a slow and rhythmic tune. Someone was here. It was a man, she found. He was clean shaven and looked like someone that Sarah Johnson would have known but Willow didn't. He may have been Mr. Black or Mr. Eggers or Mr. Thomson, but she didn't know and she didn't think about it as the knife went up slowly to his neck. She didn't know even when she plunged it deep into his jaw up into his brain. There was a shake, a jitter, the releasing of his bowels which stunk to high heaven, and then he was still. She twisted once and ripped it out, splattering thick black blood everywhere as it oozed out like pudding from the hole, soaking and inking into the depths of the white bedspread. And Willow realized. *I saw this guy in a commercial before.* And then he started to disintegrate into nothing with little flakes of this and that popping up into an unfelt wind. And then he was gone, the black pudding blood all that remained. She cleaned the knife on the blanket and left the room, shutting the door behind her.

Scarlet stood in the hallway with a look on her face. "What?" Willow asked, quiet.

"There were uh…two in your Mom's room. They weren't your parents, but…I don't know, thought I should let you know."

"Did you…"

"Yea. Their bodies disappeared." She wiped her knife on her pant leg, "You?"

"One. He's gone."

"See? They're probably fake or something."

"Maybe…he looked like someone I've seen before."

"Yeah, that's cause you were part of this fucked up little dictatorship."

"No, no…it was like something else…"

Flush. The bathroom door opened between the two of them and a tall man in his tighty whities stood with a piece of toilet paper stuck to the bottom of his foot. They all sat unmoving, like a trio of deer in a truck's headlights.

"Uh... Hello sir." Scarlet said.

"Wait, I know you two. You're the traitors!"

Scarlet burst into a speedy lunge, tackling his legs and throwing him over her back. He landed with a pound and wheeze as all the breath left his body. She turned swifty and dropped from her full height to a slamming knee full force into the center of his chest, bringing her knife into the side of his throat. She covered his mouth as his eyes bulged with dying. He kicked once or twice, sending the toilet paper flying down the stairs, and then he stopped moving as the sludge leaked from his throat. She stood and cleaned the knife on his shirt. "Guess that works."

"Yeah," Willow said. Her confidence in Scarlet's abilities rose with that single five second altercation. The man frothed and then disappeared, leaving behind the notch of ink-blood on the wooden floor. "You didn't check the bathroom?"

Scarlet shrugged, sheathing her knife, "Forgot about it. Aren't you the one who lived here anyways?"

"Yea, I guess you're right."

And the plan continued. The zipper zipped and Scarlet opened the duffle-bag once more, bringing out two earpieces. She put one in and gave one to Willow. "Check, check." She whispered into hers.

"Roger, Copter." Willow responded.

"Copter?" Scarlet asked?

"Yea, copter. Like a helicopter."

"Why?"

"We totally forgot to get cool code names, man."

"Huh...I totally forgot about those, you're right!"

"Do you like it? Copter? We can change it if you want?"

"Nah, sounds cool. I'll call you...like...Black Raven or something."

"No. That sounds way too edgy. And it should be one word to keep it quick."

"Hmm..." she scratched her chin, "Sniper."

"Sniper?"

"Yea. You're going to be the sniper. I'll just call you Sniper, duh."

"Eh, sounds good enough."

"Alright," Scarlet stood. "Let's get ready."

They split up and went around the house, barring doors with chairs and couches, locking them and blocking windows to the bottom floor. With both of their effort, they dragged the refrigerator to the hole in the glass backdoor.

"Alright," Scarlet said. "How do we get on the roof?"

"Follow me," Willow answered.

They went upstairs and grabbed all of their things. In Willow's room, they propped open the window that looked out towards Scarlets house. The treehouse was gone but it was surely the same place. Scarlet looked at it for a second as she stepped over the window seal and onto the roof. She thought of her Dad and then looked away and continued to move. The roof was slanted, but at the top there was a level spot to lay down flat. They had a view of the entire neighborhood up here and then some, their sightline stretching all the way to the dark factory that sat at the end of the road. That red carpet still slunk out like a tongue to a mouth, beckoning and consuming gluttonously. The factory was laden in silver and copper, growing brown and silver and green all around its rising body. It was taller than any of the houses, rising maybe 500 feet in the sky, hanging over everything. Willow faintly remembered loving her walks to that monstrosity each and every day. Now, looking at it, she was disgusted. And at the top of the big and twisting tower, sat a glass suite, its lights on. It looked almost art deco from down here. But it was so high up, that the two girls could not fully make out what it was. But they knew one thing about it: He was up there. And they were going to kill him.

"There he is," Scarlet said, pointing. "You ready?"

"Yea. You?"

"Yep. Alright. I'll leave the bag with you. You got a ton more ammo in there too. But keep me updated on where you are, man. If I run out of ammo, Imma have to come running back. Keep moving, roof to roof, house to house. I'll keep their attention." She grabbed Willow's shoulder, "I don't know what's going to happen out there, but let's keep it cool and we'll make it, okay?"

"Got it."

"Alrighty." Scarlet stood and adjusted everything on her person, making sure that her equipment was comfortable enough. It felt good and sturdy like her shoulders. She hung two HE grenades off of her vest. All her knives were in place and all the mags where she remembered them. She felt really good. She felt really healthy. She took a breath of the night air and came to the conclusion that that was the single greatest breath of air that she's ever taken. She grabbed the shotgun and slid two of the shells off of her bandolier, sliding one smoothly into the carrier and another into the tube. 9 shells loaded. The HK hung off of her right shoulder waiting hungrily. Everything was ready. She glanced at Willow, nodded, and went to the lowest part of the roof, dropping off of it, landing in a hearty crouch that would have broken the legs of weaker people.

Willow watched her saunter off for a second and then got prepared herself. The M24's tripod was deployed and she set it in the spot she liked the most. A clear shot down the street and towards the factory. She adjusted the scope for a second and tried to look through it towards the top of the tower. The angle was not there. *Whatever, that's not part of the plan,* Willow thought. *Wait...what even is our plan?*

"Copter to Sniper, how's it going up there, over." A voice in Willow's ear buzzed out.

"Almost done, Copter. Over. Where are you? Over." Willow adjusted her position.

"I'm in the bushes right now, waiting for you. Over."

"Copy that. Over."

"Over." Scarlet said.

"Over?"

"Over."

"We don't need to say 'over' each and every time. Over."

"Yea, but we do. Over."

"Got it, Copter. Over. I'll tell you when we're good to set off Operation Kill-Cock. Over."

"Over."

Willow checked everything on her person. She would have to move her spot once it all started but now everything was all good. The pistols were sorted, the sniper was ready, the duffle-bag was well off. Like Scarlet, Willow took a big breath and also decreed that this was the best breath of air that she's ever had circling throughout her lungs. *Ah*...she breathed out. "Commence Operation Kill-Cock. Over." They were ready to provoke him. Make him come out. Kill him like that. But, if things came to it, they were ready to storm that disgusting factory like some commando ops. *We really don't have a plan,* Willow thought. *Eh* and she shrugged.

"Operation Kill-Cock is a go. Over," Scarlet answered. She grabbed her bandana and tightened it a little around her forehead and walked out into the center of the street. Willow followed her through the scope and then moved it towards the dead street before them.

Scarlet screamed, "YO! EVERYONE! HELLO! PEOPLE! ANYONE!" Nothing. Not a peep. Absolute silence. Maybe a cricket. Or two. Or three. Or Ten. Or Fifty. Or a hundred. The constant chirping filled the entire world as thousands of chirps got louder and louder. Scarlet looked around, trying to find out where they were, Willow very much the same. But the sound continued and continued on. And then the ground began to shake.

The factory itself began to rise off the floor, floating higher and higher into the sky, no rockets no nothing. But the chirps got louder and louder and louder. Stop. It was silent and the factory was floating. A hole was left in the ground where it once was. It was maybe 1000 feet up there, just hovering, meandering up and down slowly.

"Ahhhhhhhhhhhhhhh...I see the cats out of the bag." A voice rang out over the neighborhood. "Scarlet and Willow, how nice of you two to leave that ratty ol' bunker of yours." It was The Boss. The Enemy.

The floating factory began to morph and shape itself into solid stone, the copper and iron turned to mortar and rock as parapets rose and smokestacks fell into towers that built higher and higher. Large rolling banners fell from the windows and the walls, all symbols of grueling and twisting fingers. "Jesus fuckin-" Scarlet started.

"-A," Willow finished.

"Now, why don't you two put those little toys down and come around gently." The voice boomed out.

"Fuck right off, dickweed!" Scarlet yelled.

"What can I say then? Do I really have to appeal to you two? It is already done, there is nothing you can do about it anymore."

"Were you telling the truth?" Willow asked. "Was I the Key or whatever?"

"Yes." His voice echoed like it was coming through voice comms from everywhere, the one word reverberating through all the dark houses that lined the dark road.

"Was it all real? Is everyone really dead?"

"There is no use."

"Answer my question!"

"At least here I can set things right."

"What are you talking about? Where are Third and Second? What are they?"

"They are me. All split segments that have finally been put back together. I am whole..." The Enemy took a breath out into whatever he was speaking into. "I'm sorry. Now you both really have to die."

Every door to every house down the road opened at once and an army of men charged out like a fleshy tsunami of gnarled faces and weapons ranging from war-axes to swords and shields to mauls and warhammers to tautly wound crossbows. The hoard filtered out onto the street, all wearing kilted doublets that spread out in a red gash in the shape of a finger. Some wore helmets ranging from kettle helms to full facial great helms and more and more. They plunged down the street and then stopped a couple houses down from Scarlet who snapped the safety off of her HK rifle, watching wearily out towards the giant crowd which only grew. She looked back at Willow's house and saw the scope of the rifle reflect the moonlight from above as Willow's heart jumped slightly. Their plan was to provoke, but if this is just a tap, what would a full shake cause?

Scarlet knew that she wouldn't survive out here on the street, she would have to retreat into the barricaded house and then they could make a stand in there. *We really don't have a plan, huh?* Scarlet figured. But there was no time to relent how dumb their 'plan' was as they were about to be in the thick of it all.

After a second, she saw that the wave of men had crossbows instead of rifles, shields and swords instead of pistols and riot shields. *Medieval shit.* The bodies kept piling, and Scarlet grew unsure with time. Did they even have enough ammo? Should she shoot or wait? *Stay calm, stay calm.*

The wave stopped completely still.

The Enemy started, "I don't really know what to do to be honest. You see, isn't it funny? I'm still conflicted about it all." He chuckled.

Scarlet barely even heard him as she tried to think of a way inside Willow's house, but all they had was the roof. "Psst...Sniper. Go down and unlock the front door so I can get back in. Over..."

"Roger. Over." Willow whispered. She stood swiftly.

Scarlet had to stall, let him ramble or get him to ramble *Uhhhhhh* she thought.

"I don't even know anymore," The Enemy said, his voice sounding as if he were shaking his head back and forth.

"Yo, why are they like that?" Scarlet pointed at the mass.

"Eh." You could feel his shrug.

"Why are you so, like, nonchalant?"

"What?"

"You're all sad sounding!" Scarlet said.

"Oh, sorry. Forgot that I'm trying to kill you guys or something..."

While this slow slog of an exchange took place, Willow booked it like no one has ever booked it before, vaulting through the window of her old room, slamming through her old door and down her old stairs, right through her old living room. She tried her hardest to quickly move the barricade in front of the door as she heard whatever dialogue was going on outside the walls of this old, gray, spartan house that was just waiting to turn red. Willow took a breath and pulled back the last barricade, a couch that she never sat on before, and reached over to the bolt on the door, un-bolting it and saying, with a *Bzzt*, "You're good. Over," on the radio. She turned and booked it back upstairs.

Scarlet heard at the last second.

"-Alright..." He cleared his throat as if he were getting back into the right mindset for villainous reveries, "Kill them! Mwahahahahaha!"

Scarlet grabbed her rifle without a word. She aimed and squeezed the trigger, ramming shot after shot out as she started running back to the house, the bullets slamming through this head and that, stapling the front of their skulls to the back. The sound deafened her for the moment, her ears ringing as she bounded from the hoard, her rifle poised.

The crowd roared forth, screaming and yelling, chasing Scarlet as she bolted towards the house. Willow was already back to her spot, laying down, breathing hard, she aimed the rifle and found one gaining on Scarlet. Following...fire! Boom! The gun roared back painfully into her shoulder as the bullet steamed out of the barrel, making a large hole in that man's stupid looking face. He scattered across the ground and was gone in the second as the crowd trampled and ran him over, screaming. *Chunk-chink!* The bolt slotted and Willow fired again, the stock ramming her shoulder again to lesser effect. She liked the pain anyway. *Chunk-chink!* Again, another bullet ready.

Thunk! Thunk! Scarlet was finally at the door and she grasped the handle and dove inside, slamming the door behind her, locking it. Instantly, the wood started buckling and scraping as the force of what seemed like a thousand people pounded against it. "Shit! Shit!" Scarlet swiftly set the barricade as quick as she could. She could hear the rhythmic shot, shot, shot! That rang out from the roof as Willow pulled the trigger, *Chunk-chink*ed, and then pulled again, round after round killing like fish in a barrel.

Her ear pricked up slightly as she heard the kitchen erupt with sound. "Fuck Me!" She ran over there and found that they had already surrounded the entire house. They slammed against the refrigerator which was already sliding back easily as if it were on a floor of butter. She brought up her rifle and squeezed again and again, rounding their heads into black inky goo, spreading their stuff everywhere, but more kept on coming. Her ears rang with delight.

Click! Mag empty. Within a second, her training came to boot. One quick button press, one fling of the mag, and her hand had already found another one and slid it in, *cli-tink*, and it was back in action. *Thud thud thud!* Rounding another skull and another, felling them where they stood, but more kept coming and more kept pushing. Thinking quickly, she ran back to the living room and swiftly moved one of the couches to the kitchen, pushing it as fast as she could. She tried to block the kitchen door in an impromptu barrier. *Good enough, maybe.*

Willow was picking them off easily as aim wasn't a problem, it was the sheer abundance. Mag empty. She got a new set of judgment lead in quick. *Grenades!* She thought and stuck her hand in the duffle bag, lining them up in a row before her. Ten HE, five incendiaries, and a couple smokes. With a pull of the pin she threw one of them, and then another, and then another, all deep into the crowd. Three dull thuds came ringing out, making little holes of people and blood until they got swallowed up by the tsunami once again. An arrow flew by her head and she ducked. "Oh you shitter," she whispered as she took aim, found the crossbowman trying to rapidly row the string back for another arrow, "Goodnight, bitch," and with a five pound pull the the trigger, the crossbowman's head was gone in a red haze like a morning mist.

Scarlet heard the booms on the ground from outside. *Good girl,* she thought as she continued to defend the kitchen from the growing hoard. *Wait.* She grabbed one of her own grenades. *Wait.* The fridge toppled and hit the floor. *Now!* A pin pull, a throw, another pin pull, another throw, both HE's sent into the rapidly filling kitchen. Scarlet shot another couple of times, shredding the heads of two men who both started to climb the couch barricade and then she slid behind one of the walls and...*BOP! BOP!* She took a peek and saw the kitchen torn to tinsel as hanging bodies and shredded corpses littered the entire floor. Some were dragging themselves pathetically held together by will and strings of muscle. Scarlet laughed and pulled her gun up again, taking a knee at the couch, continuing her firing into the bloody oblivion, killing more that entered. *Click!* Empty. She grabbed one of her pistols and pulled it up as her finger ticked the mag release of her rifle, dropping the empty mag to the floor with a thud that was lost in all the droning chaos of sound and gunshots and pure noise. Holding the rifle between her left forearm and bicep, she laid the butt on her knee, grabbing at her vest for another mag, firing her pistol, killing all who went through the glass hole in the kitchen. A small *tink* sounded out as the mag slid in and a loud *click* came from her pistol which just emptied itself into the fresh corpses in front of her. She dropped the pistol to the floor, uncaring, and brought the rifle up once more. *Fuck it* she thought and flipped it from semi to full auto, spraying swarths of hot lead into those cold bodies.

Pin, pull, throw. Pin, pull, throw. Willow kept hucking

them off the roof, finding the tightest formations of the mob, making sure to keep up with sniper shots, trying to find and eliminate all of the crossbowmen she could spot, lest she wanted an arrow sheathed in her skull. Some flew by, some close, some far, but they always gave their positions away. Pin, pull, throw, and an incendiary grenade went aloft in the air, filling the dark sky with light and then it crashed and burned, sending death rattling screams up from the crowd. The smell of barbeque emanated up from the burning things. She licked her lips.

And then she was back on the gun, firing, clearing headaches and fixing cleft chins with a single pull of the trigger and swift pull of the bolt. All around her rolled empty brass cylinders. Some were hot and burnt her slightly as she constantly shifted. She could hear Scarlet somewhere in the kitchen, firing and firing and...automatic machine gunning. There was no time to check in as both her hands were dealing with a gun, grenades, and the bag. The ten HE's were down to two and there was one incendiary left. *Screw it!* She grabbed the two HE's, popped them, and hucked them. Thud, thud. Waves of groans and death rolled out from the people tsunami, but they still pushed and pulled.

The front door cracked with a wood breaking slam. *Slam! Slam!* Scarlet looked behind herself for a moment and saw the door topple and splinter as the barricade behind her filled with bodies. "Shit!" She stood and retreated up to the top of the stairs as the swarm connected at the bottom, slamming together like a wave and rapidly bounding up the stairs after her. Her ears rang and her heart pumped rhythmically in her chest. She could hear the repeating sniper shots from up here even better.

Before she hit the top step, she said in the comms, "Bottom floor gone!" And she turned to see them already right on top of her. Her hand twitched and found the **BOOMSTICK** tucked across her left shoulder. She switched grips and, in a second, the entire staircase was filled with nine shells and loads of pellets blasting bone and meat. The wave stopped at her feet and fell back, all the bodies pushing the pursuers behind them down like some macabre Chaplin sketch. She switched grips again and grabbed the rifle, firing into the ones at the bottom of the steps, making sure they couldn't climb over the mountain of bodies. *Thunk! Thunk! Thunk!* They fell and stopped. For a moment the wave at the stairs stopped as it was corked full of bodies and brains.

She grabbed at the shotgun and her bandolier of red death pills, placing the butt on her shoulder, and sliding each pill in with quick precision, one, two, three, four, five, there's one! The gun went into ready instantly and blew a head clean off, painting the wall with black thick pain. And back into reload, five, six, seven, she propped another shell into the mouth and fed it well. Turning now to the rifle, she checked the mag: half full. She felt her vest and found a couple more mags to feed it. Her bandolier was still pretty full and her other glock and revolver were both ready to go. "Come on fuckers!" They came in response, filling the hall with a series of mountain climbers, this being their Mount Everest and the lead that rained down on them like snow. The air was thin up here, but Scarlet loved it and she smiled as her ears rang in pure pleasure.

Click, empty mag. Switch grip, shotgun. 8 shots rang through, the stairway being the green mile, and Scarlet their executioner. Shotgun, empty, dropped to hang as she grabbed the other Glock 34 and found head after head, firing amounts of the 18 rounds into their chests, their mouths, their eyes, everywhere, making swiss cheese out of them, making sure they were going for the 50% sale in the afterlife. *Click!* Mag throw, another, in, fire fire, kill kill. The mountain grew only bigger. Scarlet didn't think about it here, but the bodies were not disappearing like the ones before. She only thought about firing and killing and building that beautiful mushy mountain. She had another second and set to reloading everything that she had, shotgun first, firing when one popped a head out, next the HK, mag in, done. Glock next, mag out, mag in, done. She blinked and shook her head a little. The mountain was full to bursting. From the bottom of the staircase to the top, there was no room to go up or go down. "Jesus fucking Christ," she whispered. But they were there, behind that mass and still around the house, she could hear them through the ringing, droning on and screaming or chanting about whatever.

In Willow's ear, "Copter to Sniper." *Breath*. "Top floor is secured. For now. Over."

"Uh...if it's secure for now, you might wanna come up here. Over."

"Roger. Over."

Scarlet barred the door to Willow's room with a chair fitted underneath the door handle and unstrapped the shotgun, leaning it on the wall for when she had to return. She made her way out of the window and onto the roof, where a couple feet below her sat screaming husks, swinging their weapons up at her to no avail. She flashed her teeth at them and crawled up to the flat point where Willow laid down on her stomach, checking the bolt of the M24. "Hey," Willow looked at her, "look at this-" she beckoned for Scarlet to take a look through the scope.

She hoisted the HK behind her back and got on her stomach, taking sight through the tuned scope. Through it she saw the crowds of finger doubleted husks, armored slightly, carrying all sorts of weaponry. "Did they stop or something?" She asked.

"Maybe. But...look a little up."

She saw two of them wheeling out an old looking cannon, still a little off in the distance. "Really, why are they using medieval type shit?"

"I don't know. But I think I got all the crossbow dudes. Still, keep your head down for the most part. Hey, how'd you secure the second floor? Aren't they inside?" She asked, fixing her hair out of her eyes.

"Let's just say that I put a cork in their bottle for now." Scarlet stopped looking through the scope and let Willow take back her place.

She moved the gun back up, placing the crosshair over the chest of one of the cannon-movers. Her finger quivered for a second and then found itself steady, slightly pulling the trigger. She let out a breath and pulled, blowing a hole in the man, sending him reeling down towards the ground. She smirked, *Target practice.* Her hand pulled the bolt back quickly and set towards the second cannon-mover. Breath in, breath out, and he fell just as gracelessly as the other one. And then she saw the other ones. First it was one, then it was two, now there were four...six...eight- they were growing in number as they stepped out into the clad moonlight, two apiece, wheeling cannons upon cannons, getting closer and closer.

"Oh fuck me," Willow whispered as she started to set her sights on one, firing, bolting, ending.

"Shit. We're gonna have to leave this place."

"Yea but..." she shot, pulled the bolt, and aimed again, "how?"

"I'll think of something, just try to keep those fuckers at bay or we'll get blown to kingdom come. Just give me a minute."

"Minutes ticking-" Fire, bolt, aim.

Scarlet saw the two smoke grenades and the last incendiary grenade and came up with the stupidest plan she could possibly ever think of. She grabbed them, vaulted down towards the window to Willow's room and rolled in, grabbing the Benelli off the wall and kicking the chair from the door. She opened it quickly, pointing the shotgun out into black nothingness as the smell of brass blood crept into her nose. She took a couple of steps over towards the staircase and looked down to find it still clogged up with man after man. She could hear them gnawing at the pile, pulling corpse away from corpse, freeing a path.

She looked at the three grenades that she brought: Two

smokes and one fire. With a breath, she pulled the pin of the incendiary grenade and rolled it down the stairs towards the pile of fuel and blood. It sputtered and sent flames across each step it touched, fire beckoning from its growing maw which consumed with the power of hell. It hit the bodies and stopped for a second. Scarlet was worried that it wouldn't light but her worries were cast away with another shot from above as the entire pile went up and began to burn and catch on the walls and the ceiling, trailing down and making thick viscous smoke spew up towards her. She coughed and ran back to the window. "Alright, time to pack up!" She screamed into the night and the comms.

"Roger." Willow said, instantly grabbing her rifle and stoking the tripod, pulling the weapon over her shoulder. She grabbed the significantly lighter duffel bag and hurried to the window where she found Scarlet sitting on the window seal, waiting for her. She sat looking down into the husks below her as they mindlessly waved their weapons up at them. "So?" Willow asked, fearing the first shot of a cannon at any moment. She tried to cull their wave, but they kept coming, and they were coming faster than one might think.

"Look at them all," Scarlet said ponderously. Her shotgun was sat across her lap and her rifle slung across her back. Willow finally saw all the black blood that caked her clothing, spattered across her arms and her legs and her chest and her face. "Don't they remind you of something? Just looking at them all."

"I guess, but this isn't the time for shit like this, what's the plan?"

"I set fire to the house, Willow. This is our only way out." Her head nodded to the crowd below. "If we can get through them, then we can hop the fence over to my house. The treehouse is gone, but I know that place pretty well." Her hand lazily rose and two smoke grenades hung from her fingers by the pin. "I got these. We can toss one down there and just blind stride it."

"I-"

"No time to argue!" Scarlet cut her off. "It's beginning to smell like Thanksgiving!" She smiled and pulled the pin on one of the smokes, tossing it gingerly into the crowd below. In a few seconds white smoke began to froth through the crowd, more and more by the second. It wasn't a perfect cover, but it should do.

Willow's heart raced.

"Well," Scarlet readied the **BOOMSTICK**, "let me clear a little path."

Eight shells popped out of the gun within five seconds, clad in death smoke, bringing chaos to the things below, annihilating skulls and bone and brain, felling most of the ones in their path. The sound rocked their ears, the chug of the shotgun beautiful in its destruction. They would have to take their chance quickly lest the hole filled back up. Some still stood, seemingly unharmed. "Go!"

Scarlet dropped swiftly and gracefully, landing in a crouch which helped her spring off and start the short run to the fence. Willow followed behind just slightly, landing and dropping the duffel bag. Her mind never went to picking it back up as the enemies began to face and swarm them. Instead her hand went to her waist, and enclosed around a pistol, the Walther PDP, she knew by the grip alone. She began to run, firing and dodging the entire bloody way to the fence, dodging enclosed fists and weapons. A sword swung at her, but she ducked just enough to miss a body cleaving blow. In response the sword swinger got a bullet in the brain and he dropped back into the crowd as if he were made of jelly.

Scarlet wrestled through the last couple who stood, her mind annoyed at them for not dying when she rained hot lead down onto them like a storm. Two were in front of her. She gripped the shotgun more like a baseball bat, swinging at the first one with a skull cracking blow, sending him and his giant warhammer to the wet floor. The next she dodged back from a grisly maul swing. With that second, she closed in on him, getting low to the ground in almost a crouch and, in one movement, sending the barrel of the Benelli into the chin of the cladded finger-warrior. They fell to the ground, the barrel still nestled under his chin. Scarlet swiftly popped a shell from the bandolier while opening the slide, ghost loading right into the tube, blasing the entire top of his head off in a mushroom cloud of pink brain and black blood. He slid with the force. She chased after his corpse and began to hop over the top of the tall fence, pulling herself up easily with those strong arms. Willow was right behind her and started her ascension quickly, jumping a decent height and landing in a pile of herself on the other side.

"You okay?" Scarlet asked, standing up.

"Yea."

"Where's the bag?"

"Dropped it."

"Eh, whatever. Come on," she held a hand out and pulled Willow up easily. They ran to the back door and Scarlet handed Willow the smoke grenade, "Okay, now go around, fence jump, use that when you need to. Just get behind them."

"What are you doing?" Willow hurriedly asked.

"I'll be here distracting them."

"What? You're going to die!" Willow's heart jumped slightly, this lull in their situation finally letting her brain work.

Scarlet only cocked her head, "No I'm not." She smiled. "Go."

Willow sat almost stunned. She shook her head, "Good luck," she said as she turned and ran to the other side of the backyard, vaulting the fence there.

BOOOOM! The ground rumbled as an entire piece of Willow's house flew off in giant chunks of wood. *BOOOOM!* Another mess of house flew off as the cannons fired rhythmically. *Ah shit,* Scarlet thought.

Willow jumped another fence, and then another, making sure the M24 was still firmly strung across her back.

Another jump, another fence. She couldn't think about Scarlet right now, all she could think about was the cannons and how far she would have to go to effectively sneak around their asses.

Around ten houses down she decided it was a good place to cross. Down the green-grassed fenced alley, she peeked out from behind the wood and saw all the cannons. The ones she put out of commission were still void and dead while another ten were firing merrily and loudly at her burning house. Soon they would find where Scarlet was and turn their attention onto her house. Willow laid down and aimed, but the angle was off, mercilessly. *Shit! No time to think.* She crouched out from the alley and slinked across the street, *Don't see me, don't see me, don't see me.* They didn't.

Scarlet saw the first one poke his head into the open window. Then it was gone in a mist and his body slunk back outside. She popped another shell into the Benelli and waited in the living room. She sat laid back on her old couch which wasn't actually her couch. It smelled different and weird, unlike her Mom or Dad. Her ears still rang and her nose itched just slightly, maybe from the smoke. Earlier, while the mass still had their attention on Willow's house, she had completely barricaded the kitchen, locking the back door, buckling the handle with a chair. She pulled everything she could think of to cover the windows and doors from chairs to couches to tables, until the floor was bare and the walls were some weird looking art piece made of furniture. But this couch never moved. She placed the HK to her right and held the shotgun in her hands. The front door was barricaded enough and she had opened the windows wide, hoping to clog them with bodies instead of wood. Through them came a cool wind that smelled like burnt bodies, blood, and smoke. She breathed in deeper.

Another warrior poked his head through the other window. *Blam!* Then he wasn't looking anymore and would never look again. Another shell in. And then she waited. The cannons still took shot after shot at Willow's house, but soon, once the crowd all moved over here... *Maybe they're dumb and will just keep on shooting at the burning house. Keep thinking that, even when this giant crowd swarms this house. Keep thinking that even when Willow comes around and kills you all.* The kitchen began knocking as they encircled back there. Then the front door. The windows began to fill with faces and each face found another shot as she popped the barrel from one to the other, loading as quickly as she could before another showed up. In a second, a body dropped through one of the windows and he stood up. Scarlet waited for him, watching him stand, wanting to use him for later.

She blew a golf ball sized hole through his chest and he sat back down at the bottom of the window. *Another couple. Come on.* And at the other window she did the same thing. One hopped in and got a hole in their body. Another one, first his arm blew off and spun over towards the wall, splattering everything in thick blackness, and then the next shot found his lower jaw cartwheeling somewhere as he died, adding another body to the blockage. And then another, then another, and she sat for the entire time, feeling the blowback of the shotgun eating away at her shoulder, making it sore and annoyed, but she didn't notice, firing and reloading as quickly as she could.

Soon the windows were full and inaccessible with bodies. The door started battering and shaking even more. She could tell it was going to break soon. She stood, slung the shotgun over her back, and grabbed the rifle, checking the ammo quickly. She walked over to the door and kicked away any barricade she could have put there, moving the chairs and the other couches that she pushed against it. The door splintered in the center. It could not take another hit. She unlocked it and opened it, stepping back as a pile of bodies fell in on top of eachother, laying facedown, squirming like a ton of worms. They were all on the floor, right at her feet, groveling. They looked like they were all praying to God, praying for mercy. With a nonchalance, she flipped it to full-auto and held the trigger down and continued to do so as the heads turned to goo, each bullet puncturing and maiming their skulls, leaving them where they lay.

A firm *click*, resounded from her gun. She hit the mag release and slapped another in and held the trigger once more.

The cannons were starting to turn towards Scarlet's house as they saw the mass move over there. Willow spied this from the fenced alley right behind them. No time to think, she took a breath and pulled the pin of the smoke grenade, throwing it over towards the mass of cannons and their men. Ten cannons left, two men apiece, mindless husks, *I can do this*, she thought as she pulled the M24 out and laid down, flipping the bipod and aiming down the scope. The smoke was doing its job well enough. It blocked their vision while keeping hers decently clean, their backs all big square targets that bullets love to eat. She fired, killing one. *Chunk-chink*, fire. One crew down, nine more crews of two left. Two more men, down, never missing a shot. *Click.* She felt her vest and pulled another mag out and replaced the old one. *Chunk-chink,* the new round was in and she was back to killing. The other crews started to take notice and look around, confused as the smoke started really filling all of their sights. Then they found where she was as she fired another time, making it fourteen crewmen. They all began to rush her position, bare handed, uncaring if they got shot from this almost point blank spot for a sniper rifle.

Scarlet heard Willow's sniper shots and smiled. *Click.* Reload. Then firing, holding that trigger down and finally spraying into the crowd outside of the door. Reload. Firing. Mowing down more and more. Her senses were gone and the world turned into sound and death. She looked almost bored for the moment.

Crash! A window from somewhere, probably the kitchen. Her legs moved towards it, leaving them to crawl over the bodies at the front door. The kitchen was intact and perfectly fine apart from the constant banging and scratching from behind its barriers. Her mind worked for a second, trying to understand where that crash was from when she heard the creak of the stairs just above her, right beyond the bend of the stairway. And then she heard a step and then another. Above her ran boots, heavy and firm, slamming towards the stairs. *How'd they get upstairs?* She thought for a second before hastily taking the stairs down towards her old room. She opened the door and peeked in quickly to find nothing, not even feet at the small rectangular window that sat in the upper corner of the room. That was the window where she dragged Willow through when they were kids. She thought of their first conversation together and remembered being a little weirded out by this meek girl. She smiled and got to business once more, realizing that she was on her last mag for the rifle. Reloaded up, she crouched at the bottom of the stairway and waited.

Click! "Shit!" Willow whispered as she padded the vest for another mag to no avail. She was out. Eleven down. Barreling down the length of the alleyway were the remnants: five and a half men. Halfy crawled slowly, his leg hanging uselessly from a small cord of muscles and tendons, but he didn't seem to care. She stood, grabbing at the Walther PDP, aiming, and firing into the remaining group, hitting arms and legs and chests, some heads, and two more fell as the Walther ran out of ammo. She dropped it without a thought and grabbed the 1911, cocking it in one motion, bringing the bullet into the chamber and into the head of another one of them.

Then the final two were on top of her, giving her no more room to shoot as the first one swiped at her to which she ducked swiftly. The second lunged to tackle her but it was useless as she turned her crouch into a backwards roll, unsheathing the knife on her leg in the process before the first one was in arm's reach yet again. He had a flat face with a fat mouth fitted with a heavy overbite. This was a stranger, but something in his eyes made her brain tingle in recognition. She shook it away as he punched again. She pushed his fist to the side easily and wrung the knife upwards into his armpit and twisted to his wail of pain. Her boot kicked him down to the ground as the second warrior lunged again finally catching her this time, toppling her to the ground with his hands vice-gripped around her wrists, almost breaking them, the knife and pistol in her hands both useless. *Fuck! He's heavy!* He was about twice her size, twice as strong, and weighed twice as much.

She didn't have time to panic as instinct took over: Her left leg weaseled out and curled over his back as the other kneed him in the nuts which loosened his hands for but a second, allowing her to gain control of the entirety of his body as he reeled for his lost children. She rolled him over, using her leg, and wriggled just enough for her knife to find its home in the thickest part of his neck. He died soon after and she stood, pointed the 1911 handgun, and fired two shots into his head. Her wrists stung.

The other one was still reeling with pain on the ground a couple of paces down. She found him and fired a couple more shots into the back of his head. She found the Walther she had dropped and loaded it swiftly, tucking it in one of her many holsters. "Alright," she said, and started hustling towards the cannons when she found the useless half man still dragging himself on the ground. His leg had finally fallen completely off, the tendons and muscle releasing it. She put two bullets in his skull and continued moving towards the cannons which now sat completely empty. "Cannons are clear. Over." *Now how do I use one of these things?*

Now use them! Scarlet desperately wanted to say, but her hands were busy working the assault rifle as it ticked dangerously low on its last mag of ammo. Five more had died up the top of the stairs, some sliding almost completely down towards her and some flying from the impact on the further wall. She could hear more of them upstairs and more of them struggling through the wall of bodies in the living room. The kitchen's barricades fell, she heard them snap with a woody and earthy crack. And more footsteps poured in, stomping and wanting to kill her. Another showed themselves and another died, careening down the first couple of steps. *Bam! Bam! Click!* She tossed the useless rifle and picked back up the **BOOMSTICK**. From her count, she had about four shells left on the bandolier and eight loaded. 12 shots. Then it was on to the handguns. The Glock 34 on one hip and the revolver on her other. Then the knives which peppered her legs.

Everything went silent as she frantically calculated how much ammunition she had left. Willow's shooting had stopped too. Everything turned into a mass of quietness when before it had been bodies and yelling and noise from all the guns firing. She could hear her heartbeat thumping dully inside her chest as she swallowed a raspy wad of spit. *Man, I'm thirsty.* Another empty memory came when the floor had opened up to a rigorous catacomb right under her bed, it seemed like centuries ago. Anger seethed through her veins thinking about it all.

She slid up the wall, standing once again, the shotgun still pointed upstairs waiting for any type of movement to show itself. *Tick...tick...tick...tick...tick...*she heard. Just a slight little sound. A tiny little *tick* that was so small, so tiny, so incomprehensible, that she began to think that she was imagining it.

Step...step...step the floor cracked from above her head, the wood moving in accordance with the weight of someone. No, not someone, many someones. *Step step step step,* they were walking. Then it came to her. *They've cleared the barrier.* Then she heard a clink and a tink and a step and a long *creeeeeeeeeeeeeeeeeeeeeeeeeeeeeeeeeeeeekkkkkkkkkkkkk.*

They're all inside. Her heart slowed down, following that small *tick* that rang silently in her ears.

All of them at once bum rushed the stairs to the delight of Scarlet's **BOOMSTICK** that thrashed steadily through their meat, shredding and piercing multiples of them all. They fell and tripped over themselves, forcing tens down each step at the same time. Scarlet dashed into her room and locked the door, slamming the last shells into the gun. Her bandolier was empty and her gun almost full. She aimed at the wall and waited a second, listening to all of them collide down the steps, their rabble back in full ear annoying action. Then she pulled the trigger until it was done, shredding the wall and the door at the same time, leading the barrel up where she thought the stairs were, eviscerating wood and bone. They screamed and yelped as their legs got blown off and their bodies turned to swiss cheese.

Willow watched the tsunami barrel into the house as they systematically cleared the door from the dead. She turned a cannon towards the mass and looked over it, trying to figure out how to use it. The barrel was smaller than she expected. There were two boxes next to the cannon: One with ammo. The cannon balls, some whole and some filled with a ton of little balls, *grapeshot* she thought, and another held several little bags. She grabbed one and sniffed it. *Gunpowder? Gunpowder!* She rammed the bag of gunpowder to the bottom of the cannon and dropped a grapeshot ball after it. *Now what?* She found a string hanging loosely from the backside of the metal. *Screw it.* She pulled it and watched as the mass in front of her was instantly pulverized into mush, the grapeshot like a giant shotgun blast that killed and maimed fifty men in a giant spray. First she was amazed then she realized that her ears hurt so bad and her eyes seized up from the flashbang of light. But she didn't have time to think further, as what was left of the crowd looked at her and began to run, sprinting, all forgetting about Scarlet. Willow was back at it again, doing it faster this time, getting it done in no time, loading another grapeshot into the tube. But when she ran around to the back this time the string was detached. It was single use. She had no idea where to get more. They were getting closer and closer, a group of about thirty, all wanting to shred her to bits.

She looked down at the rest of the cannons and found one that looked like it was about to fire and all it needed was one good push in the right direction, one pull of that string, and god's work would take over the rest. She sprinted after it, looking over her shoulder only once to see if this would work. *It would,* she seemed to answer back. She got to it quickly, jumping and vaulting over the other cannons which sat useless, and then she slammed her shoulder into it, turning it just enough to where it pointed perfectly into the center of mass, right into the black heart of the crowd. One jump over, one grab of the string, and one thirty pound pull brought a giant flash and a chilling flow of screams that rattled over the entirety of the crowd as the mass of them got culled and split asunder, the grapeshot shredding them and cutting like a hot knife to some stinking butter. Then the sound stopped as her ears rang. And then there was silence. And then there were soft moans emanating from the crowd of broken men all around. Then she heard noise blowing from Scarlet's house, yelling and ripping. She sprinted through the field of black blood and broken bones and soft moans of death. She finally looked at her house, or what was left of it, it sat blackened and razed. She wanted to laugh.

Scarlet was too occupied to have heard the boom above her as Willow finally worked out how to use the cannon. She seemed to have gotten the mass of them congealed in the stairway. The door sat in shatters like the walls around it as maybe about ten trudged and slammed themselves upon the broken wood which still miraculously stood firm, uncaring if it was almost shredded into nothing. Some of them yelled in frustration, some in anger, and some in pain, but they all slammed and tore at the splintered wood with furious anger. The shotgun was out, but she kept it close by just in case. She shakily and quickly grabbed a foreign bed that sat in a corner and pulled it on its side, using it as some sort of cover in the corner of the room. She had reached and tried to open the one small window earlier, but it was stuck and unmoving. *Fuck it,* she thought after another failed attempt and now here she was, waiting for these ten maybe fifteen men to break down her door. In her hands she held the Glock 34 and on the ground at her feet sat one of her knives, the last mag of ammo for the

Glock, and the Smith and Wesson six shooter waiting patiently with thick and velvety 357 Magnum rounds.

Smash! Scrape! Slam! Slam! They stopped for a second and then, all at once, slammed into the door, breaking and shattering it all apart as they fell and flopped onto the carpet of the room. The Glock fired off, taking heads and bodies like a kid in a candy store. Within those eighteen shots, she caught most of them in critical places, making them stop and die. But the ones that came in were not all of them. Two more flooded through the door and rushed her little safety corner. *Click*, she instantly dropped it and grabbed the revolver and fired, *Boom! Boom!* Her wrists shot up from the recoil, hurting, the sound so loud that it reverberated the walls.

The cylinder cycled two magnum rounds out and into their heads, popping them like balloons. That gun always made her hands ache in a good way. Five more rushed in and the revolver found four more victims as she took her time, finding each target and eliminating them with a hearty shot to the chest. She knew it was out after the fourth shot and she grabbed the knife for the last one, vaulting over her little makeshift wall. He was wearing the same finger pictured doublet as the rest of them, but this one wore a hearty helmet and a coat of mail armor down his torso and legs. In his hands was held a thick war ax which looked like it could cut a tree in half with a single blow.

She kept out of its reach, slinking far away for each of his hearty swings as she constantly circled around him, making him fervently turn in frustration. All she had to do was wait until he slips up just a little bit, just one little misstep and she could get within his guard and eliminate him. She feinted up and down, forcing him to swing high and low and short and long. He overcut, letting his arms out too far and this is where Scarlet saw it. She stepped in when she would usually step out to his surprise, dodging the killing blow above her head and stabbing her knife deep into the underside of his arm. He screamed from the pain but she pushed on, slamming him to the ground with a thick shoulder strike. The ax flew with a soft pad across the carpet and Scarlet swiftly kicked him hard in the face, sending his helmet flying and his brain reeling as the world turned into a blur. She sheathed the knife and lifted the war ax up and over her head. "Goodnight," she swung it down, cleaving his head in two, the sharp blade of the ax trailing all the way down to the tip of his spine. He looked like a Picasso painting as his eyes bulged and his last breath whined out in a raspy husk. She let go of the ax and it stuck, leaving a brusque goretastic picture.

Scarlet turned towards the door and readied her knife from its sheath, waiting for more of them. Through the cracks in the wall from where her shotgun had eaten, she saw one smaller entity stepping down carefully over the many bodies and husks that lay gruesomely glued to the floor. Willow turned the doorway and looked around the room, at the dead bodies and the Picasso painting right behind Scarlet. They sat in silence for a moment.

"We killed them." Scarlet whispered, her head reeling.

"We did."

They hugged.

Scarlet realized that she was shaking. Her hands were convulsively opening and closing and her legs felt tingles everywhere as the last of the adrenaline that flowed through her body died away. She felt tired and sore everywhere, but she shook it away and took a breath.

"Hey," Willow said.

"Yeah?" Scarlet answered, still hugging her.

"Look at that."

Scarlet released her hug and looked back to the corner where her bed was all that time ago. On the floor sat a little red button that glowed softly through the black blood that covered it.

The dark maw opened up just like before. They looked down those dark steps just like before.

"Huh," Scarlet said.

"Uh huh," Willow said.

And then they went upstairs, stepping over the sizzling bodies that, all at once, began to flake and disappear into smoke as black as their own blood which utterly plastered almost everything from the steps to the ceiling to the lengths of the walls. Black sludge caked the entirety of the front door and the windows beside it, but the bodies were all gone. The damage was clear, especially in the kitchen where they saw almost the entire wall eviscerated into a gaping hole.

"Huh," Scarlet said as they stepped through it and into the backyard where the treehouse was supposed to be, where they spent so much time together when they were kids, planning to find proof of this monster in the woods. *Does Scarlet even know that that's The Enemy?* Willow thought. But she didn't say anything about it, it didn't matter either way. The castle above them still sat silent, hovering up and down at the 700 foot mark, enormous and elegant with its banners of fingers and its magnificent top floor, fully glassed and windowed, but too far to see anything clearly.

Then they went around to Willow's house and found it smoldering and blackened as the final coals of the fire died out. "That's two of my houses burned down," Willow said. They listened to the small pops and creaks of the dead wood. And then laughter barked out of Scarlet's mouth, Willow joined in, laughing at this dumb hunk of wood. "Fuck this house," Willow said.

"Where'd you drop the bag?" Scarlet asked, looking around the side, still chuckling to herself.

"Over there...oh." They walked around to the side and found where the duffel bag should have been. What sat there was a pile of smoking and burnt cloth. Scarlet kicked it a little and found some spent casings which seemed to pop due to the heat of the fire.

"Well, from my view...I'm mostly out," Scarlet shrugged.

"How much left?"

"Uh, one mag for the Glock and like fifteen hand loaders for the smithy. You?"

"The last of the M24 ammo was," she kicked the bag, "in there. But I got more Glock mags that you can have, I still have a ton of Walther and 1911 left."

"Done deal. You shoulda seen that Benelli man. My shoulder fuckin' hurts but holy shit that mother shredded."

"Well well well..." The Enemy's voice came from everywhere at once, like there were speakers sewed into the ground, in the walls, even in the burnt house that they felt the residual heat ooze off of. "You know I can just send more, right? And more and then more if need be. From alllllllll the way up here in my awesome penthouse thingy. I think I win and you two lose...again!" There was a slow clap from the speaker, "Props to you Willow! Dropping the bag! HA! Wow wow wow! Who would've known that you were going to be the one to ruin this whole little operation of yours." He laughed. "But whatever, it was doomed from the start."

"If you got more, why don't you just send them already?" Scarlet screamed out, trying to catch him in a bluff.

"Oh I would, Scarlet Miller, trust me! But you two deserve the reprieve! Have a little rest! Eat if you must."

"Eat this, dickhead!" Scarlet flipped off the castle in the sky. She nudged Willow who joined in with an equally leveled middle finger.

"How cute. Well...breaks over. Have fun you two."

They heard the screams rushing at them from down the street. "Shit. Willow, he wasn't bluffing."

"Back to your room." Willow commanded and Scarlet nodded. They both hustled double time, hopping Willow's fence and, in a moment, they were already in Scarlet's blackened room looking into the hole in the floor. Scarlet hurriedly found the Glock that she had dropped earlier and reloaded its last mag. She grabbed the revolver and put it away knowing that reloading would take too much time. The floor began to tremble slightly from the finger warriors up above, they could hear their scream more vividly now and there seemed like there were more of them…much more.

"You done?" Willow asked.

"Don't get all sassy on me, and yes. Go!" They started down the blackened steps, straight into the darkness below, this time without any flashlights to lead their path in a mirage of disco and breakdance. Scarlet stuck her hand out and pressed the button once more and the slide of the stairs closed slowly which roofed them in, blocking out all light, darkness being the only thing left. "Well," Scarlet said, her voice swirling off the walls, "We can only go forward now." She thought of breakdance.

"I can't see a thing, hey, grab my hand," Willow reached out into the darkness and felt for Scarlet.

"Ow! You just punched me!"

"Yep! Now grab my hand!"

Scarlet laughed and took it, "Well, the only way is forward, my beloved."

"That it is."

They stumbled through the dark corridors, slamming themselves against unseen walls and echoey surfaces that turned and bent this way and that. It was different than they remember, there being several wild and sharp turns compared to the one or two they experienced before as if it was intentionally trying to get them to break their noses on one of these slick dark walls. They heard the army crash into the house and run above them wildly. "Hopefully they're so dumb that they miss the button to get down here." Scarlet said.

"Eh. Not really thinking about it." Willow said. "Ow!" She slammed her shoulder on another bend.

And through some bumps and turns, some old and some new, they almost fell face first down a long stairway shrouded in darkness. "Holy shit!" Scarlet wobbled the both of them, trying to keep her balance. They settled. "Well, guess we're going down."

They heard a grinding sound that reverberated through the long inky hallways, the door just slid open. One of them hit the button, "Shit!"

They almost ran down the steps slipping here and there but for the majority of it they kept steady and firm, their footsteps finding the right length to stretch from one dropoff to the next. They could hear the many footsteps pounding behind them through the darkness, their screams echoing. They heard them slam into the walls and bump into things like some three stooges gag that almost made Scarlet burst out laughing again, but her mind was focused on going step after step, trying not to slip lest she cracked her skull on the hard stone.

They hit the bottom with an *oomph* and they both stumbled headlong into what felt like a large door. They both pushed at it and heard it creak open slightly, the bottom rumbling and scraping along the floor. They heard the mass reach the last bend at the top of the steps. They slid through the opening and with all their strength they pushed at the solid door, closing it. "This is where you went wacko that one time."

"Wacko huh? I barely even remember coming in here. We just never talked about it."

"If it was the real me, I woulda talked about it mad long, man."

"Uh huh. So..." her voice echoed.

They heard a rustle long across the lengthy complex, the sounds echoing and hitting walls far away from them. "Hey! What's so special about you people to wake the dead? I was having a good eternal rest over here!" The voice was raspy and oddly accented, Willow knew who this was.

"Chett?" Willow asked into the darkness.

Several giant flood lights flickered on at once, blinding the girls. They both shielded their eyes from the onslaught of light. Behind the artificial suns stood a massive green army tent and in front of it sat several layers of sandbags. Someone aiming a gun sat posted behind one of the bags. "Yeah, I'm Chett, who's asking?"

"Willow! Remember me? From the graveyard?"

"Eh. Name rings-a bell. Sounds like you two woke the wrath of the bastard up there, huh?"

"Yea."

"Who the hell's this guy?" Scarlet whispered.

"Shut up-" Willow whispered back.

"Why're you two whispering over there? I don't like whispering! Come closer, the two of you, hands up!"

"Nothing! Nothing at all." Willow said as they both started walking towards Chett, their hands both raised above their heads.

"That's it..." his head lifted slightly. "Is that Willow? Hey, it's me Chett, from the graveyard!" He yelled, lowering his gun and beckoning them over to where he stood.

"Uh...yea, it's me! Come on Scarlet."

Chett raised a gloved hand and took his hat off, letting the girls finally see his face. They both stopped surprised.

"Har har har! You both look like you've seen a ghost!" Chett looked like a Halloween skeleton decoration. He stood slightly taller than both of them clad in a gray green camo shirt and pants and gloves. "Well," his skeleton mouth may have tried to smile. "Why don't we deal with them first," he pointed a gloved finger towards the door which began to scrape across the ground, opening with the force of tens of finger warriors. He raised a battle hardened M16 and switched the safety to kill. "Get over there and hop on the heavy!" He nodded his head towards a corner where a very large and very heavy mounted machine gun sat on a swivel. They jumped the bags and ran towards it. Scarlet grabbed the handles and racked the thick slide. Willow picked up the belt of weighty bullets, readying them to feed into the gun. There were several other canisters of bullets, all Willow had to do was reload and feed them well enough and the entire army above them would turn to gravy even before they went through the opening door.

*Creeeeeeeeeeeeeeeeekkkkkkkkkkkk...*the door stood open. The darkness beyond it sat unbroken even with the bright floodlights gleaming through it. *Tick tick tick,* Scarlet heard that little ticking again, annoying in her ear as her hands started to cramp, her finger tapping and readying at the trigger. She was ready to feed them some thick hot lead.

They all rushed in, their weapons ready, like a cavalry-less cavalry charge.

Then they stopped as they all died in a hail of thick gunfire. Scarlet sent penetrating bursts which annihilated and shredded through body after body, the occasional tracer beaming out a lightsaber of green that caught some of their clothes on fire as it ripped through one to find another behind. Chett efficiently fired his M16, his bones chattering and clattering with each other due to the vibrations of each shot. Once it was all over, a snowfall of bullet casings rolled all around Willow and Scarlet. They went through several crates of belt fed ammunition until it was done. Chett took a breath, somehow, and wiped his bone brow with the back of his hand, looking out at the field of corpses which all started to melt away the instant the last one died. "Well, ladies, I would call that a job well done. How about some coffee?"

*

Willow's face soured as she took a sip of the void black coffee.

"Don't like it lass?" Chett chattered, his laugh like a ton of clinking bones.

"Don't think it's really my thing," she handed the cup back to Chett who unhinged his boney jaws and turned the cup on its head, swallowing the black coffee in one fell swoop. *Ahhh* his mouth steamed and his clothes became wet as the coffee trickled down from bone to bone underneath the green fatigues.

"Since I don't got no tongue, I can't taste anything, you

see. But I like the steam of it. Makes me feel something in this boney heart of mine." He chattered.

"So," Scarlet started, "How do you guys know each other?" She took a sip of her coffee, unfazed.

"Well, the lass sat on me grave. We talked and then she left. Har har, not the most eventful story but if I do recall in this empty head O' mine, there was a blasted party goings on nearby. Rumbled me bones! Har har!"

"Ohh...I remember that. I remember leaving you...and all those other times at those other parties...shit...I feel so stupid. That wasn't even me, man... Willow, I would never leave you like that."

Willow nodded and turned back to Chett, "So, Chett, why are you here? Underground? In this world?"

"Ermmm...I don't remember! Har har! But I do know one thing: I ain't resting! Har har! And I do know another thing, I hate Him, up there, above us all like he thinks he's better than us. You know, he's the one who woke me up. I'm supposed to be dead! Har har! And let me tell you two lasses, when you're dead, you wanna stay dead. I know I don't got no brain in this skull O' mine, and I know I don't have no heart or lungs behind these ribs," He rubbed his finger up and down his camo shirt which sounded like a xylophone. "But lemme tell you two, I'm tired. I wanna go rest this eternal rest I'm owed. But here I am, stuck in this hole down here, not strong enough to get out." He poured himself another cup of coffee and watched it steam with his eyeless eye-holes.

"Well Chett, good for you," Scarlet said. "We wanna kill Him too."

"Really now?" If his eyes could squint, they would. He looked over the two girls, starting at Willow then to Scarlet. "You both handled that machine gun well enough, never saw any lass do that before. And you," he nodded at Scarlet, "yer arms look almost as big as mine when I had more meat to me bones! Har har! Well, I heard the fighting above me, almost shook the walls down with me inside them, maybe then I woulda gotten some rest! Har har! Well, you lasses look like you can handle yerselves well enough. Oh, and what's the big one's name?"

"My name is Scarlet."

"Mmherm…ah you was also at me grave that same night, huh? You got much taller…and more…masculine."

"Thanks," she rubbed a proud bicep.

"And you," he looked at Willow. "You look much the same. Maybe a little leaner but with muscles beneath that skin instead O' bones! Har har! You looked almost more skeleton than me back then! Har har! But now look atcha…how old are ye lasses? I can't remember time too well."

"Uh…" Scarlet looked at Willow, "I think we're both like 18 or 19. Do you remember?"

"Not really. Time is fucked up here. Don't know how long I was wandering around as Ms. Johnson. That dumb B."

"Absolute dumb B."

"Ms. Herchel was a dumb B too."

"That she was. Still is."

They both laughed and Chett joined in even though he had no clue what they were talking about, but he liked to laugh, he liked the sound his bones made.

"Well…are we gonna get to the bastard who wont let me sleep?" Chett broached.

"Chett…there's a problem with that proposition."

"Yes, tall woman?"

"Uh…that castle is flying."

"Flying?"

"Yeah. Like…hovering."

"Flying and hovering are two different things. You gotta pick one."

"Hovering."

"Heeerrmmmm…" his bones clinked as he shifted in his seat. "How high up is it?"

"I don't know. Like a thousand feet max. Maybe less."

"Har har! Well I know just what to do!"

"You do?" Scarlet and Willow both asked.

Chett stood, his bones clinking against each other, "Follow me, lasses. I'll fly us up there."

"What?" They both asked.

Chett started clinking and clanking as he led them to the back flap of the big tent. He pulled the flap up and behind it the girls both saw that the chamber was much, much larger than they originally thought. Scarlet remembered the original one, back on Earth, was around a football field in length, but here there was seemingly a mile of space from the tent to the end. HQ headquarters rowed a long and wide length of airstrip that stretched farther back. Lights rowed down in systematic little suns that lit it up like day. Planes of all sorts and sizes sat parked at intervals from the airstrip. Some new looking and some old looking, some black and tactical and some white and ergonomic. Some were fighters and some were bombers. And, at the end, on a helicopter pad, sat an old Huey helicopter.

They walked down the strip taking it in, the smell like a new pair of shoes and freshly laden concrete. They finally reached the Huey and looked up at it. "Well, there she is, my friends. Flew one of these back in '69."

"Woah woah woah..."

"Yes, tall woman?"

"You...how...wait..." she looked at Willow. "This is just like our bunker. We had all those guns and here," she pointed at the Huey, "are all the planes and fucking flying machines! No more questions! We were meant to fuck this fucker up, that asshole in the floating castle! Chett! Would you like to be our air support?"

"Well I be, tall woman, you have my hand in battle," they shook hands, his boney glove and her large white hand. "Never did fight with lasses at me back before."

"Yo," Willow looked around. "How do we get the chopper out of here?"

"Ah!" Chett rattled. He ran around to one of the HQ buildings and the girls followed. "Right here's the control station. All we have to do is warm the Huey up, hit this button down here, then the roof opens up like a portal to hell, then we fly up and out. The problem here is, the Huey usually needs a co-pilot and, looking at you girls, I don't think either of you have even stepped inside a heli before? Am I right?"

They both shook their heads.

"Mhermm...I can fly solo, easily enough...always had me co-pilot, but I can make due." He scratched his boney chin. "Well, girls, we leaving now, or do y'all wanna rest up first, eat, get some energy? I'm dead so I don't need any of that! Har har!"

"We don't-" Scarlet began to say, but she blinked and realized how tired she was. How long were they fighting for? Was the sun coming up when they went down the steps? *Fuck me, I'm tired,* she thought, almost stumbling to the side, her shoulders both aching.

Willow saw it in her face, "We might need some food and an hour of sleep."

"Done!" Chett chattered.

"Oh, do you have guns?"

"Mmmhheerrmmm...sorry girls, I only got me trusty M16 and that heavy up front. I wish I had more to give, but all I gots are me planes and helicopters otherwise. And some rations up front in the tent."

They went to the tent and ate some random MRE's that looked straight out of Vietnam. They still tasted fine without any hint of age or mold. "If you two can do me a pleasantry, for an old dead soul, explain how those taste. I miss me food."

"Well," Willow swallowed, "I got the...ham and lima beans..." she took a bite...chewed slowly, and swallowed. "Oh...it's not bad. Tastes like...ham and beans."

"Mmmmm...I miss me ham. Meat..." he tried to lick his nonexistent lips.

Scarlet took a bite of hers, "I got the ham and eggs," she took another bite, "Jesus...that's fuckin' great!" She started scarfing it down. "Jeez, this shits almost worth going through the jungle, huh?"

"Lass...watch yer words."

"Oh...sorry."

"I don't remember much...but I do remember me friends...going in there and never comin' back." He took a boney breath, his rib cage rattling like an instrument. He looked up and tried to smile, "But here, ladies, you're coming back."

"Chett..." Willow started, "thank you."

"Oh no problem, lass. Now both of ye, eat, then get some shut eye. I'll stay watch cause we know for damn well I can't shut my eyes! Har har!"

Willow and Scarlet laughed and finished their meals. "Okay, we're only sleeping for like an hour or two. No more."

"Shouldn't we worry about the door? What if more come?" Scarlet asked.

"Ah, spit on them!" Chett said. "I'll just wake ye's up if I hear anything and set you back on the heavy."

"Okay...done deal. Soon, we're going to kill that bastard, up there."

"Alright, Scarlet," Willow said. "Now sleep. I need you in tip top shape for later."

They settled down on their military bunks while Chett held a cigarette between his boney teeth a little ways off, lounging and looking at the door, polishing his M16. The girls fell asleep, the craziness and tiredness of the day finally getting to the both of them, felling their eyelids and quieting their brains. Scarlet dreamed of firing the Benelli M4, wishing that she still had ammo for that bad boy. Willow dreamed of Mark laying his golden curls on her lap, talking about pancakes and other stuff. It was that night where he told her that the world was finally being reborn. She was still not sure if he was lying now or then or whenever. Lie after lie after potential lie. Really, she couldn't care if she was a key for some god or whatever, all she wanted now was to point a pistol at his golden hair and pull the trigger and watch the life leak from his eyes and his head. She didn't care if it worked. That would still be a victory. Winning that first battle up on the surface made her feel like a winner for the first time in her life of losing. Now she felt confident. She dreamt of other things too. She saw her Mom. She never thought of her Mom much. She remembered when they ate dinner with her that one time. She remembered how Scarlet called her a bitch and convinced Willow that her Mom indeed was a bitch. Was that the real Scarlet or was that the fake Scarlet? She felt bad for her Mom. Even if she was a bitch, she never deserved any of this. She knew her husband was cheating on her, she saw both of her sons leave her, and now her daughter was leaving too...Willow wished she tried to talk to her more. Yes, maybe she was cold or selfish after those two kids were killed by The Enemy. But she was scared too. Scared and didn't know how to deal with it all, so she pushed Willow away. That's still not right, but Willow still wanted to talk to her, show her that she didn't need to be scared anymore. She rolled around while asleep, dreaming, thinking of her fattening Mom who put all her fears right into a tub of ice cream each and every night. Willow wished she helped instead of ignored.

Chett looked over towards the restless girl as she rolled from side to side, her dreams tingling her mind. *Poor girl,* He thought. *Girl like that shouldn't be fighting.* Chett then felt a severe feeling that he never felt much anymore, well, he never felt anything anymore. But here, he felt it. He thought of his daughter and how she also had deep black hair and a spindly frame. He loved her up to the point that cancer took him from her and then he continued loving her down deep in that cold grave. But their faces looked nothing alike. And his daughter had never fired a weapon before or fought a hoard of husk men commanded by some sort of evil entity in a floating castle high up in the sky. Still, he wanted to protect her in some sort of way. The other one, the tall girl, could handle herself just right. *A mammoth of a girl,* Chett thought. Back in the field, she would've fit right in. Willow on the other hand, smaller, skinnier, but also faster and more nimble. Maybe she wasn't a bruiser but an acrobat in combat. *Well,* Chett thought, *guess I'll have to wait and see for meself.*

*

A couple hours passed until the duo woke and began preparing for the rest of the day ahead of them. They both felt light in their boots and checked each other's vests and exchanged ammo. Willow gave Scarlet her couple mags for the Glock 34 and made sure she was good with just the Walther and the 1911, which she was. Chett showed them to a bathroom that he had never used before and let them both do their humanly, non-skeleton, business. He made some joke and laughed as they followed him to the Huey. Willow was going to open the hatch at the lower HQ before sprinting back up and hopping on one of the M60 door mounted machine guns.

"Now," Chett said, "It's going to be quite loud once the rotors start a' whirrin' so pop one of these helmets on which'll allow us to talk with each other. So the plan is: We fly up to the castle, killing anything that comes at us in the air, and then I'll find y'all a nice spot to hop off. I'll come back down and open up the rest of the upper hatch which'll allow me to start one of these here planes. I'll bring one a' them up and try to take out the top glass floor. Probably won't kill 'em because he'll be hid away in some bunker. But still, it'll show him that we mean business while you two go at it from the inside. Sounds good?"

They nodded.

"Good. Let's rip 'em up." He put his hand in the middle of the three. Scarlet put hers on top of his and Willow next on top of hers. "Let's get er done ladies and get you home in time for supper. Don't kill 'em too hard, but just enough."

"One bullet will suffice." Willow said.

"Make it two. Just in case." Scarlet added.

"Two bullets then," Chett finalized. "Then I can go back to sleep."

Maybe more, I'll empty the mag, Willow thought.

They all nodded and breaked, sending their hands up.

*

The chopper buzzed and whirred, creating a whirlwind of air below its thick rudders. Willow ran up the steps as the top hatch of the hanger opened up like God to a group of priests. She hopped in through the door, slapped the helmet on, and strapped herself in behind the M60. "Ready to go!" Chett said soon after, his voice all buzzy and boney as it rattled through the little intercom in her ear. He was right, the pure sound of the rotors chopping air made speaking in no less than a scream impossible to understand. Scarlet sat at the other door mounted gun, her back facing towards her.

Then the world began to rise and become smaller and smaller as they rose out from somewhere in the forest. They saw the neighborhood below them get small. They saw the black wall surrounding them, rising higher than any of the trees and, beyond it, they saw as they rose higher into the sky, was barren nothingness. More nothing than the Sahara desert. Willow's house sat smoking and smoldering in the midday light. The castle hid the sun as it hovered in the exact same place, its eerie elegance disgusting to all the passengers of the flying machine. They cut through the air, turning heavily towards the castle, rising to meet its first level and then higher and then higher, getting closer and closer until they were above the top penthouse and they could see clearly inside. There were posh furnishings and several rooms that split off from each other. Pictures framed the bone white walls, pictures of The Enemy with his beautiful lush locks of golden silk hair and his piercing blue eyes. A dreamy monster. Scarlet began to tear through it with her M60, blowing the windows out and making holes where there weren't any before.

"Wow. Taking your misguided anger out on nothing, Ms. Miller and crew. I suspected you went down there." His voice rang out louder than the helicopter, piercing their helmets. "Keep shooting, go ahead, there's nothing in there beside dumb and stupid little things that I never loved."

Scarlet started putting bullets in all the life-sized

paintings of him, annihilating them hole after large hole.

"Ah. Real mature. Wait! Stop! That's my-well...it's not my favorite anymore. You guys know that I can shoot that little mosquito out of the sky, right?" The roof responded to him as two large panels labored out from each side of the penthouse, revealing a couple of manned AA cannons aiming directly at the helicopter. Chett pulled it low as quickly as he could while Scarlet pulled her gun to try and get a shot off at the cannons to no avail. "Look, guys, I got more than that. Please, we can resolve this like gentlemen and gentlewomen. Pickles, extend the lander and open the front gate."

At the bottom floor of the castle extended a long and sturdy landing spot fitted for a helicopter. It looked like a tongue, fitted with a long red carpet that led to the front gate which slowly lifted.

"Lassies, I don't see anywhere to land except there. Are you okay with that?" Chett spoke through the headsets.

"Can't you hover over the penthouse and let us jump in through the broken glass? We can make it!" Scarlet screamed, no longer shooting the M60 as they circled the tower, lowering towards the new platform.

"I can if y'all wanna get blown outta the sky! Look, just play his game for now and I'll be back with the bombers. I'll see about that anti air and make them some fresh hell out here!"

"Fine! Lower us down!" Willow said, unsure about all of it, but there was no other option as far as she could see.

"Oh, also!" The Enemy chimed in, "If you guys were thinking about jumping in through that broken roof up there, think again!" At the top roof another three AA guns extended out and a steel dome forked up and clasped tight around the tip, making it impregnable.

"Looks like a dong!" Scarlet screamed.

They landed softly on the helipad. Scarlet and Willow took their helmets off and hopped out onto the velvet carpet, stepping back. "See you Chett!" Scarlet screamed. Chett raised a boney thumbs up and started to fly off again. From this vantage point, it looked like they were at the top of the world, everything below looking like little ant play thingies. There was no railing where they stood so they made sure to take a good couple of steps back as they watched the Huey fly to where the underground airbase was. Cold wind bit at them as they watched. "Good thing you knew that guy," Scarlet said as they watched it go.

"Yeah..."

A missile dodged through the sky, big as a basketball. Willow froze, watching as it slammed into the side of Chett's chopper, blowing it up in a giant explosion of metal and steel and Chett. The wreck fell down almost in slow motion before making a puff of a landing somewhere out in the middle of the forest.

"Holy shit..."

"Ha ha ha! You really thought I was gonna let that dude fly back with some bombers and all of that annoying little stuff? Yeah...no!" He laughed some more. "Well, I let him come here so you guys can enter my little fun house." They both looked over to the open gate. Faint circus music whispered out from its opening. "Remember, I did say I was never good with you things, right? Ah! Ha! Ha! HA!" He coughed and cleared his throat, *AhHem*.

They didn't answer him. "Well...maybe Chett's finally sleeping again, huh?" Scarlet said.

"Yeah...." They had to move on. They turned towards the gate and started down the velvet tongue towards the circus mouth-gate. The wind picked up just slightly as if it wanted to knock them from the path into straight freefall. They kept on without a word.

The inside of the gate filled with a deep reddish yellow light that led on through a long hallway leaden with that velvet red tongue of a carpet. All through it, from somewhere, carnival music whispered out in faint little plays.

"We just play his game for now. Nothing else we can do," Willow whispered.

"Yeah, got it."

At the end of the hallway there was an old-timey looking elevator with a thin little pointer above it that sat on a small little number one. From left to right, the little dial of floors went from one to seven. The elevator dinged open.

"Please," The Enemy said, "Come in. Oh, one floor at a time, if you may."

25

"Fuck off!" Scarlet jammed her finger rapidly on the little button that read seven, then six, then five, then four, then three and then stopped annoyed. "He really wants us to go one floor at a time, huh?"

She hit seven again, "Sorry," the elevator said in a soft female voice, "Try again."

"Oh that bitch!" Scarlet said.

"Dude," Willow pressed the two. "Like I said, just play the game." The doors closed and the elevator began ticking up slowly and bumpily. It made several uncanny sounds, as if it was going to fall down, the cord breaking, but it didn't and then the doors opened back up to a new room. Completely dark and impenetrable by any type of sight, the two girls stepped through the veil into even more darkness. The doors behind them shuttered closed with a clank and then they stood, looking around, saying nothing and looking at more nothing.

"Hello?" Scarlet said, her voice stopping like the opposite of an echo.

Blank! The lights turned on at once, revealing two doors in front of them. One read 'Depravity' in big splotchy red letters while the other read 'Mentality' in the same red splotches.

"Choose one. Each of you." The Enemy said.

"What if I don't wanna?" Scarlet asked.

Nothing. He didn't respond. The girls looked at one another and shrugged.

"I could do depravity..." Scarlet started. "Hey, what if we both go through one door?" She asked the ceiling.

He didn't answer, leading them in a deafening silence.

"Alright, fuck him, lets go through mentality, huh?" She looked at Willow who had already started walking towards the door.

Willow looked over her shoulder, "What did I say about playing his game? If we don't follow the rules there's no way that we'll get to him."

"Why are you so intent on playing his fucking fiddle? Aren't you angry? He killed Chett. He killed me. Fuck man, he may have killed you too."

"Yes! I'm fucking pissed! And that's why I want to get to him and kill him! But he controls this entire fucking place from the lights to the flushes on the goddamned toilets."

"Why would he ever bring us to him willingly? Seems like a stupid thing to do."

"Well what else are we supposed to do? Jump down a thousand feet? At least this gives us a chance."

The Enemy finally chimed in, "Jeez, I wanted to keep this all silent and eerie, but you two's bickering is getting on my nerves. Here, I promise with all of my heart that on the seventh floor you will come face to face with me. Is that good enough? Now go and play my game."

"But you're a liar!" Scarlet yelled.

"Yes I am. But I have nothing else to promise with. This time, you will have to take my word. Or else I can just trap you both in this little room until starvation kills you...or dehydration. Look, there's a lot I can do to kill you, but that's no fun and that's also not fair. Say what you want about my honor or me, but you can't tell me that I haven't been fair so far."

"Oh fuck off, dickbag!"

"Scarlet!" Willow screamed. "Just go through that other door. If he wanted us dead, he could have just crashed this entire fucking place right on our heads."

"Then what does he want, huh?"

"I don't know! But let's just do this okay?" She put her hand outstretched, ready to receive a handshake. "Now are you with me or not?"

Scarlet let a breath out and shook her hand, the thick calluses rough and leathery. "Fine. Let's go." She turned and swiftly opened and shut the 'Depravity' door.

Willow shook her head and opened the 'Mentality' door, shutting it behind herself. The room, now empty, sat silent and still as both doors sucked into themselves, disappearing into the wall and pooling out into thick white paint.

*

Scarlet stood on the precipice of a cliffside drop of thousands and thousands of feet into sheer nothingness. It was silent and echoey in this dark space. Where there should have been elevation, there was nothing. Where there should have been blistering wind, there was none. Where there should have been a lengthening view across the world, there sat a steep wall, black and smooth, following all the way down the drop into the blackness below. She stood, annoyed. Her head shook as she got it together. Thinking about it all made her antsy and angry, even the thought of playing this things games made her want to heave that MRE she ate earlier right up and down to the bottom of this bottomless looking pit. Her hand caressed her stomach as she remembered being impaled. It did hurt at first, and then it felt numb and cold as she felt the heat leech from her congealing blood that trailed down the length of the pole. She remembered trying to look back at Willow, but she couldn't. She remembered forgetting all of who she was, her mind being replaced with thoughts of Ms. Herschel. But no more, her fist tightened and found itself at her side once more as she waited for something to happen.

A moment passed and the floor rose from the pit connecting levelly with the black plane she stood on. It slid up perfectly, not a sound coming from it. Scarlet wasn't surprised about anything anymore. She was angry. She stood and breathed, listening to her ragged and anger filled nostrils work.

"Scarlet Miller." That same female voice from the elevator said from no particular direction. "Now, choosing the depravity door, you must fight and survive. Have fun!"

The room slightly rumbled as the floor opened just slightly for something large to stumble out of it towards her.

"Great," she unsheathed the Glock 34.

*

Why does Scarlet have to get like that? Willow thought as she stepped into the darkness of the 'Mentality' door. She was annoyed at Scarlet's impatience. *Doesn't she know that he wants us to get to him. It's all a game. Just like how life was, it was a game of killing her and using me. I'm just as mad. Just as angry. But we just have to wade through the shit, just like I did for all those fucking years until I can get to him. That's all I need to do. That's all we need to do.* The lights flickered on. The room was small and beige without any windows or doors. She looked behind herself and saw that the door she just went through was gone, sucked back into the wall. Then she noticed someone sitting at a small desk a couple paces forward.

"Hello Willow," said a small woman with jet black hair. She was petite with small wrists and small hands. At the corners of her eyes sat small little crow's feet and her mouth donned little smile lines as she bared her teeth.

"Mom?" Willow was astonished. She looked up at the ceiling, "What is this?" She asked.

"What is what, honey? Why are you talking to the ceiling? Is someone there?"

"I...Mom I..."

"Willow," she looked over her daughter, "you're a woman now."

Willow was too struck to respond.

"Honey, please sit."

Willow took some weary steps towards the empty

chair at the other side of the desk and finally sat, her back completely straight. *This is the mentality door huh? He wants to get under my skin. Wait...if I got my Mom...what did Scarlet get?*

*

"Holy shit!" Scarlet jumped out of the way from the large spiked creature. Its head held two black eyes, the dome of it covered in little wooden spikes that jutted out. Down the length of its stomach was a thick fur that looked like it could make a million blankets there was so much of it. The thing stood bipedal, about twenty feet tall. Scarlet looked at its back and saw more, even thicker, spikes that jutted out of a black mound of fur, some of them dripping with blood and filth. Some of the biggest spikes sat skulls that bounced and jittered as the ghoulish point rammed through their bone structure. Some of them looked like Chett and some were so malformed that it was a question if they were even human at one point. Its legs sat thick and rippled with underlying muscle under a thick leathery hide. Its arms sunk and dragged along the ground with two fat fingered hands at the tip of both of them, making the creature look like some type of hedgehog-gorilla mix-match.

It rammed into the wall, just missing Scarlet as she stood and squeezed the trigger sending some bullets flying at the back of the thing. Nothing, it didn't even make a sound as the small 9mm bullets bounced off of its thick hide. It turned and ran again. Scarlet dodged again and fired some more, her mind still trying to work out what the thing was in the first place. Everything on it sat thick and bullet proof and she realized that this small baby gun in her hands would do nothing. She sheathed it and swiftly pulled her biggest knife that she had. It had to have a chink in its armor somewhere, some little thing that would be in some weird and odd place. Somewhere that no one would ever think about. It ran again-

*

"Willow...all the years...how...how are you?"

"I...you know...I'm fine I guess."

"Oh that's good...aren't you going to ask me how I am?"

"Oh yea...uh...how are you?"

"Not good, Willow. Not good at all."

"Oh..."

"Willow, do you know how I felt seeing my family destroy itself from the inside out?"

"I..."

"The house? I couldn't care about the house. You know I had you and Matt and Jeremy in my womb for nine months each. Nine awful and amazing months, and then seeing you all get older and grow and...live...it made me so proud to be a mother."

"Yea...uh..." *Why is she talking so weird?*

"And then first it was your father...I loved that bastard for twenty years and then one day I could smell it coming off of him. That's when I knew, but we never spoke about it. It's kind of hard to. And then one day he came to me when all of you were at school and he showed me the divorce papers and then left soon after. I don't know what happened to him, like some switch and he no longer cared for me or you or your brothers. Then your brothers started sleeping over at their friends' houses a lot more. At the beginning it was just little weekends and some school days here and there. I thought I was being a good mother, right? Let your kids free and they'll come back to you. But then they started sleeping over for four days, then five, and then the entire week and eventually they just stopped asking if it was alright to sleep there. And I wanted to tell them to come back and live at this new house we just spent all of this money on, but I couldn't. I looked around that sad empty house where those two poor kids disappeared and I was supposed to tell them to come back to that? I just couldn't. I don't know if it was cowardice or something else, I just couldn't let them share in that misery. And then there's you Willow. You stayed there and shared in that misery. I wanted to tell you to leave me. I wanted to send you off somewhere where you could be happy, but I couldn't. I was too weak. I think a part of me was happy that you were there to take some of that quiet sadness away from me and into you. I know we never talked much, Willow. I know you probably don't see me as your mother anymore. But I'm sorry. I'm sorry for ignoring you even when I saw how you were getting. My gosh, those black bags under your eyes, I wanted to say, 'Are you sleeping?' but I didn't want to intrude. I saw how thin you were getting and I wanted to make you a big dinner and ask you, 'Are you eating well?' but I didn't. I saw you ignoring me and I wanted to ask, 'Do you want to talk?' but I didn't. You have my eyes but I couldn't see with mine that you needed love...and I know I never gave it to you, or as much as you deserved...and I'm sorry. I wish I were a better mother, but I'm not. I remembered when those kids disappeared behind our house, gosh that was awful, and I remember being...scared to love you. It made me scared to protect you...I...I don't know how that sounds, but it makes me feel awful. And then for five years I pretended to want to push you away from me. I...I'm sorry."

What do I say to that?

*

Balls! She thought, just catching a glimpse at the giant sack that pulled in on itself. It was only visible from just the right angle if you tilted your head down just enough and she just barely caught a glimpse of that pruney looking lump. It lumbered towards her again, frustrated that the little thing below it kept dodging him. Then the lumber turned into a jog, then a pounding run. And Scarlet sat and waited the entire time, feeling the shake of the ground below her. He's been getting closer to catching her on each turn, the last time he reached his grossly elongated arms out as she jumped away, just barely grabbing the bottom of her shoe. She slipped out and fell on her face. He almost got her then, but not now. She saw what she had to do and it was going to be very, very fun. She squeezed the hilt of the knife just a little more, feeling the textured grip and weight.

Pound pound pound, the raging monster stepped closer

and closer and closer and time seemed to slow as the adrenaline pumped into Scarlet's brain as the little neurons put together her movements and sent signals to the brainstem and then down the spine and into her arms and her legs, this time sending her forward when the monster thought she was going to dodge to the side again. He didn't have enough time to react as she lunged underneath him, ramming the knife upwards into its groin. There was a slight resistance for a second before a thick *pop!* as the resistance faded into a mushy pulp, the knife ramming and pushing her entire hand up into the broken sack. She continued to push harder and harder as all the ball juices and sack juices and blood and vile substances rained down onto her face and into her mouth which she accidently opened in the second. Her lunge turned into a sure-footed crouch, her other hand found the bottom of the knife, and she stood up like at the end of a heavy squat, slamming both her arms elbow deep into the sack. The knife pushed and rammed through bone and other organs, prodding and ripping. And, in that second, Scarlet tore as hard as she could, shredding the knife out of the sack and falling onto her back as the creature made a small squeak and tumbled down onto its spiky face, squirming and grabbing at the leaking wound.

She stood and tried to wipe her face off from all the thick goo that caked it, but she only smushed the stuff around. Everything felt sticky as she tried to move. Her pants were soaked, her vest felt heavier than ever, and her short hair was plastered to her head. She listened to the monster squirm as she slowly took the heavy vest off. All the ammo and the mags and the guns that she was carrying sat thick and heavy with all the sack goo that dribbled into it. "Shit," she whispered and spit. She pointed the Glock at the monster and pulled the trigger. Nothing. "Aw come on!" She pulled again, shook the gun and cocked it for another round and still, when she pulled the trigger, there was nothing. "Your balls destroyed all my shit!" She tried the revolver next, but it had the same problem. In her little bag of naked 357 bullets, she found that it was now a 357 soup, filled to the brim with the stuff which leaked in through the sides of the bullets and ruined them. "Aw man!" She threw them all to the ground and checked her knives. The one that pierced the balls was fine as well as all the other ones that she found strapped to her legs. Her broad shoulders felt lighter now, and better without the heavy burden of her vest anymore. Still, she felt almost naked without it.

"Hrrrrrrrrrrgrrrrrrrrrrrrrrrr..." the spiked monster hummed out, still grabbing its drooping sack as it laid on the ground.

She ran around to its spiky head and found its two beady little black eyes and plunged the ballsack knife, still dripping with ball juices, hilt deep into one of them.

"Hrrrrrrrrr!" It screamed, but it didn't die.

"Sorry!" She left the ballsack knife in that eye and pulled out another large knife and sunk it into the other eye.

"Grrrrrrrr!"

"Sorry! I don't know how to kill you!" She grabbed another knife and stabbed its face and found it stuck in there, stopped thick on some facial bone. It was still alive. She grabbed another knife and stabbed down. And then another and stabbed it down even harder. And then another, and then another, grabbing this knife and that one, stabbing and striking through thick monster bone. It screamed and grumbled the entire time until it went quiet after Scarlet's final knife plunged itself into the only open spot left on its face. Now it had a good amount of industrial spikes...but sticking the wrong way.

Scarlet fell on her ass and panted, "Jesus...why didn't you just die after the first one?"

The monster dropped down into the pit as a door opened up beneath it...*plop!* It must've hit the bottom. Scarlet stood and breathed a sigh of relief until she realized that all of her knives were gone, stuck like a hedgehog into the spike monster. "Shit! Hey, come back!" She screamed into the pit to no avail. Now she was weaponless, knifeless, and covered in monster ball sack goo.

The door appeared back behind her with a whirl. She didn't even realize that it was gone in the first place. "Oh..." She mourned over her ruined equipment and lost knives for a second and then left through the reopened passage. She opened the door and then closed it behind her. It was the same room with the elevator. Her door sucked back into non-existence. Scarlet spotted Willow sitting at the bottom of one of the walls. "Yo," she said, walking up to her.

Willow looked up and scrunched her nose, "What the fuck happened to you?" she asked.

"Eh, I stabbed a monster in the nuts. All my shit got ruined though, look at me!" she gestured towards herself, "I'm like a naked baby out here." Her eyes squinted as she looked over Willow, "What happened to you? You went in the door, right?"

She nodded and stood, "Yeah. Saw my mom in there."

"Oh shit. Did you have to fight her to the death or something?"

"No..."

"Oh...you alright?"

"Yea. But I guess we're both cleared to move on, right?"

"I didn't get covered in ballsack juice for nothing."

"Ew."

"Pretty rad, right?"

"Kinda, yea."

The two walked up towards the elevator and pressed the open door button. "Ah!" The Enemy said. "You both passed the second floor I see! Well done, especially you Scarlet! I was sure that you were going to die in there!"

"Yeah, but I didn't!"

"I can see that. How did it taste?"

"Like fucking candy, now can we move on or what?"

"Yes! Yes. But let me introduce you to the future challenges. On floor three and four, you will be facing the greatest and most diabolical villains of both history and literature. They have been given the freedom to create trials based on their own knowledge to smite you both. You may enter and go on to the third floor where one of them will be waiting. I call them the LOTHWQE! L-O-T-H-W-Q-E!"

"The what?" Willow asked.

"LOTHWQE!"

"Loth-quw-ee?"

"No, loth-quee."

"Yeah, but there's a W in there. Loth-quw-ee."

"No, I made it, my pronunciation goes."

"What does that even mean anyways," Scarlet budded in.

"The LOTHWQE stands for the League Of Those Humans With Questionable Ethics! LOTHWQE!"

"Isn't that like an anagram or something?" Scarlet asked.

"No!" The Enemy said, "It's a...it's a..."

"No," Willow said, "it's a palindrome?"

"A what?" Scarlet asked.

"It's neither of those!" The Enemy said.

"Then what is it?"

"A...wait, it's right on the tip of my tongue."

"Anagram! Right?"

"No! Uh...acronym! An acronym!"

"Ohhhh..." Both girls said.

"I think it's stupid sounding," Scarlet said.

"I second that," Willow said.

"Well I don't third it," The Enemy said.

"Yeah but, majority rules bro, you said you're all about fairness over here, well, two outta three. We get to change the pronunciation."

"I...I can kill you two where you stand."

"Yea and I get to say it's pronounced loth-quw-ee."

He took a long breath, "Fine. Loth-quw-ee. It's voted on. Now can you two get in the elevator and move this on."

They both filed into the old elevator and hit the button

with the large three on it. The doors closed and it started shaking as it rose slowly. They sat silent and listened as the thing moved a little faster and then slowed down, hitting a slight bump and opening the doors once more to another dark room. They both walked in and a circle spotlight lit up half of a table. Two empty seats sat in front of it. With nothing else to do, and the prerogative that they were going to follow the rules of this little game, they sat and waited as the elevator doors closed behind them.

The rest of the lights flashed on and they saw a man dressed in black sat before them on the other side of the table. Atop his head was a bowler hat with black hair that tumbled slightly out of the sides. He had a small one button overcoat that was clasped together. Around his neck sat a gray bow tie covered slightly by a white undershirt. His hands were clasped together on top of the table and he smiled. Above that smile sat a very peculiar toothbrush mustache that reminded the girls of one very peculiar historical figure-

"HITLER?" Scarlet exclaimed. The man's smile dropped.

"Jeez," Willow said, "he's really bringing out the big guns, huh?"

"I am not Hitler, I am Charlie Chaplin."

"Huh?" Scarlet asked. "Why are you here?"

"That oaf up there, I think, mistook me for that tyrannical dictator."

"Wait wait...who's Charlie Chaplin?" Willow asked.

Charlie got a puzzled look on his face, "You don't know me?" She shook her head, "Do you?" he asked Scarlet, they both shook their heads. "Seriously? *City Lights*?"

"Nuh uh-" They shook their heads.

"*Modern Times*?"

"Nuh uh-"

"*The Great Dictator*?"

"Nuh uh-"

"*The Kid*? *Gold Rush*? Anything?"

"Nuh uh-"

"My god, what are they showing kids these days?" He wiped his face with a handkerchief.

"Look man, I don't know who you are, but how do we know that you're not Hitler in disguise?"

"In dis-" He shook his head. "I am not Hitler!"

"Yeah but...how do we KNOW...you know?"

"Do I sound German?"

"No..."

"There you go!"

"Okay, okay," Willow chimed in. "You're not Hitler. But now what are we supposed to do?"

He took a breath, "I know not. I kept trying to tell him that I was not Hitler, but he didn't listen, and now I'm supposed to make a challenge for you two to pass to the next floor."

"So what's the challenge?"

"Hmmm..."

"You don't have the challenge?" Scarlet asked.

"I was more inquired to think about how I got here..."

"Well," Scarlet started, "We're kinda in a hurry sooooooo..."

"Okay okay...let me see..." he tapped his knuckles against the table. "Oh god..." he covered his nose. "Why do you smell like that?"

"Monster Balls."

"Oh, fantastic." He looked around. "Ah!" His finger raised and then pointed at the girls, "Your challenge is to take me with you on your journey."

"What?" They both said.

"Yes...I don't think I'm actually Charlie Chaplin. I think that oaf just saw a picture of him and poof! I am here. Even now I can't say exactly who my parents were and all these other little fake memories I find faltering." He took off the bowler cap and stood, "Please, if it so pleases you two ladies, take me with you. I know you're going to see Him. I would like to meet my creator. Face to face."

"We wanna kill that dude," Scarlet said.

"Either way, I would like to meet him before you do so..."

"Deal," Willow stretched her hand out, "It's the only way." The man shook hers. "So...do you want us to call you Charlie or what?"

"I...I don't think I even deserve to be called such a beautiful name and neither am I he...that wonderful man. What are your names? You two girls?"

"I'm Willow," she pointed to Scarlet, "Scarlet."

"Hmmm...call me Wilset."

"Well," Scarlet said, standing up, looking down on Wilset, "Nice to meetcha Wilset!" They shook hands. "You gonna keep the Hitler stash or what?"

"I don't know."

"Well...maybe The Enemy will think that we were so persuasive that Hitler joined us, right?" She looked at Willow.

"Eh," she shrugged. "I think he's watching right now, man."

"Oh yea. Well, Wilset, we passed the test, time to move on, right?"

"Yes, indeed."

The three of them, Scarlet, Willow, and the newly established Wilset with his Hitler mustache all walked and stood in front of the elevator. Willow hit the open button.

"So you really weren't Hitler, huh?" The Enemy asked sincerely.

"Even if I was, I am not! Just as I was not Charlie Chaplin or whoever you made me to be!"

"Interesting...I never thought to see one of you with... sentience... Well, you girls passed the test with help from my misstep. Please, move on to the fourth floor." The mic quieted and the elevator doors sludged open.

"Hey Willow," Scarlet asked as they all stepped into the elevator, "You still have your guns?"

Willow caressed the Walther on her left and the 1911

on her right, "Uh yea."

"Guns? You guys have guns?" Wilset asked.

"We had even more, man. Rock N' roll shit, man."

"I hate guns."

"Wilset," Scarlet shook his shoulder, "Those guns are only for the enemies. And we know how to use them. It's alright."

"Yea, yea…just keep those things away from me," Wilset looked down.

"How much ammo?" Scarlet asked, turning away from Wilset.

"Walther is half empty and I got no mags for it. The 1911 is full and no more mags. I gave the rest of my Glock ammo to you but my Glock is full." She unsheathed it from her belt, checked the safety, and handed it to Scarlet. "You got around seventeen shots for whatever is coming next." Willow rolled her ankle and felt the Glock 43 micro strapped underneath her pant leg, but she didn't say anything about it lest The Enemy was listening. *Have to keep the bastard guessing,* she thought. She looked at Wilset. She wouldn't even give him one of her special guns if he wanted one. Her trust in the man was low to none, but he was here. Scarlet looked like a giant compared to him, so Willow wasn't exactly scared, but she kept a wary eye on him and his Hitler stash.

Strapped up and ready for whatever was next, the elevator doors opened to another dark room. The three stepped inside, the light of the elevator beaming around them, not enough to kill off the darkness that bided further within. The doors shut together and then they experienced nothing naught for a slight little breathing that huffed and puffed somewhere out in front of them. "Hello?" Scarlet said. "We're here for the next of the Lothquwee."

"Yes. I am here. And I see you three. A tall woman with a small woman and an even smaller man." His thick voice rasped out from beyond. "Yet, I know not what this Lothquwee is nor why you are here. Nor do I really know why I stand here amidst the darkness of this room. The light. I am afraid to turn it on and afraid to look down at myself to see my hands which feel so taught and use these eyes which feel so dry. I can feel this long hair between these fingers that stretch too big. I can feel my skin fracture along the lines and falter unto the muscles that work beneath them. I am a monster that no man should look upon, not man nor woman nor child. I have killed too many and helped too little, as that is why I deserve to be called what I am: Monster."

"You alright, man?" Scarlet said into the darkness.

"No, I am not alright. This discourse makes me yearn for another, deep somewhere away from human civilization and structure. But I cannot and I will not, for the prospect is too much for others to bide for."

"Hey, what's your name?" She asked.

"I have no name. I was not given one. I am known as a daemon or a thing and those two, as well as the many descriptives of a monster, they do not deserve to have a name bestowed upon themselves by either master or mother."

"Jeez," Willow said. "What did you do to be placed in the Lothquwee?"

"As I have said, I have killed humans not worthy of death all under the guise that I had to, as their namesake of my creator spurred me on, from slaying poor William and then Clerval and then poor Elizabeth. Maybe more, but those three stay circumstanced in my mind. All to spite my creator in a haze of rage and spite, but now, right now, all I want is to be left alone and unloved as a creature as vile as I can never find love nor a creature of my own kind."

"Wait a second..." Willow broached. "What was your creator's name?"

"I dare not say, I fear it, the man who birthed this suffering upon me. Oh I miss Felix and Safie..."

History and literature, Willow thought. "Guys, I know who this is. Hey...why don't we give you a name?"

The room and its darkness sat in pure silence for some

time as they stood and shifted. Scarlet's fist squeezed and tapped where her fresh Glock 34 was placed. Wilset cowered behind her and brushed his Hitler mustache down and licked his lips. Willow stood, waiting for a response, sure that this creature wasn't going to attack them. "A name? As I said before, I need not a name. I deserve not a name."

"Why's that? Everyone deserves a name?"

"Everyone. I am not either part of the 'every' nor part of the 'one' because I am not human. I am a filthy creature."

"I bet I'm more filthy than you," Scarlet chimed in. "Right now I'm caked in monster ball juice. Do you hear that?" There was a squishing sound, "You can literally hear the stuff in my boots."

"Filth sinks lower than physicality, beautiful child. I am filthy in this unsoul that I have been thanklessly given and bestowed."

"But you can clean filth with soap, so why don't you do that?" She asked.

"There is no metaphorical soap to clean me of who I really am."

"And who are you?" Willow asked.

"A creature. A monster."

"Then you are a creature or a monster, but who cares? I don't. Do you guys care?"

"Nah," Scarlet said.

"Uhhh, no. Nope not at all," Wilset cared much, but he dared not speak it. He was scared of monsters.

"See?" Willow said. "Maybe you are as bad as you say, but if you really were, then we would be dead right now, right?"

"Incorrect."

"A real monster would have been feasting upon our corpses after it murdered us in the darkness. But you stood and you talked. And you talk beautifully. I can hear it inside of you, you are a beautiful monster. You may look hideous as you say. All of this may be true. But don't betray yourself when you speak, because I can hear it in your voice. Now what would you like as your name?"

"Viktor."

"There you go, Viktor. That's a lovely name."

"It is undeserved."

"It may be, but now you have one. Can the lights come on now? Are you alright with that?"

"No. I am hideous. I will not have another look upon my face or my malformed body. I have been run out of villages and forsaken by many, calling me 'monster!'. I refuse to go through such torture again."

"Hey, all three of us will promise to not do any of that, okay?"

"Yeah, I got no problem with you, man."

"Uhh..." Wilset started, Scarlet stomped on his shoe right where she thought it would be. "Ouch! Yes! I promise."

"See Viktor, now, turn on the lights for us. Please?"

"What's your names if I may ask."

They said their names in unison.

"Very well...but I have warned the three of you. I promised to keep in darkness, but I have no other choice but to continue-"

The lights flashed on. They were in a small room like the last one with a similar desk in the center. No one sat at it and, instead, there stood what looked like an eight foot tall man standing in the corner, facing away. His back was large and overshadowed by a torn black shawl which catered all the way down to his ankles. His large feet were bare and both looked like two giant things of leather and meat, almost like the thick roots of a tree. Flowing down the back of his head was long and shaggy black hair that matted and clumped here and there.

"Alright, that's good Viktor. Now can you turn around for us? Please? We would like to talk to you."

Wilset's heart jittered for a second as he watched the mammoth of the man start to slowly turn towards them. He had been scared of the voice and its hideous rasp, but his heart slowed as he saw the giant man's shoulders and how they shook. It was at that moment that he saw that the monster man was horrified. More scared than he was earlier, in the darkness. He smiled a brilliant smile that was contrasted darkly by his Hitler-stache.

"There you go," Willow gestured with her hand, beckoning him to continue turning. "Come on, it's alright, you're okay..." It was like she was talking to a baby or some frightened animal.

"Are you sure you won't hate me or try to kill me?" He asked.

"I'm sure. One hundred percent, right guys."

"Abso-fruitly."

"Indeed," Wilset nodded with his smile, trying to be as cordial as he could.

"Alright," Viktor turned around fully and his face was truly a horror. Yellow cracked skin barely covered a work of arteries and muscle that moved beneath as his black hair flushed and matted even more at the front. He seemed to try and smile, showing a bright white set of teeth that only made him look more uncanny. And his eyes shone two dull yellow lights that watched them all.

Wilset continued to smile on the outside as he held back the sense to retch at this grisly creature before him. But he smiled and brushed his little mustache as he had been doing earlier. Willow's stomach caught for a second and then settled, *seen worse* she thought. Scarlet smiled and got excited looking at the creature that was Viktor.

"Cool!" Scarlet fluttered. "Holy shit, you look like...I don't know how to describe it!" She walked over to him and looked up at his yellow skinned face. He stood much taller than her, but she never shied away from his eyes nor anywhere else on him. "Dude, you look kinda jacked." She said, inspecting his shawled arms. "You have clothes under that thing right?"

"Yes, I do, Scarlet." His fake smile turned genuine, this reaction never something that he had found all those years before.

"Good. I've had enough monster balls in my face for a lifetime!" She laughed and Viktor didn't understand. He watched her face, which was covered in red and white, and then he burst out laughing himself. Wilset watched the two, surprised and Willow looked down at him and smiled too.

"Dude!" Scarlet looked over at her two companions, "We have to have him join us!"

"Scarlet, do you really want me with you? I have killed innocents and-"

"Don't care. Can't be much worse than the dude we're trying to kill at the top of this tower."

"He...you're trying to kill him up there?" Viktor asked the group.

"Yep," Scarlet nodded. "He said you were going to try and stop us, but you're pretty dang chill. Just a little shy."

"Chill? I am not cold."

"Chill as if," she smoothed her hand in front of her, "cool."

"Cool? I do not feel a breeze."

"Well, wanna join? I'm sure my compatriots are willing, right guys?"

"I only see good things from Viktor," Willow nodded.

"I don't know what's going on," Wilset said, "but I'm alright with it."

"See?" Scarlet said. "Come on!" She tried to pull his arm, but he didn't move a centimeter, stuck like a stone statue.

"Wait. Before I am able to say yes or no to such a proposition, I almost forgot that He, up there," he pointed at the ceiling, "has forced me to give you all a challenge to be able to move to the next floor. I have no able queue as to why I must follow this command, but I must, or I may not move on."

He made you and planted these actions in you, Willow thought but never spoke it aloud as Scarlet asked Viktor what the challenge was going to be.

"Before I tell you the challenge, I must ask you all a question. Are we friends?" He asked the group.

Scarlet nodded, "Oh absolutely." Willow shrugged, "I don't see why not," and Wilset nodded, "I would be glad for you to join us."

"I've never had friends before. My life has been filled with so much loneliness that I knew not that I would have a friend. But now...I feel happy." He smiled with those pearly white teeth. "Your challenge is to take me with you. I wish to help you with this journey."

"Yes!" Scarlet said.

"WHAT?" The Enemy yelled. "Another one just joined them? That's all of the Lothqee!"

"Um, it's pronounced Loth-quw-ee." Scarlet said.

"Wait? This is the entire league?" Willow asked. "There's only two of them. I feel like a league should be way more than two."

"Yes, but," The Enemy said, "league sounds really cool. But whatever! The league is kaput! And now the league is following you!"

"I will follow my friends into anything!" Viktor stated.

"I will follow them into, uh, most things!" Wilset said.

"Whatever. No problem. Please, move on to the next floor, floor number five."

The elevator became more than crowded with the giant addition of the eight foot man who slouched in the corner of the small little box. Wilset's shoulder rammed into his side and Willow and Scarlet pushed for clarity over the buttons for the next floor. Willow slammed the button that said five on it and the doors shuttered closed once more. "Everything alright with everyone?" Willow said. She saw Viktor's mouth open slightly, probably to rebuke her statement of 'everyone' but she raised a finger before he could say anything, "And Viktor. From here on, I and everyone else in this elevator, will call you a person. You may not be one, you may be one, but when you're with us, you *are* one, okay?"

"I..." he looked down at Wilset who smiled, over at Scarlet, and then back at Willow. He nodded and smiled without any teeth. "As you wish."

The elevator bumped slightly and then the door slid open like it has done over and over again. The room was alight and open and they stepped into it with some sort of caution amongst themselves. Along the floor sat a large padded mat and little silent stereos lined the outer wall. The elevator doors shuttered closed and then The Enemy spoke through speakers that lined the walls and ceiling. "Now we must break our fast. Food has been sorted in the other room. Please, enjoy and get mentally prepared for the grueling next challenge ahead of you. Since the league has been annihilated, you can only imagine what horrors are coming next!"

"Is this a dance room or something?" Scarlet asked.

"Uh...no. Have a good lunch!" The speaker went silent and at the other side of the room a door swirled open into existence to Viktor and Wilset's surprise, but Willow and Scarlet didn't react until their noses did. Out of that room wafted godly smells of meat and drink and sweets and everything that belongs in a well catered feast. "Screw it," Scarlet said. "I can eat an ox right now!" She ran towards the room and the others followed in degrees of restraint. Viktor was right behind Scarlet, Wilset a couple paces from him, and Willow dead last, not hungry enough to run headlong into a potential trap. She wanted to tell Scarlet to stop, but she was already gone with Viktor. They were in the room when Willow peeked her head inside and saw all of it plastered on several wooden benches which sat parallel with one another, laden with heavy white silk table upholstery to protect both the bench and the massive amounts of food that sat on each one.

Spreads of meat and roasts sprawled the lengths of the tables from roast duck surrounded by fields of roasted garlic and honeyed onions. Turducken stuffed to the brim and leaking oceans of grease and flavor out onto their respective dishes. Chickens galore and steaks of beef roasted in every type of cook. Salads and vegetables and teeming fruit ready to explode with one tiny little prod spread all about and shining from the fluorescent lights that shone down from above. It smelled like everything tasty put in one, and Scarlet started slamming some of it down on one table and Viktor found another, his hands knuckle deep into the turducken, ripping tendrils from it. Wilset sat down and smoothed a white napkin that he fluffed out from his coat pocket. He ate carefully and elegantly, a fork and knife, a plate right there in front of him, a wonderful dichotomy from the two others around him who ate with their hands. Scarlet seemed to forget about what she had just done a little bit earlier, her hands still caked with a thin film of ballsack monster blood, but she seemed to have forgotten about it as she munched on a leg of duck and turkey at the same time. Willow made a mental note to not eat from either of those roasts and sat down next to Wilset who was fluffing a green salad of egg and bacon.

"Hey, Wilset," she asked him.

"Yes Willow?" He answered.

"Why do you think he's giving us food?"

"I don't know, I thought that it may be poisoned or something but then I saw them," he pointed to the two monsters eating over at the other tables, "and I guessed that it was alright to eat. I'm not even that hungry per se, but I would like a little bit of a bite before we move on."

"Uh huh," she looked at a fat juicy steak that sat in front of her and shook her head, "eh, I don't think I'm that hungry." She was peckish, but unwilling. "So...what are you going to do when you meet him?"

"You know...I don't rightly know quite yet. What about you?"

"I'm going to kill him."

"Ah, right. Almost forgot about that part."

"Are you...still okay with that?"

"Hmm...maybe. I won't stop you," he looked over towards Viktor and Scarlet, two very large people, "I don't think I could stop this crusade if I wanted to either way."

"What do you remember about coming here? You know

this isn't Earth, right?"

"I pieced that together almost instantly. It was all dark and then I was here in this place and I was told my job. I was told that I was Adolf Hitler but somehow I knew I was Charlie Chaplin, or, atleast, I thought that I was. I remembered my parents back then, or Charlie's parents. I remembered doing my first film back in...1914 I think...and then it was much like that. Little memories which, right now, are fleeting. It was like the thoughts were shoved into my brain without the care to keep them there. I remember making my first talkie back in 1940-"

"Talkie?" She asked.

"Oh, talking films. Where we actually talk in them instead of cards. I explored it a little in Modern Times that I did back in '36, but, let me tell you Willow, I was scared. I thought people would hate my voice. It was scary. And it was during a scary time where the nazi's were ramping up towards the second world war. I remember we started filming right before the invasion of Poland and that's when I knew, hearing about all the destruction, that I had to go through with it lest we let men like that trample all over us. So, Willow, to answer your question from earlier: No, I won't stop you. I'm sure of that now." He took a bite of salad and patted his mouth. Then his eyes went wide like he was surprised.

"What? Are you okay?"

He coughed and cleared his throat, "Oh I'm okay," he smiled. "I just forgot myself for a second there. I am Wilset, not Charlie."

"Well, glad to have you on the team, Wilset." She stood.

"Pleasure." He responded.

Willow made her way around towards Viktor who finally sat and picked away at the entire turducken, giant piece by giant piece. "How is it?" Scarlet asked him.

"Delicious," he answered with a full mouth.

"Hey, Willow, wanna sit next to me?" Scarlet asked, she still smelled.

"Nah, I'm just making the rounds."

"Wow, just cause I'm covered in monster ball sack goo, huh?"

"Maybe, but I'm here to talk with Viktor a little."

"Me?" Viktor perked his giant head. Even sitting he was taller than all of them.

"Yea, just wanted to make sure you're okay. You're also new to the crew so I wanted to just see how it's all going before this whole weird lunch is over."

"It is going okay, Willow. I would like to ask you both a question though."

"Shoot," Scarlet answered.

"Shoot?" Wilset asked.

"No, we're not shooting a gun."

"Oh, okay, then continue on."

The girls looked at Viktor who sat confused for a second and then asked his question, "Why do you two want to kill him up there so bad?"

"He killed me," Scarlet answered.

"Ah, a noble cause then." He looked at Willow, "And what about you?"

"I...have to."

"Interesting."

Willow thought about seeing her mom earlier. She thought about this impromptu lunchtime. She thought about the whole LOTHWQE thing and how weird this whole trial system was. She thought about Chett and the guns and the fighting down below. She thought about that peculiar night and that rising sunrise. She thought about that shadow man who appeared before everything went black. First said something to her, but the memory was disillusioned. She thought about the key and The Enemy and the years of awfulness that she trudged through. She thought about Scarlet dying and being replaced with a copy controlled by a piece of The Enemy. Then she looked around at this room and all the food and the three companions they now had. She wasn't exactly sure about the conclusion that she almost landed on, she needed to see more. But she didn't think about it anymore. Either way, they had to kill him up there, no matter what. Something told her that she had to right before the black. I told her. Should I remind her? No. Not yet.

Viktor stretched his long arms out and placed his huge hands over both the girls shoulders, "I will help you then. We are friends."

"I knew that, Vik." Scarlet said.

The speakers above them conked as they turned on, "Alright! Lunchtime is over! Please file back into the other room where you will get your next challenge!"

"A dance challenge?" Scarlet asked.

"Shut up! Move!" He said and she laughed to herself. They shuffled out into the other room and padded around the dance mat. Scarlet held her stomach as she walked, "I ate too much, man." She said to no one in particular. Once they were all in place the door to the food room sucked itself back into the wall and the smells were gone in an instant. "Alrighty!" He clapped his hands together making the mic fudge and go staticky for a second. "Marrion twins, front and center!" The elevator opened at the command and those two dudes with their spandex onesies that Willow instantly remembered from the carnival trotted out. She zoned in on their giant bulges instantly and confirmed that they were, in fact, those same exact trapeze twins. Were they also dancers or something?

"Yo, yo! One two three! Mic check! Mic check!" One of the twins said as he pulled out a baseball cap and put it sideways on his head. "Hit it, bro!"

His brother picked up one of the stereos on the ground, popped a CD into the top, and started bobbing his head as a fast song with a lot of scratches and boops played out. The other twin got down and started doing a wicked breakdance, spinning on his ass, to his head, to one hand and then some. He busted some crazy ass moves on the dance pad, finishing his set with a beautiful kick into a spin on his elbow that somehow held his entire body up vertically. He spun into a standing position and, like a switch, took the hat off and bowed politely to the group of men, women, and monsters right in front of him.

"That was," *burp*, "pretty sick," Scarlet said, still rubbing her stomach.

"Sick indeed," The Enemy said. "Now, this challenge is to beat those two in a breakdancing competition. You may choose one of you from that little group. There will be three rounds and three judges."

"Who're the judges?" Willow asked.

"Ah, in all fairness, one judge may be from your little posse, one will be one of the twins-"

"Yo, keep up!" One of them said to the other as they high fived.

"And, before I was interrupted, I will be the last judge."

"Fair?" Scarlet said and burped, "Two of the three are on your side."

"The twins are not on either side, they are here for the art of dance and they will vote accordingly."

"What happens if we lose?" Wilset asked, smoothing his mustache.

"Then you will all die, yadda yadda, you get the gist. Now! Which one of you is going to be the challenger to...which one of the twins is the judge and which one is the dancer, I forget."

"Yo!" They both raised their hands at the same time.

"Uh..." The Enemy said, "yea, either one of them."

"Wait!" Willow said, "What are the rules?"

"I already gave you the rules, three rounds to beat them by any means necessary in a breakdancing competition. Three judges give scores out of ten for each round and those scores are culminated and added up at the end of the third round. Then if you lose you die, blah blah blah, okay you get it. Now choose. I'll give you all a minute to decide."

The group huddled together as the twins high fived each

other and said "Yo!"

"Okay," Willow started, "I vote that I be the judge."

They all nodded.

"Now who volunteers to be the dancer?"

"I am no good at dancing," Viktor started, "and I fear that you all may throw up if I even try. You see, I start to get..."

"Okay, okay. So it's a no on Viktor, who else?"

"I was quite the dancer-" Wilset started.

"I'll do it," Scarlet cut him off. She burped again.

"You sure? I think you ate too much," Willow said.

"True, excuse me for a second ladies," she broke from the group and bent over in the corner of the room. Out of her mouth streamed a thick spew of vomit as she hurled into the corner, "Huuuuuuuuuuuurrrrrr," more came jet streaming out, "huuuuurrrrr," more, "huuuurrrr," and she finally spit, *hack ptoo!* She walked back to the group who watched in horror. "I think I'm good." Behind her trailed the smell of vomit and stomach acid as well as the light tapering scent of ball sack juice. Wilset's face went green, Willow was used to those bad smells, and Viktor breathed in deep as if he enjoyed it.

"Uh, okay," Willow said. "I think my vote goes for Scarlet, any objections?"

Viktor and Wilset were quiet. Wilset looked at her wearily. He must have not enjoyed the red filth that plastered her skin nor the smell of vomit that trailed behind her. Viktor smiled and nodded.

"WHAT. THE. HELL!" The Enemy yelled. "I tried to slow you down with all the food, but I didn't think you would just vomit it all up in here!"

"Well I did, buster. And I'm the one who's going to win this competition!"

The group cheered for a second and then looked around and then clapped a little and then went silent, none of them really knowing how to back her up in that statement.

"Okay, so be it. Who is your judge?"

"I am." Willow said.

"Ah, the little Willow. Fine. We may start as soon as possible."

A desk with three seats rose from the ground, "Please, just imagine that I'm in the third seat." The Enemy spoke as Willow and one of the twins sat down, looking out over the mat where Scarlet sat stretching and the other twin did preliminary lunges, waiting for the contest to start. Wilset and Viktor stood off in Scarlet's corner. Viktor gave her two thumbs up and Wilset paced wearily, nervous about the whole situation, his eyes trailing off towards the brown corner where Scarlet had hurled everything in her stomach earlier. The room began to fill with the pungent scent and the twin started to take some notice.

"Yo! Who vomited in the corner yo?" The dancer twin said.

"I did. So what?" Scarlet shrugged.

"Yo, I don't deal with vomit or any other bodily fluids yo."

"Deal with it, yo. Am I going first or what?"

"Sure," The Enemy said. "Go right ahead."

She nodded, made sure the strap on the Glock in her holster was tight and secure, and then got down and dirty with it on the dance floor. Some song started busting up and Willow watched with amazement as she busted it down like she had been training for this exact day. She remembered back to when she had dared her to breakdance back at her house. Did that spur her on to practice? Willow pondered and Scarlet kicked her legs out, turning and daring into a spin and flop kick to the other side. She did a couple more moves to the music and then stood, panting. The dance mat was covered with red ball sack juices and vomit that had stained the front of her shirt. "Beat that!" She looked towards the judges and watched Willow raise a large ten out of ten above her head while the other twin raised a five.

"Eh, decent. Five." The speaker spoke.

"BS, man! That was like an eight minimum!" She screamed.

"I am a judge, you cannot tell me otherwise. Now let the other twin do his routine. Watch how a real B-Boy does it."

"Y-yo, boss, I can't do no bodily fluids and the mat is all..."

"JUST DANCE, THAT'S WHAT I'M PAYING YOU FOR!"

"You're paying them!" Wilset screamed.

"No, no. It's just a saying! Ha hahaha, now dance. Now."

The twin shook his head and began to boogie it down to some beat. He spun and kicked like he did before, his sideways hat spinning on his head somehow. Willow saw that his dance was much more pristine than Scarlet's dance, *Fuck me if I give him anything above a one,* she thought. When the dance was over, Willow raised a fat goose egg while the other twin raised up a ten, "Ten!" said the speaker. "Beautiful! That's how you do it!" The score was now an even 20-20 after the first round.

The dancing twin's face looked green and putrid as his spandex suit was soaked in vile fluids that still rubbed all around the mat.

"Second round! Scarlet, you may go!"

Viktor patted her on the back, "Don't let them get in your head."

"Yea, just think back to your happiest memory and do that," Wilset chimed in.

"Happiest memory?" She nodded, "Thanks, Wil."

She went to the bloodied mat and began a usual breakdancing routine filled with kicks and shaky headstands and a lot of spinning, all accompanied to a harsh beat that thudded out from somewhere in the room...and then it slowed into a swan song, slowing and slowing. Piano started ringing out as well as a small orchestra that swallowed the beat as the breakdance turned into an interpretive dance of the arts, the spinning turned into fluid dance. She smelled like vomit, but her movements catered more to the fresh smell of the ocean on a swell, its winds whispering and bellowing all around. And the dance ended and she put her head down as all the lights shut off at once. *Where are the production assistants?* Willow thought as she already grabbed for a score card that read ten.

The light flickered back on as Willow, Viktor, and Wilset all clapped. The twin judge clapped as well and then stopped when he saw his brother looking at him with a stern set of eyes that said 'you dick'. Willow, of course, raised the ten scorecard. The twin raised an eight and the speaker rumbled out an uncaring, "seven."

"I did say it was a breakdancing competition, right? Whatever. Twin, go ahead."

Scarlet moved off the mat towards her corner as the other twin stepped on. He moved a little slower this time, stumbling over himself as he got ready for his set to start. He tried to breath slowly so as not to inhale the fumes of vomit and blood that covered both him and the mat that he stood on. Then the beat started and he went even harder this time. His spins were even spinnier and his stands from either his head or his elbow to his shoulders and even his nose were filled with intention to win. But on his final headstand he slipped slightly, sending his face crashing down into the muck of the mat. Blood and vomit and mysterious white stuff got into his mouth as he pulled himself off of it, spitting and retching. The song ended abruptly with a *eeerrrkkk* and his set was over. His twin clapped real hard as Willow raised another zero. The twin raised a ten and the speaker yelled out, "Ten! Wonderful! Magnificent!" But still, after the scores were added up, Scarlet was winning with 45 and the twin was losing right behind at 40.

"Biological warfare," Viktor said, "excellent plan, Scarlet."

"He's basically out by now," Wilset said, looking over towards the dancing twin who was currently retching some more in another corner. "Just one more, can you do that?"

"Oh, obviously," Scarlet smiled and nodded, the blood and vomit on her face dripping and drying. Wilset smiled, nodded, and then looked away, swallowing away his want to vomit. Viktor gave her another thumbs up and nodded.

"Alright! Final round! Scarlet, take your place!" The speaker rumbled.

She took her place and got on a knee, waiting for the set to start. Music started and a spotlight beamed down right on top of her from somewhere. *Seriously, who's doing the production?* Willow thought as Scarlet started where she left off. The interpretive dance moved and flowed like a pond of water, rippling and moving with itself caused by an epicenter of disturbance. She moved and swayed elegantly to the soft piano. She was a tall and stout girl, with thick arms, giant legs, and a tight waist, someone who looked like they couldn't even touch their toes, but, on the contrary, she moved like a piece of silk flowing in the wind. Willow was impressed and Wilset even more so. He liked to dance, and would have volunteered had she not, but he was sure that they made the right decision picking her. He would have teared up watching the performance if the entire room didn't smell like vomit and blood and brass.

Then, in the middle of the dance, the beat of the breakdance song started to come in slightly and then grow, eventually overtaking the swan song as Scarlet burst back into the spins and headstands of a breakdance. She went and went, doing and busting it down. Groovalicious is the only correct word to describe it. She ran over to the empty chair at the judge table, grabbed it, and sat it down on the mat. A rope furrowed down from somewhere and she pulled it, releasing a waterfall of blood and vomit and guts all over herself. Her leg kicked up and ended the song.

Wilset vomited in his mouth as Viktor began to clap ecstatically. Willow shook her head, tried to not think about any of the possibilities of it all, and began clapping too. *Smart. Biological warfare,* Willow thought. She raised a ten. The other twin raised a zero and the speaker said, "zero."

"What?" Scarlet wiped her face and pulled a string of guts out from around her neck. "That was literally perfect!"

"Not to me. Next!" The Speaker beckoned the twin who

sat there, his face now white as he watched all the guts and blood and vomit pool to where he had to dance. He had just gotten rid of the foul taste in his mouth and now he had to do that?

He shook his head and moved onto the mat, stepping over little mounds of guts and other types of fleshy viscera that clumped together like some type of microbial mass. He swallowed and started to boogie it down and, in one spin, out from him came a swirling fountain of vomit that splattered over everyone like some green-gray water fountain that had a little too much heft to its streams. The judges got thoroughly covered as well as Wilset and Viktor. Wilset swallowed back his own flow as Viktor looked down at the lower part of his pant leg where it had gotten the worst of the spray. Scarlet wiped it down her face, uncaring and Willow did much the same. Willow blinked away the goo and found the twin crumpled over on the mat. His dance was over and she raised a zero above her head. Beside her the judge twin sat shocked, his face dribbling with the stuff. He looked up at the ceiling like he was trying to ask what to give his vomitous brother. He shakily raised a ten above his head. "Uh…" the Speaker said, "Ten! Of course! Wonderful show and very experimental indeed!"

Scarlet counted her fingers for a second, "Wait a second, that means I lose! What the fuck!" The score now was 55-60, and Scarlet had lost in the final round.

"You have! You lose! You lose! Ha hahaha!"

Scarlet walked over to the twin judge and unholstered her Glock 34 that Willow gave her earlier. She flipped the safety off, "I think you picked the wrong card up. You meant to give that performance a zero, right?"

"Uh…uh…" he looked around. "Yea, I meant to give it a zero." He raised a zero card. "That was my mistake and I own up to it!"

She holstered the pistol and laughed, "I win! 55-50! Get FUCKED!"

"CHEATER! YOU CANNOT DO THAT!"

"Sorry dawg," she shrugged, "you said earlier that we had to win by any means necessary. And I won. By any means necessary."

"What? You-you can't-I-"

"She won!" Willow said. "Can we move on now?"

"I...yes...the next floor has been unlocked." The speakers went silent and the crew walked over to the elevator. Scarlet laughed and kicked through the blood and guts on the mat, making sure to send a harsh boot into the stomach of the dancing twin on her way past. Viktor followed her, sending another much larger boot into his core, making him cough and sputter. His twin screamed in horror as he went over to check if he was alright. Wilset took a wide wide berth around all of that mess, dodging just between the brown corner and the blood spillage. Willow shuffled them all inside the elevator and squeezed in herself, pressing the six button. It lit up yellow and the doors shuttered closed.

The elevator smelled like vomit and blood and everything disgusting, a feast for a fiend. "Good job Scarlet!" Viktor boomed. "I am proud of you!"

"Yes," Wilset covered his nose with a handkerchief. "Good job indeed."

"Did you practice or something?" Willow asked.

"Yeah. After you dared me to breakdance, I thought it was pretty fun and just did it on my own for a while. Helped get me to sleep," then she frowned, "Oh wait, I don't think that was REALLY me, right? That was just some clone who's memories got implanted into me, right?"

"No. I think it was you. They say that that piece of him basically became you during that time, so it was you...at least a little bit of you." She thought of that random kiss during that one night.

"Yea, but I remember times where I really wanted to go and talk to you and ask you if you're alright when times got really bad, but something forced me to stop and stay away. I feel really guilty about all of that," her bloodied mouth parted in a smile. "I'm sorry man."

"Accepted." Willow smiled between her vomit caked lips.

Wilset almost asked for the context, but didn't. He knew that was something for them and them alone. He smiled underneath his handkerchief. Viktor smiled and was happy to have friends, even if his head was bent at an odd angle, stuck as it poked the top of the elevator. The doors finally opened and the little crew stepped through the threshold into another room that smelled like hot steaming blueberry pie.

And in that other room, there was an egregiously fat man sitting behind a large fat table. Before and behind and all around him were those steaming hot blueberry pies which sat in silver trays. He was a bald man, the sheen of his head shinier than a brand new coin. His face looked almost squashed and his nose poked out just enough from the fat folds that enveloped his face. He wore a tightly fitting vest and an overcoat which must have been custom made to have been able to fit his mass in its entirety. He smiled and beckoned the group with an inviting hand, his eyes never seeming bothered by the absolute viscosity of the people who walked up to him washed in vomit and blood and other little scents and colors. "Welcome!" He said in a thick German accent. "No formalities with me! I challenge you all to a pie eating contest!" Four chairs popped up in front of them. "Please sit."

The group looked at each other and then sat. "So, what're the rules?" Willow asked.

"Ah! The rules! Yes! I eat more pies than all of you! If I win, then you all die! If you all win, you move on to the seventh and final floor!"

Pies began to float from all over. Each person from Willow to Wilset got one to start with but more floated and lined up before them all. The fat man looked over five large pies that floated in front of him, "Are you all ready to begin or do you have more questions?"

"Hole up!" Scarlet said. "So, all the pies we eat go against all the pies you eat? Like it's cumulative?"

"Yes, indeed. Ah! You look like my sister Olga back in Germany! Ah, I miss Olga!"

"Another question," Willow asked. "What's your name?"

"Ah! My name! Augustus! That is my name! Named after my great-great-great-great-great-great-great grandfather! Ah ha ha ha ha! He made me laugh!"

"You met your super-great grandfather?"

"No! That would be silly pale woman! Ah ha ha ha! Now do we eat?"

"Uh," Willow looked at the group sitting to her right. Scarlet was right next to her, her face a mess as her stomach troubled her. Viktor sat to her right, staring right down at the pie intensely. Wilset sat at the other end, he swallowed down nervousness. Willow looked back at Augustus, "Uh...yea, I guess so."

"Great! Ah ha ha ha ha! Now...EAT!"

The five pies in front of Augustus seemed to disappear almost instantly as his mouth sucked them up like a vacuum, leaving just the silver tins to clank against the floor as it stopped floating, dead without its blueberry meat used to pad its blueberry organs used to pump its blueberry blood, all enveloped and imbibed by the enormous man that was Augustus. Willow watched the feat as Scarlet slammed her face into the blue, munching and slurping. Viktor, his mouth huge and available, was able to consume his pie within the ample time that Augustus ate his five. Wilset began, using a pair of fork and knife, but it was slow and he was still full and airy from both the feast earlier and the vomitous visceral affair that took place directly afterwards. Willow finally started, scarfing her face in the gelatinous pies. She more mushed the stuff around the sides so that they fell off and onto the floor. Scarlet ate, the vomit and blood all over her face smearing into the first couple of pies which was quickly replaced by the guts of the infinite blueberry pies. Viktor was through with many, his giant hands scooping and slamming it into his mouth with viscous intent. Viktor didn't like the look of the fat man. Augustus reminded him of gluttony, everything that made people vain and greedy. Without men like him, Viktor supposed, then the world would be a much better place. So Viktor ate quickly, his massive stomach barely filling with each large pie stuffed down his personal pie-hole.

"Aw, I think I'm going to heave-" Wilset said after his second pie was downed elegantly with a fork and knife.

"Ah!" Augustus said between mouthfuls of pie, "If you vomit, you are out!" He ate another pie in a single bite, "And no longer able to participate further!"

He shook his head a little and fixed his mustache which had a couple blueberries stuck in it.

Willow was much the same, her appetite not the most vacuous of the table. But she kept mushing the pie meat with her face, trying to push enough off so it could count as a fully eaten pie. Scarlet continued to eat, her face a dark blue. And the room was filled with just the sound of chewing and slurping and moistness as pies were slobbered and consumed. More kept appearing and floating over to each participant as they finished one pie and went on to another one. Minutes turned to tens of minutes and finally, Wilset tapped out, patting his belly as he sat back and dazed off somewhere in a food coma. The pies stopped coming to him and instead went towards Augustus or Viktor, who were almost keeping neck and neck with one another, their pie tins falling around them like snow and each pile building up like a mountain of silver. Scarlet continued to eat, she never looked up. Willow was so full she could burst, but she kept taking tiny bites and pushing the pie meat away with her face, but she was getting slower and slower as the sugar and blueberries began to digest, her veins becoming molasses as her brain was filled with melatonin. She blinked once, twice, thrice, and thought *Man, I'm tired,* and fell asleep facedown in her final pie, dreaming of pies for the first time in her life. She thought she was still eating in her dream, but in this reality, she was out.

Viktor made sure to look at Augustus as he vacuumed the pies into his gaping maw. Viktor wanted to know how many he had to keep up with. So far, to Viktor's count, he has eaten sixty pies while Augustus has consumed one-hundred, going almost five at a time, every time. Viktor took account of his friends at the table and saw Wilset dozing empty up towards the ceiling encased in a pie induced coma, while Scarlet continued to slam her face in pie after pie like some robotic oddity. He liked Scarlet much, she reminded him of the happiness and good that humanity can bring. It made him sad that he could never be a part of it. And, at the other end of the table, he spotted Willow, snoring softly, her pillow a half full tin of pie. And then he looked at Augustus and noticed something very peculiar, something that Scarlet would never have noticed with account that her face was always stuffed nose deep into a whole pie. Augustus was now only eating three pies at a time. *He's slowing down,* Viktor thought. And he was right. Augustus now only ate two at once, and then one. He still vacuumed them down faster than anyone at the table, but this was the chance that Viktor was looking for. He started slamming both his massive hands into two separate pie tins, taking entire handfuls and eating them both at once. Two at a time, Viktor began to catch up. Augustus didn't even notice as sweat accumulated all over his forehead, his full focus being on the eating part. His vest began to stretch and rip, the button straining and bulging out from his expanding mass of flesh.

And he expanded more and more, going from a human to a ball of meat and mouth with a beady little pair of eyes. But he still vacuumed them up, trying to keep up with ol' two-pies Viktor, who began to slow down himself. It slowed and slowed, Viktor still ate his two pies, but in slow motion. Scarlet still ate with her face down in some unknown amount of pies.

Eating. Eating. Eating. Eating. Eating. Eating...Eating... Eating......Eating.........Slowing.........slow...in......g...

Viktor swayed and stopped, he had never been this full

in his entire life, but he still heard Scarlet who slobbered next to him, her face still in a pie. Augustus stopped as he tried to speak, but couldn't. His eyes slowly went wider and wider and wider, like two golf balls in a giant fleshy sun that just hit its red giant phase. He was all out of steam...and hydrogen. And he began to expand and expand to where he almost touched the ceiling and pushed the table back, his tendrils of flesh oozing out all over the floor. Willow was asleep, Wilset didn't even seem to notice, Scarlet still ate another pie, and Viktor watched in amazement as a resounding *Pop!* filled the room as Augustus blew up, coating the entire room in blueberry.

It slapped against the walls and painted the floor as well as the four who sat in front of the once German man. Wilset snapped out of it and looked around at the newly painted room, Viktor tapped Scarlet's shoulder and she sat up with a "Wha- What's going on?" Her eyes looked corked and stingy and dry. Willow sat up, slapped her lips, and looked around, "Where's Augustus?" She asked.

"He...popped!" Viktor said.

"Huh..." Willow responded and looked down at herself. "Did I fall asleep?"

"Do you think that you fell asleep?"

"No."

"Then you did not, Willow. And we won."

Augustus was completely gone as if that blueberry sun had taken all of his skin and bones and guts with him. Maybe his insides were made up of sweet steaming blueberry pie. Now that's a thought. The group wearily stood and lumbered over towards the elevator.

"Aw...I think I'm gonna be sick," Scarlet said, holding her stomach.

"Hey," Willow patted her back, "Why don't you-"

She was cut off as Scarlet vomited blueberries all over her shoes. "Sorry," she straightened her back afterwards.

"Whatever makes you feel better, man." She tried to smile amidst the eye-stinging smell of stomach acid that wafted up like a humid summer breeze of awfulness.

"Aw!" Scarlet hugged Willow, squeezing her hard with those strong arms of hers. She was like a layer cake, first covered in the black blood of the finger warriors below, then covered in another layer of monster ball juice, then another layer of blood and guts and vomit, and now she was layered head to toe in blueberry. With a touch of her finger, Willow could feel through each one of those layers.

"That's weird...I don't remember him," The Enemy spoke. "Whatever! I'm waiting on the next floor for you to kill me." The doors slid open and the group, covered in everything under the sun, pushed into the small box and went up to the seventh and final floor where he was waiting. Willow blinked once, thrice, and...wait...did she ever blink a second time?

Willow

The blackness subsided as the world became white and everyone in the elevator disappeared within that second blink of an eye. And, in that second blink of an eye, I found myself in the middle of a long white hallway with a big brown door clasped shut at the other end. Lining the white wall were tens of people, all sitting in gray fold 'em chairs, all looking away, all arguing loudly with one another.

"Ey! What da fuck! How long's this wait gonna be!" Someone shouted out in a thick New York accent.

"Just wait you fuck!" Someone else shouted.

The arguing continued, on and on. They all looked familiar. All uncanny. And I barely thought about the elevator I was just in.

One looked at me.

"Whattaya lookin' at, huh?"

It was me. It was me and not me. Another one looked at me...another me. They all looked weird but the same... Some with long long hair, some with short hair, some with weird accents and some with completely different clothing. Some looked older and some looked younger, some had piercings and some had tattoos. But one thing they all had as they all quieted and looked towards my direction were my eyes. My Mom's eyes.

"My god...is she really the one that he's waiting for, huh?" One of the Willow's asked.

"I guess so," a short haired Willow answered.

"Fuck me, you little bitch. Makin' us all wait so fuckin' long," The New York Willow glared. "Says I'm the key or whatever, blah blah, jesus fuckin' A."

"Uh...what's happening?" Was all I could say. I looked down and found all that blueberry and blood and vomit gone as a pristine white tracksuit covered my body. None of them answered with their mouths as they all spoke with their eyes which all said, 'Fuck you' simultaneously.

KNOCK! KNOCK! "Gutentag! Please, Willow, come down! We need to talk!" A thick German voice shot out from the big wooden door that just ever so slightly cracked open. It sat stark and brown at the end of the hallway. I started the trek through the rows of Willows down towards the door, almost drawn to it as if it were some sort of vacuum. I tried to look down. It was hard to not glance at them as they all followed with those awful glances. Some were buff and some looked so frail and skinny that I began to pity them. Was that what I really looked like to another person? Seeing it from the outside was weird. "Um, excuse me. Pardon me. Sorry." I muttered as they still watched and watched and watched.

I opened the door and shut it behind myself which relieved a heavy weight from the center of my chest. I shook my head and looked around at the clean smelling room. It was brown and rustic looking. At the far end sat a large desk and behind it sat Augustus the German pie-man. "Please, Willow. Come sit, I must talk with you before the time has come."

What was I supposed to say? No? I don't even know what's fucking happening anymore. I sat down across from him. He really was massive. Looking at him a little more clearly, he looked like a big slice of pie. The man oozed the theme of *Pie!* If that makes any type of sense.

"You don't really think I was just some obstacle, do you?" He asked, his German accent all gone.

I didn't answer him.

He cleared his throat, swallowed, stood up with his massive size, and spoke, "YOU HAVE MESSED WITH THE PRIMAL FORCES OF NATURE!"

I didn't answer.

"AND YOU SHALL ATONE!"

I didn't answer.

"Do you understand?" He asked with a quieter voice.

"Understand what?"

"That I am...you know..."

"I don't know."

"You see...this world of worlds is a paltry place that only serves to bring me back, but you hypnotized my First, huh? Made him...defect...am I not right? We were right there... on the end of it all...and all he needed to do was kill you... bring you to me...but..." He sighed almost fondly. "I guess it's not too much trouble. There's infinite universes and there's infinite keys and only one me. I can just go over to another more suitable one...but, and here's what fascinates me about this all...you see, in each and every universe, in the infinite amount of them, this is the only time that you or any other key has made one of them defect. Now, I know, it's infinite which equals an infinite amount of possibilities which ALSO means that this is not the only time this has happened, but the deeper I look, the less I find and by that I mean that I cannot find another situation like this. Isn't it interesting? You caused even a GOD to be confused, you a little peoplething... now you're making me wonder... Well... What has been done is done. He proceeded with the ritual, killing everything in that world...except you...and I cannot understand. He doesn't even know that I can just sweep you away in an instant from his little worlds that he loves to create. Like a blink and no one even notices. Weak. You know, Willow, I can just proceed with it by myself, I can just bring you back and finish it and become that new world like I have done an infinite amount of times before…but I am intrigued. I will leave to someplace else. Some other universe with some other key and some other apostles and then, maybe there, I will achieve true godhood like I have in another infinite amount of universes. But I will keep an eye on you…you are interesting. But you are also nothing. I wish you luck." He sat back down, "Oh, and Willow…a God doesn't lend much."

I realized that I hadn't blinked once until that very second. My eyes burned like fire and my tear ducts welled. I blinked and-

Mark

Huh…she must've blinked again. She looked around all weird and then smiled a little at the others.

26

The doors opened and they filed out into a large room. A man stood by the back wall which spread behind him in a large and magnificent door that begged to be called art deco. Chandeliers lined the ceiling as a checker patterned floor stretched along their feet. Large windows with flowing velvet drapes as red and as ripe as an apple frilled down across them, washing the room in a red glow. Near the ceiling sat large stained glass windows with quasi biblical-esque art that looked down on them all in their blood and blueberry stained clothing. And large white pillars lined the ceiling to the floor. The man at the end of the magnificent room straightened up and said, "Pickles?" His voice echoed across the hall in many *pickles--ickles-kles-les.*

"What did he say?" Wilset whispered to the group.

"Fuck me," Scarlet said. "I think I remember that dude."

"Yea," Willow said, remembering the last feast she had on Earth where that man served her a bottle of kimchi at her joke of a request. "He only says pickles."

"Pickles?" He echoed.

"Cucumber!"

He shook his head, "Pickles, pickles..."

The large art deco door opened behind Pickles and out walked a plainly dressed man with golden hair, a killer smile, and deep blue eyes like the ocean. "Ladies and germs!" He echoed. "I see you're all here to kill me, is that so?"

Scarlet's hand dropped steadily towards her holster. She gently unstrapped the Glock and fingered the safety off.

"Yea," Willow said. That was all she said as her 'yea' echoed. *Yea-yea-yea-ya-y.*

"And you two brought some friends, huh? Hitler and that freak of Mary Shelly."

"I'm not Hitler! How many times do I have to tell you?"

"Yea, but...you got the same mustache."

"I-I had this before Hitler ever came to power, you twit!" His mouth twitched.

"Whatever. Pickles will sort you all out for me, isn't that right, Pickles?"

Pickles nodded, "Pickles."

Scarlet finally got a clear view of the man who she wanted to kill so badly. In her blueberry covered hands, she quickly unsheathed the Glock 34 and pointed it at him. Her finger slammed down the trigger. The firing pin, thoroughly jellied with blood and blueberry, slid forth and struck the blueberry bullet. The powder charge within the case ignited with a blueberry smell as the bullet swirled through the blueberry rifling and out into the fresh air. At 2,000 miles per hour, the small blueberry 9mm bullet coasted through the air, just missing the Golden Man by an inch. The gun jammed as the casing got caught in the jellied ejector. The hall blew up in the pure sound that quickly went extinct and its echoes died quickly right after it.

She sat there holding the gun and the man ducked down and ran back into his little room as Pickles roared and ran towards them. He was a large man, but no larger than Viktor and no faster than Willow and his skull no stronger than a bullet going faster than sound. Scarlet cocked the gun and cleared the jam, bringing the sights back onto Pickles. She pulled the trigger and a small hole jammed its way through the man's skull. He fell like a sack of rice and smacked against the floor with a meaty *thwap!* Blood leaked slowly through the hole in his head and Scarlet laughed loud and proud. "This guy was the final one?"

Willow was almost mad and then she didn't mind, "Whatever. Let's get in there and finish this." She turned to Wilset who sat shocked, "How'd it feel to meet your creator? Face to face?"

He shook his head, his ears still ringing from the sound of the pistol shot, "Milquetoast."

While those two were talking, Scarlet walked over with Viktor to the dead man. She kicked him slightly with her scoured boot and holstered the pistol once more, "Get fucked on dickhead. Serve me some more pickles."

"Why are you so angry at this man, Scarlet?" Viktor boomed, his voice echoed deep.

"I...I don't really know...I think that he was part of this whole thing. But he probably wasn't." She looked at the dead Pickles, "I'm sorry."

His hand shot out faster than a bullet and grabbed her ankle.

"Hey! What the-"

He squeezed with the force of a thousand men, breaking it like a pencil. She yelped like a puppy as he threw her off to the side, slamming her into the side of a pillar. She wriggled for a second and then lied still. Willow watched with shock. Viktor began to attack the man, but he threw him off as he stood. Pickles looked about five feet taller, five hundred pounds heavier, and five times meaner than before, with a hollow, bloodless, hole set in the middle of his forehead. "PICKLES." He stated, his voice being five times deeper. Viktor backed up to Willow and Wilset, he even looked like a child to the newly grown Pickles.

"Ha ha ha! That's what happens when you incur the wrath of Pickles!" The Enemy's voice echoed out from somewhere.

"PICKLES?"

"Yes Pickles, you may kill them all now."

Pickles smiled, slow and meaningful, "Pickles."

"What do we do?" Viktor asked.

Pickles charged at them all, shaking the ground with each step.

"Run!" Willow screamed as she dove out of the way. Wilset slunk away towards the still and quiet Scarlet. Viktor stood his ground and lifted his hands in front of him like he was about to stop a freight train. His massive legs tensed and his shoulders locked as the veins in his rapturous forehead began to flow intently as the massive man named Pickles rammed into him with the force of a man the size of Pickles. Viktor slid across the floor slightly but looked up to find that he stopped Pickles dead in his run. Pickles looked down and frowned as his hands grabbed and hugged Viktor to his waist as he bent over backwards, sending Viktor into a suplex fit for a small whale. *Crash!* Viktor's head slammed into the checkered floor, but he spun and responded as he wrapped his legs around Pickles. Pickles stood and tried to get him off. It looked almost funny with the giant man held like a baby in the even bigger man's hands. Viktor slid around to Pickles back and locked his arms in a tight chokehold over his neck. He squeezed hard, enough to easily break a wooden pillar, but his neck resisted as he screamed out a shaky "Pickles!"

Willow hid behind a pillar off to the side and looked around at the situation. She spotted where Scarlet was and saw that Wilset was dragging her off behind the pillar that she flew into. Her ankle was bent in the completely wrong direction and her face sat still. She looked at Pickles and Viktor and saw them swinging around with each other. She looked at the door and thought, for one second, of just leaving and going through it, to finish off that man. But then she heard a scream and looked back towards the catastrophe in front of her. She couldn't just leave them. "Fuck me," she whispered as she darted across the hall towards Scarlet who still sat unconscious. She was still breathing, but her eyes would not respond to anything.

"What do we do?" Wilset asked.

"Um..." Willow looked around. She leaned over and took the Glock from Scarlet's holster and looked back towards Viktor and Pickles who still wrestled over each other in several winning and losing positions. *I could shoot him, but would it really do anything? Fuck it, everyone is allergic to bullets.* She stood up and looked at Wilset, "I'm gonna need you to distract him."

"WHAT?" He yelled as Pickles threw Viktor across the room.

"Yes, go out there and make him get low enough so I can get on his back. Go!" She pushed him out into the room. Pickles saw him and stopped his advance upon the reeling Viktor.

"Pickles?" He asked, like a parent would say to a child.

Wilset looked back to behind the pillar where Willow motioned him to turn Pickles around. "Uh..." he took a couple of steps towards the center of the arena. "Well, how do you do good sir?"

Pickles face went confused, "P-pickles?"

"Uhh..." he took a couple steps to the center of the room. "Yea, sure."

"PICKLES!" He screamed angrily.

"Oh, ah, no, then. Ha ha."

Pickles took a large step towards him, turning just a little for Willow to sneak to another pillar behind him, *almost there,* she thought.

"Pickles."

Wilset took another step towards the other side of the arena, "Hey, Pickles, we're friends, right?"

Pickles shook his head, "Pi-kles,"

"Ah...acquaintances?" He took another step away.

Pickles shook his head.

"Uh...peers?"

Pickles laughed deep and happily, "Pickles!"

He took another step, "Hey, if you find that so funny, what about a joke?"

Viktor grumbled as he tried to get back up, causing Pickles to look over to where he laid. It was in an awkward spot that wouldn't allow Willow to get up on to Pickles's back.

"Hey! Pickles!" Wilset screamed. "Do you like card tricks?" He felt around his blueberry and vomit stained coat and found a deck of cards that he always kept on himself. "P-pick a card, just right over here!" Pickles turned again and took another step over towards Wilset. Wilset almost pissed his pants from how scared he was, one good squeeze from this herculean sized man would pop his head like a tomato. Wilset fanned out a deck of cards, "Come on! Don't be shy."

"Pickles?"

"Just pick a card, Pickles. That's all I care about. It's fun! Come on!" Wilset smiled his best smile.

Pickles was too tall to bend over and grab the cards, so he got on a knee and snatched a couple cards with his large fingers. He perked up as he felt someone climbing up his pant leg, up his back and onto his shoulders. He realized that he forgot about the little one and put her off as insignificant, someone that he was going to kill last as a joyous treat. He reached up angrily, screaming and stomping all around, almost killing Wilset as he dived back into the safety of a pillar. Viktor began to run over, thinking that Willow was in trouble, but he saw that she had her legs wrapped around the back of the giant man's neck and in her hands were two pistols jammed directly against his head. Willow found the triggers and began to fire both as fast as her fingers could move up and down, driving the small bullets directly into the large man's skull like a chisel. He lumbered around and screamed, the blood splashing and spurting out onto her face like an ocean spray. She shook her head and spit, but she continued firing. Her Walther was out first and she dropped it and grabbed her knife and began stabbing it wildly into the thrashing man's skull. The giant man rammed into pillars and screamed fruitless echoes that surrounded them all in a cascade of noise. Soon he fell silent just as he fell to the floor, sending Willow flying in the air. Pain resounded out from her shoulder as she landed on it directly, sending revolting and stomach churning shockwaves all around her body. Wilset helped her up, "Are you okay?" He asked and she nodded. She looked at her hands and saw that her gun and her knife were both gone, probably thrown to some random spot as she involuntarily let them go mid-air.

She looked around the room and saw Viktor prodding the dead Pickles a second time just to make sure the man wouldn't grow another five feet and another five hundred pounds. That didn't happen and Pickles laid dead.

"Owwww..." It was Scarlet's voice that echoed through the room. They all rushed over to where she sat up against a wall. Her leg was royally screwed up. "Not that bad, right?" She laughed when Willow looked at it. "Right at the end too, I get my shit kicked in," she coughed, spitting blood from her lips. "Shit, I don't think that's healthy." She laughed.

"Shit," Willow said.

"Shit indeed. But, here, help me up," Viktor lifted her up easily and held her like a bloody blueberry baby. "Ah, that's nice. Look, let's go kill that dude and then we can go see what's wrong with me."

Willow grabbed her flopping hand, "Just don't die again, alright?"

She laughed bloody, "You think I'm gonna let that dude kill me?"

"Alright," Willow looked towards the large door, "Let's go."

They walked slowly and quietly towards the door,

looking around for any other surprises, but there were none and now they were there. Willow grabbed the handle and cranked it open just enough to find a familiar smell of cigarettes waft from the entrance. She pushed just a little more. *Eeeeerrrkkk* the door squeaked open. There was that small detective's office that she remembered so well. She saw that same window froth with god rays that teemed out towards the desk. The floor was wooden as well as the brown walls. A small smoke trail danced up towards the ceiling from that one cigarette that was still stuck in the indent of that same ashtray. And behind the desk sat the man with golden hair and blue eyes and perfect teeth. He smiled at the group as they filed in. *Clair de Lune* whispered out in the corner, just like the first time they met, face to face. It died slowly as they all stood, staring.

They all sat silent. Wilset looked around, looked at his creator and then left the office without a word. Viktor held Scarlet like a baby, her twisted leg hanging precariously and uselessly to the side. She winced with each step, but still kept a stern face looking at the man. Willow started walking towards the man, her left leg tingling as she felt the weight of the Glock 43 micro pistol still strapped to her ankle, hidden under the thick pant leg. Her boots fell silent with each step across the wooden floor.

I decided to remind her of what I told her the last time we spoke. In this silent climax, in this tiny moment, in this final moment, I finally had it. That shadowman I conjured... that could never be Addasaeh, I guess she took the bait, maybe. At that point she didn't seem to care much. I made it work though. She cares. She lives. I may never be human, but at the least I get this redemption.

She turned the bend silently and came face to face with the man who stood as an icon for all the pain that she had been through for the past couple of years. Of course, the Golden Man knew she had that gun holstered and hidden behind the cloth of the left leg. His smile turned slightly sad as he watched her slowly unholster that gun as she lifted said pant leg. It was a small little thing that looked big in her quaint hands, rough with subtle calluses.

"Kill me..." It was so silent and subtle. Just a tick in her mind. "Shoot me..." Another tick. She pointed the gun at the man's head and he looked down the barrel. Her finger slid towards the trigger and found it as her thumb tightened and felt the little joints of the pistol grip that felt good between her fingers. Her right foot stood in front of her left. Her shoulders felt heavy and strained. She looked nervous below the exterior and the Golden Man saw. He slowly looked her up and down, gave another sad smile, his blue eyes welling slightly, and then he gave a small nod as she began to pull on the trigger.

It took around five pounds of force to pull the trigger back, to activate the striker pin, to ignite the cartridge that shoots the bullet out of the barrel. Within the microsecond it took to pull the trigger, Willow thought. In the first pound of force, as her finger strained, she thought of her mother on the second floor. Then she thought about her real mother. Then she thought about her father and her brothers and all of that awfulness. In the second pound of force, she thought about Scarlet, her best friend. She thought about her dying, she thought about her busted leg now, she thought about how she was about to avenge her. In the third pound of force, she thought about her life and the torture and the smell and the insanity and how much she hated this man in front of her, the man who was about to get his brains turned into soup. In the fourth pound of force, she thought about that man. And then she smiled sadly and nodded towards him as the trigger hit the fifth pound and the bullet flung out of the barrel.

It hit him directly in the middle of the forehead and he toppled out of his chair and onto the ground, his golden locks now becoming red as his blood filtered out of the back and the front of his skull. She took another step over him, lowered the pistol at his head and pulled the trigger a second time, and then a third time, and then a fourth time. Each bullet found a new spot to rest in his head. One went through his eye, one through his cheek, and one through his chin which shattered it, causing bone to sprinkle around the scene. She watched him, dead, and then dropped the gun on the ground. She looked over towards the group of friends, one old, two new, and she smiled a little more. Her face felt wet.

Wilset heard the shots ring out from where he stood outside that door. He looked down and noticed that his foot was gone. And then his hands. Then his body. He smiled, took off his bowler hat, and said something as his mouth disappeared and, soon after, his face with it.

Viktor dropped Scarlet with a *thump* as his hands went, and then his legs, he looked up, "Goodbye," he said finally as the rest of his body turned to nothing. Scarlet didn't say a word as she rolled and looked up towards Willow who was splattered in blood, vomit, blueberries, and all the stink that they've been through. She smiled as she watched little trails of tears ford their path down the gunk on her face. And then Scarlet was gone.

Willow swallowed as the world turned to darkness and the void enveloped her. First the walls turned to black, then the floor, then the Golden Man who she had killed. Her legs turned to black, her body disappeared, and her head went *poof* as it sunk into the void.

27

"Would you like to go back?" I asked.

"To where?" She answered.

"To your home."

"I don't have a home."

"You do. I can bring you back. Whole. Would you like that?"

She took a while to answer, time not being something of any noticeable degree here. It could have been a minute or two or ten; A month or two or ten; A year or two or ten or a hundred or a thousand or a million or a billion. Her mind teemed with slow remembrance. She thought about the smell of air she took before she fought the Golden Man. She thought about life. She thought about her friends. She thought about her mother. She thought about falsehoods and fakeness that she believed corrupted the world. Everything in her told her to say no. It told her to sink back into nothingness. It told her to give up then and there, her entire body teeming with that very answer. Say no, it would speak in wordless words. Then she spoke soft and silently, in nothing short of a whisper's whisper, "Yes."

"Okay..."

I thought of something for a second's second, but I didn't say it.

*

The haze faltered when the world came back around her. The cool air of the night was the first thing she noticed and then she saw the houses and the large buzzing poles of electricity that dipped up and down through the streets. She realized that she was almost dragging Scarlet down a street. She mumbled something drunkenly as she took another step with her, "Come on, we're almost home," Willow heard herself say. Scarlet responded with some more drunken mumbles. A couple blocks of dragging is serious work and she shook Scarlet's long hair out of her face. *Wait,* she thought, *I thought she had short hair?* She looked over and saw that she was noticeably smaller, not in height but in build. Her arms were thinner now as well as her jeaned up legs. Willow shook the thought away and continued dragging her friend right to the front door of her house. "Alright," Willow pushed her friend upright. "Can you make it to the front door?"

"Yea, yea," she stumbled forth and found the handle of the door, opened it, and fell inside, closing it behind her.

Willow took a breath of the cold night air and wished her luck in finding her own room. She smiled and backtracked down to her own house. The lights were on inside and she could hear scuttling and noise from beyond the threshold. She was confused, she thought no one would be home tonight. She opened the door to the smell of cooking. It smelled like meat and juicy things that made her mouth water. A weird thought entered her head, like it was wrong to be able to smell such good food, but she shook it away and closed the door behind herself. She walked into the kitchen and found her Mom pulling a roast out of the oven, "Oh, hello Willow," she said with a smile.

"Mom..." Willow said, almost shocked for whatever reason, her mind was racing with random thoughts of this and that, little memories that she never had, she shook her head as a headache began to sprout in the core of her brain.

"Hey, honey, are you alright?" She put the roast down on the counter and led Willow to a chair, "Sit, sit. Jeez, you look pale?" She smiled, "Were you out drinking tonight?"

"No, mom...no..." Willow's mind filled with everything else, she remembered hating her parents, she remembered Scarlet dying, she remembered all this pain that she never had. The intensity of it made her stomach swirl and her mind tinge out in pain. Then, like a match, the pain went out with the howl of the wind beyond the window. She looked at her Mom and realized how much she loved her, "Mom!" she said and hugged her.

"Hey, hey," her mother hugged back. "Are you okay?" She asked, surprised.

"Yes, yea..." she let go. "I'm sorry mom."

"For what?"

"I...I don't know."

"Well...I know that it's been tough without your father around, but...I'm glad that you're my daughter," she smiled and brushed her daughter's hair out of her eyes. "What happened to your hands?" She asked, scooping her daughter's hand up and looking at the palm. It was hard and callused. "You look like you were working on a farm or something. And...you look like you've been eating more."

"I'm fat?"

"No! You look healthier is all!" They both laughed.

And the night went on with a good dinner and then a good sleep. Willow snuggled under her covers, tired, and looked up at the ceiling. In the back of her mind, she remembered something being there. Some small intrepid little thing that annoyed her to sin. But it was clear of anything and she closed her tired eyes and went to sleep.

And she dreamt a dream of light and elegance. She dreamt of the Golden Man. They both wordlessly walked towards each other in a marble cladded dance hall that echoed everywhere. They both wore fancy clothes. She smiled at him, he smiled back, and they both nodded as they began to dance until the morning light woke her. As the tiredness leaked slowly from her brain, the word, 'Breakdance,' played over and over again, like a repeating stereo echoing in her mind. Breakdance.

Before she left for school that morning, Viktor called her, begging her to help him with some last minute homework. "No, Vik, I'm not even good at math, man."

"Aw! Come on, Willow! I don't want to be held back!"

"I don't know..." Willow laughed as she thought about something absurd.

"What?" He asked.

"You know who you remind me of, Viktor?" She asked.

"Is now really the time for that?" He asked. "I'm totally screwed unless you, the master, help me, the padawan."

"Stop. I hate *Star Wars* references. I am your Sifu. Fine, I'll help you. Be at the library after school, okay?"

"Ohmygosh, thank you Sifu." You could hear him do a karate kick over the phone. "Wait, who do I remind you of?"

"You ever read *Frankenstein*?"

Afterwards, Willow met up with Scarlet who was waiting by her old beat up Corolla that Mike gave to her when she got her driver's license a year back. "Why do you drag me to parties on a Sunday?" Willow asked. "And how do you not have a hangover?"

"Oh trust me, I do, very much so. But Wilset set me up with a wicked solution. Mans gave me this bread that you eat and it makes a hangover go *poof*...kinda. He's a good kid, but what kind of name is Wilset?"

"Eh?" Willow shrugged as she thought and forgot about something. Breakdance.

On the car ride Willow felt weird. Scarlet was saying something but she kept looking out the window, her daydreams loud in her head. Dreams of random little forgotten memories and experiences. "Hey, Willow!" Scarlet finally got through.

"Oh...sorry, what?" Willow shook her head.

"We're going to the same college, right? That's what I was asking you when you decided to ignore me."

"Yea, whatever we both get into."

Scarlet stopped at a red light. "Hey, you seem kinda dreamy today, you alright?"

"I'm good. Maybe kinda sad."

"Are you depressed or something?"

"No...I just feel a forlorn type of sadness. Like I miss something. But I don't know what it is."

"It's probably the end of high school fever."

"Maybe," and Willow looked back out of the window to watch the houses pass by. "Breakdance," she whispered to herself.

"What?" Scarlet asked.

"Breakdance," I answered.

Epilogue

"So…how do you feel?"

"Fine."

"You squandered yours and her potential and all you feel is 'fine'?"

"Yeah. Feel like a weight has been lifted off my shoulders."

"You don't have shoulders."

"Oh…the humanskin does that to you."

"How's the girl?"

"She seems happy enough."

"Does she know?"

"No. No she doesn't. It went to plan. I think."

"Do you regret it?"

"Maybe. But it's too late to care now, right?"

"I guess so. So…what now?"

"I don't know exactly."

"Yep…"

"Yep…"

"Hey, I have a question."

"Yea?"

"Why are we still speaking this peoplelanguage?"

Lucas writes books. I write books. Thank you for reading.

lucaswritesbooks@gmail.com

www.ingramcontent.com/pod-product-compliance
Lightning Source LLC
LaVergne TN
LVHW100513110826
845146LV00002B/618

* 9 7 9 8 2 1 8 3 4 7 2 6 0 *